Beholden To None

Jennie Cairns

The People's Friend
CLASSICS COLLECTION

Published in Great Britain by DC Thomson & Co. Ltd,
Dundee, Glasgow and London.
© DC Thomson & Co. Ltd., 2021
www.dcthomson.co.uk

Since 1869, fiction has been at the heart of every single issue of "The People's Friend" magazine. Now, through "The People's Friend" Classics Collection, modern readers can rediscover and enjoy the best-loved and most popular serials from the magazine's story-telling past, many of which have never before been published in book form.

"Beholden To None" by Jennie Cairns was first published in 1955 and the Editor received thousands of letters from delighted readers. So beloved were the stories from this writer that some of the most popular issues at the time were those featuring one of her serials.

4

CHAPTER ONE

TIIE train from Glasgow clanged to a stop. The foreman porter shouted "Kil-mar-ford" as he walked the length of the train to help with the luggage in the guard's van.

On the way he saw a young woman alight. As she turned back to the carriage to help out a little boy, he puckered his brows. He knew that face!

Keeping a grip on the boy's hand, the young woman hurried to the luggage van. The foreman watched her arrange with a porter for a trunk and a large suitcase to be sent after her.

His eyes followed her as she walked through the entrance hall into the sunshine of the August evening. Then he went to the trunk, bent down and read the label.

"I was richt!" His voice was a whisper that matched the far-off look in his eyes. "Jock Todd's daughter! Whit's brought her back? And wi' a laddie!"

Quickly he crossed the platform, went through the hall to the street outside. He saw her again halfway down the little hill, picking her out from others because she had a coat slung over her shoulders.

"She's come back gey quiet. Nae car tae meet her. And she doesna take a taxi."

He went back into the station and made straight for the luggage still on the platform. Again he read the label. But this time he read also the address.

"The Vennel! Just back to where she started." He shook his head slowly. "I wonder whit for. Surely no' for trouble. She took efter her mither, no' efter Jock."

He thought of a train that left Kilmarford several years before, and of a carriage he had labelled "Not For Public Use."

It had two occupants. A thin, middle-aged man sitting very close to a sturdy figure in police uniform. Between the two a pair of handcuffs glinted in the morning sun. Sergeant McCrindle was taking Jock Todd to prison.

Unaware of arousing such interest, the young woman and her boy made their way to the high street. She felt her coat too warm for comfort, so she walked slowly. Beneath her grey straw hat, her hair gleamed red. The boy's excited questions cascaded over her. She answered them while her own eyes noted the changes eight years had made to familiar places. Every step she took was a memory.

There was the spire of the church where she was christened, and where she and her mother had worshipped. She and Kenny would go there now. There was the Victoria Fountain.

"Mummy, is it far to Aunt Isa's?" the boy asked.

"Not too far," she told him. "Along this street where the buses are, then round the next corner and down a hill –"

As she turned the corner she stopped, catching an uninterrupted view of the far end of the busy town. Below her lay the mills that brought wealth to Kilmarford and made it one of the busiest towns in Ayrshire. There was Bone's Mill, Shaw's Mill, McCreath's Mill – and dwarfing them all in size, Laurie's. It was so big, made up of so many separate buildings, that it was never called a mill.

Folk said Laurie's as they said Kilmarford, for to most people they meant the same thing. Laurie's was Kilmarford. It employed someone from almost every family in the town. The name gleamed out now in huge white letters.

Kathleen looked in surprised. It was bigger than she had known it. New buildings thrust out in every direction from a central block, like the fingers of a giant hand. The long rows of windows glowed like fire in the evening sun.

As she looked and noted Laurie's expansions, Kathleen's full lips tightened into a firm line. But it was only for a moment. Then she gripped her boy's hand again and started to cross the busy street. Halfway over she caught sight of the bulky figure of Sergeant McCrindle, talking to a policeman on point duty.

She tried to avoid him, but too late. His face betrayed his surprise. It was a kindly face. But the memories it brought to Kathleen were not what she wanted. As she turned her head away, his hand was raised in a smart salute. Whether it was a gesture of friendliness or sympathy, Kathleen could not guess.

Monk's Vennel. Kathleen did not need to read the broken plate on the wall. She knew exactly where she was. The street was narrow, with cobble stones that had a remembered smoothness under her feet.

Her eyes went to a window where limp yellow curtains hung crookedly. She remembered her mother putting up freshly washed net curtains while they were still damp, so that they would hang evenly at that very window.

Across the years she seemed to hear a voice calling her in from play. Tears misted her eyes. Was it eight years since she left home, eight years since her mother died? Now twenty-five, Kathleen felt suddenly old – and lonely.

She hurried past Martin the grocer's and a few yards farther on stopped at No. 27. She went quickly through the pend, avoiding a joiner's barrow. Her heart was fluttering, her hands trembling. She cleared her throat nervously. She had not expected to be moved so deeply by this return.

They climbed an outside stair with a chipped green railing. The steps were worn, but she didn't see them. Her eyes were on the box on the kitchen window-sill. From it a mass of nasturtiums fell down in golden profusion. Aunt Isa was very fond of flowers.

At the top of the stairs was a wooden porch, its paint dull and peeling, and two doors with brass name plates.

She read the one on the right. It shone like a new penny. *John Duncan*. Aunt Isa had been a widow for as long as Kathleen could remember, but the plate had never been changed.

Before she could knock, the door was thrown open by a stout, elderly woman. Her cotton-print dress strained across her shoulders and hung uneven at the hem. Isa Duncan had a round, high-coloured face and an upturned mouth. She was always smiling, but her eyes were shrewd as well as kind.

"Kathy!" she cried. "It's good to see you!"

Plump arms enfolded her and drew her into the kitchen.

"And this is Kenny! Let me look at you, laddie. Well, he's certainly got your hair, Kathy – but –" Her voice wavered uncertainly and Kathleen smiled.

She threw off her coat and Isa Duncan removed Kenny's. He stood very quiet, with that stillness most five-year-olds have in new surroundings. There was so much to see and wonder at in this room.

Kathleen, too, was taking in every detail. There was much that was familiar. The sink at the window. The box bed with its looped-back curtains of clean but faded pink cotton damask. The mantelpiece crammed with ornaments and photographs. Beside the tea caddy was the letter she sent Aunt Isa a week ago.

A week ago! Kathleen sighed and turned away. The table was set and on the plates were slices of potted hough. She had not seen it since she left Kilmarford. It made her feel she was really home.

"The boy looks tired, Kathy. Do you want to give him his tea first and get him to bed? Then we can talk all night."

Kenny was too sleepy to protest, and very soon he was tucked up in the other room, with his old teddy snuggled close to him.

"I see you've got the range out, Aunt Isa," Kathleen said, coming back to the kitchen. "It's a big improvement having an interior grate."

"Alec sent me the money from Chicago. He's doing well. Wants me to go with him, but I like my own wee corner. It's not as if he didn't have a wife. Marlene seems a sensible lassie for an American, and they've got two fine boys. But there's time to talk about them later. Draw in your chair and take a good tea."

Mrs Duncan went on talking, her eyes taking in every detail of the girl's appearance. She saw dark auburn hair curling back from a broad brow. Eyes that were grey, wide-set and very clear, a chin pointed and a mouth beautifully shaped, with a short, full upper lip.

"My, Kathy, but you're like your mother! A body would think it was her sitting there, except –"

"Except what?"

But Mrs Duncan pushed across the china jam-dish and urged Kathleen to try her homemade blackcurrant jelly.

She could not say that Mary Todd's image in her memory was merely a blurred photograph in comparison to this lovely girl. There was so much more beauty here, and more strength, too. Mary, poor soul, had not been weak. But no one would have called her a fighter. Maybe that wasn't surprising, married as she was to Jock Todd.

But Mary's daughter was different. Decision showed in the direct glance of her eyes, and in the mouth above her pointed chin.

"It was good of you to take us in, Aunt Isa! As soon as I'm settled in a job I'll start looking for rooms –"

"You and Kenny are welcome to bide here always. Mind

you, I was surprised to get that letter saying you were coming back. I thought you were happy in Clacton."

"We were." Kathleen played with the handle of her teaspoon. "But I had to think about Kenny's education. I wanted him to get to his father's old school – the High, I wrote to the headmaster."

"Did you say who you were?" The bright eyes were shrewd.

"No –"

Again Isa Duncan veered away from the point.

"What about a job? Any idea what you'd like?"

"I thought I'd ask Mr Galbraith, the lawyer at the Cross, if he has a vacancy. That's where I used to work, remember? I've been doing office work in Clacton since Kenny was old enough to leave with Mrs Fison."

"She's dead now?"

"Six weeks ago. That's what made me think of coming back here. Kenny and I were so happy with her."

Kathleen turned her head away, but Isa Duncan saw the sad look in her eyes. She lifted the lid off the teapot and stirred the contents with a clean spoon from the table drawer.

"Have the extra cup of tea, Kathy. Maybe it will tell if you're to get a job."

At once the girl's face lit up.

"Of course! Fancy me forgetting! Mother always said you read teacups better than anyone."

Her elbows on the table, Isa Duncan stared thoughtfully into Kathleen's cup, her head tilted like an alert bird.

"Mercy!" she exclaimed. "This is a real mixy-maxy. But wait! There's a job for you! This Mr Galbraith, is he a tall, dark man?"

Kathy shook her head and laughed.

"Well, this man in your cup has something to do with it. There's a lot of words. As if you were argy-bargying." She tapped the cup sharply on the palm of her hand. "The words are still there – angry words, I think, but maybe no. And there's – but that's enough for now."

Isa Duncan put the cup on the table. She did it very slowly, but her mind was thinking quickly while her eyes searched Kathy's face.

"Tell me more. Who else did you write to in Kilmarford?" she said.

"I heard every Christmas from Nan Gilfillan. Her husband is at Laurie's."

"That's right. He's an incomer, but he has a good job. They've one of the new bungalows on South Road. I see her whiles when I'm shopping, but I don't know her to speak to."

"Nan and I were friends at school. Her mother was dead and her father didn't seem to mind about –" Kathleen broke off, colour tinging her cheeks.

"Have you ever heard from your own father?" Isa Duncan asked.

"No – have you?"

"Nothing since he left the town two years ago. Walked out with six months' rent owing. But I'm sure the factor thought that was getting rid of him cheaply."

"Oh, Aunt Isa!"

"Now it's no use taking that tone, Kathy! You know the life he led your poor mother. Your father was born to trouble. From the day your mother married him, she never knew when the police were to be at her door! You must remember yourself –"

"I remember." Kathleen was white to the lips.

Isa Duncan shook her head.

"Maybe I shouldn't speak like that, but Cousin Màry was as dear to me as a sister –"

"I know," Kathleen whispered, her lips trembling. A thousand small acts of kindness lay in the past; from a jug of soup to carry home on a freezing winter's day, to a remnant of printed cotton to be made up, so that she could have a new dress for the Sunday school picnic.

"Have you written to anyone else saying you were coming back?"

"No, just the letter to the school."

"The news'll not keep, dearie. Folk will soon be talking."

Kathleen shrugged her shoulders.

"There's nothing to talk about."

"That's where you're wrong! You're no longer just Kathy Todd, you know!"

Kathleen smiled and fingered the thin platinum band on her finger. Isa Duncan noticed the movement.

"You didn't write to – them?" she asked.

"I wrote twice when Kenneth was killed. I was the next-of-kin so I got the news from the War Office. My first letter was ignored. Mr Galbraith, their lawyer, answered the second. Could they have made it clearer they didn't want anything to do with me?"

"Do they know about the laddie?"

Kathleen shook her head. She started to gather the dishes.

"Kenny wasn't born till six months after –"

"His father was killed in Italy."

"At Perugia, six years ago, the twentieth of June 1944."

"You didn't have long together."

Kathleen lifted the jam dish and laid it down again.

"Just our honeymoon. Seven days in Devon. It was Easter and all the daffodils were out –"

Aunt Isa cleared her throat. She went over to the sink and peered out over the nasturtiums.

"Mercy, what's this! Oh, it's your luggage!"

They went to the door. Two red-faced men were carrying the trunk up the stairs.

"Does Mrs Kathleen Laurie live here?" asked the taller one.

"Yes," said Kathleen, standing back to let them in. "I'm Mrs Laurie."

CHAPTER TWO

ON Monday afternoon, two days after Kathleen came back to Kilmarford, James Laurie sat in the lounge of his big house on the outskirts of town.

It was seldom James Laurie was away from his mills during the day. He had, however, been to a meeting in Glasgow and the road to his office passed Finnard, his home. He had called in to get some papers and his wife had coaxed him to wait for tea.

"I should really be back at the works," he grumbled, seeing his chauffeur pacing up and down the drive. "Especially today, when Roger will be leaving early."

"The mills can get along for an hour without either of you." Mildred Laurie spoke lightly, but her husband caught a faint resentment in her tone.

He knew his wife had never liked the mill. And he didn't hold that against her. She was a woman, and women looked at these things differently.

But he loved the mill. It was his life. Started by his grandfather in a little shed, it had grown with the years until it had come to him. Now it was one of the biggest in the country, with a reputation for craftsmanship and quality all over the world.

The mill had given James Laurie everything he wanted of

life. Above all it had given him confidence to court and marry a girl above his kind. Thirty years ago there was still a gulf between a man who was in "trade" and a girl who was of "the country".

He met her on the first holiday he had ever taken from the mill. He thought the idea of a cruise to Madeira a waste of time and money. But the doctor had insisted on it after a severe pleurisy. On the trip he met Mildred Lawrence, a beautiful girl, twelve years younger than himself. It was the turning point of his life.

She was the third daughter of a poor baronet with a big family and a stately home in Hertfordshire. Her cruise was a special treat, paid for by an aunt with whom she travelled. She admired James Laurie, envied him the confidence with which he spoke of success and money and was finally a willing captive to his whirlwind courtship.

In the years that followed James Laurie quite unaware how much his wife had changed him. He never knew how greatly his attitude to people and events was coloured and shaped by her desires and her viewpoint. If he had known, he wouldn't have cared. He loved her, and always would.

He looked at her now, sitting in a low chair, her ringed hands moving among the cups. She was still beautiful, a tall woman with stately grace in every movement. Her olive skin was still unlined; her hair fair and fine, barely touched with silver, for all her fifty-one years.

The door swung open and Roger Laurie came in. He was tall and brown-haired, with an open, frank face.

"In time for tea? I hoped I would be. By the way, Dad, I had Galbraith on the phone before I left."

Mention of the lawyer made James Laurie look up sharply. "What did he want?"

"Said he wanted to talk to you privately. He didn't give me a clue."

James Laurie leaned back in his chair.

"I wonder if he's got news about Carmichael's? If only that young man would sell. I can't think what's stopping him! I've offered him a good price –"

"There's a stubborn streak in Craig Carmichael!" his son reminded him. "The fact we want his plant is enough to make him dig his heels in and hold out as long as possible."

The old man scowled.

"He'll dance to my tune before I'm finished! I know his financial position's none too secure –"

"Must you two always talk business!" Mrs Laurie broke in. "It gets very tiresome at every meal."

"Sorry, Mum! But I'd better tell you, Dad, Galbraith is coming round to see you this evening. He said he'd rather come to the house than to the works."

"What's got into him?" James Laurie asked. "It's not often he gets worked up about anything." He slapped his knee. "I'm sure it's to do with Carmichael's! He's a wily bird, Galbraith. Always too cautious to commit himself on the telephone. It looks as if we're really getting somewhere at last!"

Presently Mildred Laurie was left alone. She sat relaxed in

her low chair. Her eyes softened as she heard the roar of Roger's car in the drive. He was on his way to say goodbye to Alice Boswell before he left on a business trip. Their wedding was to be in November.

She knew she had influenced Roger's choice of a wife. The thought gave her satisfaction. It was such a suitable match. Alice's parents were personal friends, her father a retired general, her mother the sister of a baronet. It was all most satisfactory, especially in view of what happened to – But Mrs Laurie checked that thought as quickly as it came to her.

That evening James Laurie showed the family lawyer to his study.

Fletcher Galbraith was a dapper little man, who looked nervous until one met the penetrating glance of his light blue eyes. His pale brown hair was thin on the crown, but he looked younger than his fifty-eight years.

James Laurie waved his guest to a chair, having told the maid to bring coffee. For a few minutes they talked about Roger's trip to South Africa to make contact with new markets. He had already left for Glasgow to join the night train to London. Tomorrow he was to fly from Northolt and would be away about a month.

"He won't be back for your staff dance?" Fletcher Galbraith said, after accepting an invitation for himself and his wife.

James Laurie laughed.

"He'll be back. He's taking Alice! It'll probably be at the

last minute, but Roger'll make it!"

The lawyer waited until the maid laid the coffee tray on the small table and went out.

"I've got news for you, James."

"Good news, I hope!"

"Well –" The lawyer rubbed the side of his sharp nose. "I don't think you're going to like it. In fact –"

"Don't beat about the bush, man! If it's got anything to do with Carmichael's – "

"It has nothing to do with that. James – she's back in Kilmarford."

"Who's back?" he barked, unable to conceal his disappointment over a successful deal with Carmichael. "Who are you talking about?"

"Kathleen Todd." The lawyer expected an angry outburst, but James Laurie merely stared. "Your daughter-in-law."

That roused the man opposite him.

"She's no daughter-in-law of mine!" he shouted, his face purpling. "She tricked my son into marriage! A daughter of that waster Jock Todd would know how to do that!" His voice changed. "How do you know she's back?"

"She called on me today to ask if I could give her a job or help her find one. She used to be a typist with me."

"The impertinence! I hope you made short shrift of her?"

"I told her there was no vacancy, and I couldn't put her in the way of work."

Fletcher Galbraith was not only wily but far-seeing. Kathleen Todd was the last person he would lift a hand to help. Not because he didn't like her. She had been a clever worker. But he had his business to think about. It would be foolish to lose a client like James Laurie because he had helped Kathleen Todd. His advice to leave town, influenced though it was by the thought of James Laurie, had been sincere. He could see nothing but unhappiness in Kilmarford for the daughter of Jock Todd.

"You should go back south, Kathleen, back to your friends there. It's never easy to come back and pick up where you left off. For you," he smiled to take the sting out of the words, "it would be very difficult."

Kathleen returned his smile. There was a quiet dignity about her as she stood up and drew on her gloves. It seemed to Fletcher Galbraith she had grown taller, but perhaps it was only her graceful way of holding herself.

"Thank you for seeing me, Mr Galbraith. I won't take up any more of your time."

She had barely left the office before he phoned Laurie's Mill.

James Laurie put his cup down with a clatter which startled the lawyer.

"We've got to get rid of her!"

Fletcher Galbraith murmured something about it being difficult. After all, Kilmarford was her native town. She couldn't be forced away.

"Mildred will be very upset. Few of our friends knew anything about the marriage at the time. Now it's never mentioned in this house – never!"

The lawyer nodded. Among the many Laurie papers in his office was a cutting from the local newspaper announcing Kenneth's death. He had looked it out that afternoon, after Kathleen left.

"Lieutenant Kenneth Leonard Laurie, aged twenty-three years, beloved elder son of Mr and Mrs James Laurie, of Finnard –"

No mention of a wife!

After Fletcher Galbraith was gone, James Laurie sat on, putting off the moment when he would have to tell his wife.

Kenneth's death had been a tragedy; a blow made more bitter because it followed so soon after an impossible marriage. He had never understood how his son could marry the daughter of a man whose name was a by-word in Kilmarford.

Jock Todd's daughter!

Was all that to be dragged into the open again? Just when Mildred was looking forward to Roger marrying Alice Boswell? What would Alice's people think? He sprang to his feet and began pacing the floor, his eyes angry, his brows knitted darkly.

* * * *

A few days later Kathleen solved the problem of obtaining work by registering at the Labour Exchange. She filled up forms, was interviewed and finally sent to Carmichael's Mill.

"Mr Carmichael is needing a typist," the woman at the exchange said. "We are told he is difficult to suit, but you may be the very one he's looking for. You never know. It's a good place, if you get into it. Good luck, anyway."

Half an hour later Kathleen was shown into Craig Carmichael's private room. He rose from behind his desk and she noted he was tall and slimly built. His mouth looked firm with thin lips, his hair was straight and very black, in strong contrast to his light blue eyes.

He held out his hand and took hers in a firm grip.

"Sit down, Mrs Laurie." It was when he spoke Kathleen saw he had white, even teeth and his smile was charming. Her hopes rose. Surely she would suit him.

He looked at her appraisingly while she answered his questions about her experience. He noticed and liked her neat grey suit, the crisp yellow blouse, the little hat set back on her hair. She had nice hands. They were clasped loosely in her lap. They didn't fidget.

"I think you would suit me, Mrs Laurie, and I hope you'll like working here." He smiled and then asked, "Can you start on Monday?"

"Oh, well – I –"

"If it's not convenient, a day or two won't matter," he said kindly. "Only I understood you wanted to start as soon as possible."

"I do! But I have a little boy and Monday is the day for enrolment at the High School. I'd like to take him, if possible – "

22

"Of course! Make it Tuesday, then."

"Thank you." Kathleen made a movement to rise from the chair, but his voice detained her.

"So you're sending your boy to the High? That's where I went – not that I'm a good advertisement for it!" He grinned.

"Kenny's father went to the High, so naturally –"

Kathleen's voice went on, but Craig Carmichael scarcely heard her. Until now the name Laurie had not meant anything to him. But her boy being called Kenneth seemed more than coincidence.

"There was a Kenneth Laurie in the class below me at school." His voice was deliberately casual. "He was the son of James Laurie, the millowner."

"He was my husband," Kathleen said quietly.

Craig Carmichael didn't try to conceal his surprise.

"Your – your husband!"

He took out a silver case and offered her a cigarette. She refused with thanks. Until now, his interest in this girl was no more than he would have shown in any prospective employee.

But she was no ordinary girl! And this was certainly no ordinary situation!

The daughter-in-law of James Laurie applying for a job in Carmichael's! So that talk of a hasty war marriage was true! And there was a child now! The Lauries had certainly kept that dark.

The breach must still be unhealed. Otherwise this girl wouldn't be looking for work. Craig Carmichael smiled. The situation would be amusing if it weren't so tragic for this girl! He saw she was ill at ease and realised his sudden silence had disturbed her.

"You must excuse me, Mrs Laurie. But I had no idea till just now who you were!"

"I hope it won't make any difference, Mr Carmichael. I need the job, for I need to work."

He leaned back in his chair, his mind busy. He liked this girl; admired her honesty and courage. But her coming to Carmichael's could create problems for him, as well as herself. He wondered if she knew what the position might be. He must certainly warn her. He leaned forward to tell her.

"I've offered you a job here," he said. "And that stands. It will be for you to decide if you will work here after I've told you about myself and Carmichael's – and your father-in-law!"

He told her how after the war he had gone to Australia. He had been there only a short time when his uncle died and left him the mill. He had flown back from Australia meaning to sell up the mill and return. But once home again he had somehow liked Kilmarford and the mill had worked its way into his blood.

He liked, also, the people in the mill. They were good folk, happy to work for him as they'd worked for his uncle. So he had changed his mind and stayed.

This had annoyed James Laurie, who was hoping to buy the mill at a cheap price. He kept trying to buy it. But pressure from Laurie's served only to deepen his own determination.

"I mean to stay," he concluded. "But how long I shall is still in the lap of the gods. Carmichael's have very little money. Your father-in-law knows that. He might force us to close down. There are ways he could do so, and I would be forced to sell. If you come here you will be working against your father-in-law. He hates me already. He may get to hate you, and that wouldn't be good for you or your boy.

"Do you understand what I'm trying to tell you, Mrs Laurie? Don't you think you would be better to get work elsewhere?"

He saw Kathleen moisten her lips, but her answer came without hesitation.

"I am a Laurie only by name, Mr Carmichael. I'm living with a relative of my mother's in Monk's Vennel. Mr Laurie doesn't even pay me the compliment of hating me. I just don't exist – for him."

It was her answer. He accepted it, admiring her for the calm and quick decision she had made.

He stood up to end the interview.

"All right, then. You'll start on Tuesday." He smiled and came round the end of the desk. "Kenneth was a good chap. I'm sorry about – that."

"It seems a long time ago now." Her voice was very low.

He paused with his hand on the doorknob, peaking lightly to dispel her sad mood.

"You know, I still can't believe you're James Laurie's

daughter-in-law."

She raised her head and looked straight at him.

"I think it is only fair to tell you, I am also the daughter of Jock Todd!"

He looked blank.

"You want a job and I need a good typist. It doesn't matter whose daughter you are! I'm not interested in pedigrees!"

After Kathleen had left he rang for his typist. Effie Gemmell was a thin woman in her early fifties, with tidy brown hair and neat features. She looked as efficient and as cold as a filing cabinet, but Craig Carmichael knew no heart in Kilmarford was kinder than Effie Gemmell's.

She'd been a tower of strength to him. Without her and Andrew Tosh, the works manager, he would have been lost at one time. He had leaned on them and they had never failed him.

"I want some information, Miss Gemmell," he said. "Sit down and tell me what you know about Jock Todd."

Effie Gemmell folded her hands in her lap. She'd lived in Kilmarford all her life and knew everyone.

"So that's it! I was sure I knew her." Then she told him all she knew.

"Poor girl," Craig Carmichael said when she'd finished. "What a mess to come back to. There's a child –"

"A child?"

He nodded.

"A five-year-old boy. She's going to need a helping hand, Effie. I hope you'll look after her?"

Miss Gemmell primed her lips with difficulty. Mr Craig only called her Effie when he had something important on his mind. She didn't always agree with him. Some of his methods were unusual, but like everyone in the mill, she thought there was no one like him.

"Ours is a happy office," she said. "I don't see why she shouldn't be happy here."

And over the desk they exchanged a look of understanding.

CHAPTER THREE

ON leaving the office Kathleen made for the Cross to meet Mrs Duncan and Kenny. These two were already close friends, and the boy was perfectly happy to be left with "Aunt Isa".

"Have you been waiting long?" Kathleen asked, her eyes sparkling. "The interview took longer than I expected. But I got the job! I start at Carmichael's on Tuesday. He must have been the dark man you saw in my cup, Aunt Isa. But there were no angry words!"

"That's grand! I am so glad for you, Kathy. Kenny and I put in time watching the buses."

"It's four o'clock now. We'd better get along to Fenwick's. I told Nan –"

Mrs Duncan put a hand on her arm.

"I've got to go to the factor's. This is the last day for the rent. Then I've shopping to do. I saw some nice fish in Calder's. It will be all ready by the time you get back. Nan will be pleased to see you. I promised Kenny an ice-cream, though. Here's the money –"

"Don't you dare!" Kathleen shook her head and watched Isa Duncan's sturdy figure vanish into the crowds.

She and Kenny crossed the street to Fenwick's. It was a baker's shop with a tearoom above, old-fashioned but one of the best known meeting-places in Kilmarford.

"Can I get an ice-cream, Mummy?" Kenny pleaded as they climbed the stairs.

"Of course, darling. But just one! There's Nan, over in the corner. The lady with the fair hair."

The two girls greeted each other affectionately, taking in at a glance the changes of the years. Nan was pretty in a colourless way and had grown stouter. After the usual first awkwardness, talk flowed easily. Kenny applied himself silently to the ice-cream set down before him.

"He's got your hair, Kathleen, but –" Unconsciously Nan echoed Mrs Duncan's words.

"In features he's like Kenneth," Kathleen finished for her. "I know. You haven't any family yet, Nan?"

Nan Webb, as she was now, shook her head.

"I wish we had."

Time passed quickly as they talked about old times and the reasons for Kathleen's return. When Kathleen mentioned her job at Carmichael's, her friend's face showed surprise but she made no comment.

For some time Kenny had been growing restless. He slipped from his chair and stood watching people entering and leaving the tearoom. A tall, well-dressed woman dropped her umbrella on her way to the cash desk. Kenny picked it up and handed it to her.

"What a nice little boy! It was very good of you to pick up an old lady's umbrella." She turned to the young woman beside her. "Hasn't he got lovely hair, Alice? I've always loved that dark auburn hair."

She patted Kenny's head.

"Tell your mummy a lady gave you this to buy a toy because you were a good boy." Into Kenny's hand she put a shilling.

At the table Nan Webb caught the scene with surprised eyes.

"Did – did – you see that, Kathy?"

"I did." Kathleen said, feeling motherly pride in her little son. "He did it quite nicely."

"Yes, of course! But don't you know who that was?"

"No, should I?" Kathleen looked after the tall figure and noted her clothes were expensive.

"That's Mrs Laurie! Your boy's grandmother! The girl with her is going to marry Roger Laurie."

Just then Kenny came back to the table to show his mother the shilling.

"For a toy, for being good," he told her.

"I hope you said 'Thanks' to the lady, Kenny. Yes, we'll buy a toy on the way home."

These were the words she spoke. But her thoughts were very different.

What a strange meeting! Grandmother and grandson, yet neither knew the other! It was in keeping with the many strange things that had happened to her since she became a Laurie. But she didn't want such strange things happening to Kenny! But he would get his toy. The first, and probably the last present he'd ever get from his grandmother!

Six weeks later Kathleen walked home, happy after her day's work. She was in no hurry. Since she had started at Carmichael's Aunt Isa had given up her part-time work in the afternoon. She loved to bath and put Kenny to bed. So often Kathleen lingered on the way home so that Aunt Isa could do what made her happy all evening.

Although only a short time at Carmichael's, Kathleen felt quite at home there. She liked the work and the people she worked with. Everyone was friendly. If any knew who she was, Jock Todd's daughter, or Kenneth Laurie's widow, it made no difference. Everyone was kind, Miss Gemmell especially so.

Kathleen thought she had much to be thankful for, and every night prayed for things to continue "just as they were." Kenny was at the High School and liked it. His enrolment had been accomplished very smoothly. The rector was a youngish man, recently appointed, and the name, Kenneth Laurie, was just another name to him.

Her thoughts were broken when she came to a crossroads where traffic was heavy and quick. She stood on the kerb at a crossing until the lights changed. A waiting car sounded its horn sharply and a man waved to her. Craig Carmichael. He opened the door of the car and signalled her to come in.

"Jump in, before the lights change," he said, when she went forward.

She got into the front seat beside him. "I'm just on my way home, and it isn't far, you know."

"Then I'll drop you at the Cross. You're late, aren't you?"

"I was finishing these schedules for – "

He was obviously not listening. "I meant to ask you something this afternoon when you were taking down these letters, but that phone call came."

He glanced at her sideways. She was wearing a navy woollen dress with a white collar, and over it a loose coat. She was hatless and he thought he'd never seen such lovely and unusual hair.

"Laurie's are having their staff dance next Friday. They've sent me two tickets. Merely a courtesy gesture, I assure you! Will you have dinner with me that night and come to the dance as my partner?"

The invitation held her speechless. They reached the Cross, but he didn't stop. Instead he turned to the right and took the road down to the river. He stopped at the bridge.

"Thank you, Mr Carmichael, but I couldn't!"

"Why not? It would be an opportunity for you to meet the Lauries."

"But I don't want to meet them! Why should I? They've shown no desire to meet me – or their grandson. No, I couldn't!"

He turned in his seat so he could face her.

"Listen, Mrs Laurie, you've come back to this town and you mean to stay in it! At this dance there won't be the Lauries. There'll be everybody else, all the people who could be friends with you. You want to have friends, don't you?"

"But I don't see – "

"You'll be with me," he broke in. "So Laurie will have to accept you even if he finds out who you are. But you'll meet everybody else. I'll see to that. Forget about the Lauries. Don't let them rule your life! But don't ever run away from them. We needn't stay long unless you don't want to."

He was insistent, and because she knew he was trying to help her, Kathleen promised to think it over.

But she wasn't happy about it. She was more worried when she confided in Aunt Isa. That wise woman not only shared her misgivings, but gave them voice.

"I don't like it, Kathy! You're far better to keep out of James Laurie's way! Going to that dance will be like a challenge. And you can't fight a man like that! Stronger people than you have tried, and where are they today? Don't go, I'd say!"

So the next day she told Craig Carmichael.

"Well, if that's how you feel, that's the end of it, Mrs Laurie. Perhaps you're right! I don't particularly want to go myself and quite understand. I'll tell you what! I'll excuse myself because of a previous engagement; and that engagement will be with you! We'll have dinner somewhere and then run down to Ayr, where we can dance. How about that? It gives me a good excuse, and it won't run you into any of the Lauries."

He was so friendly, Kathleen felt she could not refuse. He had tried to help her. The least she could do was to help him establish his excuse. She accepted.

Aunt Isa agreed that she did right. So days passed and the

evening came.

The one evening dress Kathleen possessed was of "hunting green" velvet, cut with a square neckline. Her skin was dazzlingly fair and her hair shone.

"My, but you're bonnie!" Aunt Isa said, while helping her dress. "Have a nice time dearie!"

Kathleen smiled and slipped into her coat. "I'll wait downstairs. There's not much room for parking a car in the Vennel." Impulsively she threw her arms round Mrs Duncan and kissed her.

Once downstairs she drew her coat round her and stood in the shadow of the pend. She didn't have long to wait. Craig Carmichael was on time. He would have got out to open the door, but she was too quick for him.

"I booked dinner for half-past seven. If we arrive at Ayr around nine, that'll be early enough."

He looked handsome in his dinner suit. They had a corner table in the hotel on the Glasgow road. The food was excellent and the service good.

Kathleen was surprised at how quickly the time passed. She felt at ease with Craig Carmichael. He had the gift of making people believe they really mattered to him. He was her employer by day, but now he slid into a friendly, yet impersonal relationship which made conversation easy.

It was after half-past eight when the waiter came to say Mr Carmichael was wanted on the phone. Craig excused himself and went. When he returned Kathleen instantly saw the change in him. Something had happened.

He pushed aside his peach melba. "That was our manager, Andrew Tosh. He's at Laurie's dance. My housekeeper told him I was here."

Kathleen looked at him questioningly.

"James Laurie has sent word that the dance is to go on, but he cannot be present. That's all that's being said just now." He hesitated and looked at her closely before going on. "But Andrew Tosh says there has been a train crash near Carlisle this afternoon."

"It was on the six o'clock news," Kathleen said.

"Roger Laurie was on that train. He died after he was taken to hospital."

Kathleen's eyes closed in horror. "Oh, no!" she whispered in a moan.

Craig looked at her in silence. She had no cause to love the Lauries. But she was feeling for them as few would feel.

"Poor Mrs Laurie. Her two boys!"

Kathleen whispered the words, and thought of the regal woman who had given Kenny a pat on the head at Fenwick's. A son, a second son, taken from her.

They talked of the tragedy, then Kathleen said: "I – couldn't go dancing now. I'd rather go home."

He suggested a run to Ayr, anyway, but did not press her. "Did you ever meet Roger?" he asked, as they walked out to the car.

"No – "

"He was a grand fellow. What a tragedy!"

The car stopped at the entrance to No. 27. It was barely

dark. They said good-night in subdued tones and Kathleen wearily climbed the stairs. Aunt Isa was dismayed to see her.

"That's dreadful news, Kathy, terrible," she cried, when she heard the reason, then she clapped her hand to her mouth to stifle her cry, while tears filled her eyes and ran down her cheeks.

"What is it?" Kathleen asked her.

"This death, Kathy. I saw the sign of it in your cup the night you arrived. I never mentioned it, of course. But I've worried about it every minute since. I knew it wasn't you, but somebody near you. Oh! How I've watched Kenny every day, always fearing something might happen to him if I was late meeting him at school. But – this – is it."

The last words were a whisper. A simple acknowledgment and relief that God had spared her the worst of her fears.

Kathleen went into the other room to take off her dress. There was just light enough to see Kenny lying on his back with his knees drawn up and half the bedclothes down the front of the bed.

Kathleen turned him over and tucked in the clothes. He murmured in his sleep and she whispered something reassuring, bending to kiss his hair.

"Your poor grandmother!" she whispered, her eyes filling with tears.

CHAPTER FOUR

FLETCHER GALBRAITH looked at James Laurie, slumped in his chair in his study. It was three weeks since Roger's death. But James Laurie was still stricken. The change showed most in his face. It was grey and lined, almost lifeless.

"James, you must try to go out! You haven't been to the mill since – well, you owe something to the people there. There are men who have worked forty years with you! Men who –"

"Stop going on about the mill!" James Laurie's voice was bitter. "There's no one to carry it on now. Roger was the last one of the Lauries."

"He wasn't!"

James Laurie raised his massive head to look at his lawyer.

"Are you out of your mind?"

"I said he wasn't!" Fletcher Galbraith rubbed the side of his sharp nose. "I'm a governor of the High School. I was speaking to Miss McNabb, the infant mistress, and she told me there's a Kenneth Laurie in the school again. He's your Kenneth's son."

Slowly James Laurie straightened in his chair. He gulped in a deep breath.

"Are you trying to tell me –"

"I'm saying your son and Kathleen Todd had a child. The

boy's in this town. Living in Monk's Vennel." The last four words were said with deliberate emphasis and it had its effect.

The millowner heaved himself out of his chair and stood over the lawyer.

"In Monk's Vennel! But – but how do you know he's Kenneth's child?"

The lawyer gave a dry cough.

"He's Kenneth's son He has hair like his mother, but he has Kenneth's features and his eyes – your eyes! I've seen him! He's your grandson, all right. *He's* the last of the Lauries – the last of the name."

James Laurie began to pace about the room and the lawyer was relieved to see awakening interest in his face. Any emotion, even anger, was better than the apathy which had gripped him since the news about Roger.

"It's worth thinking about, James. He seems a fine boy. You could do a lot for him. And he could do something for you and your wife."

"Mildred." James Laurie stopped his pacing. "I must tell her!"

"Yes, do. Talk things over with her. Get in touch with me if I can help. Maybe arrange a meeting or something."

When Fletcher Galbraith left he was well pleased with himself. He had jolted the old man out of his self-pity, given him something to think about. Something would come of it, he was sure.

He was right. The following Tuesday he drove Kathleen to

the Laurie home. She was dressed, as he had first seen her, in her grey suit with a smart matching hat and a yellow blouse. Her burnished hair was shining. She looked cool and self-possessed.

But actually Kathleen was nervous. Galbraith's approach to her and his invitation had surprised her. It was Aunt Isa who had put her finger unerringly on the truth.

"It'll be about Kenny, mark my words. James Laurie must have heard. Now, don't you let them talk you into anything, Kathy!"

"What could they talk me into?"

All Mr Galbraith told her was that the Lauries wanted to talk about Kenny's future. Beyond that he knew nothing. But surely nothing but good could come from the Lauries asking her to their home! It was the first sign of friendliness. She should welcome it.

Yet her knees trembled as the car stopped outside the pillared front door of Finnard.

Kathleen now knew Mr and Mrs Laurie by sight; but her appearance was a surprise to them. This straight-backed girl with the dark flaming hair had appearance and character.

Fletcher Galbraith made the introductions and then withdrew. He would wait in the next room, he said. Better they should talk without strangers.

Mildred Laurie motioned Kathleen to a chair. Kathleen was hardly aware of anything in the beautifully appointed lounge except the older woman's sad face.

James Laurie was never a man to beat about the bush.

"You married my son in the spring of nineteen forty-four?" he began quietly.

"On Easter Monday," Kathleen replied.

"You were in the A.T.S.?"

She nodded.

"We met when we were stationed in the same camp near – "

He held up his hand to stop her.

"I want you to know that all this is still painful to me and my wife. We disapproved of the marriage. But that's in the past. It's the future we have to think about. I had no idea you had a boy."

The accusing note in his voice nettled Kathleen, but she answered him calmly.

"You never showed any interest, Mr Laurie. Kenny was born six months after his father's death. By that time I was well aware of your attitude to me. I remember a very formal letter from your lawyer –"

"The boy," Mildred Laurie broke in quickly, "alters all that."

Kathleen looked from one to the other, and waited.

"I'll be frank with you," James Laurie went on, and Kathleen noticed he refrained from addressing her by name. "I want to do something for Kenneth's boy. You know – what's happened to us?" Out of the corner of her eye Kathleen saw Mildred Laurie's face go white.

"I know. I'm – deeply sorry."

He brushed aside her sympathy and hurried on.

"Your boy is a Laurie. I should like him brought up as one. My wife and I can give him the kind of upbringing he should have. When I go he'll have all I leave – the mill – and all else."

"And he'll have a home here, with everything a boy could wish for." Mildred Laurie spoke with almost passionate eagerness.

"I feel – feel overwhelmed," Kathleen stammered. "I – I never thought – " Her voice trailed away.

For the first time James Laurie relaxed. Things were going more smoothly than he had anticipated.

"Now, if you'll ring for tea, Mildred, I'll get Galbraith in. Have to tell him what to put in the papers." He turned to Kathleen, "You'll hear all I say."

"Papers?" Kathleen raised her head. "What papers?"

"Papers – agreement, you know, to make everything legal," he replied. "Since you've come back to Kilmarford, the best thing you can do is to sign this paper and give up all claim to your boy – our grandson!"

But even before James Laurie had finished, everything was suddenly clear to Kathleen. His words and their meaning seared into her mind. She rose from her chair, her eyes aflame, her whole body shaking with anger.

Afterwards Kathleen could never remember all the things she suddenly felt, all at the one time, as she rose and faced James Laurie.

There was deep anger in her heart. She felt righteously insulted that the Lauries could imagine she would ever part with Kenny – to them or anyone. She suspected now her visit to Finnard had been a trick, to trap her into something the Lauries and their lawyer had arranged.

All these, and then, a feeling of pity for the Lauries. For all their scheming, as she alone knew, would come to nothing. She would never part with Kenny.

"All you have to do is to sign that you give up any claim to the boy."

That's what James Laurie had said. As Kathleen remembered, anger surged through her again, and angry words rose to her lips. But before she could speak them James Laurie's voice barked out again, his bushy eyebrows rising and falling like heavy shutters.

"You heard what I said, didn't you?"

"I certainly did!" To her surprise Kathleen found she was suddenly calm. Her voice sounded cold even to her own ears. "You want me to hand over my boy to you! I've always thought you were a foolish old man. Now I think you must be mad!"

The words jerked James Laurie upright in his chair. No one had ever spoken to him like that before. He raised a pointing finger, and opened his lips, but Kathleen went on.

"Please don't interrupt. What I have to say, I want to say quickly. I feel so ashamed coming here that I want to get out of this house as soon as possible. But understand this, once and for all. Kenny's my son. And my son he will remain, so long as I live."

"Can't you forget yourself and think of the boy? It's all for his good. You shouldn't be selfish."

Kathleen's eyes held James Laurie unflinchingly.

"Selfish! If it is selfish for a mother to keep her own child – to love him and work for him so that he will grow up to be as good a man as his father – then I'm selfish – and proud to be so, Mr Laurie."

"You are standing in your boy's way. We can give him – "

"You can give him nothing that matters. You can give him a kind of upbringing I never had. The kind of home I've never known. What else? Better clothes, maybe. After that – nothing!

"But I can give him what he can't get from anyone else. A mother's love and care. And you ask me to deny him that! If I did I'd deserve to be whipped out of the town." She lowered her voice to a whisper. "My father went to prison for doing less."

She saw the look of pained surprise on Mrs Laurie's face.

"You don't like me mentioning my father, I see. But you needn't wince. My father did things I could never do. Just as you do things my husband wouldn't do, if he were alive today. Kenneth would never ask any mother to give up her child. Not for any reason in the world."

"Fine words. But you should be practical. Do you think you can give your boy all he deserves – all that is his right as Kenneth's son?"

"I've done it for five years," Kathleen said firmly. "I was alone in the world when Kenny was born. My mother was dead, as dead as I was to you! I've worked to give Kenny a

43

home, to feed him and clothe him. He now goes to the school where you sent his father. We've never had much! We never will. But, thank God, we've never wanted."

"We don't deny that," James Laurie conceded, "but your best isn't good enough for my grandson."

Kathleen smiled wryly.

"He's your grandson. But he's my son! And nothing in the world will make me give him up!"

"You don't let me finish, you know," James Laurie said. "You would get a lump sum for giving us the boy. Enough to keep you for the rest of your life – in comfort."

Kathleen was angry again, and spoke now without choosing her words.

"So I wasn't just to give up Kenny. I was to sell him to you! How dare you!"

Her words echoed round the room and then fell into a pool of silence. It could almost be felt as Kathleen picked up her gloves. But her anger quickly spent itself. Again a feeling of pity took its place. Unlike Kenneth's parents, she had a son – and a future.

"And we have never seen him." It was the first time Mrs Laurie had spoken. Her words, like a cry from a broken heart, reached Kathleen as she made for the door.

"But you have, Mrs Laurie! You have seen Kenny. You've talked to him."

The older woman looked up, a wistful expression on her saddened face.

"You were in Fenwick's Tearooms the other day,"

Kathleen reminded her. "On your way to the cash desk you dropped your umbrella. A little boy picked it up and handed it to you. Remember?

"You patted his head, talked about his lovely hair. The dark auburn hair you like so much. And you gave him a shilling for being a good boy. That was Kenny! Your grandson! The boy you want me to sell to you! Would you?"

Colour ran into Mildred Laurie's face. Her hand went slowly to her open mouth.

Kathleen didn't wait for an answer. Her head high, she walked from the room, closing the door quietly behind her.

Fletcher Galbraith was in the entrance hall, his thin face betraying his anxiety. He had overheard enough to know that his scheming had misfired.

"I'm leaving," Kathleen told him. "I think you know why. You drove me here, but I'd prefer to leave alone."

She walked past him and he could only marvel at her dignity and bearing.

But for all her outward calm, Kathleen scarcely realised she was out of Finnard until she was at the front gate. Then her self-control deserted her. She began to tremble, her knees sagged under her. She leaned against the wall to steady herself, closed her eyes as though to shut out the vision of James Laurie's hard face.

"Are you all right, Miss?"

Kathleen didn't see the chubby-faced telegraph boy dismount from his red bicycle and look at her with concern. She smiled wanly and raised her hand in an assuring gesture.

He returned the smile, jumped on his bicycle and went whistling down the road.

Kathleen walked slowly to the centre of the town, her cheeks scarlet and white by turns. Her mind tried vainly to place the scene with her "in-laws" in some kind of coherent order.

That they should entice her to their home on such a cruel pretext! Of course, it was all part of their scheme. Finnard, with its luxury and spacious comfort, was meant to dazzle her, to impress upon her the world that separated it from Monk's Vennel. That was bad enough. But that the Lauries could ever imagine she would give up Kenny – her own son!

Hot tears spilled over her cheeks. She brushed them away. Before reaching the High Street she stopped to powder her face, to remove any tell-tale marks. They were nice folk at Carmichael's, but they had sharp eyes.

Miss Gemmell looked at her searchingly when she entered the office. But her greeting was as friendly as usual.

Kathleen sat down at her desk and stared in surprise. A red rose, a joy of deep colour and rare perfection, glowed from a small vase. She touched its rich petals and felt their velvety warmth. As she took the cover off her typewriter, Kathleen looked round at the other desks. Hers was the only one with a rose.

CHAPTER FIVE

TEN minutes after her return, Kathleen was called into Craig Carmichael's room. He had given her time off that morning and knew where she was going. He looked up from a pile of letters as she came in. At a glance he took in her pale face, and the trembling hands that held her notebook and pencil, and understood an ordeal had been faced and conquered.

"Sit down, Mrs Laurie, and put your notebook away," he said kindly. "Would you like to tell me what happened at Finnard? Just a moment!" He picked up the inter-office phone and spoke to Miss Gemmell. "Please bring two cups of tea, Effie."

He sat back in his chair and lit a cigarette.

"I can see you haven't had a happy time." He slowly waved away a cloud of smoke to give Kathleen time to compose herself.

"It was dreadful!" she began in a whisper. "I should have known better than to go."

Without prompting she told him everything. Once or twice her eyes flashed, but all the time her voice was low and calm. As Craig Carmichael listened his attention transmitted a sense of sympathy Kathleen felt and appreciated.

"And that's all," she finished. "But do you know, before I walked out of that room, I was beginning to feel sorry for

Kenneth's parents. In spite of all they've got, they are lonely and sad. They've lost two sons. Can't they understand how I would feel to lose mine – even to them?"

She looked across the desk at her employer and their eyes met.

"You think I did right?" she asked. It was a challenge rather than a question.

"You couldn't have done anything else," Craig Carmichael replied. "You are Kenny's mother and no real mother gives up her child to anyone. I'm surprised at Laurie! He's never tactful, but he's rarely just foolish.

"Of course, that's the trouble with a man who always gets his own way. You can't argue with him. He only sees what he wants. But I'll bet right now he realises his mistake and has made up his mind what to do about it."

"I'm afraid I – I lost my temper with him," Kathleen smiled.

"Well, don't ever apologise to him," Craig Carmichael's eyes twinkled. "Soft words are lost on your father-in-law. He doesn't believe in mincing words himself – or in the right of anyone to have an independent mind."

Miss Gemmell brought in the tea, raised her brows at her employer and went out quietly.

Kathleen sipped the tea gratefully.

"You know, I feel quite limp – as though I've wakened from a nightmare."

"I understand. That's why you are going to take the rest of the day off. Now, please don't start arguing with me! I like getting my own way, too!" He laughed and she joined in. It was a safety valve to her pent-up emotions. It eased the strain and she felt better after it.

"Go home and tell your aunt all about it," he went on. "You'll feel much better after talking to someone you really know."

"You are very kind. Oh, and thanks for the lovely rose. It meant a great deal to me."

He shrugged, still smiling.

"Now, off you go, but remember – "

"Yes?" Kathleen was already halfway to the door.

"Don't be surprised if Laurie makes another approach. Once he gets his teeth into a thing, he never lets go. And next time don't cut him off completely. After all, there's your boy's future to consider. Laurie's Mills aren't something to throw away lightly."

"All the mills in the world wouldn't make me give up Kenny!"

"You wouldn't be the woman I think you are if you did," Craig Carmichael replied with conviction. "But don't get up against Laurie any more than you can help. Always remember he is an old man, and old men don't easily change their ways. But you never know. Laurie may soften in time. Perhaps when he gets to know Kenny and you – "

Kathleen shook her head.

"He doesn't want to know me! He regards me only as a means to an end. He wants my boy – but he'll never change towards me!"

"'Never is a long day'," Craig Carmichael quoted with a smile.

* * * *

That talk with her employer put new life into Kathleen. As she walked home to Monk's Vennel she felt the sunshine returning to the day again.

Sympathy is a never-failing balm to a heavy heart. She had known little of it in the past. At the time of Kenneth's death she was in need of comfort. But those who could have extended it in healing measure, withheld it from her. The Lauries shut her out from their own grief; as though it were something she had no right to feel or share.

But in Kilmarford she now had friends. Craig Carmichael was one. Beneath the rather cynical surface the world saw, there lay qualities kindly and gracious. He had the gift of understanding, and an understanding heart always had room for the cares of others. Just like Aunt Isa!

An added spring was in Kathleen's step as she ran up the stair at No. 27 and threw the door open. Isa Duncan was standing at the table baking, her hands flaked with flour.

"What are you doing back at this time?" she asked anxiously. "Has that man upset you?"

Kathleen slipped off her coat and stood at the window. Between many interruptions she told what had happened. Aunt Isa's reaction was what she expected.

"I felt in my bones while I was tidying up this morning,"

the older woman said, her floury hands akimbo on her plump waist.

"I felt sure Laurie was up to something nasty. Fancy him thinking he could have our bairn! The nerve of him!"

Kathleen smiled.

"He's right in one thing, Aunt Isa. The Lauries could give Kenny everything – "

"There's only one place for a bairn, and that's with the mother."

Kathleen's eyes filled with tears. She leaned against the sink with something approaching peace in her heart. She needed no assurance that she had done right. But Craig Carmichael and Aunt Isa had put the seal of approval on all she had done.

"Well, that's enough of the Lauries for one day," Mrs Duncan said. "It'll be something to put in Alec's letter tonight. Show him strange things can happen here as well as in Chicago. But forget about them now. Would you like to come with me and meet Kenny from school? Or would you rather sit and – "

"I'll come with you," Kathleen said eagerly. "It will be a nice surprise for him."

When they arrived at the gate the smaller children were already streaming out. Kathleen had no difficulty in picking out Kenny. He was talking excitedly to two boys. She was pleased to see how easily he was fitting in to this new and important phase of his life.

He caught sight of her and shouted, "Mummy."

"Hello, darling! I've come with Aunt Isa to meet you today. Now stand still a minute. You've buttoned your coat the wrong way."

They started for home, Kenny skipping along in front of them, his school bag dangling from his shoulder. Since he started school, he saw no need for anyone to take his hand. Although her heart sighed over the baby she had lost, Kathleen rejoiced in his boyish independence. God willing, it was something she meant to protect.

* * * *

The weeks slipped by. The clash with the Lauries receded further and further into Kathleen's memory. Although she knew correspondence was exchanged between the two firms, Craig Carmichael never referred to the matter again. Kathleen was grateful.

She was now firmly established in the office. She enjoyed the work and the measure of her popularity was reflected in the frequent use of her christian name. Only Miss Gemmell continued to call her "Mrs Laurie".

But it was in Kenny she found her greatest happiness. From a shy, sensitive child, he was growing into a lively, independent boy. Never a night passed but she had to listen to an excited account of something that happened at school or on the way home. Aunt Isa no longer met him at the school gates every afternoon.

Kathleen got back from the office one evening and found

Aunt Isa greatly excited. Her round cheeks glowed like peony rose.

"You'll never guess what happened the day, Kathy!"

Without waiting for an answer she rushed on, her words tumbling out helter-skelter.

"I was paying my rent and Mr Wilkie, the factor, fair took my breath away. 'Mrs Duncan,' he said, 'if you'd like a change of house, I've got the very thing for you.' Did you ever hear the like? Rented houses in Kilmarford are as scarce as blue snow!"

"Where is the house?" Kathleen asked.

"It's one of the bungalows off the South Road. Four rooms, a modern kitchen and bathroom. I told him the rent would be too heavy. But he said it wouldn't be much more than I'm paying now. He'd heard I'd got you and Kenny staying with me, so he thought I'd be glad of the extra rooms. That's right enough – but, of course, we could never go. I can't see myself anywhere but in the Vennel!"

"I'm not so sure!" Kathleen's expression was thoughtful. "Think what it would mean, Auntie. A nice modern kitchen and a bathroom. No stairs to climb or wash. If it's a bungalow, there'll be a garden. You'd have all the ground to grow the flowers you love – not just a window-box. Think of it!"

"It would be nice, I know, but – "

"It would be lovely for Kenny. I'm never happy when he's playing in the Vennel. It's so narrow and busy."

"That was the first thing I thought about." Aunt Isa tied the strings of her apron round her ample waist.

"But I can't understand it – a bungalow, to rent! I'd like to know why Mr Wilkie gave me the first chance of such a house. There must be plenty on his books he could give it to. It wasn't because I cleaned for him in the war, surely? My, your uncle and I often spoke about moving. But never to a bungalow! Oh, it's no' for the likes o' me!"

"That's nonsense, Auntie," Kathleen argued. "You've been a good tenant all these years and Mr Wilkie wants to help you. There's nothing to worry about. If it's a rented house, you couldn't be put out. And I'm sure we could manage the little extra."

Aunt Isa beamed.

"Maybe you're right, Kathy! Anyway there's no harm in going to look at it."

Kathleen nodded.

"Could you make it tomorrow afternoon?"

"Mr Wilkie said I could get the key any time. Oh, Kathy! Do you really think it would be right? Imagine me flitting to a bungalow after all these years in the Vennel! It's like a dream. I keep thinking I'll wake up –"

Kathleen put her arm round the plump shoulders.

"You deserve it, Aunt Isa, if anyone does! If the house is suitable, I'll lift some money out of my post office account. I saw some pretty curtain material in Sandiland's."

For the rest of the evening they talked and planned. They were like children with a new toy.

The following afternoon was damp and grey. But nothing

could dim their enthusiasm. Dalreoch, the name on the gate, was small and compact, with red slates and little fat chimneys. There was a small garden and Isa Duncan wandered round the neat flower beds, pausing now and again to gasp in delight.

The house was empty so they could explore every corner. They missed nothing. In the end it was the labour-saving kitchen and modern bathroom with its chrome fittings and pink tiles that delighted them most.

"It's beautiful," said Aunt Isa, a tremor in her voice. Kathleen noted it and quickly changed the subject.

"We'll have the Webbs quite near us. Their bungalow is only about ten minutes from here."

"Is their house rented?"

"No. Nan said they're buying it through a building society."

They wandered into the kitchen again and Isa Duncan stopped at the window, a frown creasing her brow.

"That's the one thing against the place. Look! You can see Laurie's Mill from this window. I could think of better things to look at! But there's not many places you can go in this town and not see Laurie's! I wonder how they're enjoying their holiday?"

Everyone in Kilmarford knew that James Laurie and his wife had gone on a cruise to the Bahamas. It was their doctor's suggestion and James Laurie had actually welcomed it. Perhaps away from Kilmarford he and his wife might forget the past and learn to face the future.

By the time Aunt Isa and Kathleen left the bungalow, there was no doubt in their minds. They were going to live in Dalreoch.

"But I'd still like to know why Mr Wilkie gave me the first chance of this lovely house. It wasn't because I cleaned for him in the war."

That thought had also been with Kathleen, but she kept it to herself. The night before she lay awake turning it over in her mind. If it wasn't the factor's doing, who was behind it? Who had used his influence?

One name did jump to her mind. Craig Carmichael! Yet why should he? She could never mention it to him, because if she were wrong, it would embarrass them both. Still –

She walked thoughtfully beside Aunt Isa, watching Kenny scuffing through the wet leaves on the road. Perhaps there was nothing in it after all. It could be just a stroke of luck! Yet doubt persisted . . .

She tucked her hand into the crook of the older woman's arm and squeezed it.

"Stop day-dreaming, Aunt Isa," she smiled, "and tell me when we're going to flit?"

"What a lot I'll have to tell Alec in my next letter. I never thought I'd be flitting at my time of life. But let's get it over before the cold weather really sets in. I'll see Mr Wilkie tomorrow. Then I'll start scrubbing the place out. I'd like your bedroom painted, I think. The rest will do fine."

CHAPTER SIX

DAYS and weeks passed in rising excitement. While Isa
Duncan emptied cupboards and drawers, Kathleen was busy
making new curtains on the old treadle sewing machine.
There was also shopping for extra furniture. But everything
was ready the day they were due to move into Dalreoch.

Kathleen was happier than she had been for years. Amid
all the preparations the Lauries were forgotten by everyone.
Kathleen was content to let them remain so.

She'd heard no more from them or Fletcher Galbraith,
their lawyer. Things were just as they had been when she
first arrived in Kilmarford. She had lost nothing, but had
gained a great deal. She was back home. People were
forgetting she was Jock Todd's daughter. Neither her old
name nor her new one seemed to count for much. People
accepted her as herself.

She made new friends, among them Jenny Taylor at the
office, and several she met through the church. There, too,
she had renewed old friendships.

On the day they moved from Monk's Vennel to the
bungalow, she received a note from Nan Webb, inviting her
to spend Friday evening with her and George. They were
entertaining a few friends.

There was still much to do in the new home, so Kathleen
decided not to go. But Aunt Isa was instantly up in arms.

"This is only Monday! By Friday we'll be settled fine. You're needing a change and a party is just the thing. You're too young to be spending every night in the house with only me for company. I get gey dreich at times!"

So Kathleen spent the evening with the Webbs. To her surprise she enjoyed every minute of it. George Webb was a stoutish man with a faintly superior air. But he was pleasant to Kathleen, obviously doing his best to make her feel at home.

Kathleen wore a blue dress and her dark red hair glittered in the light. Even Nan remarked on it. She wore no jewellery, except her thin platinum wedding ring and an old-fashioned pearl brooch which belonged to her mother.

There was present another young married couple, by the name of Mason. But it was Ewen Gilmour, a young farmer, who paid Kathleen most attention. Fair-haired and tall, he seemed to tower over her, but his voice and manner were surprisingly gentle for a man of his size. He talked enthusiastically about his farm, just twelve miles out of Kilmarford.

It was striking ten o'clock when Kathleen rose to go.

"Must you?" Nan Webb asked. She was naturally pleased that the evening had been a success.

"I'm afraid so – "

"But you can't go yet! It's raining heavily," George Webb said. "Listen to it lashing on the window –"

"Stay a little longer," Ewen Gilmour broke in. "I'll run you home."

"Thank you," Kathleen smiled. "But I really must –"

"What's the hurry?" he insisted. "It's early yet!"

"I've got a job to go to in the morning. Besides, I've got a little boy at home, too!"

A few minutes later Kathleen and Ewen Gilmour were saying good-night to the Webbs, who saw them to the door. Then they drove away into the darkness and Kathleen gave her companion directions for finding Dalreoch.

Ewen Gilmour drove very slowly. When they reached the garden gate he switched off the engine, then he turned in his seat so that he was facing her.

"So you have a little boy, Mrs Laurie."

"I'm a widow. My husband was killed during the war."

There was a momentary silence, then he went on.

"I gather from the conversation tonight that you're new to Kilmarford."

"Not really. I was born and brought up here, but I've been away for some years. I came back in the summer."

"Do you know the part where I live?"

She shook her head.

"I don't think I've ever been that way."

"It's rather nice. I think you'd like it," he said with simple directness. "Now, I've an idea –" His voice took on a note of enthusiasm. "You must come and see Carnbo. That's my farm. And bring your little boy. There's plenty to interest him – and you."

"That's very kind of you –"

"We'll fix it up later. I'm in town every Tuesday for the

market. I won't forget. My sister, Aileen, will be pleased to see you, too."

Kathleen slipped out of the car and let herself into the house. She expected Aunt Isa to be in bed. But she was sitting at the fire, her grey hair streaming down her back.

"Come and give me all your news! I've been washing my hair. Did you have a nice time? Who brought you home? I didn't know the Webbs had a car."

Kathleen smiled at the bombardment of questions. But she knew they were not asked out of idle curiosity.

"First of all, I had a lovely time. Second, the Webbs don't have a car. A young farmer, Ewen Gilmour, drove me home. Anything else, Auntie?"

Isa Duncan raised her brows and looked interested.

"I thought the car sat a long while at the gate."

Kathleen laughed. She sank into the chair opposite the older woman and slipped off her shoes.

"He was telling me about his farm – Carnbo. Now this will really interest you! He invited Kenny and me to go to see it; and to meet his sister." She forestalled her aunt's questions by hurrying on, "I'm quite sure it was just one of those polite invitations that are never meant to be taken seriously. Probably by this time he has forgotten all about it."

Aunt Isa went on brushing her hair.

"You think so?"

Kathleen nodded.

"Still, Kenny would love to visit a farm."

"Ay, he would like that fine."

"But as nothing will come of it, we won't mention it to him. You know how excited he gets!"

"Just as you say, Kathy." Isa Duncan's voice was almost a whisper, but her eyes were deeply thoughtful.

* * * *

The weeks following "the flitting" were as paradise to Kathleen.

She was happy Aunt Isa liked the bungalow, complaining only that winter wasn't a time for gardening. She felt Kenny was safe from hurt or harm in his own garden, or in the one just a few yards away with his new playmate, a boy who also went to the High School.

Then suddenly, three weeks before it was due, Christmas came to Dalreoch.

It began with a letter and a ten-dollar bill from Alec in Chicago.

"I am sending this early so you can change it and have the money ready to pay any charges the Customs make on the parcel Marlene is sending. Hope Kenny's present suits. We had to guess the size."

Of course Kenny was told nothing about it. And a very good thing! For when the parcel arrived two days before Christmas Aunt Isa had not enough to pay for it! She and Kenny had to watch the postman carry it back to the van.

"It was a pity," Aunt Isa told Kathleen. "But he'll bring it again tomorrow. It's been so long in arriving I've spent most of the money Alec sent. You leave me a pound tomorrow, Kathleen."

With the parcel next day there arrived another addressed to Mrs K. Laurie. Kathleen opened it that night and found a plump, plucked chicken and a note from Ewen Gilmour.

"I have been down with pneumonia so haven't arranged that visit yet. But there'll be more to show your boy later on. A happy Christmas to you both."

Aunt Isa took charge of the chicken. About the note she nodded her head with strange satisfaction.

"That explains a lot. I couldn't understand why he did nothing. But maybe I was just fearing too much." And before Kathleen could ask what she meant she stalked off to put the chicken in the pantry.

So Christmas came. Kenny got the cowboy suit Alec sent him. Kathleen got several pairs of nylons. And Aunt Isa from Marlene got an assortment of gifts for the bungalow that delighted her.

In the early weeks of the new year, Andrew White, a foreman at Carmichael's, who was also superintendent of the Sunday school of the Parish Church, asked Kathleen if she would help at the children's party. Kenny attended the primary, so Kathleen readily agreed.

There is nothing in all the world quite like a Sunday school soiree, even if it has changed from what it used to be. Kenny was soon in the thick of the fun, wearing a pair of grey shorts and a new white shirt Aunt Isa gave him at Christmas.

Kathleen tried to subdue her pride in her boy every time

she saw him. She was sure he was the nicest-looking boy in the crowded hall.

Although the children never showed signs of having enough, some of the mothers who had come to help the teachers were soon exchanging tired looks. One of the little girls lost a sandal, and Kathleen lifted her on to a chair to buckle it, when she felt a hand rest on her shoulder.

"Excuse me. You're Mrs Laurie, aren't you? I've been trying to get a chance to speak to you. I'm Alice Boswell."

Kathleen knew her by sight. Aunt Isa had pointed her out on their way to church one Sunday. She was a striking-looking girl, pretty and tall, without being clumsy. She was very fair and her hair was knotted loosely at the nape of her neck. Her eyes were a soft blue. On her face there was an expression of sweetness which was instantly attractive.

"Yes, I'm Kathleen Laurie." Kathleen took the extended hand and felt its warm clasp.

"I've been hoping to meet you – ever since I knew –"

"Then you do know about me?"

"Oh, yes! Your father-in-law told me everything."

It was strange hearing James Laurie referred to as her "father-in-law." It took Kathleen a moment to recover.

"Actually, I'm unpopular with him at the moment," Alice Boswell went on, ending in a soft laugh.

"I – I don't quite understand."

Kathleen felt all at once out of her depth. She found Alice Boswell's habit of going straight to the heart of things slightly disconcerting.

She was to grow used to it in time, and to realise her sincerity was one of her greatest charms.

"Mr Laurie told me he wanted to take your boy away from you. He wasn't pleased when I didn't agree with him, and that I'd never heard of anything so heartless."

Kathleen felt her stiffness melting.

"Thank you, Miss Boswell. But I'm sorry if you've made yourself unpopular on my account. There have been times when I've wondered —"

She broke off as two boys dodged between them and Kathleen was spun around.

"I understand the Lauries are back home," Alice Boswell went on.

Kathleen raised her eyebrows in surprise.

"You haven't seen them?"

"No. My mother has, but I think — it's better for me to stay away — at least for a time. I'm a constant reminder of —"

Kathleen saw the white, ringless hand clench slightly and knew that, beneath the outward calm, deep feelings tormented.

"I — never knew Roger," she said hesitantly. "But if he was like Kenneth, we have both suffered a great loss."

Alice Boswell's blue eyes misted, but she blinked the tears away.

"Yes, but you have — something left." She turned to look at the crowd of noisy children. "That's your little boy."

"Yes — the one with the red hair."

"As if I didn't know! He's the image of Kenneth." She

sighed. "Sometimes I can't believe it, even yet –"

"I'm sorry," Kathleen whispered, and felt how inadequate words could be. She, too, had loved and lost. She knew all it meant.

"I'm so glad to have met you." Alice Boswell's voice changed. "And I hope we'll meet again – often. Well, I suppose I'd better get back to the piano. I persuaded one of the girls to play for the last game, but I see Miss Robertson signalling to me."

"Mummy!" Kenneth rushed up to them, his eyes shining and his cheeks flushed.

"Are you having a good time, darling?"

"Smashing! But, Mummy, I've got something to ask you. That boy over there – the one with a blue shirt and the balloon – you know what he said to me?"

"No, dear, what was it?"

"He said I'd got a grannie in Kilmarford!" His voice rose. "I told him he was wrong. But he said it again. I haven't got a grannie, have I?"

Kathleen felt her mouth grow dry as she looked down at her son. It had come at last. One of those questions she had always feared had come when it was least expected!

Into the pause fell Alice Boswell's gentle voice.

"Your little friend is right, Kenny. You have a grannie staying in Kilmarford. A grannie and a grandfather!"

"Oh!" Kathleen gave a gasp, then realised Alice Boswell was looking at her, an embarrassed expression flooding her eyes.

65

"Doesn't he know?" Alice Boswell whispered.

Kathleen shook her head, glad that Kenny's attention was taken up by a passing balloon.

"Oh, I am sorry," Alice stammered. "But I'm afraid it's done now."

"Yes," Kathleen echoed, "it's done now."

She knew Kenny wouldn't rest until he knew the truth. And he had a right to know the truth now.

"Does my grannie and grandfather live in Kilmarford, Mummy?"

"Yes, darling," Kathleen tried to keep her voice steady. "They live here and – and one day you – you'll see them!"

CHAPTER SEVEN

THOUGH spoken in a whisper, Kathleen's words seemed to be as firm as a challenge. But she knew there was little chance of her having to face it.

To promise Kenny he would meet his grannie and grandfather was one thing: to see it ever happening was a different matter. But she knew Kenny would hold her to her promise. He wouldn't forget.

"Some day soon, Mummy?" His voice broke into her troubled thoughts.

He looked up at her so appealingly that she was forced to smile. But she must not promise something she could not fulfil.

"Look, darling. The other boys and girls are going to play musical chairs. You'd better go and take someone's arm before you're left out."

He rushed away to join in the fun. As Kathleen watched him her smile faded. What a sorry tangle it was!

After six years the Lauries' attitude to her no longer hurt. They didn't want her. She didn't want anything to do with them. She wanted Kenny's life to be free from all that unpleasantness.

But now the past had reached out and touched him. He was now involved, as much as she was herself. Kenny had all the persistence of a five-year-old with a naturally questioning mind. In his childish way he would go on probing, asking questions until he stumbled on the truth. And that was the last thing she wanted.

She closed her eyes as if to shut out a vision of things to come. She had forgotten all about Alice Boswell until she felt a hand on her arm.

"What a clumsy fool I've been," Alice said with sincere apology. "I never realised –"

"Please, don't blame yourself. This had to be faced sometime."

"That may be, but it doesn't excuse my blundering." The pressure on Kathleen's arm increased. "Why are some people so blind – and cruel? Oh! I do wish things could be different for you."

Kathleen smiled wanly.

"Perhaps they will one day, when there – there's a change of heart."

It was a pious hope. At that moment Kathleen had little faith in it.

"There's Miss Robertson signalling frantically," Alice said. "I'll have to go. Good-bye, Mrs Laurie – no, I'm going to call you Kathleen. Good-bye, Kathleen. I hope we meet again soon."

The evening wore on and the fun and games reached a joyous crescendo. The floor shook with happy, pounding feet as Kathleen's eyes sought Kenny, always in the thick of things. For the time being at least, all thought of his grannie and grandfather was forgotten.

The thought was with her as she helped with the washing up. It stayed with her during their walk home under a moonlit sky. Kenny talked all the way, proudly flourishing a big Donald Duck balloon and a wilted paper hat.

He ran ahead as they neared the bungalow and burst into the kitchen excitedly.

"Aunt Isa!" he said. "See what I won in the musical chairs." He dropped a tartan-covered diary and pencil into her lap. "I'm going to write something in it every day."

The old woman smiled as she listened to his chatter. Watching their heads together, like two friendly conspirators, Kathleen wondered if any boy could have a better "grannie." Isa Duncan had a big heart, filled with kindness and love.

"It's a cat's wash for you tonight, Kenny," Aunt Isa said, and Kathleen was glad. She was tired. It was a good thing for grown-ups, she reflected, that Sunday school soirees didn't happen every week.

When Kenny was finally asleep, his balloon dangling from the end of the bed, his diary and pencil under his pillow, Kathleen slumped into a chair by the living-room fire. She brushed a strand of hair from her forehead and sighed.

"It's amazing where the bairns get all their energy," Aunt Isa said, raising her eyes from her knitting. "You're looking tired, lassie."

"I am, rather." Kathleen stared into the fire. "It was quite an afternoon, one way and another."

Isa Duncan sat back and looked at Kathleen's thoughtful face.

"You were very quiet when you came in. I noticed it while Kenny was giving me his news. Did – did something happen, Kathy?"

"You're an old witch!" Kathleen laughed, but there was no mirth in it. "Actually, something did happen. And I'm very sorry about it."

She leaned forward, her chin cupped in her hands. In a low voice she told her aunt about Alice Boswell.

"It would have been better if Miss Boswell had kept a still tongue in her head!" Isa Duncan stabbed her darning needle into a stocking with an expressive gesture. "Oh, I'm not saying she meant harm! But it was none of her business!"

"She was most upset about what she had done," Kathleen defended. "After all, how was she to know Kenny hadn't been told about his grandparents?"

"Ay, and she's not the only one. It would be a shock to a lot of folk in this town. But I'm not worrying about them."

"Neither am I. I'm wondering what I'll say when Kenny starts asking more questions?"

"Cross that bridge when you come to it, Kathy. A bairn soon forgets. We'll just have to wait and see. But it makes me angry! There's nothing I'd like better than to put the whole clacking of Lauries clean out of my mind. I've got that man setting at the back of my head like a hoodie crow on a dyke!"

Kathleen smiled and Isa Duncan stifled a yawn as she rose to her feet.

"The only time I forget James Laurie is when I'm in bed.

And that's where I'm going this very minute! It's where you should be, too – to forget all about this. Maybe you're making a mountain out of a molehill."

Kathleen leaned over and patted her hand.

"Away you go and I'll bring you a hot drink."

Within half an hour Kathleen was in bed, to fall asleep to the sweet sound of Kenny's soft breathing. Her last thought was of what Aunt Isa had said. Perhaps Kenny would forget he had a grandmother.

But Isa Duncan couldn't sleep. At half-past two her dumpy figure padded silently through the living-room and into the kitchen. She'd got up to make herself a strong cup of tea. Quietly she went to the sink with the kettle, then drew up with a start.

A bright glow in the sky caught her attention. She blinked, then leaned forward until her nose almost touched the glass.

"A fire!" Her eyes widened as she recognised the outline of the buildings against the glow of flames. She turned away quickly.

Kathleen came out of the mists of sleep with an insistent hand on her arm. She started into wakefulness and sat up.

"Aunt Isa!" she gasped. "What – what is it? Are you feeling ill?"

"Come at once, Kathy!" Her voice was breathless. "Laurie's is on fire. You can see it from the kitchen window. I've never seen such a blaze!"

Kathleen got out of bed and slipped into her dressing-gown and slippers. Drawing the bedroom door behind her, she joined Aunt Isa at the kitchen window.

"How awful!" The words were a moan.

The huge name of the mill stood out luridly in the red glow now filling the whole sky.

"It looks as if it's the new buildings," Kathleen said. "I do hope they can keep it under control. It would be terrible if the whole place were gutted."

"That's what I was thinking!" Aunt Isa's words were thoughtful. "And yet it's a wonderful lesson, if you can learn it, isn't it? All that money, and the power money can bring, just going up in flames and smoke. Maybe old Laurie will learn something from it."

Kathleen made no answer.

"I just pray nobody is injured – or worse – trying to save anything for that old fool," Aunt Isa went on. As Kathleen remained silent she lit the gas under the forgotten kettle.

"I got up to make myself a cup of tea, so we'll have it now."

Kathleen spoke for the first time as she sat on the draining board, sipping her tea and watching the glare, staining the sky like a sunset.

"Surely enough has happened to the Lauries without this!"

"Why be sorry for them?" Aunt Isa asked. "James Laurie won't thank you or anyone else for pity. He'll get over this. His kind always do. He'll be well insured against fire. Give your sympathy to those who'll be put off their work. I mind the time of the depression –"

Kathleen was only half listening now, letting Aunt Isa's

voice flow over her. The letters, L A U R I E, that glittered white in the daytime now looked red beside the flames. As she watched a pall of smoke obscured the name, leaving only the letters "S O N."

Kathleen stared, fascinated, then turned her head away quickly.

"My, but Kenny would love to see this," Aunt Isa was saying. "Shouldn't we get him up? It's the biggest bonfire he's ever likely to see!"

"No – no! He's had enough excitement for one day," Kathleen said. She lifted down the dish towel to dry the cups she had just rinsed. "Besides, it's not the kind of thing I want him to remember."

"Maybe you're right, Kathy," Isa Duncan said apologetically. "At times I'm just a spiteful auld besom!"

"I think the fire is dying down," Kathleen said after a while. "They'll have got it under control – thank goodness! Let's get back to bed or we'll not be fit for anything in the morning."

But Kathleen found sleep eluded her. Too much had happened in the last twenty-four hours for her to sleep. Her meeting with Alice Boswell. Kenny's questions about his grandparents. Then the fire. All three were linked with the Lauries – and herself. She felt that she hadn't heard the last of any of them.

* * * *

Next day the whole town was talking about the fire. A recently built section of the mills, containing the newest machinery, was completely destroyed.

After church Kathleen and Mrs Duncan walked into the town to see the damage. From early morning there had been a steady stream of sightseers.

In the cold daylight wisps of smoke still curled up from the burnt out part of the sprawling buildings. The blackened walls and twisted machinery presented a picture of desolation.

"Mr Laurie was here a few minutes after the alarm was raised," a mill employee was telling one of his mates. "And he didn't leave until the fire was under control. He's an amazing man."

"It's a bad business with so many orders to meet and the mill working at full pressure," the other replied. "Wonder what will happen?"

"I don't know – but James Laurie will think of something."

As she moved among the crowd Kathleen overheard many expressions of sympathy. All of them were mingled with an unfaltering faith in James Laurie's ability. He would find a way out of this misfortune.

The fire was also the topic of talk at the office on Monday morning.

"Thank goodness it wasn't Carmichael's," Jenny Taylor said. "I shudder to think what would have happened –"

"It'll be a big loss to Laurie's –"

Kathleen tried to keep outside the flow of conversation. But she fully shared their feelings about Carmichael's.

In these few months she had developed a deep sense of loyalty to this small firm – and to Craig Carmichael. He'd given her a job when she needed one badly. Unlike many others, he wasn't interested in her family history or background. He had accepted her on face value and she returned that trust by diligent work.

Yet that day Kathleen could not settle to work. She was all on edge, and couldn't account for it. It was as if she were waiting for something to happen. Lunch was a welcome break. Yet she did poor justice to the steamed fish and apple pie Aunt Isa had prepared on her new gas cooker.

When she got back to the office Jennie Taylor, bubbling with excitement, followed her into the cloakroom.

"You'll never guess who's in with the boss!" she said. "Mr Laurie! Wonder what he's after?"

Colour flooded into Kathleen's face and she tried to keep her voice steady.

"I – I don't know, but we'd better not be caught gossiping here."

She went to her desk and tried to concentrate on her work. But her eyes kept straying to the door leading to Craig Carmichael's private room.

Beyond that door James Laurie sat with his knees crossed, facing the younger man on the other side of the desk. His deep-set eyes were red-rimmed, his voice raw with the effects of smoke.

"I'm in a fix, Carmichael," he said, "and it would be foolish to pretend otherwise. At the same time, I want to be perfectly honest with you. I've been to others before coming here, because you and I haven't seen eye to eye in the past, and we may not now. I've tried Bone's and Shaw's. They're both on late-work already so that rules them out. McCreath's willing to help. But they can do so little that it won't matter."

He paused and drummed his thick fingers on the arm of his chair.

"If I can't get help, I can't complete my orders. It's the South African one that's worrying me. Roger signed it up before he – and there's a time clause in the agreement. You know what that means! If I can't make it, I stand to lose thousands – as well as my reputation for never failing with an order!"

Craig Carmichael listened, his eyes thoughtful.

"That's why I'm here," Laurie went on. "That's why I'm asking you to forget what's happened between us. A firm's reputation is more important than personal ambition. I need your help." He leaned forward. "Is there anything you can do? Can you see your way to take over even part of the South African order?"

CHAPTER EIGHT

I'LL do anything to help, but –" Craig Carmichael shook his head and stabbed the blotter with the point of his pencil. "We've got our own problems, Mr Laurie, and we're working to high capacity. But – but I wonder if it's possible! Just a minute." He lifted the inter-office phone. "Ask Miss Gemmell to come in."

It was Jenny Taylor who answered.

"She's off this afternoon, Mr Carmichael – "

"Oh, I forgot! Well, ask Mrs Laurie to come in."

Craig was aware of a faint movement from James Laurie, but scarcely realised its significance. In the urgency of the moment he forgot Kathleen's relationship with the man before him.

Kathleen came in, neatly and simply dressed, her hair brushed smooth above her broad brow. She gave a quick look at her father-in-law, but his eyes were fixed on Carmichael.

"Kathleen, what is the position with overtime just now? You're in charge of the sheets, I think."

"We are almost on full overtime now. We will be on full when we start the Bristol order next week."

Craig looked at James Laurie. He had slumped in the chair, his face grey with fatigue and disappointment.

"I can't ask my men to do any more," Craig said. "There's

only so much men can do. But we might tackle it another way."

The slumped figure sat upright in the chair and a gleam flushed into the red-rimmed eyes.

"If there's any way out I'm ready to try it and pay for it. What do you suggest?"

"If you like to work a nightshift here, you can put in your own men and do it – "

"But I can't spare the men," Laurie broke in. "They're working full-time already."

"But you have men laid off because of the fires?" Craig explained. "They should be quite familiar with our machines. Could you not get enough together to make a nightshift?

"It could have a full twelve hours every night running the Bristol and the South African orders until they're completed on time. What's required first to have priority."

James Laurie's fist bounced off the arm of the chair; colour mounted again in his grey cheeks.

"I'd never have thought of that! My men and your machines! Of course! You'll not regret this, Carmichael. I'll pay you well –"

"You'll pay me only what it costs and not a penny more, Mr Laurie. This isn't a business arrangement. It's to help you – as I would help anyone at such a time. I'd like to think you would do the same for me if the need arose – but I hope it won't!"

For a moment James Laurie was speechless. He wasn't

used to generosity in business. He cleared his throat and faced the younger man squarely.

"That's very – very generous of you," he muttered.

Craig smiled.

"Not generous, Mr Laurie, just human. Now, I think you'd better have a talk with my works manager before you go." He turned to Kathleen. "Get Mr Tosh and send him in right away. Oh, and tell him I'll want to speak to all the foremen later."

Before Kathleen was out of the door, the two men were huddled together in quick discussion. In that moment the antagonism of the past was forgotten.

As she went back to her desk she thought how wonderful it would be if all misunderstanding and distrust could be swept aside as quickly. Why did it take misfortune – and sometimes heartache – to make people come to their senses?

When James Laurie had gone, the foremen gathered in the main office. Craig Carmichael sat on the end of Miss Gemmell's empty desk and told them what he had arranged. He had already discussed it with Andrew Tosh, and the manager's face wore a slightly troubled frown.

There were also doubts among the men.

"When are we to get time for maintenance?" an engineer asked. "The machinery'll never stand up to it – running day and night! It's asking for trouble – "

"Some of your stuff's old," another broke in. "It needs nursing. Put some of Laurie's men among it, and – "

"Now, now, let's be reasonable," Craig pleaded. "I

appreciate all you say, but it's just for a few weeks till they get this South African order out."

"But why bother, Mr Craig?" A small figure with broad shoulders and a pointed chin pushed himself to the front. "What's it to us whether Laurie's get their orders out or not? Hasn't he been trying to put you out of business for a long time?"

Craig blew a smoke ring and let it drift away before he spoke.

"Maybe! But we all need help sometime, Willie. Even the biggest of us! Where would we be today if the fire had happened here – and no one gave us a hand?"

"I suppose you're right," Willie Scott said grudgingly, and the others nodded approval.

"But we'll need to keep on a skeleton night staff of our own," Andrew Tosh said. "We must watch our own machines."

Craig nodded.

"We'll work out a suitable arrangement. So long as I know you're with me, we will manage. Thanks, boys. The office staff will have to do a spot of night work, too."

The men left and Craig instantly got busy. He issued orders that kept every member of the staff on tenterhooks till teatime. In the cloakroom there was a lot of talk. But the general opinion was that the "boss" had been very kind to James Laurie – maybe too kind.

Even Aunt Isa could only praise, thinking not so much of the mill, but of the men who would have been idle. But she did not like the idea of Kathleen having to work late every Tuesday and Friday.

"You work hard enough as it is; then you come home here and do more," she grumbled.

"But I enjoy it. And think what we can do with the extra money! I'll put it aside so we'll have a day in Glasgow on the spring holiday!"

Aunt Isa laughed and began cutting the bread.

"What did Laurie say when you were called into the office?"

"I'm quite sure he didn't even see me!"

"He would see you, all right!" Aunt Isa's smile vanished. "There's not much that man misses when it concerns him –" She broke off as Kenny came running in from the garden.

* * * *

On the first Friday she worked late, Kathleen came home from the office just after ten o'clock, to see a car parked at the gate. Ewen Gilmour rose to his feet when she went into the living-room. He seemed to tower over Aunt Isa, who was obviously on the best of terms with the visitor.

"Mr Gilmour came about half an hour ago, so I told him you'd soon be home. I've been thanking him for the chicken he sent at Christmas."

Ewen took Kathleen's hand.

"Thank you for your letter."

"You're thinner," said Kathleen, taking off her coat.

"So my sister says, but I'll soon put it on again. There's nothing wrong with my appetite."

The table was set and Aunt Isa hurried into the kitchen to make tea.

"I'm here with a special invitation," Ewen said. "I'm hoping you'll come to Carnbo a week tomorrow. I'm sorry the visit has been delayed by my illness. Can you come?"

"Yes – I think so."

Ewen Gilmour smiled.

"Good! And you'll bring your boy, of course. He'll like the farm. If you get the two-ten bus from Kilmarford, I'll meet you at the end of our road."

When he left, after a pleasant meal, Aunt Isa was full of praise.

"That's a fine young man," she observed. "No airs or nonsense about him. Made himself at home the minute he came in. You'll have a nice time at Carnbo. It will do you and Kenny a lot of good getting into the country. Mr Gilmour was telling me all about the farm. There's a housekeeper and –"

"You seem to have got on well together," Kathleen broke in with a smile.

"He's easy to talk to and I don't need much encouragement! He was saying his mother died when he was at school, and his father five years ago. There's only him and his sister – Aileen's her name. They're twins."

"Oh – I didn't know that."

Aunt Isa paused as she washed the supper dishes. From

Ewen Gilmour her thoughts suddenly switched to Kathy. It was as if she were seeing her in a new light – a new and disturbing light. Except for Kenny and herself – an ageing woman – Kathy was alone in the world. She had never known much happiness.

What she had shared with Kenneth Laurie was tragically short, and it wasn't right that young folk should live on memories. They were compensations that helped to mellow old age and give it dignity. But Kathy was young with a lifetime ahead of her. She was wise and loving, and these gifts – precious gifts from God – were meant to be shared.

"A penny for your thoughts!" Kathy's voice broke into her thoughts.

"I think Ewen Gilmour has a real notion of you," Aunt Isa said.

"You read too many love stories." Kathleen smiled.

Isa Duncan hesitated for a moment.

"Do you never think about marrying again, Kathy? It's not right for a girl as young and as bonnie as you not to have a man in your life – "

Kathleen laughed and put her arms round the drooping shoulders.

"But there is a young man in my life, Aunt Isa! He is my life – and yours, too, judging by the way you spoil him."

Isa Duncan knew the value of silence. She slipped out of the enfolding arms and busied herself with the remainder of the supper dishes. She had dropped a tiny seed and was content to let it lie – on what she hoped was fertile soil.

Until the new nightshift scheme got properly under way, Kathleen was back at the office three and four nights a week. She didn't mind the work. Her only regret was the time spent away from Kenny. She saw little of him during the day, and their evenings had always been a joyous reunion.

Seated on the rug by the fire, he monopolised the conversation. Every day was a new experience for him; and Kathleen and Aunt Isa were content to listen as he described the wonder of life opening to him. New friendships in the playground; new games to play; fresh discoveries in the park on his way home from school. All found a place in his life and his talk.

They were happy evenings and Kathleen grudged every one spent away from Dalreoch. Besides, it gave Aunt Isa extra work. Kenny was a good boy; but his high spirits could be tiring.

But Isa Duncan never complained. She enjoyed it, and often declared she'd taken on a new lease of life since there was a bairn in the house. There was nothing she liked better than giving Kenny his bath and putting him to bed – and if the bath took longer than when Kathleen was at home, who was to object?

It was one of those evenings that Kenny pushed an arm into his pyjama jacket and announced: "I've something special to put in my diary, Auntie. Will you help me write it? Do you know who I saw today? My grannie!"

Aunt Isa pushed back a wisp of damp hair and looked at him suspiciously. By now she was accustomed to his flights

84

of imagination.

"Now, Kenny –"

"But I did! Scout's honour! It was when I was coming home from school. I was feeding the swans in the park and she came over with another lady. She said she was my grannie."

Mrs Duncan's lips drew together.

"The other lady, did you know her?"

"I – I think it was the lady who spoke to Mummy at the Sunday school party. I don't know her name."

Mrs Duncan lifted the damp towel and tried to sound calm.

"What did your grannie say?"

"She asked me all about school. And I showed her the swans. Can I take my diary to bed with me, please?"

Aunt Isa looked down at his pleading face and nodded.

An hour later she was sitting at the fire reading the paper when the doorbell rang. The tall, fair girl on the doorstep was known to her by sight. She introduced herself as Alice Boswell, and asked for Kathleen.

"She's working late tonight, and I doubt if she'll be home before ten. Will you come in, Miss Boswell?"

Alice Boswell sat in the living-room and smiled her winning smile, but it had little effect on the older woman. Isa Duncan had not forgotten that it was this girl who had told Kenny about his grandparents.

"I wanted to explain to Kathleen about what happened this afternoon," Alice began. "But perhaps –"

"This afternoon?" Mrs Duncan was on her guard at once.

"Yes, I was in the park with Mrs Laurie. You've probably heard she's not been keeping well. We met Kenny, quite by accident. I told Mrs Laurie who he was and naturally she wanted to speak to him."

"She's taken a long time to show any interest in her grandson," Isa Duncan retorted.

"You've no idea how much good it did Mrs Laurie!" Alice went on. "She was like a different woman afterwards. I'm going to take her back there so that she'll see Kenny again. But I wanted to be perfectly honest with Kathleen. I wanted her to know everything."

"Miss Boswell –" Isa Duncan planted her small, plump hands on her knees. "Maybe it has done Mrs Laurie good. But what's it going to do to Kenny? That's more important."

Alice Boswell was obviously taken aback.

"But – what harm can it do?"

"I'm only saying what I think. Maybe Kathy will think different, for she hasn't lived as long as me! I don't like this. Kenny's just a bairn and he shouldn't be getting mixed up in the quarrels of older folk."

"But he'll grow up one day, and he is a Laurie –"

"Ay, and what's he going to think of the treatment his mother's had? From the very woman you want to see him?"

"I'd think any breach was the better of being healed –"

"This breach is not going to be healed with Kenny on one side of it, and his mother on the other!" Mrs Duncan said firmly. She looked up suddenly. "There's Kathy now. You can tell her yourself."

CHAPTER NINE

IT was raining and Kathleen's soft hair was curling round her brow. She was tired, but she welcomed Alice warmly and persuaded her to stay for a cup of tea. She was sensitive to atmosphere, and knew at once something was displeasing Aunt Isa, who let Alice Boswell do all the talking without once interrupting.

"Quite frankly, I hoped this was a step in the right direction," said Alice. "It happened quite by accident, but it seemed almost providential."

Aunt Isa sniffed – a sniff which implied that providence, for once, was moving in the wrong direction.

"I don't like it, Kathy," she said, "and I'll tell you why – just as I've told Miss Boswell."

Kathleen stirred her tea thoughtfully before she replied.

"If it makes Mrs Laurie happy to see and talk to Kenny, then I can't see any harm in their meeting."

"That's what I was thinking," Alice agreed.

"I can't tell Kenny never to go near the park – or say he mustn't speak to his grandmother!" Kathleen went on. "That would only make me as – as hard-hearted as James Laurie! Two wrongs don't make a right, you know. Surely a few minutes in the park isn't going to make any different to Kenny – "

"But it is going to make a wonderful difference to Mrs

Laurie," Alice agreed.

"Well, if that's the way you feel," Aunt Isa admitted grudgingly, "I don't suppose there's any use me saying more. Let the boy talk to his grandmother.

"But I'm warning you! If it does him any harm I'll put a stop to it. I'll meet Kenny at school and walk home with him myself!"

But the fire was gone out of Aunt Isa, and Kathleen knew it. She smiled at Alice.

"Would you like Aunt Isa to read your cup? She's very good!"

"I'd love it!"

So all traces of seriousness vanished, and there was good-humoured talk during the remainder of the visit.

But the following afternoon Aunt Isa dressed herself and went out. She had a shopping bag on her arm, but she deliberately avoided the shops and sauntered towards the park. She was no sooner there, keeping out of sigh behind some bushes, than she saw Alice Boswell walk along the path with Mrs Laurie clinging to her arm.

How stooped the older woman was, she thought. And how pale. She looked an old woman, though she must still be only in her fifties!

Aunt Isa cowered back. All at once she felt ashamed of herself for spying on others. She saw Kenny run along the path, and Mrs Laurie put out her hand to touch his head. She saw Alice Boswell turn and walk away, to leave them together, and Kenny put his hand in his grandmother's and led her to the swans.

Aunt Isa sniffed. The way Kenny slowed his usually hurrying steps to the slow movements of the old woman brought a lump to her throat.

She nodded her head.

"Aye, Kathy's right. What ill can come to him? And that poor soul with not a body in the world but that old bear, James Laurie."

Isa Duncan slipped from behind the bushes and hurried away.

"I'm just a selfish old woman, looking for ill where none is!" she reproached herself. "Two sons she's lost, and here's me with Alec still spared to me. And I've got Kathy, and Kenny as well – yet I'm grudging her a sight of her ain flesh and blood. You can think black burning shame of yourself, Isa Duncan!"

That night Kathleen was late in getting home. Before sitting down to supper she slipped quietly into the darkened bedroom. She could hear Kenny's regular breathing. As she moved forward to switch on the bedside light her feet hit something on the floor.

She looked down and saw Kenny's diary. It was lying open. She picked it up, a feeling of guilt surging over her as the sleeping boy stirred and turned over on his side. Instinctively her hand went behind her back. After a pause she drew it back. The open page proclaimed the day and date. At the top, in childish block letters, sprawling over the opposite page, stood out clearly the words "MY GRANNIE

FO – ." Then, written below, in a firm hand Kathleen had never seen, was written: "Tomorrow I'll remember to bring bread to feed your swans. – Grannie."

Tears trickled down Kathleen's cheeks. She left them unheeded. The writing told her much – yet told her nothing, for only Kenny and Mrs Laurie knew why and how it was written. Had Mrs Laurie promised something and forgotten? Had Kenny made her write it, so she would remember? He did that with Aunt Isa sometimes.

She would never know, because she would never ask. But it was plain these two were friends, united by a bond both could feel, but only one understood.

She placed the diary on the edge of the bed, switched off the light and left the room.

* * * *

Kathleen rose from the desk and put the cover on her typewriter. It was after nine o'clock on Friday evening. She lifted the typed lists from her desk and tapped at the inner door.

"Come in." Craig Carmichael was still at his desk, surrounded by papers. "Thanks, Kathleen. I'm afraid I'm working you too hard."

"Oh, no – although I'll be glad to get home tonight."

"So will I! But the worst is over now. Everything is running smoothly, and Laurie should be able to deliver that South African order in time. Everyone has done marvels, and I'm very grateful." He looked up at her, and his voice grew more personal. "You're really looking very tired, Kathleen. I know this has meant a lot of extra work for you girls in the office."

"We don't mind –"

"I've got an idea!" His blue eyes lit up. "How about coming for a run with me tomorrow in the car? It would do you good. We could go to Ayr and round the Burns country – "

"I'm sorry," she broke in, "but I'm going out tomorrow. Kenny and I have been invited to a farm – Carnbo."

"You mean Ewen Gilmour's place?"

"Yes. Do you know him?"

"We've met," he replied with what Kathleen felt was an unusual lack of enthusiasm. "Well, I hope you both have a very nice day."

When Kathleen was gone, Craig Carmichael started on his work again. But he could no longer concentrate. He gave it up and sat back, a deep frown on his brow.

Kathleen was on friendly terms with Gilmour! That was news! Well, why shouldn't she be? She was entitled to make her own friends. A girl like her would make plenty. And Ewen Gilmour was a good chap. Only – he wondered – how much genuine regret was there in her voice when she declined his own invitation. He thought about that for a long time. Then suddenly he got up, pushed his papers into a drawer and set off home. It was only when he reached home he remembered he had left his car in a garage in town.

Saturday was a lovely day, with a refreshing hint of spring in the air. Having seen Kathleen and a very excited Kenny off, Aunt Isa went into the back garden in a serious frame of mind.

She had a busy day in front of her. She had bought seeds, and she was going to sow them in the boxes she'd got from the grocer when they were flitting. They would be ready to transplant when she knew for sure what was coming up in the garden.

She put on an apron and a thick cardigan and went up to the shed for the boxes. At the end of the path she stopped to look back at the house, a thing she never did without a thrill of pride. Who would ever have thought that she, Isa Duncan, would ever have her own house and her own garden!

She was struggling out of the shed with a box in each hand when she saw a tall, middle-aged man come up the path.

"Mrs Duncan?"

"I'm Mrs Duncan," she said, with a look which plainly told him she disapproved of men who came into her garden without a by your leave.

"My name's Chalmers. I saw your front door was open, so I knew you must be somewhere about. I rang three times."

Aunt Isa unbent a little.

"What do you want?"

"Do you mind if we go indoors? I'm a plain clothes policeman."

One of the boxes dropped from Aunt Isa's nerveless fingers. Her face paled as she led the way inside. They sat in the living-room, perfumed with the hyacinth bulbs Kathleen had given her at Christmas.

"You're related to John Todd – known hereabouts as Jock Todd – aren't you?"

Isa Duncan was immediately on the alert.

"In a way – he's a cousin by marriage."

"You have his daughter staying with you?"

She nodded, a wary look creeping into her eye.

"Why are you asking that? What's happened?"

"Has he been to see you – or written to you?"

"No."

"He's out of prison. He got the usual remission for good conduct, and he was supposed to report regularly to the police. He's never done so. The Glasgow Police have asked us if he's in Kilmarford."

"He wouldn't know to come here unless he went to the Vennel first and got our new address."

"I've made inquiries at the Vennel, Mrs Duncan. No-one has seen him there. If he comes here, will you get in touch with us – at once?"

Isa Duncan almost sprang to her feet.

"I will not – and you've a cheek asking me to do such a thing. Jock Todd's nothing to me. I've no love for him, and I pray God he never darkens my door for the sake of his daughter and her laddie! If he ever does come I'll give him short shrift and get him out of here. But I'll not inform on him. The police can do their own work, Mr·Chalmers!"

"I'm sorry you feel like that, Mrs Duncan," he said,

making for the door. "But we can't force you."

"No, and you needn't try!"

Aunt Isa let him out, carefully closing the front door after him, and returned to the garden. But she had no heart for it now, so she put the boxes back in the shed. Her face was clouded and her mouth drooped.

"This means trouble – maybe sore trouble," she whispered to herself, going into the house and shutting the back door.

She filled the kettle and put it on the gas automatically. She would have a cup of tea. She had found a way out of many a problem over a cup of tea.

She sat and sipped the strong and well-sweetened brew, her mind disturbed and herself alarmed at the intensity of her own feelings. What a day to hear about Jock Todd again. There was Kathy, having the good time she well deserved at Carnbo, without an inkling of what might be in store for her. And for them all.

Of course, Jock Todd didn't know about Kathy's marriage, or about Kenny. But he knew about Kathy and herself. If he ever learned Kathy was earning good money and they now lived in a bungalow, he would be down on them like a ton of bricks, to take all he could from them.

And Kenny would come into it then. Jock Todd would make the most out of Kenny being a Laurie – and would do it in his own clever, hard way.

It was all a puzzle. Only one thing was clear. It boded no good to any of them.

It would be a real shame if Kathy's father turned up now

– or later – to spoil her happiness. It was quite clear Ewen Gilmour had a notion for Kathy. If nothing happened to spoil things, they might marry.

At that thought Isa Duncan rose and poured herself another cup of tea.

And why shouldn't they marry and be happy? It was what Kathy deserved. But if she knew of the threat of her father she wouldn't marry Ewen Gilmour – or anyone.

Well, Isa Duncan was never one to spoil romance. She would keep to herself what had happened that day. She wouldn't tell Kathy. She'd just pray nothing happened. God would be on her side, she was sure. He did everything for the best. He would know very clearly what was the best way out of this problem.

Her lips moved slowly and wordlessly, and as they moved her head bowed in silent submission.

CHAPTER TEN

WHILE Isa Duncan wrestled with the problem that Jock Todd presented to all of them, Kathleen and Kenny were having an interesting journey to Carnbo. To please Kenny they were in the front of the bus. He was so interested, watching and talking to the driver, that the "Beano" Kathy had bought him lay neglected on her lap.

They got off where Ewen Gilmour had arranged, and found him waiting. He was dressed in breeches and leggings, and although still thin from his illness, was healthily tanned.

As they got into the car they were unaware of the interested glances and speculating voices of the passengers in the bus. Ewen Gilmour was known to them all. They liked his easy friendliness and respected his position in farming and county circles.

His companions that day were strangers to them. But obviously not to Ewen. The laughter in his voice as he answered the lively youngster and the courteous manner in which he helped the attractive young woman into the car were not lost on the country people.

They were still speculating among themselves when the car drove away on its two-mile journey to Carnbo. Ewen and Kenny became instant friends, and Kathleen was happy to let their easy conversation flow over her head.

A feeling of content filled her, and, not for the first time, she felt grateful for the blessings of life. Since returning to Kilmarford she and Kenny had known nothing but heart-warming kindness. Aunt Isa had stretched out her hand and gently guided them from a world of loneliness into the heart of a home. Her love enfolded them like a warm plaid.

But she did more. In her wise and forthright manner she had helped to restore Kathleen's faith in herself; to give her new hope for the future. There were others, too, whose friendship took all of the humiliation and hurt out of her return to her native town.

Fletcher Galbraith, her old employer, had tried to remind her of unhappy days. But Craig Carmichael never did. He had no thought of her family name, nor of her father's reputation when he engaged her.

She enjoyed the hospitality of Nan Webb's home and the companionship of the girls at the office. Most surprising of all, she'd found a new friend in Alice Boswell. She had risked a life-long friendship with the Lauries by disagreeing with their attitude.

And now there was Ewen Gilmour, this frank, quiet-spoken young farmer. Kathleen turned her head and studied his face as he pointed out a mare and young foal to Kenny. It was a fine face, sharply etched with character and breeding, the face of a man one could trust.

He turned suddenly and their eyes met.

"You seemed so occupied with your thoughts that I didn't want to disturb you," he said. "I'm afraid you haven't been seeing much of the countryside."

"Oh, but I have!" Kathleen assured him. "It's lovely – so beautifully fresh and peaceful."

That seemed to please him and he smiled.

"Well, here we are! There's Carnbo on the right."

Kathleen had expected a small farm, so the gracious, well-proportioned house and extensive outbuildings in an attractive cream, came as a surprise. Carnbo was a large, up-to-date, prosperous farm.

Aileen Gilmour, waiting at the front, also presented a picture quite contrary to Kathleen's expectations. She'd expected twins to be alike; but Ewen was as fair as his sister was dark. She was dressed in a green, tailored tweed, and her greeting was warm and friendly. She had all the appearance of a strong-minded, capable woman.

The interior of the tree-sheltered house was gracious. The fine old furniture and modern curtains of rich Glamis fabric gave an instant impression of good taste. It was a house with atmosphere, and an honest sturdiness that stamped those who lived in it.

"You have a beautiful home, Miss Gilmour," Kathleen said frankly as they returned to the sunny sitting-room.

Aileen smiled.

"Thank you. But if we're going to be friends you must call me Aileen."

Susan Hay, the elderly housekeeper, served tea with lovely girdle scones and freshly made butter. Kathleen learned she had been at Carnbo since Ewen and Aileen were children.

Nowadays she had slipped into the position of a doting aunt who saw to their every comfort.

After lunch the afternoon flew past all too quickly. Kenny was in his element. Seldom off his feet, he ran in and out of the house to tell his mother in almost speechless excitement of all he saw and all he was allowed to do. It was after they had afternoon tea that he ran in to tell about the puppies.

"Mummy, there's little black puppies! Will I bring one in and show you? Uncle Ewen says I can. Oh, Mummy, will I?"

"I'd better come out with you and see them. You're wearing the carpet thin with all this rushing out and in."

"It's a nice change to see a bairn in this house." Susan Hay smiled as she cleared away.

Kenny clung to his mother's hand as they went out to the yard. Ewen walked with them, his eyes full of amusement as he looked down at the bright red head.

"They're Scotties, Mummy! Real Scotties! Aren't they lovely!" They were delightful, with fat little bodies and absurd tails. Ewen stooped down and put one into Kenny's arms.

"And there's one for you!"

Kenny couldn't speak for a moment.

"You – you mean to keep? He – he's really mine?"

"If your mummy doesn't mind."

Kenny's eyes fastened themselves on Kathleen's face with a heart-rending expression.

"It's all right with me, darling," she said. "But we'll have to ask Aunt Isa. It's her house, you know."

"Oh, but she'll say yes! There's room in the house for him," said Kenny confidently, letting the puppy lick the point of his nose. Then he smiled appealingly. "Aunt Isa will say yes, won't she?"

"Just wait and see!" Kathleen's gaze met Ewen Gilmour's over Kenny's head and they smiled. "Now we'd better be getting back."

And, surprisingly, Kenny made no protest. He was impatient to get home to plead with Aunt Isa.

There was room in the car for Kenny and the puppy beside Kathleen in the front seat. The Scottie snuggled in the crook of his arm. Kenny's eyes never left it. It was a case of love at first sight – on both sides.

Ewen Gilmour drove slowly, and he and Kathleen talked lightly and companionably. She was thinking how much she had enjoyed the day. What nice people the Gilmours and Susan Hay were. There was genuine warmth in Aileen's voice when she invited them to come again soon.

When the car drew up at the bungalow Kenny shouted, "Good-night" over his shoulder and rushed indoors with the puppy. They walked up the path after him.

"Will you not come in for a little, Ewen?"

"Not tonight, Kathleen. I must be getting back."

"Well, I can only say thank you again. I think it's been the most wonderful day in Kenny's life. And he has something to remind him of it."

"But have you enjoyed it?"

"Every minute," she said sincerely.

"Then you'll come again – soon?"

"I'll be very happy to. A day in the country is a lovely change."

For a moment his hand rested on her arm, and she could feel the pressure of his fingers. She stood at the door until the car was out of sight. Then with a contented sigh she went into the house with the eggs and fresh butter Aileen Gilmour had given her.

"And I can keep the puppy, Aunt Isa?" Kenny's excited voice reached Kathleen as she took off her coat.

"Well – I suppose you can. There's times when a dog about the place might be handy – even if it's only for keeping unwelcome visitors away!" There was a harshness in her aunt's voice that was not lost on Kathleen. It was unlike Aunt Isa, and "unwelcome visitors" suggested something had happened.

"Have you thought of a name for him?" her aunt went on.

Kenny stroked the puppy's black ears.

"Uncle Ewen says he's a Scottie. We'll call him Jock!"

"Jock!" Aunt Isa's voice rose. "There's nothing by that name coming – "

She broke off quickly when she caught sight of Kathleen. Their eyes met and held for a moment. There was a look in the older woman's eyes that puzzled Kathleen. Was it impatience or anger? She didn't know.

Isa Duncan lowered her head.

"All right, Kenny," she said. "If that's what you want –

Jock it will be. Take him through to the bathroom and we'll christen him with some of your bath water."

Kathleen could almost feel the edge in Aunt Isa's voice. Even the atmosphere in the room had changed since they'd left. There was a tenseness that gripped her and added to the confusion in her mind. But when she would have spoken, the older woman shook her head decisively and gave all her attention to Kenny.

They got him bathed and into bed quite quickly. Even the christening of the puppy passed off briefly and without comment. And if Kenny noticed the lack of ceremony and enthusiasm, he was either too excited or too tired to say anything.

"Jock'll sleep at the bottom of my bed, won't he, Aunt Isa?" he asked, the puppy wriggling joyfully in his arms.

"Indeed he will not! He'll sleep in the kitchen."

"But he'll be lonely – "

"Not a bit of it! We'll make him a grand wee bed all to himself. There's an old jersey of mine will do him fine for a blanket – "

Half an hour later Kenny was asleep, and Kathleen and Mrs Duncan sat at the fire and tried to keep an uneasy conversation going. All the time, as she told about the visit to Carnbo, Kathleen grew more and more convinced that Aunt Isa's attention was divided. Her fingers twitched as if she were on edge. Her brightness seemed forced; her replies were slow and hesitant.

At last Kathleen could stand it no longer. She leaned

forward and looked straight into the older woman's eyes.

"What is it, Aunt Isa?" she asked. "What's wrong? I've felt there was something from the moment I got back tonight. Are you feeling all right?"

"There's – there's nothing wrong." The reply was too hurried to deceive anyone so sensitive to feeling and atmosphere as Kathleen. She rose and laid her hands on the old woman's shoulders.

"You've got to tell me what's happened, Aunt Isa! There must be no secrets between us at any time."

In the brief silence that followed, the regular tick-tock of the clock sounded like a strange overture to a symphony of fear.

Isa Duncan moved uncomfortably in her chair, then slowly raised her head.

"Oh, Kathy, lassie! I wasn't meaning to tell you. There was no sense in worrying you."

Kathleen's frown deepened.

"You know I'll only imagine all kinds of things if you don't tell me. And what concerns you concerns me."

So Mrs Duncan folded her small fat hands in her lap to keep them from trembling, and poured out her recital of the policeman's visit.

As she listened Kathleen began to understand the reason for the older woman's strange behaviour earlier in the evening. The harshness in her voice when she spoke of unwelcome visitors. Her objection to calling the puppy Jock. Even Kathleen felt herself growing cold and depressed, as if some icy hand had been laid on her.

Like Aunt Isa, she was sure her father would try to find her again one day, if ever he learned about her. She had no illusions about him; no reason to remember him with any feeling of affection. All that had gone years ago.

But Jock Todd was her father. Little as she relished the bond, it was there. It could never be broken. It was the tie of blood, demanding certain duties she could never ignore.

It could threaten her happiness, Kenny's happiness and future. Yet through the cloud of her dark thoughts there came a glimmer of light and hope.

"I don't expect he'll come here." She tried to speak lightly. "If he's anxious to keep out of the way of the police, Kilmarford would be the last place he would come to. Don't you agree?" She hoped she sounded convincing. "Besides, he doesn't know where we live."

"He can ask at the Vennel. Jock Todd always had a good tongue in his head. He'll no' want for lack o' speering."

"We'll face that when it comes," Kathleen said.

"That's right, lassie. We'll face it when it comes. But if Jock Todd dares show his face near this house, if ever he tries to make trouble for you and Kenny I'll – "

Kathleen made no reply. She just stared into the fire, her lips twisted in a little cynical smile. What a difference a few hours could make to people's lives.

On her way to Carnbo that afternoon she was counting the blessings of life. Giving silent thanks for new friends, fresh interests; and for a future bright with the promise of hope for herself and her boy. Now, like something out of the blue, came this shadow from the past, glooming the present and the future. Threatening all she was trying to rebuild.

"Marrying Jock Todd was the worst day's work your poor mother ever did." Aunt Isa's voice seemed far away.

It scarcely broke through the barrier of Kathleen's troubled thoughts. She sighed, striving to keep her mind from slipping back into the past. The past didn't matter. Or did it? Wasn't the past bending back into her life to threaten her new-found security, to cast its shadow on her son's unclouded childhood?

Despite herself a tear trickled down her cheek. And she was unaware of Isa Duncan rising from her chair and slipping into the kitchen.

At the doorway the older woman paused and looked back. There were moments when even to be present was an intrusion. It was better to leave Kathy on her own for a while, much as she wanted to put her arms round the lassie and comfort her. Kathy had never been one to cry – not even as a child. The news tonight had gone deep. . .

"I'm a foolish woman," Isa Duncan reprimanded herself as she filled the kettle and placed it on the gas stove. "I should have kept a still tongue in my head. I should have kept my mouth shut and my worries to myself."

Yet in her heart Aunt Isa knew there was no consolation in that thought. Sooner or later Kathy would have heard about the police inquiries. It was better she heard from her than from outsiders. And tonight was as good as tomorrow or the next day. Kathy had a right to know.

"But the world's not coming to an end because that rogue's name has cropped up again," she assured herself with some of her old spirit. "Jock Todd's not going to spoil her happy day. Ewen Gilmour has a real notion of her or he wouldn't have invited her and the bairn to his home."

As she infused the tea the smile in Isa Duncan's eyes spread to her face. She was humming happily to herself as she carried the tray through to the room.

Kathleen looked round in surprise, all trace of tears gone.

"When are you going back to Carnbo?" Aunt Isa asked. "It seems a grand place, and Aileen Gilmour sounds a real sensible young woman. I think she's taken a notion to you and the bairn. But it must be lonely whiles for her –"

"For her?" Kathleen asked and smiled.

"Well, for both of them," Isa Duncan replied. "I was just thinking –"

"As if I didn't know," Kathleen broke in, and the sound of her laughter rippled through the room. And as the little waves cascaded over her head a feeling of peace, of confidence in the future, crept into Isa Duncan's heart.

All things worked together for good, her old minister used to say. Kathy wouldn't be the first woman who had to walk through the shadows before reaching the light and warmth of the noonday sun.

CHAPTER ELEVEN

KENNY was restless all that night. Kathleen thought it was due to over-excitement after the visit to Carnbo. All Sunday he was kept in bed. But by Monday morning it was obvious that it was something serious.

"I'm sure it's mumps!" Aunt Isa declared over the breakfast table. "I remember my Alec having it when he was Kenny's age."

"I'll phone Dr Dallas on the way to the office," Kathleen said. "Oh, dear, I wish I didn't have to go out at all."

"Now, don't worry yourself. Just leave everything to me."

"Mummy! I want you!" The fretful cry came from the bedroom, and Kathleen rose from the table.

Mrs Duncan was clearing away the breakfast dishes when Kathleen returned.

"I'm going to phone now," she decided. "He's fevered. I can't go to the office till I hear what the doctor has to say. I'll be back in a few minutes. I'll – " She broke off and moved forward quickly. "Is something wrong, Aunt Isa?"

Mrs Duncan straightened herself at once, dropping her hand from her side.

"No!" She smiled reassuringly. "It's all this excitement, or I must have eaten my breakfast too fast. Away you go and get Dr Dallas. I was just saying to myself last week it was uncanny the way the bairn was getting through his first year

107

at school with never a day's illness."

Dr Dallas arrived soon after ten o'clock and confirmed Aunt Isa's opinion of mumps. He was a tall, white-haired man, with courtly, rather old-world manners.

He had a few words alone in the living-room with Kathleen before he left.

"There's nothing to worry about, Mrs Laurie. Kenny's not the only one off school with mumps this morning. There's quite an epidemic in the town just now. Keep him warm and give him plenty to drink."

Kathleen smiled at the old doctor.

"I'm afraid – I must have sounded very alarmed," she said. "But Kenny's all I have."

"Yes, yes, I understand. He's a fine boy. He'll get over this quite easily." Dr Dallas tore the sheet off his prescription pad and handed it to her. "It must be nearly thirty years since I brought his father into the world. Kenneth Laurie was a fine boy!"

"You knew him!" Kathleen said eagerly. It always pleased her to meet someone who knew Kenneth.

"I knew him all his days – and they were much too short, my dear." Dr Dallas pressed her hand, then turned and left the room.

When she reached the office, breathless after hurrying along the road, Kathleen apologised to Miss Gemmell for being late. Craig Carmichael was in Glasgow on business for some days.

Now that Kenny was in bed there was a lot to be done at

Dalreoch. Kathleen did as much housework as she could in the evenings to take the burden off Aunt Isa's shoulders.

It was actually Friday before Craig Carmichael returned. Kathleen was in his room taking letters to be done in a hurry when he suddenly leaned back in his chair.

"I'm driving you too hard," he said. "You're not looking well. You haven't been since that extra work came along after Laurie's fire. What about tomorrow or Sunday afternoon for that run in the car? I haven't forgotten about it."

"I'm very sorry," she said, and told him about Kenny's illness.

"Of course, I understand. But you will come when he's better?" he asked with an eagerness which surprised her.

She nodded.

"If the invitation is still open."

"Take tomorrow morning off," Craig said. "You look as if you could do with some rest yourself."

"Oh, but – "

His brilliant smile flashed out.

"There are no buts. I've just given an order and I expect it to be obeyed. If I see you here tomorrow morning I'll give you a week's notice."

Kathleen took charge on Saturday morning, and all that was needed to crown her relief and gratitude was Dr Dallas's assurance that Kenny was making excellent progress. She accompanied the doctor to the door and saw him drive away. But she didn't see the thoughtful look in his eyes as he drove off to Finnard.

Ten minutes later he was seated opposite Mrs Laurie in her beautifully furnished sitting-room.

"What have you been doing to yourself these past few weeks?" he asked. "I've never seen such a change in anyone. You look a different woman. What's the secret, Mrs Laurie?"

Her eyes sparkled.

"I – I believe I've found a new interest in life, Doctor."

He rose to his feet and smiled.

"Don't ever lose it," he said. "It's the best thing that's happened to you for a long time." He picked up his bag and hat but made no move to go. "By the way, do you know where I was this morning? Visiting your grandson – Kenneth's boy."

He saw her start and the colour flood her cheeks.

"Visiting him? Does that mean he's ill?" she asked anxiously.

"Mumps! But he's over the worst. He's a fine boy. The image of his father."

"Yes – I know. I've seen him. Everything about him is Kenneth, except for his hair. That way he has of turning his head – "

The old doctor listened attentively, watching her animated face.

"It's a pity you and James don't see more of him."

The face lost its animation and grew controlled – almost mask-like.

"We would have taken the boy. Given him a home. Done

everything for him," she said. "We offered months ago, but his mother refused."

Dr Dallas raised his brows but made no comment. He had heard stories but never repeated them or took sides. He had enough to do healing bodily ailments without being involved in family troubles.

When he had gone Mrs Laurie moved to the window and looked out to where the daffodils were nodding in the garden. It would soon be Easter. She fingered the lilac chiffon scarf at her throat. So little Kenny had mumps. She was sorry. But it was a relief to know.

She had imagined he was being deliberately kept from the park so that she would not meet him. Three times she had gone, looking for the lively little red-haired figure in the blue coat. Three times she had returned home unhappy and depressed.

But the doctor said he was making good progress. That meant he would soon be out again. The thought kept her happy for the rest of the day. . .

At Dalreoch, Kenny put the last piece of his jig-saw into position and pushed away the tray with an impatient gesture.

"Mummy," he asked suddenly, "why doesn't my grannie come to see me?"

Kathleen lifted a discarded book and laid it on the chair.

"Oh, well – maybe she's busy, darling."

"But why doesn't she? Didn't you tell her I had mumps?"

"What a boy you are for asking questions! Do you know what Jock did this morning? He chewed the pompom off

Aunt Isa's slipper!"

"Did he?" Kenny said in a disinterested voice, and turned his head to the window.

"I heard him," said Isa Duncan when Kathleen joined her in the kitchen a few minutes later. "I know you don't agree, of course, neither you nor Alice Boswell, but I still think it was a bad day for Kenny when he got to know Mrs Laurie. It's unsettled him!"

Because she had no answer Kathleen avoided the issue.

"Aren't people kind?" she said. "These eggs from Ewen, grapes from his sister. The jigsaw from Nan and George – "

"But not a thing from his ain flesh and blood!"

"Oh, Aunt Isa – "

"I'm sorry, lassie. There are times when I let my tongue run away with me. But it vexes me to think of anyone upsetting our boy – or yourself. But I'll away to the garden and do some weeding. I wish it were as easy to pluck out the weeds that stunt the growth of kindness in some folk's hearts."

* * * *

"Do you really like my hat?" Kathleen came into the living-room on Easter Sunday morning. Isa Duncan drew on her brown gloves and picked up her Bible.

"It suits you," she said, putting her head on one side like a plump bird, the better to study her niece. "That bit of green velvet ribbon on the plain straw sets it off. Now, Kenny, have you got your collection?"

Kenny nodded sulkily.

"I wish I could sit with Malcolm. I don't see why I – "

"Darling, it's because you've had mumps," Kathleen explained, straightening the collar of his coat.

"It's a special service for Easter! Miss Fulton, the teacher, told me when she came to see me yesterday. Everybody in the Sunday school is s'posed to sit in the middle of the church and – "

"Well, you'll be upstairs so you'll be able to see everybody."

"Mercy, Kathy, how the laddie's stretched since he was in bed! That coat'll have to be let down."

"Mummy, that's the bells ringing. We'll need to go quick!"

It was a lovely morning. The sun was shining colourfully through the long memorial windows as they joined the other worshippers in the church. Kenny was consoled when he realised that, by sitting in the front seat of the side balcony, he had no difficulty seeing all his friends. The mellowed church was beautifully decorated, with tulips and daffodils massed on the Communion table.

Kathleen could remember when she, too, had taken part in such a children's service, a shy and lonely figure, tucked away in one of the corners. The memory came unbidden and Kathleen's eyes filled with tears.

A few minutes later she saw Mr and Mrs Laurie take their places in their family pew. It was the first time she had seen Mrs Laurie at a service for many weeks.

When the service ended and they came out into the sunshine, little groups of people stood round the main door. Aunt Isa caught sight of an old friend from the Vennel and moved away to talk to her. Kenny wanted to go, too, but Kathleen kept hold of his hand.

It was only then she realised that she had dropped one of her gloves. She looked on the red-chipped path, but there was no sign of it.

"Wait here, darling," Kathleen told Kenny. "Mummy's lost one of her gloves. I must have dropped it on the stairs. Now don't move away!"

As she went back through the doorway a large car drew up at the church gate. A chauffeur jumped out and opened the back door as James Laurie and his wife approached.

"Grannie!" Kenny's clear, childish voice rang out as he ran forward.

At his call the buzz of conversation suddenly ceased. People turned their heads and stared, first at the excited little boy, then at the Lauries.

Mrs Laurie's hand came up for a fraction of a second, then she dropped it, turned away, and stepped into the car.

"It's me – Kenny!" He stepped forward, then checked himself as the shadow of the tall man fell across his path. He looked so big and strong. And why did he look so angry?

Mildred Laurie was now hidden inside the car, but the silent groups saw the colour surging into James Laurie's face. They saw, too, the bewilderment in his eyes as he looked at his wife, then at the red-haired boy. Then, conscious that people, among them some of his employees and their wives, were watching him, he gave a curt order to the chauffeur, hurried into the car and slammed the door.

Kathleen caught sight of the car moving away as she came out of the church carrying both gloves.

"Kenny! What are you doing there?"

"Oh, Mummy," he cried and ran towards her. "I've seen Grannie. But she didn't speak to me. She just went into the car."

"Perhaps she didn't hear you, darling."

"But she did!" his little voice persisted in protest. "She turned round and saw me. So did the big man."

The big man! James Laurie!

Kathleen felt her cheeks go scarlet. What had happened while she was inside the church? Had Mrs Laurie deliberately ignored Kenny, or had James Laurie said something?

Kathleen would have given much to know. But she couldn't question Kenny with people looking on. In any case, to question him at all would exaggerate the importance of the incident and might leave a painful memory in his mind.

"Come along, darling." She forced herself to smile as she tried to shut out the covert looks and penetrating eyes of people around her.

"We'll walk on slowly and Aunt Isa will soon catch up with us."

There was an electric atmosphere in the Lauries' car as it

sped towards Finnard.

"I'm waiting," James Laurie said gruffly. "I recognised that boy. Kenneth's boy. Knew him the moment I clapped eyes on him. But what was it all about? Why did he call you Grannie? Did that woman put him up to it?"

His wife's sallow face was pale, and she was breathing deeply. She put her gloved fingers on his hand and nodded towards the chauffeur in the front.

"Wait till we get home, James."

The few minutes it took to reach home did nothing to check his impatience or anger. He paced up and down the lounge, giving full vent to his feelings.

"Of course that minx put him up to it! I saw her in church this morning. How else would the boy know who you were? Affronting us on the very steps of the kirk – "

"Please, James!" Mrs Laurie's voice was almost shrill.

She took off her hat and slumped into an armchair. She looked tired, and he felt ashamed of himself for his outburst. Dr Dallas had warned him against upsetting her over anything.

She leaned back in her chair, looking up at him as he stood in the middle of the floor.

"You're quite wrong, James. Kenny's mother had nothing to do with what happened. And I'll tell you why."

Slowly, haltingly, she told him of the meetings in the park. When he tried to interrupt she silenced him with a wave of her hand.

He sat down, trying to grasp what all he was hearing really

meant. Obviously it meant a great deal to Mildred. Even as she recounted the meetings with Kenneth's boy there was an animation in her voice, a sparkle in her eyes, that he hadn't known in months.

"Why didn't you tell me about this before?" he asked. "Why have you kept it to yourself all this time?"

"I should have told you, James. But I thought it would upset you." She smiled with an effort. "IBut he's so like Kenneth! He's a darling boy –"

The smile vanished and her eyes filled with that contradiction of tears that only a mother can shed, tears of sorrow and of joy.

James Laurie cleared his throat, but in such moments words did not come easily to him.

"If only we could have had him," she murmured. "It would have made up for so – so much!"

James Laurie gripped his hand on the edge of the chair till the knuckles showed white. All their married life he'd tried to give Mildred everything she wanted. He prided himself he had succeeded in all things – but this one big thing. Only a red-haired snippet of a girl stood in the way of completing Mildred's happiness! He'd get Kenneth's boy if it was the last thing he did! No woman was going to defy him!

"Just be patient, my dear." His voice was quiet, almost pleading, but there was a hard glint in his eyes. "Be patient and one day – perhaps quite soon – I'll bring our grandson home!"

CHAPTER TWELVE

THERE was nothing he wouldn't do to please Mildred. He always had been able to please her so far. Please God he always would. She understood his words and his tone as no one else could.

His wife looked at him. A half-smile drifted across her features, but there was only pity in her eyes.

"James, that girl will never give up her boy! She's a mother, a real, good mother, and she'll keep him. I don't blame her! I'd have done exactly the same."

James Laurie's expression did not change. He only shrugged his massive shoulders. Of course, Mildred wouldn't have given up her children to anyone. But that didn't mean his ideas were wrong. Mildred had never needed to work for her sons. She had high principles and fine feelings no-one could wear down with argument, maybe temptation. But that red-haired girl wasn't Mildred Laurie. She was Jock Todd's daughter!

He put his strong, thick fingers together and drew down his brows in deep thought.

"I'm not going to have that snippet stand in your way!" he growled. "She's not going to keep what you want. It won't be easy, but –" He stopped for a moment, then he went on, almost inaudibly, "Perhaps Fletcher Galbraith –"

The pity in Mildred Laurie's eyes deepened. She

understood her husband, knew how ruthless he could be. Short of kidnapping Kenny, no idea or plan would be discarded whatever the cost. He would wield his power and use his money without scruple.

Until now this trait in her husband had scarcely affected her. Since it was never used against herself, she had found it something almost to admire. He always got what he wanted. But since Roger's death she had learned that power and wealth meant little in the end. They were not the abiding things . . .

She pulled thoughtfully at the fingers of her black suede glove.

"James, there is nothing you can do to get our grandson here," she insisted gently.

He raised his head.

"Isn't there? You wait! I haven't started yet!"

Mildred Laurie sighed, but persisted.

"She'll never give the boy up, and we might as well face that, James. Unless –" Her voice trailed away, and again she examined the finger of her glove.

"Unless what?"

She looked at him for a moment without answering, laying the gloves aside on the small table beside her.

"Kenny is our grandson, James, but, after all, she is Kenneth's widow. Our only chance would have been to –"

"No!" His fist bounced off the arm of the chair. "As long as I have my way she'll not be counted as a Laurie! We want to get the boy away from her influence –"

Mildred Laurie went on as if she had not heard.

"You made a mistake offering her money that time. That put her against us."

"What difference does it make if she is against us? She always was."

His wife shrugged her thin shoulders.

"We can't say she isn't doing her best for him. In fact, she's doing very well. He's at the school Roger went to. She's in a good job. They have a nice home, in a good district –"

She broke off when her husband turned and walked to the window, standing with his back to her, his shoulders hunched.

Moodily he stared out at the nodding daffodils, his thoughts bitter. If ever a man got back evil for good it was he. What he'd done, he'd done in good faith for his grandson. But it was a poor reward to find he'd merely put a weapon in Kathleen Todd's hand to use against him!

His one idea at the time had been only to get the boy out of the Vennel into a more suitable environment.

Far better if he'd left Kathleen Todd to struggle away in the Vennel. She'd have come to heel more quickly! All he and Mildred could offer the boy would have been more attractive by comparison if he'd left her to stew in her own juice!

Yet Fletcher Galbraith had agreed it was a good idea when he put it to him. In fact, Fletcher had finally arranged the thing very cleverly. He had said he would have a talk with

Wilkie, the factor, and see what could be done. Then it had all worked out neatly, with that old woman, Mrs Duncan, having done some charring for Mr Wilkie during the war.

Of course, Mr Wilkie was a bit bewildered at first. He had a tenant all lined up for the bungalow. But when he realised there was money in it for him he'd agreed to sell, and still factor the place at a ridiculously cheap rent.

It had all been very discreet. No-one except Wilkie and Galbraith knew whose was the guiding hand behind it. He ground his heel into the thick pile of carpet. It angered him to have this hitting back at him in a way he'd never foreseen! He should have left them in the Vennel. All he'd done was make her path easy.

"You must admit the girl is getting on well," Mildred said again behind him.

He admitted it all right, but only to himself. Nothing would drag him into an open admission, not even to Mildred. He remembered now seeing Kathleen Todd in Carmichael's office when he went about the fire. She was a smart one all right. Had all the information about orders and dates at her finger ends. No junior typist her!

Settled, that's what she was! Settled into a good job and settled into the town! Settled into the home his generosity had stupidly provided for her. And now she was ready to flourish like a weed.

He'd shift her! He'd shift her if it was the last thing he did. Kenneth's boy would come to Finnard. It was the right place for him.

He lifted his chin from where it had sunk on to his thick chest and turned to his wife. He opened his lips, then checked himself.

How pale she was, her eyes black-ringed. That cruise in the winter had been a complete failure. She had never roused herself from her listlessness. He'd sensed all the time her desire to come home.

Yet home was now an empty place, full of memories for both of them. He had the mill and the balm of work. But what did Mildred have? He cleared his throat and said gently, remembering the small figure at the church door.

"He seems a fine little chap."

"Oh, he is!" He saw her eyes light up. "He's just Kenneth all over again at that age!"

Her quick enthusiasm touched him. It also rekindled his anger against the young woman standing between Mildred and happiness. Mildred was dearer to him than anyone or anything in the world. But he knew his devotion had not been enough to lift her from the shadows since Roger's death. It was a small boy who had given her an interest, an aim in living.

She spoke now in a low, strained voice.

"James, believe me, the only way was through her, that day she came, and it's too late now. If we'd offered her a home here – "

This time there was no outburst.

"If that's what you want, Mildred –" he began with deceptive mildness, and then broke off because she was shaking her head.

"It's too late, James! She's formed other attachments. She has that old woman who took them in. Aunt Isa, Kenny calls her. He thinks the world of her. She's like" – she swallowed – "like a grannie to him."

James Laurie swung back round to the window, restraining himself with difficulty. Thoughts churned in his head, but when he turned again a few minutes later his wife's chair was empty. She had slipped from the room and he hadn't heard her go.

* * * *

Meanwhile at the bungalow Mrs Duncan was looking at the "Sunday Post." She had read Francis Gay and had turned to the news. The table was set, and the potatoes boiling on the stove in the small kitchen. Kathleen was admiring the hyacinth bulbs on the window ledge.

Aunt Isa crossed her fat little feet and looked up from the paper.

"Do you know who's coming to Glasgow next month – on the twenty-eighth? Princess Elizabeth!"

Kathleen turned from the flowers with a smile.

"The twenty-eighth? That's a Monday. In fact, it's our spring holiday!"

Aunt Isa read aloud from the paper.

". . . to open the Festival Exhibition of Industrial Power in the Kelvin Hall. My, I wish I could see her – "

Kathleen turned again.

"There's not reason why you shouldn't! Remember I said we'd use my overtime money to have a real day out?"

"But you bought the new plastic curtains for the bathroom and – "

"Auntie!" Kathleen laughed. "I've still got enough left to have a day out in Glasgow. We'll go on the early train and we'll make a day of it – and we'll see the Princess, too!"

Aunt Isa dropped the paper.

"Do you mean it? Do you think we could?" In her round face her bright eyes grew excited as a child's. "There are sure to be awful crowds. But it would be worth it. If we were there early enough we could get a good place to stand – "

"Of course we'll go!" Kathleen was infected by the older woman's enthusiasm. "It'll be a real holiday for me, too. You know, I've been here since last August and this will be our first outing together. I'd like to get Kenny a new coat, too. He's growing out of everything – "

But for once Aunt Isa wasn't deeply interested in Kenny. She was leaning back in her chair, a faraway look on her face. Already she was savouring pleasures to come.

"I'll better see to the potatoes," said Kathleen, "or they'll be away to mush!"

Mrs Duncan nodded and smiled, barely comprehending.

Kathleen drained the potatoes into the sink. She could see Kenny in the back garden, playing with Jock, the Scottie. She pushed open the window.

"Dinner's ready, Kenny!"

She had to call twice before he heard. He came running up the path, with the black puppy nosing at his heels and giving little, high-pitched barks. Kenny's cheeks were pink and his eyes bright. How wonderful it was to see him completely recovered. It had been only mumps, but she had many an anxious hour over him for all that.

Kathleen turned away from the window with a smile, wondering fleetingly what James Laurie had thought of his grandson that morning. It would be interesting to know. Not that it mattered – really.

* * * *

It was nearing the end of the week when Craig Carmichael spoke to Kathleen. It was a sunny day. The feeling of spring was everywhere, even in the office at Carmichael's. He stopped her as she rose from the chair beside his desk after he was finished dictating his letters.

"How about tomorrow, then, for that run in the car – or Sunday afternoon! Kenny's better, isn't he?"

Kathleen nodded and smiled in answer to his last question. She was wearing a lime-green blouse, and the colour brought out the dark-red lights in her hair.

"He'd be back at school if it wasn't for the holidays." Her smile widened and she said frankly, "I'd love a run in the car."

Her naturalness pleased him. He smiled back, a boyish smile completely unexpected on such clear-cut, manly features. "How about Kenny – would you like to bring him?"

Kathleen hesitated.

"I'd better not. He's better, but the doctor said I must be careful of draughts, and in a car – "

"We'll take him another time, then," Craig said. "If Saturday's all right I'll pick you up at two."

When Kathleen sat down at her typewriter in the outer office a few minutes later she looked long and thoughtfully at it, her hands idle in her lap.

"A penny for them, Kathleen!" Jenny Taylor whispered in her ear.

Kathleen started, then joined in the laughter.

"They weren't worth a penny, Jenny. I wasn't thinking about anything! I was just in a 'dwam,' as my mother used to say!"

It was early evening, when the tea dishes were cleared away, that she mentioned the outing to Mrs Duncan.

Kenny was playing in the garden. They could hear his shouts mingling with those of Peter Balfour, who lived a short distance down the road. Peter was a month older than Kenny, and his parents had just moved from Hawick to Kilmarford. The boys had struck up an instant friendship, in the manner of children.

Kathleen had spoken only a few words in passing to Mrs Balfour. But she liked the look of both her and her husband, who was a banker. Peter was their only child.

Aunt Isa digested Kathleen's news in unexpected silence.

A slight frown went over her usually smiling face.

"I'd have thought," she said finally, "if you'd been going anywhere on Saturday it would have been to the Gilmours at Carnbo. Ewen was in last week inviting you."

Kathleen looked up from her sewing.

"But that was when Kenny was in bed – "

"I know, but we didn't fix anything definite."

Aunt Isa's small mouth tugged inwards at the corners. Kathleen looked across at her, reading in the familiar features an expression of displeasure. The round mouth was tight, the brows drawn. In Aunt Isa's fat hands the knitting needles were stabbing in and out of the grey sock wool with angry little clicks.

It was clear she disapproved of this outing with Craig Carmichael. Kathleen wanted to ask why, but didn't. It would be better not discussed. It was only natural Aunt Isa should have romantic notions, and she'd always liked Ewen Gilmour and made no secret of it.

Aunt Isa didn't realise that all that was over for her – buried in Italy. That kind of love can come only once in a lifetime. Ewen was a friend. Craig was a friend. But that was the end of it.

Kathleen sewed in silence until she rose to call Kenny in and send Peter home. Mrs Duncan went on knitting. Click, click went the needles, and her thoughts kept time with them. Why couldn't Kathy encourage a fine man like Ewen Gilmour instead of keeping him at arm's length all the time? It wasn't natural, a young woman like Kathy behaving as if her life was over before it was well begun!

Kathy was neither as old nor as sensible as she thought she was, or she'd realise it wasn't for her to be seen going off for motor runs with Mr Carmichael. He was her employer, and Aunt Isa believed firmly in folk keeping their own place in this world.

Besides, he wasn't like Ewen Gilmour. There was nothing "couthie" about him. Not that she'd ever spoken a word to Craig Carmichael. She wouldn't want to, anyway! She didn't like his black-browed type, and the way he had of looking down his nose. And he was a mill-owner, and Kathy had enough trouble with mill-owners already!

But Aunt Isa's storms never lasted long. By the time Kathleen had put Kenny to bed and returned to the living-room the knitting needles were no longer clicking at top speed. Kathleen sensed the difference in the atmosphere at once, and was glad of it. Impulsively she put her arm round the plump shoulders, straining out of their brown crepe dress.

"Darling, you're so good to us – Kenny and me!"

That was too much for Aunt Isa. Her eyes filled with tears.

"You're good to me!" she sobbed quietly. "I've not been so happy since Alec went to the States and John died. It's been like a new lease of life to me having you and Kenny." She cleared her throat. "Pity help anybody that harms either of you!"

Kathleen smiled gaily.

"Who's going to?"

CHAPTER THIRTEEN

NOTHING more was said about Saturday. Aunt Isa accepted it with the best grace she could manage. She didn't approve. But she decided to bide her time.

On Saturday afternoon when Kathleen ran out to the car Kenny had already gone to play in Peter Balfour's garden. He hadn't minded in the least being left. But it was strange not to have him waving to her.

"Hello, Kathleen! Right on time!" Craig Carmichael was smiling at the neat figure in the grey suit and crisp white blouse. Kathleen was hatless, her hair shining in the sunlight.

The car drew away from the gate Kathleen turned to wave to Aunt Isa, but she was nowhere in sight, an unusual thing. Kathleen soon forgot that pinprick. This was a holiday and she was going to enjoy herself.

It was as lovely an afternoon as it had been a morning, and Craig Carmichael did everything to make her happy and at ease. She had noticed before how easily he could slip from the role of employer to that of friend, calling her Kathleen as naturally as he called her Mrs Laurie in the office.

She found it less easy to address him as Craig, but only at first. So the hours flew as they explored the lesser-known byways of Ayrshire with interest and enjoyment.

They went through Ayr and on to Alloway, to see the "wee

clay biggin'" where Robert Burns was born. Craig showed
her Kirk Alloway and the Brig o' Doon. He even quoted her
a few lines of the song: –

Aft ha'e I roved by bonnie Doon,
To see the rose and woodbine twine,
And ilka bird sang o' its love,
And fondly sae did I o' mine.

It was so unlike him to quote poetry that Kathleen found it
oddly touching. She had always liked him, but now she
found herself warming to him as never before. Here was a
side of the practical business man she had not known
existed. He seemed years younger and his slightly cynical
air was gone, as if it had never been.

From Alloway they took the Maybole road to Turnbery.
Later they ran on to Girvan, then along the lovely coast road
to Ballantrae. At Kathleen's request Craig drove slowly.

"It's so beautiful," she said.

He looked at her closely as they ran along, the sea now
level and then sometimes far below them. He marvelled that
with her recent worry over Kenny, and the task of bringing
him up, she could find such happiness in things he and many
others took for granted. The sea, the sun, the greening of
hedgerows, the burgeoning of trees. She was always
showing him something new about herself. The tragedy of
widowhood, the cares of motherhood seemed only to make
her a more delightful and desirable woman.

At Ballantrae they had a meal. When they started back

twilight was hushing the day to rest and quiet, a full moon dusted the sea with silver, and the lights at Ailsa Craig, Davaar and Pladda were stabbing their warnings across the firth.

Just after they left Kennedy's Pass behind, Craig drew the car on to a grass verge. He stretched over and let down the window on her side. The rustling of the sea on the shingle rose to them like a whispering chorus.

"You know – you were right. It is beautiful."

"Oh, it is. It's the one thing I miss at Kilmarford – the sea!"

"Wasn't it Clacton where you lived?"

She nodded.

"Do you think – could we go out for a few moments?"

"Of course!" He stretched over and opened the door and followed her out.

The night was deceptive. It had been warm in the car, but now Kathleen felt the chill in the wind. She lifted her head, feeling the breeze blowing the ends of her hair.

"Are you sure you're not cold, Kathleen?" They were standing on a hillock of tussocky grass above the rocks and shingle.

"A little," she admitted, drawing her jacket round her, "but it doesn't matter. It's so lovely here. Look at the moonlight right across the water!"

"Kathleen –" he said softly, and she was conscious of a deepening warmth in his voice.

"Yes?" she asked, a little uncertainly. Her face was as pale as a pearl in the moonlight. She looked up at him. The wind was ruffling his hair above his brow. When he drew her to him she did not resist. But there could be no response on her lips. He felt them cold, unyielding.

"Craig –" she whispered.

He released her at once, standing very straight in the moonlight.

"I'm not apologising for that, Kathleen."

She looked past him to the whispering water. There was nothing she could say, nothing she wanted to say. But his next words startled her so much that she swung back to face him.

"Ewen Gilmour – is he a particular friend of yours?" Craig asked.

"I visit the farm, that's all. They're nice people, he and his sister. Ewen gave Kenny a Scottie pup," she added as an afterthought.

"Is that all there is to it? Oh, I know I shouldn't be talking about him to you like this! I haven't the right! But I'd like to have the right. That's what I'm trying to tell you, Kathleen! And I'm doing it badly, I know!"

She had never seen him before when he wasn't sure of himself and completely self-controlled. She shifted her position on the coarse grass and sought for words.

"Craig, I wish you hadn't –"

He brushed that aside.

"I've known for some time now, Kathleen. I admired you from the first day we met. But it's more than that now. I love you. I'm asking you to marry me."

She drew a quick breath.

"Craig, I like you very much. You've been a – good friend to me – and I'm grateful. But I – I've never thought about marrying again.

"Kenneth and I – it's like a wonderful dream – "

"That's all it is now!" he said earnestly, taking her hand in his. "A dream! It must be nearly seven years since Kenneth was killed, and you told me you had only a week or two together. What's that, in a lifetime? You're just a girl, Kathleen. Your whole life's in front of you. What's past is past – "

"There's Kenny," she said simply.

A boyish smile flitted across his pale face.

"I haven't had much practice at being a father, but I'll do my best. I promise you that, Kathleen." His voice deepened. "I love you, my dear."

He saw her eyes fill with tears. Gently he pressed her hand and then released it.

"I'll ask you again. Don't let this make any difference between us. That's all I ask at the moment. We're still friends?"

"Of course." Her voice wavered uncertainly, but she smiled.

They were both quiet on the way back, and when they did talk, it was of generalities. It was late when they reached Dalreoch, and Kathleen did not ask him in. He said goodnight almost casually and drove off.

Kathleen went into the house to find Aunt Isa still up at the living-room fire. She seemed to look rather pointedly at the clock as though to emphasise the lateness of the hour, but she made no comment. Neither did she ask anything about Kathleen's outing.

Instead she launched into an account of the visitors who had come that afternoon.

"Ewen Gilmour and his sister! What a pity you missed them. They were that disappointed! Ewen brought a tartan collar for Jock. It's got his name and the address on it – Dalreoch, South Road. Kenny's fair away with himself about it!"

"How nice of Ewen!" Kathleen examined the collar, which was at the side of the fire.

"They want you out there next Saturday. I said I was sure it would be all right."

It was warm in the living-room. Kathleen slipped off her costume jacket and hung it over the back of a chair.

"But I can't go. I'd need the morning off, and I couldn't ask off again so soon – "

"You could go in the afternoon. Kenny would like it!"

"Not next Saturday," Kathleen returned with what Aunt Isa considered unexpected stubbornness. "I'll drop a note to Carnbo."

Aunt Isa made a sudden movement in her chair. Then put her hand to her side with a cry which stopped Kathleen on her way to the kitchen.

"You all right, Aunt Isa?" she asked anxiously.

"I'm fine. It's just a stitch. I get it now and again. Away you and make the tea. I could do with a cup."

* * * *

A few weeks later Kathleen came out of the baker's on a Saturday afternoon. She all but walked into Alice Boswell, tall and graceful in soft blue tweeds. Kathleen did not envy but always admired the other's clothes.

Alice's face lit up into a smile.

"It's ages since I saw you! Have you time for a coffee?"

Kathleen smiled.

"Not really – but I'll make time!"

They threaded their way back into Fenwick's and upstairs to the tearoom. They got a table for two and chatted animatedly, two good-looking young women towards whom many threw interested glances.

"I wanted to ask if you and Kenny would come out and visit us. My mother would like to meet you. You have the Monday holiday on the twenty-eighth, haven't you? I could call for you in the morning with the car, and we could make a day of it."

"We'd have loved to come," said Kathleen, but went on to explain about the promised visit to Glasgow. "Aunt Isa means to see the Princess!" she finished with a smile.

"It'll have to be a Saturday, then? We'd better fix one right now. How about the next after the holiday – that'll be the first Saturday in June? I could phone you at the office."

It was left like that when they parted.

Alice did not mention Mrs Laurie, so Kathleen didn't. She knew Mrs Laurie was still meeting Kenny in the park on his way home from school. But now Peter Balfour was always with him and sometimes Malcolm Guthrie, an older boy in South Road. She wondered if Mrs Laurie felt the other boys spoiled things. She hoped not. She wanted Kenny to have plenty of friends.

She crossed the park and turned into South Road. Kenny was hanging over the gate.

He came charging along the pavement to meet her, having carefully closed the gate on Jock. The puppy was not yet traffic trained.

His face was sparkling with excitement.

"Peter's going to Saltcoats with his mummy and daddy on the holiday – and I can go, too! Peter's mummy asked me to as you. They're going to have a picnic on the sands." His voice cracked with sheer excitement. "I can go, can't I?"

"But I thought you were coming to Glasgow with Aunt Isa and me?"

"Mummy – but they're going to the sands!"

"We'll see, then. I'll need to speak to Peter's mummy."

That evening she did have a word with Ray Balfour, a slim, brown-haired young woman with bright hazel eyes. She confirmed the invitation.

"We'd like to take Kenny if it's all right with you. It'll be more fun for Peter having another boy to play with. That's the bother with an 'only', isn't it?" She ended with a note of regret.

Kathleen agreed. She liked Mrs Balfour and the tall, sandy-haired husband she called Don.

"I'm sure Kenny will be a lot happier at Saltcoats than in Glasgow," said Mrs Balfour.

"You and your aunt can have a real day on your own. We'll look after Kenny."

* * * *

It was a "real" day. From the moment in the early morning when they stepped on the train, Aunt Isa in her best brown coat and her brown straw hat with the raffia flowers, Kathleen in the grey suit and white blouse she had worn the Saturday she was out with Craig, everything went well for them.

Later on Kathleen was to be astonished at the details Aunt Isa remembered. Over lunch she described almost everything about the Princess's dress, from the deep powder-blue coat to the diamond bow in the shawl collar, from the little blue hat with the matching flowers to the grey glove on the hand which seemed to give Aunt Isa a special little wave.

But at the great moment Aunt Isa was dumb. When Kathleen looked at her she saw a tear trickling over her cheek.

"Bless her," whispered Aunt Isa. "She looks that young – just a lassie –"

Kathleen took a firm hold of her arm.

"We'd better look for some place to eat. You must be

dying for a cup of tea."

"I'll remember this day if I live to be a hundred!" said Mrs Duncan. "What a lot I'll have to tell Alec when I write on Sunday."

The hours flew. The Princess had lunch in the City Chambers with Sir Victor Warren. Aunt Isa and Kathleen had lunch in Craig's. They spent the afternoon shop-window gazing, and Kathleen bought herself some blue material to make a summer dress, and one or two odds and ends for Kenny.

There was a train soon after five. They mustn't be any later because of Kenny. They went to have tea, but Aunt Isa said she wanted nothing to eat.

"I'm not hungry. A cup of tea will do me," she said. But she left half of it, which was unlike her.

They had plenty of time to get to St Enoch's. Kathleen paid the bill and they started to walk out to the street.

"Kathy – I –" Aunt Isa's fingers dug into Kathleen's arm.

"Auntie!" Kathleen dropped her parcels and tried to catch the slumping figure, but she was too late. Aunt Isa's face was ashen. She was unconscious.

The next few minutes were a nightmare Kathleen was never to forget. The gathering crowd. The voice which said, "That's not just a faint –"

"A doctor –"

"Better an ambulance. Poor body, she looks far gone –"

Someone phoned for help. Kathleen knelt on the floor beside Aunt Isa, whose raffia-trimmed hat had slipped pathetically sideways on her grey hair. She would have hated to be stared at like this.

The ambulance came and the old woman was lifted gently into it. Kathleen picked up the parcels, including the small toy motor Aunt Isa had bought for Kenny. She sat beside the still figure. There was no movement; the colourless face was waxen.

The Western Infirmary received them. Aunt Isa was wheeled away and Kathleen was put into a room to wait. The minutes ticked on and on. They became hours. Kathleen sat on the edge of the chair, her eyes strained with watching the doorway.

Finally a doctor, his hair as red as her own, came.

"Are you a relative?" he asked.

He told her there was no definite news. It was too early to say anything. It would be better if she went home and rang the infirmary in the morning.

"Is she – is she –" Kathleen's dry lips trembled with the words she could not speak.

"You ring tomorrow morning," he repeated with kindly firmness.

They gave her a parcel with Aunt Isa's clothes.

"Will we get a taxi?"

"Yes – yes, please." She was dazed. In the taxi, running down from the infirmary, she could see the Kelvin Hall where Princess Elizabeth had opened the exhibition. Was it this morning, or another lifetime ago?

It was almost ten o'clock when she reached South Road.

She was worrying again about Kenny. Ray Balfour opened the door to her, and as soon as she saw Kathleen's face she knew something was wrong.

"Come in! What is it? We didn't worry – we thought you had missed the train."

Kathleen told her and asked about Kenny.

"He's fine. Come into the bedroom and see him."

On the pillow were two heads, side by side, one red, one fair, and on the old cushion on the floor was a round black body which whined a welcome to Kathleen and went to sleep again.

"It's a shame to waken him," said Ray Balfour, smiling. "Just leave him and I'll send him round after breakfast."

"You're too kind –"

That was swept aside.

"You look all in, Mrs Laurie. I'll get you something to eat. Then Don will take you home. He's out, but he'll be back any minute."

The kindness brought stinging tears to Kathleen's eyes. She was afraid she would break down if she stayed.

"Please – I'd rather go home. It's only a few yards."

Ray Balfour did not press her. Kathleen felt dreadfully weary as she let herself into Dalreoch. The fire was out. How empty the house was without Kenny – and Aunt Isa. Her eyes went to the clock. She could hardly ring the infirmary before seven – that was nine hours to wait.

She suddenly realised that she had never felt so lonely in her life.

CHAPTER FOURTEEN

IN the quiet and loneliness of the empty house Kathleen felt suddenly cold. It was quite a mild night, but she shivered. The old superstition "someone walking over my grave" jumped to her mind and was chased from it at once. Her lips moved silently in a prayer for Aunt Isa.

The only sound in the house was the tick-tock of the eight-day clock in the living-room. In time its slow regularity became monotonous, frightening.

She shivered again. Her shoulders ached because of the tenseness with which she held them as she waited in the hospital for news of Aunt Isa. Her head ached, too, and her eyes felt gritty. But her exhaustion was only physical. Her brain seemed to be spinning in endless circles.

There was no fire, but Aunt Isa had set it before they left that morning. It seemed a century ago to Kathleen since she had cooked breakfast while Aunt Isa, in her flowered overall, knelt at the hearth and dealt energetically with the cinders.

She knelt and lit the fire. Her fingers trembled so that matches showered from the box on to the hearth rug. She drew the curtains against the unfriendly darkness and went into the empty kitchen to put on the kettle. She was not hungry. She felt she never wanted to see food again. But she was very thirsty.

It was strange to see Jock's basket empty. To hear no

scrabbling of his sharp paws on the kitchen linoleum. Aunt Isa kept it so well polished that Jock was for ever skidding.

She took off her jacket and went into the bedroom for her dressing-gown. There were the two single beds with the blue quilts neatly arranged. Kathleen looked away from the emptiness of the one nearest the window. Kenny had never slept a night away from her since he was born.

Yet she could only be thankful he was where he was; thankful he would not have the memory of Aunt Isa's collapse and the scenes at the infirmary imprinted on his little mind for all time. It had been a blessing he had not been with them in Glasgow. In the midst of all the worry, that was one very tangible thing she was grateful for.

She would still have to tell him, of course. That would be difficult because he adored Aunt Isa. But it would be easier for him to listen and understand than to have actually experienced the shock of his aunt's terrifying collapse.

She made tea and sat down with it at the fire. It was now beginning to send glowing tongues of flame from the coal. Gradually she grew warmer and felt better. It was only half-past ten. The hours between now and morning stretched before her like an abyss. What was happening to poor Aunt Isa now? What news would she get when she phoned the infirmary in the morning?

The hot tea was refreshing, but she could not relax. Her troubled mind was full of problems, questing solutions she could not find. What lay ahead? What had she to do? Well, she must give up her job at Carmichael's for one. There was no doubt about that. When Aunt Isa came home she would need care. But supposing Aunt Isa didn't come home?

She pushed that thought feverishly from her, as she had done hundreds of times since she saw the inert figure lifted into the ambulance. Aunt Isa must come home!

She remembered now the times she had caught Aunt Isa in pain. "It's just that stitch – " The familiar voice sounded in her ears, and now she blamed herself bitterly. She should never have let it pass. She should have insisted on Aunt Isa seeing Dr Dallas. Perhaps, if she had, before it was too late. . .

Too late!

It was after midnight when Kathleen climbed stiffly into bed. She slept only in restless snatches and she was glad when daylight crept through the curtained window. It would be hours before she could phone for news, but she got up and dressed.

It was just a few minutes before seven o'clock when she slipped on a coat and ran along the road to the phone-box. It was a bright morning, with high, puffy clouds and an early, cool breeze. From farther along the road Kathleen could hear the cheerful clatter of milk bottles; a boy delivering papers interrupted his whistling to greet her with a friendly, "Hello!"

She had the exact money for the call. Her heart was fluttering as she inserted the coins. After a series of slight delays she was put through to a ward and a nurse answered her request for news. She was told Aunt Isa had undergone

143

an emergency operation the previous night.

"Mrs Duncan is as well as can be expected," the voice said, with a slight Highland accent.

"But, please –" Kathleen swallowed "– can't you tell me any more?"

"If you care to speak to Sister when you come up to the ward –" The soft, attractive voice trailed off.

"But – she has had an operation?" Kathleen found herself repeating, willing the voice at the other end to say Aunt Isa would be all right.

But there was no reassurance. Only the repetition of the staid words, "As well as can be expected." And they could mean anything, or nothing.

She hung up the receiver and stepped out into the morning sunshine. It was too early to go for Kenny, so she walked back to the house. The phone call had been such an anti-climax. All night she had longed to make it, and dreaded what she might hear. The words she had heard were comfortless.

She was not hungry for breakfast, but she put on an egg to boil, one of the eggs from Carnbo, and lit the grill to make toast. It was not worth setting the table. She put a tray on the end of it. The house was so oppressively quiet that she switched on the wireless. But the cheerful sounds of the morning music grated on her mood. She turned it off, preferring the silence.

The brown paper parcel containing Aunt Isa's clothes was still on the chair where she had put it the night before. She cut the string and shook out the brown coat. The creases would have horrified Aunt Isa. It was her best coat. The brown hat with the raffia flowers had been pressed out of shape.

She hung the coat on the back of the bedroom door where it would get the air, laid the rest of the clothes on Aunt Isa's bed and put the hat on the dressing table. Later, she would stuff it tightly with paper to get the shape back. In the meantime, she must go round for Kenny.

* * * *

Ray Balfour answered the door and her husband rose to his feet as Kathleen went into the room. Kathleen thought how cheerful it was with the sun streaming through the yellow curtains and the two small boys facing each other across the table.

"Mummy, I slept in the same bed as Peter!" Kenny greeted her joyfully. He was halfway through a large plateful of porridge, and was obviously in the best of spirits.

Ray Balfour was asking if she had had breakfast. Kathleen said she had.

"It's so good of you to have looked after Kenny – "

"That's been nothing!" Ray was smiling, but there was a question in her eyes and Kathleen answered it.

"No news. I've just phoned. 'As well as can be expected' – that's all the nurse would say."

"That's all they ever say, Mrs Laurie. But she'll get the

best of attention there." Don Balfour's kind blue eyes were full of sympathy and comfort.

"There, I've poured you a cup of coffee! You'll manage that, anyway." Ray Balfour handed it to her.

Kathleen was aware of the two small boys talking about Saltcoats, as she and Peter's parents spoke in undertones.

"But you're not needing to give up your job on account of Kenny!" Ray Balfour said. "We'd look after him till you got back from the office at nights, and be glad to!"

"You are kind, but it wouldn't work out. I mean, I don't know what's going to happen. How long it might be for.

"But I would be obliged if you'd keep an eye on him after he's out of school today. I'm going to Glasgow, and I don't know just when I'll get home. But I'll be no later than seven."

So it was arranged. In a few minutes Kathleen was leaving the bungalow which was so like Dalreoch, pausing at the gate to have a last word with Ray Balfour, while Kenny went darting along the road. Jock panted along beside him, arrayed in his new collar and lead.

Kathleen had left the back door open and Kenny had found it. The first thing she heard when she went into the front garden was Kenny's voice shouting: "Aunt Isa!"

He met her at the kitchen door.

"Mummy, where's Aunt Isa?"

"She – I left her in Glasgow, Kenny. She's to stay there for a little while. She's – ill."

The brightness left his face at once.

"Isn't she coming home tonight?"

"No, Kenny – not tonight."

"Tomorrow then?"

"Not tomorrow – but soon, maybe," Kathleen said weakly. She saw his eyes fill with tears, and added hastily: "She sent something to you. It's on your bed."

He brightened at once, with one of the quick changes that blesses childhood. He came running back from the bedroom clutching the toy motor car. So he listened with only half an ear while Kathleen told him she was going to Glasgow again that afternoon, and that he was to go home from school with Peter and have his tea at Mrs Balfour's.

"You'll be a good boy, Kenny?"

He nodded his red head and spun the wheels of the car.

"I'll be seeing Aunt Isa. Will I give her your love?"

That made him look up.

"Oh, yes – and tell her to come home quick!"

"I'll tell her," said Kathleen.

It was after half-past nine when Kathleen reached Carmichael's. She went at once to Miss Gemmell and explained her lateness, saying, too, that she would like to leave at once. Miss Gemmell's shrewd eyes were kind, and her rather dry voice was warm.

"I don't think you should be too hasty about that!" she said. "Take time and think it over. In any case, you'd better see Mr Carmichael and talk it over with him. I'm just going in. I'll tell him."

So when Kathleen entered the familiar inner room a few

minutes later, Craig Carmichael already had the outline of what had happened. He rose from his chair and came towards her, his face concerned.

"Kathleen – this is bad news! Sit down and we'll talk about it. Miss Gemmell tells me you're leaving, but surely that's not necessary? Your aunt may be home quite soon!"

Kathleen shook her head. Her face was pale, her eyes heavy with lack of sleep.

"I don't feel I can go on. You see – there's Kenny to think about. I couldn't have him coming home to an empty house every day. I never knew how empty a house could be until last night."

His eyes searched her face and what he saw did not please him. It was some time before he spoke. When he did his tone was lighter than his heavy thoughts.

"Well, just as you like, for a while. We won't make a real decision about it now." He smiled, and she did her best to respond.

As he went on talking she found herself drawing at least a small measure of comfort from the bracing quality of his sympathy. He was practical. When she mentioned she was going to Glasgow that afternoon he broke in at once.

"I'll run you up, then. I've an appointment at Carstairs and Denholm's today. You made it for me on Saturday morning, remember?"

Kathleen nodded vaguely. Saturday, and Carstairs and Denholm's were a thousand miles away. So much had happened since Saturday.

"I'll call for you at two o'clock."

"But," she protested, "I can go by train!"

"But you're not going to! You be ready at two o'clock!"

She was ready long before two. When the grey saloon car drew up at the gate she was waiting.

"I'm not late, am I?" He opened the door for her.

"No." She slipped into the seat beside him. "I was early. I couldn't rest."

He glanced quickly at her. Then having asked who was to look after Kenny when he came out of school, he talked in generalities during the speedy run to Glasgow. Kathleen was grateful. It kept her mind occupied.

Craig insisted on driving her to the infirmary gates.

"I'll be free by five. It's just after three, so you ought to be finished by then," he said. "I'll meet you outside the subway entrance at St Enoch's at five. I'll park the car somewhere about there. Can you find your way?"

She nodded.

"I think a tram from here goes to Argyle Street. But I can ask."

She was walking away when Craig called her back. He reached over the back of the driving seat and brought out a bouquet of long-stemmed roses wrapped in paper bearing the name of Kilmarford's best florist.

"These are for Mrs Duncan."

"Why – Craig – how nice of you!"

He coloured faintly and shrugged.

"Five o'clock, then."

Kathleen turned in at the gates and looked across the huge grey building which was the university. The pointed spire towered through a blue sky. But she was hardly seeing it, and for all her anxiety she was almost smiling. The paper rustling against the delicate, colourful buds was suddenly like music in her ears.

How charmed Aunt Isa would be. Only they were from Craig! And Aunt Isa didn't like Craig!

The smile faded, but the lightness remained in her step as she walked up the hill.

CHAPTER FIFTEEN

CRAIG CARMICHAEL looked at his watch, and scanned the busy crowds thronging Argyle Street. It was seven minutes past five and a frown of anxiety furrowed his black brows.

All at once his expression cleared. Kathleen was threading her way towards him, a slim, straight figure in grey, with a soft blue hat and a matching blouse. He went forward to meet her. Her expression was so revealing that involuntarily he put his hand under her elbow, speaking lightly but with decision.

"Now we're going to have a meal. Don't argue! If you couldn't do with some tea, I could. I've had a most trying afternoon. We'll just go into the hotel. It's the nearest."

Her pallor alarmed him, and he was relieved when they were safely seated at a table. He spoke with deliberate matter-of-factness, feeling that if he showed too much sympathy she would become more distressed.

"The news isn't good, then?"

Kathleen shook her head.

"I didn't even see her! The sister said I'd – better not. I spoke to the doctor in charge of the ward, Dr Soutar. He was very nice." She swallowed, and stopped.

"Yes?" Craig prompted her.

"He said the operation had been successful – so far."

"Then it's not too bad!"

"I told the doctor where I lived."

Kathleen's voice was flat and expressionless. She was in thought back in the infirmary, hearing again the doctor's kindly, clipped accents, and trying vainly to read the expression on his face. She felt he was evasive. Yet he was definite, too. He'd said there was no point in trailing all that distance every day. Perhaps by Saturday there would be more definite news . . .

"But I can't wait all that time!" she had said.

"You can phone, Mrs Laurie. In fact, when you do phone you can ask for me and I'll tell you if there's any real change. Phone me between –"

Then she remembered where she was and began to explain to Craig.

"The doctor was very kind."

The tea was bringing a touch of colour to her cheeks, Craig noted, but the violet shadows beneath her eyes were like bruises.

"You mustn't look on the black side, Kathleen! I've never met Mrs Duncan, but from what you've told me I'm sure she's got a streak of real toughness in her. She's a fighter, now, isn't she?"

He was rewarded by a faint smile.

"I suppose she is!"

"And she's where she's getting the best of care. She couldn't have better attention anywhere!"

"I know," Kathleen murmured, "but she's very ill, Craig.

They told me that. It was all they did tell me."

"She'll pull through," Craig assured her, with a confidence he was far from feeling.

Kathleen tried to believe him.

"I don't know how I'll manage through the days till Saturday," she said when they were nearing the end of the meal.

Her voice was less jerky. She no longer felt oppressed by the fear which seemed to be smothering her when she left the infirmary. The fear was still there, at the back of her mind. But now she had shared it it seemed less foreboding. There was something comforting about Craig. She could not express it in any way except that she had a feeling of hidden strength.

She was aware now, more strongly than on the night when they had stood on the shore at Kennedy's Pass, that there were depths to Craig of which she knew nothing. He was not a man to reveal himself except in brief flashes.

She found a moment to wonder, even in the midst of anxiety, if she would ever know the real Craig. At the same time she did not know if she really wanted to. To have him as a friend. Surely that was enough.

Craig dropped her at the gate of Dalreoch at ten minutes to seven.

"Have an early night, Kathleen. Take a couple of headache tablets and get to bed."

"All right." She found herself responding with unexpected meekness.

But after Kenny was safely in his bed she sat down to write to Alec Duncan in Chicago. He had to be told of his mother's illness. She was halfway down the first page when the door bell rang, and she started to her feet. Could it be news from the infirmary?

Alice Boswell was on the door step.

"Come in, Alice!" Relief made Kathleen's voice shaky, but her welcome was genuine.

Alice drew off her gloves and sat down at the fireside.

"I see you're busy. I won't stay long. I've just come to ask about Mrs Duncan. Is it anything serious?"

Kathleen gave her the details. After Alice had expressed her sympathy Kathleen asked her, "But how did you know?"

"Mrs Laurie told me. She saw Kenny in the park today and he said his Aunt Isa was sick and didn't come home from Glasgow. She wondered about it, and so did I. I was at Finnard just now with some plants. My father grows a lot under glass." She dismissed Mrs Laurie from the conversation.

"This means you won't be out on Saturday, then?"

"No – I'm going to Glasgow." Kathleen went on to say she had given up her job for the time being.

Alice crossed her slim ankles.

"You know I'll do anything I can to help. If you'd like me to look after Kenny –"

"Thank you." The offer was so genuine that Kathleen smiled spontaneously. Alice's friendliness was like a lamp. One could almost feel its warmth.

"How about me taking Kenny on Saturday, while you're in Glasgow –"

The door bell shrilled again. This time Kathleen was more relaxed. She did not jump up nervously to go to open the door.

She found Ewen Gilmour's great bulk filling the doorway. His fair head was bare and he was smiling.

"Come in!" Kathleen held out her hand and it was immediately engulfed in his.

"But you've already got visitors! There's a car at the gate. I just stopped to ask if you'd fix a date to come out to Carnbo. Aileen is beginning to think you're never coming back! So I got strict orders to call on my way home from the market – not that I needed much ordering –"

By this time he was in the living-room, and Kathleen introduced him to Alice Boswell. Then he had to hear about Aunt Isa, and his concern wiped all the smiles from his tanned face. For Aunt Isa he had conceived genuine affection.

When he heard that Kathleen was going to Glasgow on the Saturday he said that Kenny had better come out to Carnbo.

"He can spend the whole day, and – oh, no, I can't come for him! I can run him home at night, but I won't be free to collect him."

"Where is your farm, Mr Gilmour?" Alice asked. "I could run Kenny out."

They talked over directions while Kathleen slipped into the kitchen to put on the kettle. She heard their voices mingling pleasantly, and was glad they had taken an obvious liking to each other. It was fine to know that Kenny would be at Carnbo on Saturday. He would be in the seventh heaven of rapture when he knew.

When they were gone Kathleen carried her tray into the kitchen and returned to her letter. But it was some minutes before she began writing again. She was thinking how fortunate she was in her friends. Craig, Alice, Ewen, the Balfours – for all she had known the latter such a short time, she was already in their debt. Yes, she was fortunate.

But as she bent her head over her letter her expression changed, and the pucker of anxiety came back to her face.

* * * *

On Friday Kathleen almost danced her way back from the phone-box. But her brief moment of joy was gone almost before she reached her own gate. It was followed by such an overwhelming wave of weak thankfulness that the lines of the neat bungalow wavered before her eyes.

Dr Souter had said that Aunt Isa had more than held her own. She had a fair chance of recovery now. In fact, it was to be expected that when Kathleen visited her on Saturday she would find her weak but able to talk a little.

Kathleen's weakness passed, but the exaltation remained. She gave vent to her feelings in doing a washing and hanging it out in the back garden, where it flapped joyfully in the June breeze. Housework was no trouble to her. The small bungalow was soon gleaming.

By afternoon restlessness still possessed her. She decided to meet Kenny from school. That would be a surprise for him. She was at the gate of the park before she remembered about Mrs Laurie.

Twice, sometimes three times a week, Kenny's grandmother met him in the park. It was a meeting on which Kathleen had never intruded, because it was Mrs Laurie's only contact with her grandson.

She could not intrude now. Quietly she turned at the park gates and walked home. If she had been earlier she would have walked to the Vennel, because several of Aunt Isa's friends had been to inquire about her. But that would have to wait till after tea. She would go home now, and bake something. That would please Kenny.

It was almost nine o'clock when Craig parked his car at the gate. It was still broad daylight and Kathleen was weeding in the front garden, but she stopped and went to open the gate for him.

"I'm just looking for an excuse to make myself a cup of coffee. Come in, Craig!"

He smiled, the elusive smile that took the hardness from his features.

"I can see you've had good news!"

Her eyes were bright, but he was not blind to the fact that her face was thinner and faint lines were marking the smoothness of her brow. Yet she was beautiful to him, more than beautiful. The office had been an empty place all week.

"When are we leaving tomorrow?" he asked, taking the cup of coffee from her.

She raised her finely etched brows.

"I'm going by train, Craig. There's one just after one o'clock that will suit. The visiting hour is between three and four – I've got cards."

He stirred his coffee, and said calmly: "We'll leave about eleven, take it very easy and have lunch somewhere. We'll take Kenny, of course. He can stay in the car with me."

"Kenny's going to Carnbo. To the Gilmours'. He's spending the day there."

Craig's spoon jarred in his saucer. His brows drew together. But he only observed quietly: "Can you be ready at eleven?"

"I suppose so. But Craig, I don't want to – to cause any upset in your life like this. You must have other plans – "

"Kathleen, haven't I let you know – you are my life – "

Then Kathleen began to talk brightly, almost feverishly, of other things, and he suited his mood to hers. He left shortly afterwards, with the understanding that she would be ready to leave with him soon after eleven o'clock.

Kathleen had slept badly all week, and this Friday night was no exception. Now her rest was disturbed by thoughts of Craig Carmichael. She found him disturbing, as no man had been in all the years since Kenneth's death.

They arrived at the infirmary just at three o'clock.

"I'll wait for you," Craig said, handing her a small basket of fruit. "Have you got the card?"

He watched her until she was out of sight, and then opened his paper and rested it on the driving wheel. Mrs Duncan might be allowed a visitor for only a few minutes. On the other hand, Kathleen might be able to wait for the whole hour.

It was twenty minutes later that he caught sight of Kathleen's auburn head, and opened the car door for her. She hesitated, then said unexpectedly: "You're to go in. Aunt Isa wants to see you."

"To see me?" he asked blankly.

"Yes, she wants to thank you for the fruit – and the flowers."

"I'm not going in," he protested.

"Please, Craig! I promised I'd ask you, and she's not in any state to be upset."

He grumbled about it, easing himself out of the driving seat. Kathleen gave him a card and told him how to find the ward.

"I'll be no longer than five minutes," he said firmly.

But he was much longer. He had no means of knowing that the change in Aunt Isa was considerable, and that in a few short days she had become a frail old woman. He was conscious only of a strong personality, even in a weak body, and of a will that reached out to do battle with his own. It showed in the look in her eyes, although her voice was only a thread of sound.

"Is the bairn all right, Mr Carmichael?" That was her first question after he had taken her limp hand and sat down at the side of the bed.

He assured her that Kenny was perfectly all right. He hadn't seen him, but at this very moment he was enjoying himself on a farm.

"Aye, at Carnbo. Kathy told me so. That Ewen Gilmour – he's a grand man. I'm that – " Her voice faded and then regained strength, "that glad him and Kathy are good friends."

The effort of speaking was tiring her. Her eyes closed and Craig laid her hand gently on the bed, but her grasp tightened and her eyes snapped open.

"I want to thank you for the fruit you sent in. It was a kind thought for an old body. And you never been over the doorstep of my house –"

He leaned closer to her, and spoke with deliberate gentleness.

"Oh, but I have, Mrs Duncan! I was there last night, and I hope to be there many more times! So it's up to you to hurry up and get well, so you'll be there to welcome me!"

He smiled at her, but she only answered fretfully.

"I just don't like millowners – " Now her voice was stronger than it had been since he entered the ward.

"Oh, well – there's millowners and millowners –"

Her eyes were full of the ready tears of weakness.

"I'm just an ill-natured old woman –"

Craig patted her hand.

"You're nothing of the kind, and we're going to be good friends, the best of friends, you and I."

But this time the eyelids did not lift, and he tiptoed away, thinking she had fallen asleep. But she was not asleep. She watched his dark head till it was out of sight, and then she looked at his beautiful roses. Now she'd spoken to him he seemed nicer than she'd imagined.

But he wasn't Ewen Gilmour!

CHAPTER SIXTEEN

MEANWHILE at Carnbo Kenny was having a wonderful time. He was in his element, and tagged after his "Uncle Ewen" like a small shadow.

He and Alice had arrived in the forenoon, and Ewen crossed the yard to meet them, in leggings and an open-necked shirt.

Kenny catapulted out of the car followed by the puppy.

"Uncle Ewen – I'm here!"

Ewen laughed.

"So I see!"

Alice smiled at them both. She looked very pretty, with her smooth, fair hair shining in the June sunshine.

"Well, I'll be getting along now. You'll see Kenny home –"

"Just a minute! You can't go off like that! Aileen's expecting you," Ewen told her. "She'll have my head off if you run away right away! Now you're here you must stay for a little. We don't have so many visitors."

Alice looked round the prosperous farm, bright and peaceful in the warm sun. She wasn't much interested in farms. She never had been, but the invitation was pressing.

"Here's Aileen now –"

Alice climbed out of the car and shook hands with the dark-haired, vivid girl who was Ewen's twin. From that first instant of meeting she and Aileen recognised each other as kindred spirits. They had much in common, and were to find increasing pleasure in each other's company.

Alice stayed, not only for lunch but for tea as well. And it was she who ran Kenny back home in the evening, with many promises to return to Carnbo.

It was not until the great, sprawling mass of Laurie's mills came into view that the happy curve of Alice's lips drooped, and a half-wondering expression crossed her face. This was the first day since Roger's death that she had not thought about him, with an ache of loneliness she never mentioned to anyone.

But this day she had just been happy.

She turned into South Road and smiled at the top of Kenny's red head. He was blissfully tired, his head nodding. There was already a grey car at the gate. Kathleen must be home, so there was no need for Alice to use the key she had given her.

Alice had often met Craig Carmichael and knew him quite well. They greeted each other and chatted pleasantly. Kathleen was tired, rather overwhelmed with mingled joy and surprise that Aunt Isa was improving. The release from strain was telling on her, and she felt almost light-headed. She put Kenny to bed as quickly as possible, and for once he was more than ready to go. The long day in the open air was taking its effect.

It was Alice who bore the brunt of the conversation. She was animated and happy, her eyes sparkled. She was full of her visit to Carnbo.

"I thought you told me you were scared of cows!" Kathleen smiled at her as she crossed the living-room.

"I am, but I kept away from them! Ewen wanted me to cut through a field, but I wouldn't. He laughed, but I didn't mind, and didn't go."

Craig watched her animated face and his own grew first thoughtful then cheerful. Few men are particularly perceptive of a girl's emotions, unless she interests them personally. Alice's delight in her day out was as transparent as glass.

It was surprise to Craig that she and Ewen Gilmour had not met before. But now they had, they'd obviously taken to each other. Well, that was the best thing that could happen. The more they took to each other the better he would be pleased.

It did not occur to Craig Carmichael that Alice spoke of Aileen Gilmour more often than she did of Ewen. Man-like, he accepted the obvious, because it suited him, and having accepted it, did not probe beyond it.

When he drove away from Dalreoch a short time afterwards he felt a pleasing satisfaction at all that had happened that day. He had been of help to Kathleen; had been with her all day. He had seen Mrs Duncan. It was true he'd made little progress with either. But that would come. Meantime Alice Boswell had met Ewen Gilmour.

It often happened that indirect methods solved a puzzling problem. Once a road was clear of obstacles progress was always quick. He pursed his lips and began to whistle with contentment.

* * * *

While Craig Carmichael drove away from Dalreoch, in a happy mood of contentment, Kathleen and Alice Boswell still sat talking at the window. Both would have been surprised, and alarmed, if they had known that Craig Carmichael's contentment came from his linking Ewen Gilmour's future with Alice Boswell's.

Some of Alice's earlier animation had faded. But there was a quality of relaxed happiness about her which did not escape Kathleen's notice.

It pleased Kathleen, even in the midst of her tiredness, to see Alice happy. Not that Alice, in the months Kathleen had known her, had ever outwardly appeared otherwise. With the exception of one or two occasions, Alice had hidden her grief over Roger Laurie from the world at large.

But Kathleen knew this was only because Alice had turned her thoughts to helping others. In her concern for them she had kept her sweetness of temperament under a blow which would have turned others bitter. Kathleen herself, and Mrs Laurie, were two cases in point.

Now Kathleen smiled at Alice, leaning back in her chair. "You'll be glad you went to Carnbo, then?"

"I am. The Gilmours are the nicest people I've met for ages. And Mrs Hay is an old dear!"

165

Kathleen smiled again, hoping Alice would not notice the stifled yawn. How sleepy she was!

"You'll be going back?"

"Aileen asked me, and I've asked her to visit us," Alice said frankly. "She's keen on gardening, so she and Dad will have lots to talk about." She clasped her fingers together on her knee. She had long hands, white-skinned and beautifully shaped. "Aileen and Ewen aren't a bit alike, to be twins."

"No, but there's a strong bond between them."

"I noticed that. I don't think they have many secrets from each other. Aileen was saying she was so glad Kenny had taken to Ewen –"

Kathleen's heavy eyelids opened in surprise. The tone of Alice's voice, rather than her words, was full of meaning. But she said nothing and Alice went on:

"Carnbo's like a second home to Kenny already. Aileen told me she won't stay on there, of course, when Ewen marries. She's got plans of her own –"

As she listened, Kathleen watched Alice's face and read the expression in her wide-set, tranquil eyes. Honesty and friendliness glowed in them and told her a little of what had happened at Carnbo that day.

Both Aileen and Alice were her friends. They had talked about her, as friends will, sincerely and sympathetically. They were happy about the way affairs were seemingly shaping, hopeful for the future. Like Aunt Isa they sought only happiness for one they loved.

"But, Alice," Kathleen smiled, "you mustn't jump to

conclusions. Ewen Gilmour and I are only friends."

Alice looked at her, shaking her head while the corners of her mouth curved into a friendly smile.

"Yes – but that's not his fault, is it?"

Kathleen let the question pass unanswered. She knew what Alice was implying was true. Ewen was such a transparently honest person. It was she who had, more than once, kept the atmosphere light between them when he had wanted it otherwise.

Alice was looking into the South Road where the shadows were lengthening.

"Today has been a strange day for me, Kathleen. When Roger died, I thought that was the end of living for me. Last winter – wasn't easy –"

"I know," Kathleen murmured.

Didn't she know, only too well, every step of the tortuous path Alice had trod – alone? Her own loss had been, perhaps, more bitter, since she was a wife. But later she had been given Kenny. She had, in fact, never really been alone. Without Kenny what would there have been but desolation!

Alice's lips trembled.

"Today was the first day I forgot him. I didn't think about him at all! Then when I did remember, it seemed like betrayal – forgetting him –"

"No!" Kathleen sat forward impulsively. "Alice, you mustn't think like that! You ought to be happy! It's only right. You're young. You'll fall in love again –" She broke off, feeling a strange familiarity about her words, then

167

realising they were an echo of those used by Aunt Isa to herself.

Soon afterwards Alice left, her brief moment of revelation gone as swiftly as it had come.

"When are you and Kenny coming to visit?" she asked, drawing on her gloves at the car door. It was decided that the following Sunday would be best as Kathleen would be going again to the infirmary on Saturday.

Kathleen stood at the gate until the car was out of sight. A light breeze had sprung up and she shivered in her thin blue blouse. She was cold, but realised it was mostly tiredness. Tonight she knew she would sleep without rocking, as Aunt Isa would have said.

Dear Aunt Isa! How shocked she had been at the change in her, and yet how thankful to find her conscious and clear-minded. It was like a miracle.

Yet before she drifted into sleep, it was of Alice Boswell she found herself thinking. Of course love would come again for Alice! For Alice – but only for Alice –

* * * *

A couple of days later a letter arrived from Craig. Kathleen recognised the firm handwriting at once, but the London postmark was unexpected. She drew out the tightly folded sheets of notepaper.

Accustomed to Craig's short, business letters, these closely written pages were a surprise. So, too, was what they contained. The details of his journey south, a description of the hotel he was staying at, the people he met. It was so different from the Craig she knew, the man who never used two words if one could do.

"I was called away in such a hurry I had no time to let you know. But I should be back at the end of the week and I'll see you then. London is full of talk about the King's illness. It doesn't sound too good, poor man. The bulletin issued tonight says he must have complete rest and no engagements for at least four weeks. Hope nothing happens to him. He and the Queen have done a wonderful job."

He went on to talk about Aunt Isa; how sorry he was not to be able to drive Kathleen to Glasgow on Wednesday. The first place he'd call when he got back would be Dalreoch.

Kathleen folded the letter into the envelope and laid it on the sideboard. Her face was solemn; her mind raced with deep thoughts.

She saw Aunt Isa again on Wednesday and Saturday afternoons. On Saturday she took with her Mrs Torrance, one of Aunt Isa's oldest friends, a neighbour in the Vennel. Mrs Torrance was very stout, and her breath came short as she followed Kathleen along the polished corridors to the ward.

Aunt Isa was propped up a little that afternoon. She looked considerably better, to Kathleen's loving eyes.

"I was beginning to think you weren't coming!"

Kathleen stooped to kiss her.

"We're five minutes late – that's all!"

"That's a long time when you're lying watching the clock! Hello, Nessie – I'm real glad to see you!"

They sat at the bedside and Aunt Isa's first questions were about Kenny. Kathleen assured her that at that moment he was playing happily in Peter Balfour's back garden.

"Did you get the card he sent you? He printed it himself."

"Aye, I got it. Bless his heart! It's in my locker. I had a lovely one from Ewen Gilmour, forbye, and these grapes. Did you ever see their like, near as big as some tomatoes! My, but folk are good to me."

"There, there, Isa." Mrs Torrance patted the hand nearest her as tears came to Aunt Isa's eyes, trickling down cheeks which had lost all their plumpness.

They began to talk of cheerful generalities, and Kathleen found herself smiling as she listened to Aunt Isa's trenchant remarks on hospital life. Her interest in the other patients and in everything round her showed she was improving.

It was some time later Aunt Isa asked if "Mr Carmichael" had run them up from Kilmarford. Kathleen was at once aware of Mrs Torrance's quickening interest and answered very evenly that he was in London.

"But he can't be! I had these gladioli from him this morning – and the roses still as fresh as they day they came in."

Kathleen smoothed down Aunt Isa's bewilderment by explaining how flowers could be sent by telegram from anywhere. But she could see this talk about Craig was not lost on Mrs Torrance. That embarrassed her quite a lot, for

Mrs Torrance, thought a kindly body, loved to talk.

But even that was forgotten when Kathleen saw Sister on the way out. Mrs Duncan was doing very well – very well, indeed! She was out of danger now. Provided there were no unforeseen relapses, she was well on the way to recovery. Kathleen's spirits soared. She took Mrs Torrance to tea in the Cadora before they caught the train home.

"Isa's had a bad shake," observed Mrs Torrance over her fish and chips, "but don't you worry your head over her now, Kathy. She's on the mend."

"That's what Sister said. I hope you're both right."

"I'm right." Mrs Torrance nodded, her homely face red and moist beneath her old-fashioned black straw hat. "When you've lived as long as me, Kathy, and seen as much, well, you get to know. Aye, I've buried three – " She sighed heavily, then smiled. "My goodness, I nearly forgot! Emmy Gibb and her sister want to come up with you next week, Wednesday or Friday, they thought."

"Wednesday would be better. The visiting hour's not till seven on a Friday."

"You'll be glad of a rest tomorrow, Kathy. You've had a lot of rushing about!"

"I'm going visiting tomorrow. To Miss Boswell."

"Oh!" Mrs Torrance's eyes filled with kindly interest. "That's her that was engaged to young Laurie? My, that was a sad business. Have you been out there before?"

When Kathleen said she hadn't, Mrs Torrance went on: "The Croft they call it, but there's no' much of a croft about it! It's a big place and the gardens are a fair picture. The general's a great man for his gardens. I mind last year they opened them one Saturday for the Nurses, and Tom and I took the bus out. I've never seen the like o' the rhoddies."

On Sunday the gardens of The Croft were beautiful. Mrs Torrance did not exaggerate. The rhododendrons were lovely enough to take one's breath away. Kathleen took an immediate liking to Mrs Boswell, a sweet-faced woman with Alice's friendly charm, and something more besides. There are people in whom one confides instinctively. Elizabeth Boswell was one of these. Kathleen was drawn to her from the first moment of meeting.

The white-haired general was tall and straight as a poker. Kathleen rather expected Kenny to be scared of him. But with the unerring instinct of childhood, Kenny knew where he would be welcome. He was soon walking hand-in-hand with the general, having his unending questions answered with unfailing patience. Jock had been left at home, but there was a big Airedale to pad along at the heels of the tall man and the red-haired boy.

Kathleen and Mrs Boswell watched them from the window.

"I do hope Kenny won't be a nuisance."

"Don't think so for a moment, my dear! My husband's very fond of children. We'd hoped for grandchildren close at hand when Alice –" She sighed and did not finish the sentence.

Mrs Boswell studied Kathleen as they sat together in the

long, panelled room. Mildred Laurie was her friend, and from Mildred and Alice she had received different reports about this girl; although it was what Mildred had not said that was most telling!

But Alice was right. Kathleen Laurie was a daughter-in-law anyone could be proud of. There was intelligence in her broad forehead. She had a natural ease of manner that was most attractive. She was quite beautiful. And her boy was a credit to her.

Elizabeth Boswell went on talking quietly to Kathleen, showing her photographs of her only son, Michael, now farming in Rhodesia, but her thoughts were busy elsewhere.

She was glad Alice was friendly with Kathleen Laurie. Under happier circumstances they would have been sisters-in-law. They had both suffered bereavement. That was a bond between them. Alice's interest in Kathleen and the little boy had helped her. Mrs Boswell was the only one who knew the real depth of Alice's grief, bravely though the girl tried to hide it.

The afternoon passed pleasantly. They had tea in the rose-garden, with a sun-umbrella shading the table. Kenny was entranced by the goldfish in an ornamental pond. In the evening the sun vanished and it was beginning to drizzle when Alice drove them home.

"I won't come in, Kathleen! Thanks all the same. I'll be seeing you soon."

When Kathleen unlocked the front door, there was a folded slip of paper on the mat, a leaf torn from a diary.

"Sorry you're out. Hoped to take you and Kenny for a run. Didn't think you'd be out on a Sunday. Hope it doesn't mean bad news about Aunt Isa. Will call tomorrow night. – Craig."

Kathleen pushed it into her coat pocket, bending to pat Jock, jumping wildly with excitement over their return.

Was she sorry she had missed Craig? Or was she secretly relieved? She asked herself the question. But she could not answer it.

CHAPTER SEVENTEEN

THE following afternoon Kathleen opened the door to Nan Webb with a feeling of genuine delight. She had been sitting at the front window when she saw her old friend turn in at the gate.

"How brown you're looking! Did you have a good holiday? I got your postcard last week."

Nan was full of her holiday in Morecambe with her husband's parents, but first she wanted to hear about Aunt Isa's illness.

"I just heard about it this morning when I was in the grocer's."

Kathleen gave her the news while she put on the kettle and set a tray.

It was not until Nan was stirring her second cup that she suddenly sat forward and said, half-shyly, her round face glowing: "Kathy, I'm – I'm going to have a baby!"

"Nan!" Kathleen set the teapot on the stand with a click. "Oh, my dear, how lovely! I'm so glad for you, Nan."

Nan nodded, her cheeks pink.

"I've had to wait five years. I was beginning to think we never would have one. In fact, I tried to talk George into adopting a baby, but he wasn't keen –" She chattered on and Kathleen's heart warmed to her.

Nan was her oldest friend in Kilmarford, one of the people

she had longed most to see when she returned. There had been something vaguely unsatisfactory about the renewed relationship. When Kathleen thought of it during the winter months, she had wondered if it was because she had idealised the friendship.

So many of her childhood memories were unhappy, and Nan had been one bright spot. Although things had improved, and she had often been in Nan's home, the old intimacy had seemed lacking.

But because of the miracle of love and motherhood they slipped effortlessly into the old, easy comradeship. The hands of the clock flew round as they talked and talked.

"I'll knit a pram suit!" said Kathleen. "I've a good pattern I used for Kenny. Can I tell Aunt Isa? She'll be thrilled. She loves babies –"

"Well, wait a little, Kathleen. I haven't told anyone but you, yet. Is Mrs Duncan allowed visitors? I'd like to go and see her."

When Nan finally left, Kathleen looked at the clock and hurriedly got out an air-letter to send to Alec Duncan in Chicago. She wanted to catch the afternoon post. But she was scarcely settled to writing it when a violent screeching of brakes in South Road made her jump to her feet. Kenny! He was due home from school. Not Kenny –

She darted to the front door. A lorry was slewed across the road, the driver just climbing down from his cabin. Kathleen ran to the gate. No sign of a red-haired boy anywhere – thank God! But what was that pitifully small bundle lying on the road? Oh, poor Jock!

"Is it yours? I'm sorry, lady. I couldn't do a thing. It just flew out of the gate like a bullet and went right under the wheel. I tried – but I hadn't a chance!"

Kathleen knelt down, heedless of the dust.

"He's dead?"

"'Fraid so. I'm sorry."

The driver was young, hardly more than a boy. He looked shaken and Kathleen scarcely heard him. She was thinking of Kenny, whose heart Jock held between his little black paws.

"I'll need to put in a report," said the driver. "The firm's particular about that. You own the pup?"

"My son does. The name and address is on the collar. Could you – could you take him away quickly? My boy'll be home from school any minute. I don't want him to see –"

"Of course. I'll do that, lady. I'm sorry –"

Kathleen wanted to say it didn't matter. But she couldn't, because it did. She could only worry over how she was going to tell Kenny, and blame herself for not reminding Nan to shut the gate. She could imagine Jock's bright eyes spotting the open gate, his short legs scampering down the path, and then his joyful dash across the road . . .

She closed her eyes in agony at the noise as the driver started up his engine. When she opened them again the lorry was driving away. She read the name on the tailboard. "Laurie and Son." She might have known. There was never anything but trouble from Laurie's Mills.

She went back to her letter, but she had lost taste for writing.

Five minutes later she thankfully heard the clatter of Kenny's feet coming round to the back door, heard the "plop" of his schoolbag dropping on the kitchen floor. Today she did not tell him to put it in its proper place.

"Mummy, where's Jock?"

She laid down her pen and drew Kenny to her. She had to tell him. There are times when even a mother's love cannot shield her child from tragedy. And the tragedies of childhood are deep and often heart-breaking . . .

* * * *

It was almost nine when Craig Carmichael called. He explained he had been late at the office, making up for last week's absence. It was not long before he was saying: "I expected to find you brighter. When your aunt's so much improved. Is something worrying you?"

She told him about Jock.

"Is Kenny very upset by what's happened?"

Kathleen nodded.

"He cried himself to sleep. I'm afraid it will be a long time before he forgets."

"Poor little chap. Never mind, I'll get him another puppy."

"Oh, no, Craig!"

"Why not? Take his mind off –"

"But it wouldn't! It's not just any puppy. It's Jock he has

178

lost. Another puppy wouldn't help. Not just now."

"Maybe you're right."

"I know I am." She sighed. "Nothing but time will help Kenny. It's his first grief."

Craig did not pursue the subject. Kathleen made coffee and they sat chatting.

"You'll be going to Glasgow on Wednesday, Kathleen. I could make it fit in with business. Shall I run you up?"

Kathleen handed him another cup of coffee.

"I'm going by train, Craig. I've promised to take two of Aunt Isa's old friends. We've made the arrangements."

"Saturday, then. And we'll take Kenny."

"Kenny's going to the Sunday school picnic on Saturday. Kathleen brushed a wisp of hair from her brow.

"He'd rather come with us, I'm sure. He'd love to see Aunt Isa and she's always asking about him –"

Kathleen was shaking her head.

"I'd rather not take Kenny to the infirmary, Craig. He's too young. He'll see enough sorrow and trouble in his life. Anyway, it's all settled he's going to the picnic with Mrs Balfour and Peter. We can't alter it now."

He smiled.

"But you'll let me take you?"

It would have been ungracious to refuse. But once again she had the familiar feeling of uncertainty as to whether she was pleased or not.

Craig did not wait long. When he went she washed the coffee cups and thought about him. He disturbed her, as no man had done since Kenneth's death. She felt she knew him. Yet at the same time thought she did not know him at all! Beneath his kindness, his obvious desire to help her make decisions, even to make them for her, she could sense he was holding something back.

He had told her he loved her that night on the shore at Kennedy's Pass. But he had said little or nothing about it since. Was it the expression of his love he was holding back? Was he trying to convince her by his deeds, by showing her that her troubles were his, that his love was true?

That night on the shore she had not been receptive to him. Tonight she had felt a subtle difference in him. There was a gentleness, a readier acceptance of her wishes.

He had not even shaken hands at the door. Yes, she did not doubt he was in love with her. Had he been influenced by his head instead of his heart, he would have realised she was the last person he ought to become attached to – the unwanted daughter-in-law of James Laurie – the daughter of Jock Todd whose name had been a byword in the town.

Was she falling in love with Craig? She did not know. Yet there was something about him that moved her deeper feelings.

She undressed without putting on the light, afraid of disturbing Kenny. She kicked against something in the half darkness, and realised it was Jock's empty basket. Kenny had insisted on having it at his bedside that night. She picked it up and carried it into the kitchen. In the morning before he was awake, she would hide it in the shed.

Tomorrow would be a new beginning. For Kenny, she prayed it wouldn't be a sad one.

As she pulled the bedsheets up to her chin, she began to think. How often people thought of tomorrow as a new beginning. But the tragedies of life are not so easily forgotten. They linger past today till tomorrow, and beyond tomorrow till next year. The scar heals. The grass grows green again. But the pain that has been is never quite forgotten.

Even little Kenny would never really forget. He might think he had. Yet one day, perhaps when he was a grown man, he might glimpse a black Scotty pup with an impudent tail and a lolling tongue. Then he would remember Jock and there would be a hint of sadness, like a ripple on a smooth pool.

Kathleen lay still. Now she remembered Kenneth, without conscious effort, as she not done for years. The clarity of the image was almost a shock. Every line of his face, his smile, the tone of his voice saying: "Katie – Katie, darling!" He had always called her Katie. He was the only one who ever did.

She remembered their brief honeymoon in Devon. The daffodils and the starry violets, the scent of lily-of-the-valley mingled with the tang of the sea. The elderly woman at whose cottage they spent those brief golden days away from everything – especially from the war and all its fears. It was a low-roofed cottage with thick walls and tiny panes of glass in the windows. Through them you could see the waves chasing each other to the shore, like children racing out of school.

She could see the pink paper flowers in the fat pottery jug on the mantelpiece; hear Kenneth's voice shouting: "Come on for a swim, Katie! Come on!" Twenty-three he was. Twenty-three he would always be. She might grow old, but Kenneth never!

No pain is ever quite forgotten. Could women, especially wives and mothers, ever forget? Would those memories linger on all through her tomorrows? Tears seeped through her eyelashes. She cried without bitterness, without remorse. Not because Kenneth had been her husband and she had lost him, but because he was so young to die.

* * * *

"Poor Jock!" said Aunt Isa sadly, propped up on her pillows on Saturday afternoon. "I'd got fair attached to the wee thing."

But her sorrow was really for Kenny. Kathleen assured her he had cheered up at the thought of the Sunday school picnic, that he had gone off smiling with Peter Balfour, a cup slung round his neck on tape.

"Not one of the good cups?" Aunt Isa asked anxiously.

"Of course not!" Kathleen was smiling.

Craig and she were sitting at the bedside. Craig took little part in the conversation, although he listened with every appearance of interest. Aunt Isa was much better, and some of her old spirit brightened her talk. She had many questions to ask, was obviously wearying to get home. She spoke of other visitors who had been during the week, including the minister and Nan Webb.

"Have you seen Ewen Gilmour again?" she asked Kathleen.

"He looked in on Tuesday on his way to market. Just for a minute. It's his busy time just now. He sent you his love."

Aunt Isa beamed at that.

"What a nice man he is!" she turned to Craig. "You're not saying much, Mr Carmichael?"

"No." His eyes met hers frankly. "But don't you worry about that! One day you'll hear me saying plenty."

For a moment their glances held. There was an unwilling glimmer, it might have been humour or it might have been admiration, in Aunt Isa's eyes. She returned to Kathleen.

"You did right to cable Alec not to come. He must have mair money than sense, sending a cable to you! He could have a better holiday in America, and not spend half –"

"He wasn't just coming for a holiday, Auntie. He was coming to see you!" Kathleen opened her handbag. "Here are all your letters. Three from Alec. You'll have a fine time reading them when we're away.

Aunt Isa tucked them under her pillow, agreeing she would.

As Kathleen was leaving the ward, a nurse stopped her and said Sister would like a word with her.

"I'll wait for you in the corridor," Craig touched her arm.

It was ten minutes before she appeared, and he saw her face was bright.

"Aunt Isa is to get home in a few days. They're to let me know when to bring her clothes."

The radiance remained, but she was quiet and thoughtful as they walked to the doors. She'd seen Dr Soutar and he'd told her Aunt Isa would need a lot of care and attention. She could see a difficult time ahead. If she couldn't return to work, there would be nothing coming in but their two pensions, her widow's pension and Aunt Isa's. But that was a bridge to be crossed later. At the moment there was only thankfulness for present blessings.

Craig started up the car.

"I'll run Mrs Duncan home when the time comes, Kathleen. Just let me know when you get the word."

Kathleen sat back as they turned into Dumbarton Road. How good Craig was.

"I'm looking forward to tomorrow," he said, slowing up behind a tram. "I hope it's a good day, for Kenny's sake. I thought we'd run down to the coast and have a picnic. You'll be at church in the morning?"

Kathleen nodded.

"Half-past two, then?"

CHAPTER EIGHTEEN

THE following afternoon the grey saloon car, now familiar to the neighbours in South Road, drew up at the gate of Dalreoch. Kathleen had changed when she came in from church. She was wearing a green summer dress, with a light coat in case it was breezy. Kenny was carrying a basket.

"I see you've packed some food, I brought some. My housekeeper made up a basket. We'll have enough for two Sunday school picnics, Kenny."

Perhaps it was having Kenny with them that let Kathleen relax and be just happy in Craig's company. They went through lovely country, across open moor, past shadowed woods, right to the coast where the Firth of Clyde sparkled in sunshine. At West Kilbride they took a side road westwards. Its hedgerows were heavy, but here and there the blue of Ardneil Bay shone through the tracery of green leaves in mingled beauty.

"We'll soon be there," Craig said. "You'll like Portencross. I came here for a holiday when I was a boy. There was a hotel then. There isn't now. So it's completely quiet."

They parked the car in a farmyard, carried their baskets past the old castle and along the rockbound shore until they found a place to picnic. Craig had brought his field glasses and he was soon showing Kenny the passing steamers and the floating gulls in magical nearness. Kenny was fascinated.

In a way, so was Kathleen. Somehow she had never imagined Craig having any patience for children. But that afternoon he was an undemanding companion, more interested in Kenny than in her.

When Kenny fell on a sharp rock and cut his knee, it was Craig who bandaged it with his own big handkerchief. He distracted Kenny from his wound by telling him that Portencross Castle was where the Bruce landed when he crossed from Arran. Did Kenny think Bruce had maybe fallen on the rocks? Perhaps he had. Where was Arran? Why, that was it, away over the water. Once they got the bandage on they would look at it through the glasses and see Goatfell and Glen Sannox and the Holy Isle.

It was Craig, too, who produced an empty toffee tin for Kenny to use as a pail, and suggested he try catching little fish in one of the pools. That was after Kenny had said suddenly: "Wouldn't Jock have loved it here! He could have gone swimming –" And he choked on the last word.

Afterwards, watching Kenny playing among the rocks with his tin, Craig leaned back on the grass, propping himself up on one elbow and eating another sandwich. Then he told Kathleen the story of the parish minister on Cumbrae, who used to pray for the people of "Great Cumbrae, Little Cumbrae, and the adjacent islands of great Britain and Ireland."

Kathleen laughed. Her eyes were dancing and the breeze tossed the soft hair above her brow into tendril curls.

Kenny came running towards them, water splashing from

the tin.

"See, Mummy! See – I've caught a fish! Can I take it home to keep? They're like General Boswell's goldfish. Oh, please –"

It was Craig who explained that, without salt water, the little fish would die, and that tap water and kitchen salt wouldn't do. But goldfish were different. Would Kenny like a goldfish? He would love one? Well, he could have two, because one might be lonely.

Kathleen's eyes met Craig over the little red head. The little ghost that was Jock had retreated . . .

On the way home, Craig let it drop that his housekeeper had the evening off.

"Then you'd better come in with us, Craig, and have a meal!"

Kathleen gave Kenny his supper, and Craig announced he would put him to bed. Kenny accepted this with high glee, and Kathleen started to fry some bacon. Later when she cleared up the shambles in the bathroom and hung two sopping towels on the pulley, she wondered if Craig's help was worth it. But when she heard a voice from the bedroom saying, "I'll call one Jonah, Uncle Craig. You know, like Jonah's whale! Isn't that a good name for a goldfish?" – she decided it was.

It was an hour later before they rose from the table, and it was at that very moment the doorbell rang. Kathleen's eyes flew to the clock, pointing to ten minutes to nine. It was late for callers. She pulled Kenny's door close as she passed it, and opened the front one to find James Laurie standing on the doorstep!

Kathleen stepped back in surprise, all sorts of things flashing into her mind. What could he want? This father-in-law of hers who refused to recognise her, or her marriage. Rather flustered for the moment, she could not utter a word.

James Laurie took Kathleen's step back in surprise as an invitation. He walked past her into the house. Still surprised, Kathleen closed the door after him. Then she heard him say, "Thank you. You lead the way."

She showed him into the living-room.

Immediately she was aware of three things. The used dishes still on the table. The hesitation in James Laurie's step when he saw she was not alone. The slow way Craig rose from his chair.

"Evening, Mr Laurie," he said with an easy composure Kathleen envied.

"Evening," James Laurie grunted. There was surprise in his eyes at Craig's presence. But he said nothing.

Kathleen drew forward a chair.

"Do sit down, Mr Laurie." She felt she should explain affairs and went on. "Mr Carmichael kindly took my boy and me to the seaside this afternoon. He came in to supper because his housekeeper has the evening off."

James Laurie didn't sit down right away.

Craig Carmichael remained standing.

"I'd better push off, then, Kathleen."

At the words Kathleen turned in quick desperation. She

was behind James Laurie, at the moment unseen by him.

"You needn't hurry, Craig. Or must you?"

Her voice had a lightness she was far from feeling. From the moment she opened the door and saw James Laurie she had felt comforted that Craig was with her. Her eyes signalled her desperation, willing him to stay. To make sure she motioned him with her hand to sit down.

"Please don't run away because I happen to have called," James Laurie said. He said it quietly but unconvincingly.

Craig knew his presence was unwanted by the older man. But a feeling of warmth gripped him. Kathleen wanted him with her. She felt she might need his help. He was hers to command. He made up his mind nothing would dislodge him until Kathleen told him he could go.

For the first few minutes conversation was stilted.

"I was sorry to hear about your troubles," James Laurie said, having cleared his throat noisily. "How is your – your aunt?"

"She's much better, thank you. I think most of our troubles are over now. Aunt Isa will be coming home quite soon."

James Laurie indicated he was pleased to hear it.

"My – er – my wife told me about it. Your boy told her. I – we were wondering if you needed any help?"

Kathleen shook her head, smiled vaguely, and asked for Mrs Laurie's health. She felt quite sure the old man was only waiting for a chance to say why he had really come. Something lay behind this visit, but what?

"The boy asleep?" James Laurie asked.

"Yes. It's long past his bedtime. He went to sleep as soon as his head was on his pillow. The sea air had made him tired."

James Laurie's deep-set eyes flickered to Craig, impelling him to go. But Craig was not to be got rid of. He took out his cigarette case and leaned forward.

"Cigarette, Mr Laurie?"

"Thanks – never touch them. But if –" His face was impassive, but he stumbled over the name. "If Mrs Laurie doesn't mind, I'll fill my pipe."

"Please do!" Kathleen smiled more naturally than she had done since he entered the room. It was the first time James Laurie had given her a name!

As he filled his pipe he turned to Craig.

"I was going to see you at your office tomorrow." He lowered his beetling brows. "What game are you playing with Beltons of Amersham? Sticking out for a bigger profit?"

Craig smiled and shook his head slowly.

"How do you know I refused an order from Beltons?"

"They've written me. Told me all about it and given me the order, at the best price I've ever got from them. What's your game, Carmichael? Where's your common sense? Beltons are the biggest –"

"The point is, Mr Laurie, they're not my customers. They're yours," Craig put in smoothly.

Kathleen could see the old man was shaken, so greatly that he was at a loss for words. She knew nothing of what they were discussing. She sat back, aware and content for the time being that she was quite forgotten.

Finally James Laurie prodded the bowl of his pipe with a broad forefinger.

"You're more of a fool than I thought," he said bluntly. "You'll never get on in business with these high-flown notions! How do you think I got where I am? It wasn't by turning down orders and letting someone else snap them up!"

Craig shrugged, his dark brown eyes slanting above his blue eyes.

"It's not a question of being a fool, Mr Laurie. It's a matter of being honest in business. You and I, in a way, are business rivals. Because I helped you after your fire I became known to some of your customers. They liked what Carmichael's did for them. They wanted more."

"Are you suggesting your stuff is better than mine?"

Craig smiled.

"I'm not saying so. But what I do suggest is that when they order from me direct it could look that I was stealing customers from you. And I've no need to steal customers. I'm working to capacity for my own."

"Well, I'll have to see you about Belton's order again. I don't want anybody but ourselves to get in with them. That would be bad business, if you like."

James Laurie relit his pipe, then, turning to Kathleen, spoke in more natural tones than he had ever used to her before.

"I really came about the dog. When I saw the report I knew it must be Kenny's puppy. I'm sorry about that."

"It couldn't be helped. It was an accident. Someone left the gate open –"

James Laurie made to rise from his chair.

"I've got a spaniel pup for the boy. I've left it in the car. Shall I –"

"No, please." Kathleen held out a restraining hand and the old man sat down in astonishment. "I'd rather you didn't."

"Why not?"

Kathleen looked at Craig for help.

"It's much too soon to give the boy another dog," Craig said right away. "Surely you must see that."

James Laurie still addressed Kathleen.

"It's a good pup," he declared. "Fully pedigreed!"

"It's most kind of you." Kathleen spoke gently to offset Craig's abruptness. "But Kenny's grief for Jock, that was the puppy's name, is too personal yet. Just giving him any other puppy wouldn't help. Would it, Craig?"

"It wouldn't," he agreed, as though he had never suggested replacing the puppy himself. "Not just yet. He'll have to forget Jock first. He's getting a goldfish," he added, to James Laurie's further bewilderment.

With a word of excuse, Kathleen slipped into the kitchen. She poured milk into a saucepan to heat for coffee. From the adjoining room she could hear the sound of voices, with James Laurie's predominating.

"Maybe you're right," he rumbled, but his tone reflected

disbelief. "I'm certainly learning a lot tonight! Having my eyes opened, in fact! First there's your queer notions about business. Then this about the dog.

"When I was a boy I'd have been thankful to get something to replace what I'd lost. But I never did. Maybe I'm wrong. Folk seemed to have changed without me noticing it. But I can't see –"

Kathleen looked out biscuits and set a tray with one of Aunt Isa's hand-embroidered cloths. She went back into the living-room and cleared the table as quickly and quietly as possible.

"Anyway," James Laurie was saying, "I'll keep the spaniel till it's bigger. Kenny might take to a grown dog. What do you think of that?" he demanded of Craig.

"Meantime you could have it traffic-trained," said Craig.

"Now that's a good idea! I'll just do that. I'll take it to the kennels."

When Kathleen handed him coffee he knocked out his pipe and took the cup with a brief word of thanks. Kathleen reflected that it was the first time he had set foot in her home, or Aunt Isa's home. She wondered what Aunt Isa would say. But surely it was a good omen for the future?

She was more sure about that when she saw him to the door not long afterwards. He turned to her almost diffidently.

"Could I – see the boy?"

Without a word she opened the bedroom door and switched on the shaded light between the beds. Kenny lay on his back, and the blue quilt was on the floor.

James Laurie came no nearer than the foot of the bed, leaning forward to study the small, sleeping face. It had all the sweet defencelessness of childhood asleep. Kathleen saw the blunt-fingered hands knot on the end of the bed.

"He's the image of Kenneth," he murmured, half unbelievingly. "Mildred's right! Except for the hair –"

Kathleen drew the bedclothes over Kenny's pyjama-clad shoulder.

"He's got my hair," she found herself saying, almost excusingly.

James Laurie raised his eyes and looked directly at her.

"Aye – I can see that. He's a fine boy – does you credit."

The unexpected words caught Kathleen off guard. They brought a prickle to the back of her throat. She smiled, but James Laurie was already turning and walking out of the room.

* * * *

"I'm sure everything's going to turn out all right!" Kathleen told Craig when she went back to the living-room. "He was nice tonight – like a different person."

"Don't build your hopes up too high, Kathleen."

"Why not?" She had expected him to share her optimism. "You were the one who told me he'd probably come round – in time."

Craig looked doubtful.

"I don't think I said that exactly, but –"

Kathleen's eyes were glowing and she refused to listen.

"What will Aunt Isa say when she hears James Laurie had coffee out of her best Indian Tree design china?"

He grinned, his eyes sparkling.

"That," he said, "is something I should like to hear!"

Kathleen did the washing-up after Craig left. It was an easy task. Anything would have been easy to her that night. It had been a day of many surprises. And it had been a day of happiness.

CHAPTER NINETEEN

IT was a June day when Aunt Isa came home. Craig drove Kathleen to Glasgow that morning, arriving at the infirmary about eleven o'clock. Kathleen had raised no objection when he said he was going to do it. By now she knew there were times when it was better to take the line of least resistance with Craig.

They were talking about Kenny's goldfish as they passed through Crookston.

"He's called them Mr Gold and Mrs Gold!" Kathleen said. "When it came to the point he didn't like Jonah."

Craig laughed.

"But can he tell them apart?"

"He says Mr Gold's bigger and fiercer, but I can't see any difference! It's a lovely bowl, Craig. You shouldn't have bought such an expensive one."

He edged out to pass a lorry and made no response.

"I saw Alice Boswell in Kilmarford this morning," he remarked when the road in front was clear. "She was early in town."

"Did you speak to her?"

He nodded.

"I met her in the doorway of the bank. She was saying she had a card from Ewen Gilmour. He's in Aberdeen for the Highland Show."

"Yes. I had a postcard from him yesterday."

"Oh!" Craig frowned and changed the subject. "By the way, I discovered the teller in the bank is a near neighbour of yours. Peter Balfour's father."

"Yes, they're a nice couple, and they've been so good to me these past weeks. Once we get back to normal I must have them round for an evening."

When the time came for Kathleen to go into the ward with Aunt Isa's clothes, Craig waited outside in the corridor. Aunt Isa greeted Kathleen with unconcealed delight. It had been a long wait for her that morning.

When she was dressed she made a tour of the ward, saying good-bye to all the patients. She maintained she felt fine. But to Kathleen's eyes her clothes "hung" on her. When they left the ward, and Aunt Isa turned for a last cheery wave, Craig rose and went towards them.

"You'd better take my arm, Mrs Duncan. These polished floors are slippery. The first time I came here I thought I was going to break my neck!"

Aunt Isa looked as if she would refuse. But her legs were weaker than she was going to admit, and the corridors were frighteningly long. She took Craig's arm rather gingerly and allowed herself to be led. By the time they were crossing the court and getting into the car, she was leaning more heavily on him than she realised. He packed her into the back with Kathleen beside her.

"Well, all I can say is I'm glad to see the back of that place!" Aunt Isa announced, sinking into the seat with a sigh of relief. "Not that they haven't been good to me. But I'm wearying for my ain fireside! I suppose the weeds are rampaging in the garden –"

"Indeed they are not!" Kathleen pulled the rug over Aunt Isa's knees, although it was quite warm. "In any case, you'll not be gardening for a while!"

"I thought you might have brought Kenny with you," Aunt Isa said a trifle wistfully as Craig started up the engine.

"He's at school. There's to be a concert on Friday and he's in a little play. There's a practice today."

Craig drove straight to Dalreoch and helped Aunt Isa into the house. She was pale now, the flush of excitement having faded. Kathleen noticed the change and hurriedly put on kettle to make her a cup of tea. But before Aunt Isa would settle in her chair at the fireplace she had to make a tour of the house. She had to satisfy herself that all her household goods were in their places.

"I see you've put away Jock's basket. He was the first thing I missed when I came through the door."

Kathleen made her sit down and sip the tea she had specially sugared.

"You'll take a cup, Craig?"

"Thank you. Then I must go."

Mrs Duncan stirred her cup and tasted it. "There's nothing like tea out of one of your ain cups!" she announced with a sigh of satisfaction. Then she looked at Craig. "I'm much obliged to you for bringing me home."

"It was a pleasure, Mrs Duncan. I hope to have you in my

car again before long."

Aunt Isa smiled vaguely but made no response.

Craig's strong white teeth bit into a biscuit.

"What you really should have is a holiday – a complete change."

"That's what I was thinking," said Kathleen.

Aunt Isa disagreed at once. But before long she was wistfully confessing it was a good idea if it could be managed.

"It's funny what you think about when you're lying in bed. I often thought about the holidays I had when I was a lassie. We went to a wee village called Kirkmichael. A lovely place. I played about with a girl called Annie MacCrae. I still get a Christmas card from her every year."

"You mean Kirkmichael – about three miles from Maybole?"

"That's the place! We drove from Maybole station in Johnny Leckie's waggonette. Annie's married now. Annie Simpson she is. But she's still there. I might go to her."

"It seems the very place for you. Nice and quiet," Craig encouraged her, and in no time at all had everything fixed. But later in the day, when Kathleen referred to it, Aunt Isa was too concerned with ways and means.

"Don't start worrying about money now," said Kathleen, as if money had not given herself much concern of late. "We can manage all right. Here's Kenny! At last!"

The back door banged open and in the happy reunion more serious considerations were forgotten.

Aunt Isa went on her holiday to Kirkmichael at the beginning of July. By then she was almost herself again, so much so that she insisted on taking Kenny with her.

"Don't talk nonsense about him being too much for me! He'll be company, and Annie loves bairns. Forbye, he's needing a change, and you said yourself it would mean you could start at the office again.

Kathleen gave way. The last consideration carried considerable weight. Craig had said to return when it suited her.

"You'll remember to feed my goldfish, Mummy?"

"I'll remember."

Aunt Isa and Kenny went to Kirkmichael on a Saturday, and it was Ewen Gilmour who drove them there. He had dropped in the previous Tuesday, and immediately offered his services. Aunt Isa beamed on him, but said, wasn't he too busy in the month of July?

Ewen assured her he could take a Saturday afternoon off. If Kathleen would come with them he'd run her home, too – calling in at Carnbo for tea on the way.

Kathleen suspected Craig had every intention of taking them to Kirkmichael. But it was too late for her to say anything when Aunt Isa and Ewen were making their plans. She could only agree to the arrangement.

She had not seen Craig for a few days, so she sent him a note. She told him about Saturday, and confirmed that she would start work on Monday.

Aunt Isa was as excited as a child over her holiday. It was

a beautiful run to Kirkmichael. The village had an old-world air about it which Kathleen at once loved. The smiling-faced woman whom Aunt Isa referred to as "Annie," gave them a royal welcome.

Kathleen saw the holiday-makers settled, and left them with considerable regret. Kenny waved her away cheerfully. He was an independent boy, which she had cause to be thankful for in the past. He made friends readily and adapted himself to new environments.

Ewen drove slowly on the way back.

"It's a long time since I had a chance to talk to you, Kathleen. I was sorry I wasn't able to help when Aunt Isa was ill."

Kathleen smiled.

"You were very good, Ewen. Look at all that lovely stuff you sent in from the farm!"

He moved his hands on the wheel. They were strong hands, weather-beaten, but not rough.

"I wish Carnbo was a bit nearer Kilmarford! I'd like to see a lot more of you!"

Kathleen smiled again at that. There was something so transparently honest and uncomplicated about Ewen. She liked him, and she enjoyed his easy-going company. He never disturbed her as Craig did.

They drove into Carnbo and Aileen met them, her dark head bare and her yellow dress belted in at her neat waist. She was tall and well built, but she was always neat.

"Kathleen! How nice to see you! Tea's just ready. I've

been picking strawberries. My hands are a mess."

She led Kathleen into the cool house, and Kathleen was struck again by its peaceful atmosphere. Mrs Hay smiled at her from the background. The housekeeper was inclined to be shy in the first moments of meeting.

"You've just missed Alice Boswell," Aileen said as they sat down to tea. "She brought me that book she told us about. I told her you two were to arrive for tea, but she said she couldn't wait."

"That's funny! It's quite a way to run out here with a book and not wait for tea," Ewen said. "She was quite well, was she?"

"Yes, oh, yes," Aileen told him. "I suggested she could wait and run Kathleen home. But she said she had to get back. Must have been something pressing, I think. She seemed on heckle pins to get away again."

"Strange," Ewen murmured. Then, remembering he was host, "What will you have, Kathleen? Try those. They're usually good."

The hours flew past so quickly that Kathleen was amazed when she realised the time.

"I shouldn't have stayed so long!"

"Of course you should." Aileen beamed on her. "In fact, there's no reason why you should go home to an empty house. Stay the night, and Ewen will run you home tomorrow."

Ewen pressed the invitation, and in the end Kathleen was persuaded. She had been up very early, and now the combination of sunlight, a good meal and pleasant company was making her loth to move. The thought of Dalreoch deserted by Kenny and Aunt Isa did not draw her.

So she found herself in a well-appointed guestroom with natural oak furniture and a softly blue fitted carpet.

"I feel I'm taking advantage –"

"Nonsense!" Aileen drew the thin, blue-flowered curtains. "We're happy to have you! We love visitors. Alice Boswell was here last weekend."

"Yes – she told me. She had a lovely time."

"Now" – Aileen looked round – "have you got everything you need? My pyjamas will drown you. You'll need to turn up the legs and the cuffs. There are magazines on the table if you want to read, but maybe you'd better get to sleep, because the cockerels will wake you early enough in the morning! Good-night, Kathleen. Sleep well."

Kathleen did sleep well. Not even the cockerels wakened her. It was after seven, with the sun streaming through a chink in the blue curtains, when she opened her eyes.

CHAPTER TWENTY

IT seemed to Kathleen the rest of the summer took wings. It was difficult to believe it was now more than a year since she came back to Kilmarford and sought out Aunt Isa in the Vennel.

There was a great change in Kenny in that year. His self-reliance had increased. He was taller and more boyish. He was growing up. He would be seven in January.

Aunt Isa, too, had changed in that year. She had aged, although her general health was much better than Kathleen had expected, considering the seriousness of her collapse. She had picked up a lot since her holiday. But she was not the woman she was. An outsider would have seen little difference. But Kathleen noticed it, as the person living in the house always does. The tiny signs are never missed by loving eyes.

But Aunt Isa's tongue was as smart as ever. One of the first things that set it going was James Laurie. Kathleen had not seen or heard of him since he had come with the spaniel puppy. Aunt Isa had said plenty about that! But she said much more when a formal note arrived requesting Kenny be allowed to have tea with his grandparents on a Sunday afternoon.

"You'll never let him go!" Aunt Isa declared.

"But Auntie – I can hardly refuse!"

"Well, I wash my hands of it. I've said it before, and I'll say it again. You'll live to rue the day you have any truck with James Laurie! I wouldn't trust him as far as I could fling him! If he wants the laddie to tea, what's to hinder him asking the two of you? He's deliberately going past you! It's a slight, that's what it is –"

Kathleen said little. She agreed it could be a slight. But mothers endure much for their own, in silence, in hope. She remembered James Laurie as he was in the bedroom, looking at Kenny asleep. That guided her to her decision. So one Sunday she dressed Kenny in his grey shorts, white shirt and blue blazer, and saw him off in the car sent to collect him.

"Mr Laurie said to tell you the boy will be back at six o'clock, madam," said the impassive chauffeur.

Kathleen stepped back and waved to Kenny, sitting in the back of the car. Then she went in to face Aunt Isa's disapproval, no less telling because it was now silent.

Kenny returned promptly at six o'clock, clutching a toy tractor, full of chatter about Grannie and Grandfather, and about the trifle he'd had for tea. Aunt Isa sniffed loudly. Trifle for a bairn's tea – well!

But Kathleen continued to let him go, and in time it became a fairly regular thing. There were times when she was doubtful herself. They gave Kenny too many toys, for one thing. But they were not expensive or elaborate toys. Kenny still loved his old ones. And the Lauries never encroached on Kenny's life or upbringing. He was collected at three and brought back punctually at six. It was ony for three hours now and again. And he was their dead son's child.

What possible harm could come from Kenny's visits to Finnard, Kathleen asked herself.

* * * *

When school started again Kathleen arranged for Kenny to have dinner there. Aunt Isa and she didn't see eye to eye on that, of course. Aunt Isa had firm ideas about a child eating at home. But Kathleen wanted to free Aunt Isa from the strain of cooking a midday meal. She carried her own lunch to the office. Then they all had a cooked meal when she came home and had more time to help.

Aunt Isa took a light meal herself in the middle of the day and, after her preliminary grumbles, admitted she liked the arrangement fine. For one thing she had more time to go out of an afternoon. There hadn't been any afternoon at all from the time Kenny went back to school till he was home again.

With staying at the office, Kathleen found herself getting to know Miss Gemmell much better, and became quite attached to her. Miss Gemmell brought her lunch with her, too, as she lived in a small village outside the town. Her outward reserve hid a warm heart, as Kathleen had suspected from the beginning, and she had a dry wit which enlivened all their conversations.

She had a great interest in people, and when Kathleen

invited her to Dalreoch one evening she was not surprised that she and Aunt Isa got on like a house on fire.

It was only with Craig Carmichael that things seemed unsatisfactory during those weeks. It dated from the time Ewen Gilmour took Aunt Isa and Kenny to Kirkmichael. Craig had not said anything. But Kathleen sensed his displeasure. He told her he had called at Dalreoch on the Saturday night, and again on the Sunday, hoping to take her out because she was alone.

When she told him she had stayed overnight at Carnbo he made no comment. She found herself beginning to explain how pressing Aileen Gilmour had been, then stopped abruptly. Why should she made excuses for herself to Craig? Why should he give her the feeling that she ought to excuse herself? She felt annoyed at the idea, but at the same time was unhappy that the atmosphere between them was strained.

"Gilmour bring you home on Sunday?" he asked.

"Yes."

Nothing more was said, and it was not referred to again. But it lay between them for weeks. The fact that Ewen Gilmour also brought the holidaymakers back from Kirkmichael did not help matters, although that arrangement had nothing to do with Kathleen.

At the beginning of August Craig went on holiday himself. He told Kathleen one day at the office that he was meeting an old friend of his R.A.F. days and they were to tour Italy.

"How lovely – you'll send me a postcard?"

"I'll send you more than a postcard if you really want me to?"

The question was put with such gentleness, almost humility, that Kathleen felt colour rising in her cheeks and looked down at the papers she held.

"Do you want me to, Kathleen?" His face was grave, and when she raised her eyes she could not avoid his searching glance.

"I – I'd better get these typed right away." Her confusion showed in her face.

Craig looked at the door she had closed after her. His face was still unsmiling, but his expression had changed. He looked hopeful.

While Craig was away the postman brought so many foreign letters and postcards that Aunt Isa was heard to declare that a fool and his money were soon parted! Still, her own highly-coloured postcard of La Scala di Milan had pride of place on her bedroom mantelpiece.

Nor did she comment on the brooch Craig brought back to Kathleen. It was an exquisite painted miniature which delighted her. It was good and yet sufficiently inexpensive for her to accept without embarrassment. Aunt Isa just said it was "bonnie."

The first thing Craig told Kathleen on his return was that she needed a holiday.

"You'd better take next week."

"But I've been off so much. I didn't expect to holiday at all!"

"One week's holiday – with pay," Craig smiled. He was deeply tanned and looked well. "Get away for a few days, too"

For once Aunt Isa was in complete agreement with Craig.

"You've had that cold hanging about you for a fortnight, and it's never lifted. Kenny and I'll get on fine on our own."

"And where would I go?" Kathleen asked. "It's almost September now."

"Go to Kirkmichael, where I went. Annie'll spoil you and give you your breakfast in bed. There'll be nothing for you to do. It's just what you're needing."

So it was arranged. Aunt Isa wrote to her friend and received a favourable reply. Craig was to drive her down. So Kathleen came home from the office on Friday evening to do her packing and get ready to leave the following afternoon.

But she found a letter waiting for her. She read it silently.

"What is it, Kathy? Mercy, you've gone as white as a sheet!"

"It's – " Kathleen cleared her throat. There seemed to be an odd buzzing in her ears. "It's the superintendent of a prison hospital in Manchester."

"Your father? I felt in my bones he was back in jail. But why the hospital?"

"He's had a heart attack. He's not expected to recover. The – the letter says I can go – if I wish to see him."

Aunt Isa's legs gave way. She sat down in the nearest chair.

"You'll not go, of course! It's no' a place for you!"

Kathleen moistened her lips.

"I shall have to, Aunt Isa."

"But you were to go on your holiday!" Aunt Isa wailed. "It's dreadful, I know, but it's a pity spoiling everything like this – could you no' wait and see?"

Kathleen shook her head.

"He's my father, Auntie. I'll go tomorrow."

Torn from a stricken heart, the words completely silenced Isa Duncan.

She wanted to tell Kathleen that she didn't understand; that there was no need for her to sacrifice her holiday and go rushing off to Manchester. Jock Todd had never been a good father. He had walked out on her nine years ago, why and where to no-one knew. He had never cared what happened to her. His silence all those years, when the love and support of a real father could have helped her, showed what he was. Yet it was the best thing that could have happened. Kathleen had been better off without him.

But now he was back into her life, upsetting all she had done, perhaps spoiling all she might do. It might only be for a short time. But it would leave its mark. Not only on Kathleen, but on Kenny, too.

In all her life Aunt Isa had never felt so thwarted. Silently she turned towards the kitchen. The movement was like a safety valve to her pent-up feelings. She wouldn't add to Kathleen's worries by arguing about them.

Kathleen had made up her mind. So she needn't waste any breath on Jock Todd. Some day he would meet a greater and more merciful judge.

She came back a minute later with the ironing board.

"You'll need some fresh things with you, Kathy," she said in a gentle tone. "I'll just do them now."

Kathleen raised her brows in surprise. It was not what she expected. Since announcing her intention of going to Manchester she had steeled herself to meet Aunt Isa's protests and anger. Yet Aunt Isa had said next to nothing. Now here she was eager to help her get ready for the journey. She went to her and squeezed the older woman's arm in unspoken gratitude.

"I'd better phone Craig and tell him I'm not going to Kirkmichael," she said after a time. She turned towards the door, then paused. "But what about your friend, Aunt Isa?"

Plugging in the iron, Aunt Isa said she'd send a telegram in the morning.

Kathleen hurried through the rain to the foot of the road. There was a man in the telephone box. She drew her scarf over her head and waited, the edges of the pennies cutting into the palm of her hand. She tried to picture her father. But after nine years it was a blurred and hazy image.

She had not seen him since the day after her mother's funeral. That was in Aunt Isa's house in the Vennel. Always he had lain across her life like a dark shadow. Her childhood memories of him were all linked to sad events.

Now all things were forgotten, wiped out by the grave news in the letter from the prison chaplain. She could only think of him now as a helpless man, lonely on a narrow hospital bed . . . dying.

The door of the phone-box slammed. She hurried into it, glad of its shelter, glad of something to do to chase the memory away. Her fingers trembled as she inserted the coins, dialled Craig's number, and waited. Craig's voice came almost at once. She could feel the tenderness in it when he recognised her own. Haltingly she explained her change of plans.

"Manchester?" His voice was blank with amazement. "Whatever are you going to do there?"

Kathleen moistened her dry lips.

"I don't want to talk about it over the phone, Craig. I'll write –"

"Write?" he broke in quickly. "Look here, I'm coming to see you. I don't understand all this, Kathleen. I'll be over right away."

When Kathleen came out of the box the rain was heavier. A plump figure stepped across South Road, half hidden beneath a grey, plastic umbrella. Kathleen's mind was busy with all her problem. Her eyes failed to recognise the woman. But Nan Webb both saw and greeted her.

"Oh – hello, Kathleen!"

Kathleen stopped and returned her greeting.

"Isn't it an awful night?" Nan went on. "How's Mrs Duncan? I was just on my way to see you both. George is at his men's club tonight."

For a moment Kathleen's heart sank. Neither she nor Aunt Isa were in any mood for visitors that night. But here was

Nan, and Craig was coming soon. It might help to ease the atmosphere. It would give them something else to talk about. So she ducked her head under Nan's umbrella and they walked along, side by side.

"I met Kenny yesterday and he told me you were going for a holiday," Nan said.

"I was going to Kirkmichael," Kathleen said wryly, "but I'm – not now. I'm going to Manchester to – to see my father."

She added the last words because Nan was staring at her in surprise.

"Oh! You've heard from –" Nan broke off, and Kathleen smiled sadly as she recognised the note of curiosity in her friend's voice.

She remembered how close they had been before she left Kilmarford. That friendship had meant much to her. Nan knew all about those unhappy days. There was no need to pretend about things to Nan. She was someone she could trust. Hurriedly Kathleen told her about the letter and of her decision to go to Manchester.

"I'm so sorry, Kathleen," Nan said sincerely. "I wish I could say something that would help you. But whatever happens, I hope it will be for the best."

Kathleen nodded silently. She wasn't sorry she'd told Nan. She was her oldest friend. There was something about an old friendship, about the shared experiences of growing up together, which made it different from newer ones. It wasn't to be expected that new friends would understand.

CHAPTER TWENTY-ONE

AUNT ISA was putting away the ironing board when they went in. At any other time she would have been pleased to see Nan. But that night Isa Duncan was out of tune with the world. Her heart was sore with anxiety.

It was not until Kathleen was putting Kenny to bed that Nan told Aunt Isa about the coming baby. For the first time that night Isa Duncan smiled.

"Now, isn't that grand news!"

The pleasant murmur of their voices reached Kathleen as she folded Kenny's clothes in the bedroom. She went to the window and looked out before she drew the curtain. It was still raining. She leaned her elbow on the sill, as Kenny knelt by the bedside and said his prayers.

"God bless Mummy and Aunt Isa –" His voice seemed far away.

Tomorrow! Where would she be tomorrow at this time? What was waiting for her at the end of the journey?

"Mummy! Why're you going to Manchester instead of Kirkmichael?" Kenny's voice reached her from the darkened corner of the room.

She drew the curtain and turned round from the window.

"I – I'm going to see – someone."

"Who?" The small voice insisted.

"Someone – you wouldn't know, dear. A – friend." His

little face was puzzled and she stooped down and kissed him.

"I'll soon be back, darling. And if you're a good boy while I'm away I may bring something for you. Now go to sleep, dear."

After she had closed the bedroom door, Kathleen stood quite still in the narrow lobby. They said you should always tell a child the truth? Always? About everything? But how could she?

The atmosphere in the living-room was warm and friendly. Aunt Isa and Nan were talking about babies. Both were smiling. Kathleen went to put on the kettle.

"No, I'm not waiting, Kathleen." Nan began gathering her things. "George said he wouldn't be late and he hates to come into an empty house. Aren't men funny about some things?"

Craig Carmichael's car drew up at the gate as Kathleen was seeing Nan away. Kathleen introduced them, and after a few words Nan went off, umbrella tilted against the wind and driving wind.

Craig followed Kathleen to the room where Aunt Isa was poking the fire, making the flames leap up. It was not cold, but the rain made everything depressing. The older woman greeted him with more than her usual warmth. Here was an ally, she thought. Here was someone who would think as she did; someone who would voice her unspoken thoughts. If he had any real feelings, he would surely advise against Kathy going.

But he didn't. He listened carefully. At the end he made no comment till Aunt Isa could keep her silence no longer.

"Do you think it's wise for her to go to Manchester on her own?"

Craig looked at Kathleen. Her face was so pale that every vestige of colour seemed concentrated in her hair.

"If Kathleen feels she must go, then she has to go," he replied slowly. "However close we may be to her, we can't just feel as she does about this."

The rain lashed against the window, but the three people in that room did not hear it. Craig watched Kathleen and his heart was wrenched with pity because he could not help her. He remembered her standing, straight and slim, beside his office door a year ago. He heard her voice, honest and yet full of hurt, telling him she was the daughter of Jock Todd.

She must have suffered agonies in the past with her pride and her sensitiveness which showed now in her full-lipped mouth. He loved her for what she was. He would have wished her parentage different. But in the balance it was nothing to his love for her.

"When do you go off, Kathleen?" he asked.

She answered him quietly, saying she would go to Glasgow in the morning. When he offered to drive her there she shook her head so definitely, that he did not argue with her. He could understand her wanting to be alone.

Aunt Isa retired to the kitchen and moved around noisily. Her anger against Craig rose in her like a wave. She had expected support from him. A man, a real man, like Ewen

Gilmour, would have put his foot down and forbidden the whole thing. And that would have been the end of it! But that wasn't Craig Carmichael's way!

But while she upbraided him in her mind, she evaded the thought which upset her most of all. Kathy and Craig had said little to each other. Yet they seemed to understand each other without words. She sensed that understanding – and knew she was outside it.

She knew it was wrong for Kathy to go to Manchester. She felt it in her bones. No good would come of it. She couldn't understand why a man, obviously fond of Kathy, failed to feel as she did. Surely folk who loved the same person would want for her the same thing.

Craig did not stay long, but it was already dark when Kathleen went with him to the door.

"You'll let me know how things go?" he said.

"I'll write," she promised.

He took her cold hand.

"Look after yourself, darling." He lowered his head, searching her face in the poor light. "You're very pale."

She smiled, with an effort.

"I've got a cold."

He bent and kissed her. Her lips were soft but unresponsive.

"Kathleen –" he whispered.

She turned her face from him. But he held her, his cheek against the soft mass of her hair.

"It's all right, darling," he murmured. "I'll wait."

217

It was raining when she left Kilmarford. It was raining again when she reached Manchester.

Kathleen stood at the window and looked out at the wet pavements. The bedroom behind her was dark-papered and a little depressing. But it was clean. She was lucky to have got such a place. The charge was moderate for all the kindness she had received.

Kathleen played with the fringe of the net curtain and her thoughts drifted. She saw herself arriving at Victoria Station the previous night. She remembered the bewildered feeling of being pushed and jostled in a crowd in which she knew no-one. Then she had grasped her small suitcase firmly and looked round for someone to direct her. She caught sight of a policeman.

He was tall, quite young and looked as if he would snap at the waist if he bent. But when he spoke his voice was soft and kind. It had the lilt of the Highlands, and reminded her fleetingly of the nurse in the Glasgow Western Infirmary.

She'd asked about a small hotel, a quiet one, not too expensive. As he rubbed his chin thoughtfully she went on, haltingly:

"Somewhere near – Strangeways? I've to visit – my father. He's ill."

The policeman's expression did not change. In the course of a day a man in his job gets many surprises. His eyes were used to judging, and he'd already read what was to be seen in the lovely face beneath the green hat.

"You're a Scot," he said. "I wasn't sure at first."

She nodded.

"But I lived in England for a number of years."

"Has it got to be a hotel? My wife's cousin lets rooms. You'd be comfortable there. Quiet, too. Mrs Midgely will look after you. Tell her Jim Donaldson sent you."

He led her to a taxi and gave the driver the address. When he stood back and raised his hand Kathleen felt sorry to be leaving him. He was her one human link, quickly made and as quickly broken, in the throbbing city.

The middle-aged woman who greeted her at the end of the five-minute journey was small and thin. Her hair was turning grey, and she had a slight limp. Mrs Midgely was quiet and made no attempt to pry into Kathleen's affairs. She had a room vacant. Her practical kindness included giving Kathleen a hot-water bottle in bed and asking if she'd prefer her meals served in her room, which she did.

Kathleen turned from the window and slumped into an old armchair, leaning back against the overstuffed cushion. Her head throbbed. Cold shivers ran down her spine. The electric fire glowed and she stretched out one hand to its warmth.

What would they be doing in Kilmarford? The churches would be in and the Sunday stillness would be like a blessing on the small town. Aunt Isa would be in church, Kenny beside her.

Kathleen thought of many things, trying to keep her mind from the coming interview. But the hands of her watch crept round to the hour arranged in her phone call to the prison hospital the previous evening.

When she left Mrs Midgely's her inward worry showed on her face. Her mouth was tightened to an unaccustomed firmness, her eyes were dull and clouded.

The rain had stopped, but the pavements were still wet and shining. In her green travelling coat and matching hat she looked no different from the other Sunday walkers in the Strangeways district of the city. But she felt a thousand miles separated her from the people she passed.

She even felt detached from herself. It was as if someone else, not Kathleen Laurie, was making her way towards the prison, until yesterday no more than a vague name to her.

She looked at her watch. In ten minutes she would see her father! The thought brought no stirring of emotion. It was as if the thought had never registered in her mind.

In ten minutes she did not see her father. Instead she faced a middle-aged doctor, who spoke to her with impersonal kindness. Her father's condition, he said, was grave. At that moment he was under the influence of drugs. As she already knew, he had suffered a heart attack – a coronary thrombosis, to give it its medical name. But in addition there was another condition which caused some anxiety.

"Can't I see him?"

"Yes, but don't expect him to recognise you, Mrs Laurie. He's only semi-conscious. Would you like to go to him now?"

Kathleen clasped her hands tightly round the handle of her handbag.

"Yes, please," she said quietly.

He held open the door for her and she preceded him into the corridor. She walked steadily, her head high.

* * * *

Kathleen wrote to Aunt Isa that evening as she sat shivering in the old armchair beside the electric fire. She had put another shilling in the meter, glad of its warmth and its companionable glow.

It was hard to write, because there was so much more in her mind and heart than could be put down in words.

"He didn't know me, Auntie. He thought I was Mother."

That was all she wrote, still almost feeling the plucking fingers which fastened on hers, and the eyes which focused and then moved again, to come back, recognition struggling in them.

"Mary – Mary – "

A thread of a voice. The voice of an old, ill man. Yet he was not old – barely sixty.

Her pen moved slowly.

"I would not have known him. He has aged so much . . ."

It was only nine years, but she had remembered his hair as jet black. Now it was thin and greying and he looked shrunken.

She bent her head again over the letter.

"I tried to talk to him, but his mind was wandering. I've no idea yet how he learned I was living with you, or that we have moved to South Road. I only stayed a few minutes. I'm going back tomorrow."

In the end it was not a long letter. But it took a long time to write. Kathleen was finishing it when Mrs Midgely tapped at the door and limped in with a tray.

"I've brought you some tea and biscuits, Mrs Laurie. Is that enough, love, or would you like – "

"Thank you – that will do nicely." Kathleen smiled at the thin face beneath the greying hair. She was becoming accustomed to this Manchester habit of addressing everyone as "love."

"You haven't much of an appetite! You've hardly eaten and it seems to me you're in for a cold. You should always feed a cold, love. Now, there's nothing you fancy?"

"You're very kind, Mrs Midgely, but there's nothing – really."

Mrs Midgely did not linger. But the small, human contact had warmed Kathleen. She screwed the cap on her fountain pen and lifted the hand-sewn cosy from the brown teapot.

After she had finished Aunt Isa's letter, she must write to Craig. She put milk in her tea and stirred it. With so much on her mind, she had not dwelled on those revealing moments with Craig at the door of Dalreoch on Friday night. But they had been at the back of her thoughts all the time.

She loved him. All her doubts were suddenly blown away like chaff in the wind, leaving only a shining certainty. This was the second blooming she had never thought possible. It was a different, a more mature love than she had known for Kenneth. But it was the same emotion.

She had fought against her attraction to Craig, believing her feelings could have no permanent roots. Thinking that because she had loved before, and lost, the flower was withered for all time.

But that was wrong! The capacity for loving never died. She remembered suddenly the words on the hand-sewn sampler which had hung above Mrs Fison's parlour mantelpiece in Clacton.

"God gives us love. Something to love He lends us."

She thought of Craig now, remembering all the things a woman does about the man she loves. Not the big things, but the small, heart-tugging details. His smile, the deeper tones of his voice, the quick movement of his fingers as he flicked open his cigarette case.

She loved him. And he loved her. Was she not blessed then in spite of her worries? The past and the present would pass. They were but stepping stones leading to a future together, her future and Craig's – and Kenny's.

She wrote Craig a short letter and went out to post it with Aunt Isa's. She could have made it a love letter. That would have been easy. But she did not. Circumstances and her natural restraint made her write only of facts. There would be time to speak of love later. There would be time for loving.

But there are times when the golden hour strikes out of time, when the words which could be spoken easily today must remain unsaid tomorrow.

CHAPTER TWENTY-TWO

ISA DUNCAN came out of Fenwick's in the high street and slowed her pace. She'd always been a quick walker, her little feet taking short, busy steps. Nowadays the effort to remember to go slower was a ceaseless thorn to her.

It was Tuesday afternoon. A strong breeze swirled round her ankles, making her glad she'd put on her heavier coat. It was strange, but since her illness her clothes seemed to have added pounds to their weight.

The high street showed the usual extra stir of market day. Usually when she was in town on a Tuesday, Aunt Isa kept an eye open for Ewen Gilmour. But today her mind was full of other things.

Kathleen's letter had come with the first post. She'd watched for the postman for twenty minutes before he finally appeared. She had been relieved to get the letter. It eased her conscience. Hadn't she been tempted to hope that Kathy would arrive in Manchester too late to see her father?

"May God forgive me!" Aunt Isa murmured to herself as she stepped off the pavement. It wasn't Christian, wishing anybody away like that. Her husband had always said we shouldn't judge, because we never know enough! But that was her John all over. He'd a heart of gold and eyes that could see some good in the worst body.

But he was taken away in his prime. And a worthless

rascal like Jock Todd had been left! The ways of God were inscrutable as the minister said on Sunday.

Aunt Isa reached the opposite pavement and looked up at the clock on the Town House tower. Twenty minutes to four! Kenny would be out of school and she'd meant to meet him at the gate. She hadn't walked home with him for months.

He'd dawdle through the park, though. He and Peter Balfour always did. She'd catch up on them. She quickened her step, her string bag swinging from her arm and all the warnings about hurrying forgotten.

She nodded and waved to a friend, but she did not stop. She hadn't gone twenty yards into the park when she made up on the two boys. They were playing round the old fountain, splashing water from the chained metal drinking cups.

After mildly rebuking them, Aunt Isa let them share her poke of "granny sookers" and walked between the bright flower-beds, while the boys scampered in front of her. She looked at the shaggy-headed chrysanthemums with the eyes of an enthusiastic gardener. Next year she'd grow them as big in her own garden! Being laid up she hadn't had much chance this year. But she had it all planned in her mind.

When she became aware of Kenny speaking to a black-clad figure sitting on a bench, it was too late to hang back. Even if she hadn't recognised the woman, Kenny's clear voice made it only too plain.

"Aunt Isa!" he called. "Aunt Isa! Here's Granny!"

Mrs Duncan pursed her small mouth. There was no

avoiding a meeting. Mrs Laurie had already risen to her feet.

"Good afternoon, Mrs Duncan!"

"Good afternoon," Aunt Isa replied stiffly, taking the outstretched hand and wondering how Kathy's mother-in-law knew her name.

Mildred Laurie was sallow and black did not become her. Even the touch of lilac at the throat was not enough to relieve it. Her eyes were sunken and dark-rimmed.

"She's no' looking weel," Aunt Isa thought. "She's not half the woman I am, for all I've been through!" She settled her string bag more comfortably on her arm and prepared to move on, but Mrs Laurie addressed her.

"I hope you're keeping well now?"

"Thank you. I'm feeling much better."

"Kenny was telling me his mother's away. I was surprised."

"To Manchester, Granny!" Kenny piped in.

"Manchester!" echoed Mildred Laurie, obviously taken aback. "And left you alone with Kenny. But you've been ill – "

Aunt Isa stiffened her plump shoulders.

"Aye, but that was some time ago. I can manage fine with the bairn. He's no bother!"

"Manchester," the well-modulated voice repeated thoughtfully. "Not just the place I'd choose for a holiday –"

"Mummy's gone to see someone. She told me."

Aunt Isa frowned at Kenny, who moved across to where his little friend was hanging over the parapet of the ornamental bridge. Aunt Isa's cheeks were hot. She regretted the impulse which had brought her through the park to this awkward meeting. She was keenly aware of Mrs Laurie's eyes on her.

"Kenny and me had a holiday earlier on. Now he's back at the school, so, of course, he's got to bide with me." She gave the explanation grudgingly.

"Will Kathleen be back from Manchester soon?"

"Well – that all depends. I'm not just sure – " Aunt Isa broke off in confusion, feeling annoyed with herself. She was getting flustered. She wasn't feeling so good, either. That rush along to the park, or maybe just this upset . . .

Mildred Laurie noticed the older woman's sudden loss of colour, but did not fully understand its cause.

"I'll need to be away then, Mrs Laurie!" Aunt Isa managed to smile. "I'll say good-day!"

"Good-bye." Mrs Laurie smiled. "I'm so glad to have met you."

"No doubt!" reflected Aunt Isa, her smiled vanishing as soon as she turned away. She called to Kenny and Peter. "No doubt," she thought again, "speiring news frae the bairn like dabbing at a whelk with a preen! But you didn't get much change out of me!"

She sat down on a seat round the first bend and five minutes later she was herself again. But she was by no means easy in mind. She was worrying about Kathleen and wondering if she could expect another letter tomorrow. She put her meeting with Mrs Laurie out of her mind and decided she wouldn't mention it to Kathy when she wrote to her.

"Least said, soonest mended."

Not that there was any harm done! But she had a feeling the fewer folk knew where Kathy was the better. It was a pity Mrs Laurie knew anything at all. But what she did know didn't amount to much.

Not that it mattered. Manchester was a big place. But she hadn't liked the talk of Kathy leaving Kenny with herself. Who else would Kathy leave the bairn with? She would have had plenty to say if Kathy had suggested leaving him with anybody else!

As for the Lauries of Finnard, she could snap her fingers at them! As for Kathy being in Manchester, that was none of their business!

Isa Duncan turned into South Road with Kenny and Peter on either side of her and a smile on her face. But she wouldn't have smiled if she could have heard the conversation which took place over tea at Finnard later that afternoon.

Mildred Laurie moved the trolley into place between herself and her husband and handed him a cup and saucer. He balanced it on the broad arm of his easy chair. They always had afternoon tea like this if he was home early from the mill. There was a log fire snapping in the grate and the lounge was pleasantly warm.

"A rather odd thing happened this afternoon, James." Mildred Laurie halved a small oven scone neatly. "I met that woman with Kenny – Mrs Duncan."

"Oh." James Laurie had been thinking about a problem he had at the mill, but any mention of his grandson now had the power to fix his attention at once.

"Kathleen's in Manchester."

"Manchester? What is she doing there?"

His wife shrugged.

"I don't know. But I thought Mrs Duncan seemed uneasy about her. She gave me the impression of trying to hide something. Perhaps it was just my imagination. But I felt there was more to it than she cared to tell me." She moved her expressive hands. "You know what I mean?"

James Laurie smiled.

"Are you sure you weren't imagining things? Kenny's mother lived in England for several years. She'll have friends –"

"But she didn't live in Manchester! It was Clacton. Alice told me. Besides, I've a feeling Mrs Duncan was trying to cover up something! Why should the girl suddenly dash off to Manchester? Kenny said she was all ready to go to Kirkmichael. What do you make of it, James?"

"It seems strange." He leaned his chin on his chest, sitting back in his chair and sipping his tea. He sat up so suddenly that the tea slopped into his saucer.

"Good gracious! I've just remembered! I met Wylie – you know, the factor – a couple of days ago and he said he'd had that old woman – what's her name –" He snapped his fingers.

229

"Mrs Duncan," supplied his wife.

"Mrs Duncan up paying her rent. He's asked her if everything was all right at the bungalow on South Road. Any repairs needed and such-like. She seemed to be quite satisfied, but –"

"But what, James?" Mildred Laurie was impatient, her eyes fixed anxiously on his face.

"She said maybe it wouldn't matter a lot anyway because she might be moving!"

"Moving! What did she mean by that?"

"I don't know – unless they are all moving."

"But that would be terrible! I couldn't stand it if they took Kenny away. Can't you do something, James? Couldn't you find out where his mother's gone? What about Craig Carmichael? Remember that night you called about the puppy. He was there. You were surprised."

"I was very surprised. Not so much at seeing him there as their friendly attitude to each other. It was 'Craig' this and 'Kathleen' that. It was an eye opener to me."

"You could ask him."

James Laurie's brows furrowed.

"I suppose I could. As a matter of fact, I've got to see him anyway. I want to see if I can't get him to change his mind about that Amersham order."

"You'll see him soon?" Mildred Laurie was not interested in business. Her urgent concern was Kenny and the prospect of losing him.

"I'll ring him and make an appointment for tomorrow." He

heaved himself out of his chair. "Now, don't worry yourself, my dear."

If Craig Carmichael was surprised at James Laurie's sudden interest in Kathleen the following afternoon he gave no sign of it. He looked steadily at his visitor, measuring his words carefully.

"Yes, Kathleen is in Manchester."

"What's she doing there?" James Laurie asked bluntly. "My wife met Kenny in the park and he told her about some sudden change in her holiday plans. Seems strange, rushing off like that and leaving the boy with a woman hardly fit to look after herself. My wife was quite upset."

Craig slanted his dark brows upwards, but made no reply. James Laurie was forced to go on.

"Do you know why she's gone?"

Craig took out his cigarettes and offered one to James Laurie. He refused with an impatient shake of his head.

"Yes, I was told. But it's a personal matter, and I'm not at liberty to talk about it. It concerns only Kathleen."

"Is she coming back?"

"Of course!"

The old man gave a sigh of relief and relaxed, but he still wanted reassurance.

"You're quite sure about that? We thought maybe she was after a job – "

Craig smiled.

"Kathleen's visit has nothing to do with a job. She is coming back here. I can assure you of that."

James Laurie put his blunt fingertips together and stared at the younger man.

"It's all very mysterious. But I suppose we'll have to leave it that way. Now, what about that order from Amersham – Belton's – "

"I told you already I wasn't interested!"

"I know you did! But need you be so hasty, man!" He leaned forward. "Think what you're doing and listen to me! I've got a proposition to put to you. We can work together. We did it before when I had that fire. I haven't forgotten how you helped me, or how smoothly everything went. We could do the same again. But this time on a permanent basis."

Craig narrowed his blue eyes.

"You've tried buying me out before," he said flatly.

James Laurie grunted.

"I'm not talking about buying you out. Times have changed and a lot has happened in the last eighteen months. I've lost Roger and – "

Craig's voice softened.

"I don't want Carmichael's to be swallowed by Laurie's – not the way other small mills in Kilmarford have been."

James Laurie hunched himself forward in his chair.

"Buying! Swallowing! Stop putting words in my mouth, man! I want to amalgamate! That's what I'm trying to tell you. I'm getting on in years. The work's getting too much for me.

"I never knew how much I depended on Roger till I lost him. If you ever lose a son" – some of the colour left his florid face – "you'll know what I mean. It's like losing an arm."

"I think I can understand," Craig said gently.

James Laurie sighed.

"You don't." He roused himself with an effort. "I could do with young blood in the firm! A younger man with new ideas. I don't agree with some of your methods, but I respect you for sticking to your ideas. That's why I'm asking you to come in – " He broke off because Craig was shaking his head regretfully.

"I'm sorry, Mr Laurie. I appreciate what this offer could mean. It's generous. But it wouldn't work. It couldn't for several reasons. In the first place I want to keep my independence. That's why I've stood up to you and rejected your previous offers.

"I like the family feeling in a smaller concern like this. But there's something else. Something more important and I'm afraid you won't like it."

Across the desk both men stared at each other, but neither wavered.

"When Kathleen returns from Manchester, I'm going to ask her to marry me," Craig said. "And I hope more than anything else in the world that she will."

As Craig Carmichael finished speaking, two pairs of eyes met across the desk.

James Laurie did not move, did not bat an eyelid. He did not know what to say. The news left him speechless. Carmichael and Kathleen! He had never suspected this.

Poor Mildred! This meant the end of all her hopes – of Kenny ever finding a home at Finnard. Carmichael was in a position to provide both the boy and his mother with a good home.

Home! James Laurie sat up with a start as the word left his lips in a long, drawn-out whisper. They would set up home – here! In Kilmarford! Kenny would be within reach of his grandmother. She would be able to see him any time – every day.

The door which James Laurie had seen closing a few minutes before was now being thrown wide open. He and Mildred were not going to lose Kenny. His mother and Carmichael could marry. But he would still be their grandson, still be a Laurie! And perhaps one day . . .

"You appreciate the position, Mr Laurie," Craig's voice broke into his thoughts. "You understand now why I can't accept your offer."

James Laurie heaved himself out of the chair.

"I see the position – quite clearly." He spoke with the voice of a man who was well pleased and satisfied with himself. "Now I had better be getting back to the mill."

Craig came from behind the desk and held out his hand.

"Thanks again for the offer. I appreciate it."

"That's all right, Carmichael." Laurie grasped the extended hand and shook it warmly. Holding himself erect, he marched out of the room, leaving Craig Carmichael staring after him thoughtfully.

CHAPTER TWENTY-THREE

THE following morning the long train drew out of Victoria Station in Manchester. It was crowded. But Kathleen had a corner seat. Usually she was interested in her fellow travellers. Today she was hardly aware of them. Her head ached and her mind refused to rest.

She could scarcely believe it was only five days since she had left Kilmarford. It seemed like a year; a year of bitter experience. She now knew the details of her father's conviction and sentence. Nine months. He'd been arrested three weeks ago and collapsed the day he went to prison.

She bit her teeth into her lower lip and stared blankly at a picture of Llandudno above the seat opposite.

The train thundered on. Preston. Lancaster.

Paper rustled as her companions unwrapped sandwiches. Mrs Midgely had insisted on her accepting a small parcel of sandwiches, but Kathleen left them untouched. She would never forget the little woman's kindness, and her endearing habit of addressing her as "love."

Before she left she had told Mrs Midgely why she was in Manchester. That had only made the little woman more kind.

"But the darkest cloud has always a silver lining, love! I got this" – Mrs Midgely touched her limp leg – "in a street accident. I lay in hospital for weeks feeling sorry for myself.

I thought my life was finished. Then one day I had a visit from the bus driver who knocked me down." She smiled. "That was Midgely! And look at me today. The happiest woman in Manchester."

Kathleen went on staring at the picture of Llandudno, hearing Mrs Midgely's kind Lancashire voice.

"If you have to come back again you'll always find a corner here."

Kindness. Kindness and courage.

Carlisle . . .

A young soldier brought Kathleen a cup of tea from the trolley on the platform. She took out her sandwiches but only took a bite.

The scene in the prison doctor's office the day before kept recurring in her mind. She could almost hear his voice.

"Your father is not likely to die now. He's got over this attack and will live, perhaps for years. An invalid –"

Kathleen was glad he was going to be spared. But what was to happen in the future? He would be discharged at the completion of his sentence. He would need care and attention. From whom? He would have to be kept. Where? He had nothing, and no-one in the world but herself.

She closed her eyes. They were hot and gritty.

No-one but herself. Who else was there to look after him?

Kathleen couldn't wait to see Aunt Isa welcoming her father with open arms. It was doubtful if she would even let him enter her home. No-one could blame her. He was no kin to her.

Aunt Isa could not live alone at Dalreoch with nothing but her pension. And she herself couldn't keep a separate home without going out to work. But she couldn't do that with an invalid father and a small boy to look after!

Kenny! Always Kathleen came back to him. The idea of Kenny growing up with a cloud over him was unbearable. Jock Todd's grandson. Folk would talk. None more readily than children. They would be cruel without knowing it. Kenny would be singled out as "different," as she had been different.

For herself, she could bear it. But not for Kenny!

People had long memories, especially in a small town. The news of Jock Todd's return would spread like wildfire. The old stories would be raked up and magnified. Kenny would suffer. As she had suffered.

She had endured it before and she would again. But it was hard. She had made friends, made a small niche for herself in Kilmarford. Would her father's return spoil these friendships? There was Alice Boswell, Ewen and Aileen Gilmour, and – Craig . . .

She looked down at her hands and was surprised how tightly they were clasped in her lap. She widened her eyes, straining to hold back the tears.

Craig!

Kathleen had sent a telegram telling Aunt Isa when she was leaving, but she expected no-one to meet her at Glasgow. When the train steamed into Central Station she lifted her small suitcase from the rack and joined the crowd of passengers streaming along the platform to the barrier.

Then she heard her name spoken. She turned and saw him and a wave of tenderness, of love, engulfed her. She wanted to fall into his arms, rest her aching head on his shoulders and pour out her heart to him. It would have been so easy, and Craig would not deny her the comfort of his strength and compassion. But she checked the impulse.

"Craig!" she whispered simply.

She looked up at the familiar, thin-featured face, the slightly narrowed blue eyes beneath the slanting, dark brows. But his welcoming smile vanished, changing to unconcealed anxiety as he caught her arm.

"Kathleen – darling!" He was shocked at her appearance. He had never seen her look like this. Except for two vivid patches on her cheek bones, her face was colourless, and dark shadows lay beneath her heavy eyes. She looked ill, exhausted.

Craig took her case.

"I've the car outside. We'll get out of the city. My dear, are you all right?"

Kathleen nodded, trying to smile. His tenderness, the concern in his voice, seemed to weaken her. She loved him! She knew that now. This moment of meeting told her where her heart lay. But it was impossible. She must go on closing the door on his love, on his assurance that theirs could be a perfect marriage. Dreams don't come true so easily.

She could not think of a future with Craig. She must shoulder the responsibility of her father alone. He was an insurmountable barrier to her marriage.

When they were in the car, driving over Jamaica Bridge, Kathleen began to talk, forestalling the questions she felt sure would come. She must be honest with Craig. She must tell him the truh. He had a right to know. Deliberately she kept her voice flat, willing herself to speak calmly. She was so tired.

Craig never interrupted once, driving slower than usual, his hands firm on the wheel. Kathleen kept nothing back. But she did not look at him as she told him her father was out of danger and expected to recover.

"When he is released," she said, "I shall bring him to Kilmarford. There is nowhere else he can go; no-one else to turn to.

"So you see, Craig, we – we can never be more than –"

"When did you last have a meal?" he broke in.

It was so unexpected it startled her. More than that, in her overstrained condition, it irritated her. This was the last kind of response she had expected. She was nerved up to withstand his protests, to show him her mind was made up, to try to be brave.

"I don't remember." She wrinkled her aching brows. "ButI'm not hungry."

"We'll stop at a place before we reach Kilmarford. It's after five and we should be in time for high tea."

Kathleen protested. She'd rather go home. He didn't argue, but twenty minutes later he drew into the drive of a country hotel.

It had been a mansion-house, and there was an air of solid elegance about it. The entrance hall was panelled and had deep window embrasures. The fireplace was massive, and the newel posts of the staircase were heavily carved.

It was Craig who took charge of the conversation during the early part of the meal, talking lightly of general things and coaxing Kathleen to eat. But he was met with little success. The fish was beautifully served, but Kathleen barely touched it. She drank the tea, however, and it seemed to brighten her temporarily.

The dining-room was quiet, and they were in a secluded corner overlooking the garden. There was no chance of being overheard. Finally Craig dropped his lightness and became serious and determined.

"Kathleen, you and I are going to be married. The only thing that really matters is that I love you! I want you, darling, and the day you become my wife will be the proudest in my life."

"Please, dear," Kathleen protested. "Don't make it harder for me. Are you forgetting about my father?"

He leaned forward and took her hands in his.

"I knew about your father when I engaged you a year ago. It made no difference then. It makes no difference now!"

"But it must!" she insisted miserably. "He'll be living with me – "

"Dearest, your problems are my problems! I want to take the burden off your shoulders. I want to look after you and Kenny – and I'm going to!"

She tried not to look at him, fixing her attention on the unused cutlery on the table. She wanted to give in. She wanted so much to give in!

"There's another thing," he went on firmly. "If there are to be any more journeys to Manchester I'll make them – not you. It's a man's job!" He pressed her cold, unresponsive fingers. "Darling, we belong together, you and I. Nothing and no one can come between us!"

She was too tired to protest. Although she tried not to listen he went on talking, painting a picture of their future together. Enthusiasm lighted his face; her heart ached almost unbearably.

It was all so hopeless. She could not ruin his life. She could not burden him with a father like hers. It was no ordinary responsibility. Jock Todd was no ordinary man.

No, Craig could have no place in her future, and she could have no place in his. He needed a wife of whom he could be proud, not a wife at whom the finger of scandal could be pointed.

His voice rose on a crest of enthusiasm. It was too much. She couldn't let him go on.

"No – no! Oh, I'm so tired, Craig. Please take me home."

"Of course, darling!" He stood up at once and held her coat for her. "I've talked too much! But I had to make you understand." He smiled tenderly. "You'll feel a lot better after a good night's sleep. I told Mrs Duncan I'd have you home no later than six o'clock and it's almost that now."

Kathleen walked out to the door while Craig paid the bill.

There was a large copper beech at the side of the drive, and the leaves were shining in the mellow September sun. Two men were walking from a parked car, and Kathleen moved aside to let them into the doorway, hardly seeing them. Then one of them spoke her name and she recognised him with a start.

"Ewen –"

Ewen Gilmour closed his hand over hers, bending his fair head. "This is a surprise, Kathleen! I heard from Alice that you'd gone south."

"I'm just on my way home. I – we – stopped for a meal."

Craig joined them just then, and the two men greeted each other pleasantly. Ewen introduced his friend, a neighbouring farmer at Carnbo. For a few moments conversation was general, and then Kathleen moved to go.

"Now if you'll excuse me, Ewen. I'm feeling rather tired."

"Will you be in if I call on Tuesday evening – after market day?" he asked, and Craig noted the eagerness in his voice.

"Yes, I – I think so." She coloured slightly. "Good-bye. Remember me to Aileen."

On the short journey home Ewen Gilmour's name was not mentioned. Kenny was hanging over the garden gate watching for the car. His face lit up into such a beam of joy that some of Kathleen's despondency lightened. She was back home. The sight of it was like being folded in the comforting arms of some beloved one.

Kathleen hugged Kenny so fiercely that she felt him wince. Then he drew away and danced round her when Aunt

Isa came hurrying to the door.

Aunt Isa beamed a welcome. But only for a moment. Her eyes quickly widened into anxiety at the sight of Kathleen's strained face.

Craig carried Kathleen's suitcase into the house.

"I'll not stay, Kathleen," he whispered. "Get to bed soon and have a good night's rest. I'll see you at the office on Monday. Good-night, darling."

Aunt Isa did not press him to stay.

"I've got the kettle on," she told Kathleen as soon as he was gone. "It's just on the boil."

"I'm not hungry – really. We stopped for a meal at some place."

"You can always manage a cup of tea!" Aunt Isa said firmly. "Here, I'll hang up your coat. You go in and sit at the fire."

Kathleen was thankful to do so. Kenny leaned against the arm of her chair talking excitedly. It was wonderful to be home again. The feeling of "belonging" enfolded her like a blessing.

"Mummy, Peter and me –"

Kathleen listened to him, hiding her weariness behind a wan smile of interest.

"I brought you something from Manchester, darling. It's in my case." She rose to her feet, and Kenny ran ahead of her out of the room.

Watching her, Aunt Isa shook her head, then went into the kitchen to make the tea.

"What have you brought for me, Mummy?"

"It's a game called hidden treasures. You can play it with Peter."

His eyes brightened in wonder as he removed the wrapping paper, revealing a colourful box with exciting pictures.

"Can I show Peter it now, Mummy?"

"Aye, off you go," Aunt Isa broke in unexpectedly, having followed them into the bedroom. "It'll give us a few minutes' peace to talk," she said to Kathleen as they went back to the living-room.

Kathleen sat down at the fire.

"This is a poor welcome for you," the older woman remarked, setting a tray at the end of the table. "But Mr Carmichael said he was going to take you for a meal, although I told him you'd be wanting to come right home."

"Thank you," Kathleen took the cup and saucer and Aunt Isa noted the tremor in her hands.

"Lassie, you're dead beat!" There was gentleness and worry in her voice. "Was it that bad? I'm near feared to ask you about things."

Kathleen told her everything, holding nothing back. Aunt Isa listened without saying a word, letting her own tea stand till it was stone cold.

"I'll have to look after him, Aunt Isa. There's no other way!"

CHAPTER TWENTY-FOUR

MRS DUNCAN at last shifted her eyes from the strained, unhappy face to the snapping flames in the grate. She tightened her small mouth and shook her head helplessly. What a mix-up it all was! And what a burden for poor Kathy! Jock Todd had been a drag and a heartbreak to Cousin Mary all their married life. Now he was going to be the same to his daughter! Some folk were born to make trouble, and some born to bear it for them.

"How did he find you were here?" she asked.

Kathleen roused herself.

"When he was arrested he told the police he came from Kilmarford. They got in touch with the local police here when he became ill to see if he had any relatives."

Aunt Isa nodded, then leaned forward to lift away Kathleen's cup and saucer.

"I'm going to fill a piggie for you and you'll get right to bed! I built up the fire, thinking you'd want a bath after your journey. By the looks of it you'd better just have a quick wash and into bed. I'll see to Kenny."

"I'll be all right in the morning," Kathleen smiled uncertainly. In spite of the warmth of the fire she was cold, and her head throbbed painfully. "I'd better unpack."

"Never mind unpacking! I'll see to all that."

Aunt Isa hurried into the kitchen. Above the sound of

running water she filled the kettle her voice rose in forced cheerfulness.

"I had a letter from Alec. He and Marlene are coming over sometime next year, and bringing the bairns with them. I was that excited when I got the letter I never slept a wink the whole night. Isn't it wonderful news?" She was silent for a moment, moving around the kitchen. Then she went on, "I'm saying, isn't it wonderful news?"

When there was still no reply she thought Kathleen had gone into the bedroom and made to follow her. But she stopped short in the kitchen doorway.

"Kathy!"

The name was a cry of fear as she rushed forward to the still figure slumped on the floor.

Isa Duncan was not a woman to panic in an emergency. She realised at once Kathleen had fainted. But there was also something about her laboured breathing that sent a pang of alarm through the older woman's heart. She had heard that once before. She knelt stiffly beside her niece, her eyes fixed on the colourless face.

How pale she was. Her cheek bones stood out far too sharply! She slipped her arm under the slim shoulders to raise her. But at once she realised her own lack of strength.

The sound of feet clattering on the stone flags at the back door made her start in alarm. Kenny! Kathleen's eyelashes fluttered as though the approach of her boy had brought her round. Aunt Isa scrambled to her feet and hurried to the back door.

Kenny mustn't see his mother like this! It would give him a shock he would never forget. Isa Duncan summoned a smile to her wooden lips and spoke cheerfully.

"Kenny! I've just been looking for you! Run back and ask Mrs Balfour if she'll come round a minute, and – and ask if you can stay a wee while longer with Peter."

"But Peter's gone to bed!"

For a moment the old woman was at a loss. She couldn't let him into the house while she wrote a note. Nor could she stand at the back door a second longer.

"Just say Aunt Isa asked if you could stay," she said firmly.

"Where's Mummy?"

"She's having a bath," Aunt Isa lied. "Now be sure and ask Mrs Balfour to come round at once!"

To her relief he ran off without further argument. Isa Duncan rushed back into the living-room, breathless with anxiety. Kathleen was coming round. But the eyes that looked up at Aunt Isa had no recognition in them.

"Kathy, dearie –" Aunt Isa caught her hand, helping her to sit up. "You'll be all right. You fainted."

But Kathleen went on looking blankly at her, babbling words which made no sense to the listener. Now Aunt Isa noticed the hands she held were burning hot.

Ray Balfour arrived in a few minutes. The older woman was never so glad to see anyone. And her hazel-eyed smiling young neighbour was capable and calm in the sudden emergency.

Together they got Kathleen undressed and into bed. Then

Ray Balfour went to phone for the doctor.

"I'll do it from the box," she said. "Kenny might overhear me in the house. I'll come back and wait till the doctor's been."

She returned soon afterwards.

"I spoke to Dr Dallas himself. He'll be round immediately after his surgery, he said. I ran in and spoke to my husband. He's going to keep Kenny there for the time being. Don't you think he should stay with Peter for the night? It's no trouble. This isn't the place for him." She looked at the restless figure in the bed.

"I know," Aunt Isa smoothed back Kathleen's red hair. "Poor lassie! She's burning up with fever. It's very good of you, Mrs Balfour, but Kenny might wonder and get upset if we didn't let him come back. He's been looking forward to his mummy coming home. I'll tell him she's asleep and put him in my bed for the night."

"Perhaps you're right."

Dr Dallas arrived half an hour later. Aunt Isa was thankful to see the kindly face beneath the silver hair. Ray Balfour slipped into the living-room to wait, and Aunt Isa took the doctor into the bedroom.

"Well," she asked later when she followed him out of the room. "What ails the lass?"

He looked grave.

"It's not too good, Mrs Duncan. It's pneumonia."

"Pneumonia!" Aunt Isa repeated.

She belonged to a generation for whom the word still had

a dreaded sound. Pneumonia! That's what had struck down John in his prime! She'd sat with him for long hours waiting for the crisis – the crisis he never survived.

"More than that," the doctor went on, "she's completely run down. What's she been doing with herself, Mrs Duncan?"

Aunt Isa told him. The doctor would respect her confidence.

"I see! Some get more than their fair share of trouble." Dr Dallas shook his head. "I'll give you a couple of prescriptions. You won't be able to get them till tomorrow so I'll leave you something just now. Now this is what you must do . . ."

"You'll be back, Doctor?" Aunt Isa asked when he finished.

"First thing in the morning," he promised, and Aunt Isa was comforted. In Dr Dallas she had absolute faith.

When she was opening the front door for him she said, "Do you mind, it was pneumonia with my John, Doctor?"

He patted her shoulder.

"Yes, I remember. But don't you be thinking things! Pneumonia isn't the danger it was, you know. We've got things now we didn't have years ago – things that keep it from going too far. Kathy is going to get better."

Aunt Isa saw the car drive away, and turned to find Mrs Balfour beside her. She told her the doctor's verdict.

"Would you like me to stay with you?" Ray Balfour asked.

"Thank you, but I'll manage tonight fine. If you'll just

send Kenny home –"

It was not easy to get Kenny to settle in bed without saying good-night to his mummy. Aunt Isa allowed him to peep in at the door. When he was assured that his mother was lying in her usual place his protests dwindled. But he couldn't understand why he had to sleep in Aunt Isa's bed.

"I'll put in the goldfish to keep you company," she said. By this time she would have promised anything to get him settled for the night.

The long hours of darkness dragged on. Kathleen was still restless, her head turning and turning again on the pillow. The old woman sat beside her, trying to keep the covers close round her. Kathleen kept pushing them off.

The hoarse voice, so unlike Kathleen's, made Aunt Isa bend over the tossing figure. She held Kathy's hand firmly, speaking soothingly as she would to a child.

"Craig! I can't marry you now – I can't!"

Isa Duncan stared at the flushed face and bit her lip.

"Craig – Craig – darling –"

The old woman's fingers tightened on the hot hand.

"Wheesht, Kathy! It'll be all right. It's going to be all right!"

"Craig –"

Craig! Not Ewen! Through the long hours Isa Duncan sat and listened, and learned she had been building a dream that could have no reality. Always she had hoped Kathy would fall in love with Ewen Gilmour. He was a fine young man, and she was convinced he would have made Kathy happy.

Earlier in the night she'd even let herself think it could solve the problem of Jock Todd. There were always quiet places about a farm. If he were a semi-invalid he would find enough things to take up his interest, maybe keep him out of trouble. He'd be far enough away from Kilmarford to be out of the way of gossip. Folk in the country wouldn't know him for what he was.

It would have suited herself, too! If Kathy married she couldn't live on at the bungalow on her own. But Ewen was a good friend, the kind who would help. There was always work about a farm an extra woman could do. There would have been a corner for her, too. Ewen would have seen to that.

She'd thought about it that day when she was paying her rent.

"Changes are lightsome," she'd told the factor.

But that was a dream that would never happen, either. It was a lesson to her not to be so selfish, not to be thinking so much about herself and her comfort.

"Craig –" Kathleen whispered again.

Aye, the poor lass was in love. Well, Isa Duncan had hoped it would happen and it had. But not like this! Not with Craig Carmichael! But what ever does turn out the way we plan? Rabbie Burns was right, "The best laid schemes . . ."

Isa Duncan laid a cold compress on Kathleen's forehead, and reflected that no one had the power or the right to mould another's life. Yet that's what she'd been trying to do.

But now nothing mattered but that Kathy should get well.

And God willing, she would get well. As if to give voice to the hope in her heart, Isa's lips moved silently in prayer.

* * * *

The following day as Isa Duncan peeled potatoes to make chips for her own and Kenny's tea, she thought about what Dr Dallas had said. A frown furrowed her brows. She was tired after a sleepless night. But she would admit that to no one.

"You can't carry on alone, Mrs Duncan, not with a boy about the house!" the doctor had said firmly.

"Kenny's no bother – "

"He's an added responsibility when you have enough on your hands. Don't forget you were a sick woman yourself just a few months ago. I'm not having two invalids on my hands!"

"I'm fine, Doctor – "

"Maybe you are at the moment. But this isn't going to be a short illness. Mrs Laurie is going to need a lot of nursing. I still think hospital – "

"She's not needing to go to hospital! I'll look after her – "

Remembering his warning, Isa Duncan dug an eye out of the potato with some fierceness. She could manage. Kathy was not going to hospital, not if she could help it.

Craig Carmichael called in the afternoon. Aunt Isa had asked Ray Balfour to phone the office in the morning about Kathleen.

"But you can't see her just now, Mr Carmichael," she said firmly. "Dr Dallas says no visitors, and she mightn't know you anyway."

"How is she?" His face was so serious that the old woman's stiffness melted and her eyes filled with tears.

"It's pneumonia – "

"Oh – " His face whitened. "I wasn't surprised to hear she'd collapsed. I'll never forget how she looked when she stepped off the train in Glasgow. She's had a terrible time with all this worry about her father. She was overtired – but pneumonia – "

"I blame myself," Aunt Isa sniffed. "She had that cold hanging on her before she went away."

Craig patted her shoulder as the doctor had done the previous evening. She did not resent it. It comforted her.

"Who's nursing her?" Craig asked.

"I am!"

He smiled, that oddly boyish smile Kathleen had always found so attractive.

"Then she's in good hands," he said gently, which made Aunt Isa give a louder sniff and blow her nose.

"Now if there's anything you want or need you'll ask me, won't you?"

Aunt Isa nodded, pushing her handkerchief into her apron pocket.

"Can you manage on your own?"

When she assured him she could, he went on to speak of the future.

"I'm going to marry Kathleen, Mrs Duncan. I'm going to look after her and Kenny. That is" – again the quick smile made him look years younger – "if she'll have me."

Isa Duncan looked at him. He wasn't Ewen Gilmour and she was convinced she'd never feel the same towards him as she did to Ewen. But he loved Kathy. He'd make her a good husband. He'd look after her and that was what Kathy was needing.

"I think," she said gently, "she'll have you. She was delirious that first night. She said your name often."

She saw the warmth in his eyes.

"I wish I could see her, Mrs Duncan!" he said. "I feel terrible – knowing she's so ill –"

"Maybe in a day or two," she promised. "Dr Dallas said she was to be kept absolutely quite. No visitors."

"I'm not just a visitor!"

"We'll see what she's like tomorrow, Mr Carmichael. Maybe you could just peep in the door."

A few minutes later she saw him to the gate. It was windy and the leaves were swirling in the front garden.

"Just do one other thing for me," Craig said as he turned to go. "Call me Craig."

"I will – if I mind." It may have sounded a trifle ungracious, but he didn't notice.

While he might make things lighter for others, he was weighted with worry. When he drove away from Dalreoch his face was set in hard lines.

Pneumonia! His Kathleen! And he could do nothing.

CHAPTER TWENTY-FIVE

KENNY spent most of Saturday with Peter. Kathleen was sleeping deeply under the influence of drugs, and Aunt Isa lay down on the other bed in the afternoon, covering herself with the quilt. She dropped into a doze, but wakened with a start when the front door bell rang. She slithered off the bed. It might be the doctor. But he usually tapped at the door and walked in.

Instead of the doctor's bulky figure it was Mrs Laurie standing on the doorstep, a sheaf of flowers in her hand.

"I've just heard Kathleen is ill," she said.

Aunt Isa hastily smoothed her ruffled hair and opened the door wide.

"Come in, Mrs Laurie." She spoke softly because the bedroom door was open.

Mrs Laurie explained she had heard of Kathleen's illness through George Webb – rather Mr Laurie had heard of it at the mill. Aunt Isa told of Kathy's collapse. She told her only facts she thought Mrs Laurie should know, only those and nothing more. All Kathy's personal affairs she kept to herself.

Mrs Laurie seemed truly concerned. But Aunt Isa went on looking at her with some suspicion. This was Mrs Laurie – Kathy's mother-in-law, the woman who had slighted her.

"Is Kenny out?" Mrs Laurie asked, drawing off her gloves.

"He's playing with one of his chums."

"How are you managing? I mean, having a boy in the house where there is illness must make things more difficult!"

"Kenny's a good boy." Aunt Isa knotted her plump fingers together and raised her chin aggressively.

"He is!" Mrs Laurie smiled. "But he's also a very lively little boy and he can't help being noisy sometimes. Then there's yourself. You've been ill."

"I'm fine now." Aunt Isa was breathing rather deeply. In her own mind she could see where this was all leading. And it did.

"How would it do if Kenny came to Finnard for a short time – till his mother is over the worst."

"Thank you, Mrs Laurie, but Kenny's staying here. In any case, I couldn't let him leave this house without asking Kathy; and she's not fit to be asked."

"It's not as if he would be strange. He's visited us often, and we'd take good care of him."

"I'm not doubting that, but –" Isa Duncan broke off as the familiar tap sounded at the door.

"Excuse me, that's the doctor."

Mildred Laurie smiled.

"That's all right, Mrs Duncan, I'm in no hurry."

Dr Dallas spent some time over Kathleen and then turned to Aunt Isa.

"How are you feeling yourself?"

"I'm fine," she maintained stoutly.

He shook his silver head.

"You can't do it day and night with a growing boy in the house –" He broke off because as they came into the hall he caught sight of Mrs Laurie through the open door of the living-room.

She came towards him.

"Good afternoon, Doctor."

"Good afternoon, Mrs Laurie. I saw the car outside but I didn't recognise it."

"How is Kathleen?" she asked.

"She's holding her own," he said briefly. "It's Mrs Duncan I'm concerned about at the moment."

Mildred Laurie nodded.

"I was trying to persuade her to let us take Kenny for a few days – till his mother's on the way to recovery."

"That's an excellent idea!"

"But, Doctor, I can't let Kenny go. Not without Kathy knowing!"

"You leave Kathy to me. It's either that or I'll have to send her to hospital. You're not completely fit yet, Mrs Duncan, and your niece is going to need all your attention for weeks! But if you'd rather keep the boy I'll put her into hospital –"

"I don't want her to go to hospital!"

"Please be sensible, Mrs Duncan," the doctor said firmly. "Kenny will be in good hands."

"I'll look after him well, Mrs Duncan," Mrs Laurie broke in. "I promise you. You needn't worry.

"As soon as Dr Dallas says Kathleen is well enough I'll

bring him back to see her."

Isa Duncan looked from one to the other but refused to commit herself.

"I'll come back for Kenny about six o'clock," said Mrs Laurie gently. "I'll bring a case for his things."

Isa Duncan straightened her back.

"You needn't bother with the case!" she declared with a touch of her old spirit. "I'll pack them in his mother's."

"Six o'clock then, Mrs Duncan. I'll come for him and take him – home."

* * * *

"I'll come for Kenny and take him – home." Mrs Laurie's words echoed in Isa Duncan's mind.

Home! That word kept hammering in her mind as she set about packing Kenny's belongings. Her thoughts flew quicker than her hands. Finnard would never be his home! It would always be here – here with his mother.

But at the back of it all was a feeling of relief. In the end the decision had been taken out of her hands. This last day or two she'd been made aware of her own bodily weakness; and Kenny was a responsibility.

He needed attention as all good, healthy laddies did. Attention and mothering.

What a beautiful word that was, she suddenly thought. Mothering. What a lot it meant. With Kathy so ill she hadn't time to mother Kenny properly.

Mrs Laurie had the time, if she could do it properly. She should. She'd brought up two boys of her own.

Well, since she couldn't mother Kenny and look after Kathy, too, it was just as well Dr Dallas spoke as he did. She hadn't liked it. But she was funny about some things and some folk. And often she was wrong about both. She knew that fine. No-one better. But she had to have her say. And she always tried to think for the best.

She poked two fingers into a grey sock to make sure there were no holes. But if things had been normal Mrs Laurie wouldn't have got Kenny out of the house!

But she must not think like that. Things weren't normal. And she wasn't one to deny Kenny the mothering a laddie needed. There always came a time when you had to do things you didn't like.

Dr Dallas had stopped at the door after Mrs Laurie had gone off in her car.

"It's all for the best, Mrs Duncan. It's natural for the boy to go to his grandparents at such a time. They'll look after him."

"I'm not doubting that!" she answered dourly. "It's just that –"

She stopped as his lips curved into an understanding smile.

"It'll leave you free to nurse Mrs Laurie. She'll need all the care you can give her. And she's the first consideration. Other things don't matter."

Dr Dallas was a deep one! He could twist a thing so you found yourself agreeing with him in your heart – if not always in your head.

Isa Duncan finished the packing and looked into the bedroom. Kathleen was asleep. She went into the kitchen and started preparing tea for Kenny. She could hear him outside playing with Peter Balfour. She'd have to call him soon and get him washed and dressed.

It wasn't going to be easy telling him he had to go. He might ask questions she would find difficult to answer. As she lit the grill to make toast she wondered about the best way to approach it.

But, like most dreaded tasks, the telling was something of an anti-climax. Kenny received the news with almost unclouded delight. He always enjoyed his visits to Finnard. The prospect of going to stay there all on his own was an adventure to him.

Besides, though he didn't say so, home wasn't quite the same place these days. With Mummy in bed, and having to creep silently about the house all the time, there wasn't much fun for him.

But thoughts of Mummy made him look at Aunt Isa rather doubtfully over his boiled egg.

"Couldn't Mummy come, too?"

"Not just now, dearie. Your mummy's been very ill and she still needs lots of sleep – and quietness. But you'll come and see her every day, won't you?"

Kenny nodded his head seriously then brightened suddenly.

"Grandpa's got a dog, Aunt Isa – a spaniel."

"Has he now?" She spread raspberry jam on her wheaten scone. She'd heard about that spaniel from Kathy.

"His name's Roy. He's nice – but not as nice as Jock!" Kenny drove his eggspoon through the bottom of the empty eggshell, because Aunt Isa had told him the story of the witches using eggshells for boats.

"D'you remember Jock?" he asked wistfully.

"Aye, I remember." Aunt Isa gave him a bright smile. "What about your goldfish? You'll need to tell me how many ants' eggs I've got to give them each day.

"Maybe you'd better feed them yourself when you come to see your mother."

The sun came out on the small, intent face beneath the red hair, and the meal ended in a burst of animated conversation.

* * * *

Promptly at six o'clock the car arrived, and with it Mrs Laurie. Kenny was all ready. The goodbyes were as brief as possible. He tiptoed to the bedroom door and whispered goodbye to his mummy, but she didn't hear him.

"You'll be a good boy now, Kenny," Aunt Isa said as Mrs Laurie took his hand.

Kenny smiled and did not seem to think a reply was necessary. He was, to his own way of thinking, always a good boy. He was all smiles, but Isa Duncan had to blink fiercely once or twice as she watched him sitting in the back of the car with his grandmother.

Mrs Laurie smiled and waved her hand, then the car drove away.

Half an hour later Kathleen called weakly and the old woman went in with a sinking heart to tell her Kenny was away. Once again it was something she dreaded. But if Kathleen grasped what she said, it barely registered. She just accepted the news and asked no questions.

Isa Duncan bathed her face and hands and combed back her soft, auburn hair. Kathleen's eyes were heavy and clouded. Fever still painted a hectic flush on her cheeks.

Sitting on the bedside chair Aunt Isa remembered Dr Dallas's words. He was right! Kathy was her first consideration. For the time being Kenny – and anything the Lauries did – must come second.

Later that evening Aunt Isa was rummaging in the sideboard drawer for an air letter to write to Alec when Ray Balfour tapped at the back door.

"I've brought some calves' foot jelly. I thought maybe Mrs Laurie would manage a little. Yes, I'll come in a minute. But I won't stay. My husband's out and I've left Peter reading in bed. How is she today?"

Isa Duncan gave her the latest news and told her about Kenny going to Finnard.

"I think that's a sensible arrangement, Mrs Duncan, though Peter will miss him. It's too much for you with all the nursing. Besides, it's not good having a boy in the house where there's serous illness. Now if you have any washing I'll take it with me."

"Washing?" Aunt Isa echoed doubtfully.

"Yes, I'll do it with my own on Monday. I've got a washing machine and it's no work at all –"

"Thank you, lassie, but I can manage fine." Aunt Isa tried to keep her voice calm. The idea of anyone doing her washing!

But Ray Balfour was smiling broadly.

"I suppose you're just like my mother! She always says no washing machine could do the works as well as she could do!"

"It's not that!"

"What is it, then? You'll have a lot of extra washing just now."

Aunt Isa's stiffness melted. She liked Ray Balfour, and she'd been a good friend during these anxious days. No-one could have had a kinder neighbour.

"You've done enough for us already, lassie," she murmured weakly.

But Ray Balfour wouldn't be put off. She saw the heavy lines on the old woman's face, heard the tiredness in her voice.

"Please don't argue, Mrs Duncan. I won't go until I get the washing."

Meekly Aunt Isa went to do as she was told. Mrs Balfour followed her into the bedroom where she was stripping Kenny's bed.

"Did you hear the six o'clock news, Mrs Duncan?"

"No." Aunt Isa eased a pillow out of its cover. "I missed it.

It was just when Kenny was leaving. Was there news of the King?"

"Nothing new. It said yesterday he was to have an operation."

"Aye." Aunt Isa sighed. "Poor man! But the way he has kept going is an example to all of us. It's no' always the smiling face that has the lightest heart."

Ray Balfour looked at the old woman's shadowed features and changed the subject.

"Don't you overdo it. Take it easy tomorrow. Get your feet up for a while. You're not expecting visitors?"

"Mr Carmichael will maybe look in but he'll not stay."

Ray Balfour tucked the bundle of clothes under her arm.

"I'll come round tomorrow afternoon. I'll sit with Mrs Laurie and you can have forty winks."

Aunt Isa's lips trembled and her voice faltered.

"You – you're very kind."

Ray Balfour smiled.

"Nonsense! Besides, what are neighbours for? Now I'll away or Peter will be coming out to meet me! You get to bed early and don't worry yourself."

Then she was gone, and the house seemed an emptier place without her.

CHAPTER TWENTY-SIX

THE weekend passed quietly. Aunt Isa heard the announcement of the King's operation, and despite her own worries she shared the concern of the English-speaking world. Seated by the fire the knitting needles slipped from her tired fingers. Her thoughts flew to Buckingham Palace, to the Queen and her daughters.

At this moment they were a family united in loving anxiety. And that, Aunt Isa decided, was what made the Royal Family so beloved and revered. They were just like any ordinary family, sharing the same hopes and fears, the same joys and sorrows.

It was just after teatime on Tuesday when the bell rang. Aunt Isa opened the door to find Ewen Gilmour standing in the tiny vestibule. He made to speak, and then hesitated when he saw Aunt Isa's expression.

"Didn't Kathleen tell you I was coming?" he asked.

"Come away in, Ewen," she told him soberly, and opened the door wide.

Ewen sat at the fire in the living-room while she gave him the news about Kathleen. As he listened his pleasant, frank face grew deeply concerned. He was sympathetic and anxious to be helpful.

"If there's anything I can do – anything at all – just let me know, Mrs Duncan!"

"I'll do that," she promised. She was always at her ease with Ewen.

He was by nature optimistic. His views and outlook cheered Aunt Isa up.

"Now," he said, "as soon as Kathleen's on her feet again we'll get her to Carnbo for a real holiday. Aileen will look after her, and the change of air will do her good."

Aunt Isa returned the smile warmly.

"I saw Kathleen on her way home last week. She was with Craig Carmichael." He said this with such casualness that Aunt Isa would have been amused if her sympathies were not always with him.

To her relief she was spared the necessity for comment by another ring at the door bell.

"This'll be the minister, like enough."

But it was Alice Boswell in a blue tweed suit with a lighter blue beret set jauntily on her smooth fair hair.

"I just heard about Kathleen from Mrs Laurie," she explained. "I came to ask –"

Aunt Isa brought her into the comfortable living-room, gratefully accepting the dahlias General Boswell had sent from his garden.

Ewen rose to his feet and greeted Alice with unassumed friendliness. Aunt Isa went to put the flowers in water, leaving them for a moment, but hearing the low, pleasant murmur of their voices. They both had the gift of friendliness, these two.

Not that she'd ever taken to Alice Boswell as she'd done

with Ewen. But it was difficult to be stiff with Alice for all that. Only she was so friendly with the Lauries . . .

"So Kenny's with his grandparents!" Ewen was saying when she came back into the room. "I was just going to ask about him."

"Aye," responded Aunt Isa with a marked lack of enthusiasm which may have been lost on Ewen but was not on Alice. "He's at Finnard."

"Could I see Kathleen?" Alice asked.

"Well – the doctor said no visitors." Aunt Isa's hesitation was due to her slight feeling of guilt at having let Craig look into the room the previous day.

But Alice did not press the point. She sat back in her chair, her long, well-shaped hands loosely clasped. There was a faint flush on her cheeks and her eyes sparkled. She was more animated than Aunt Isa had ever seen her.

"Could I come some afternoon and sit with Kathleen?" Alice asked. "It would give you a rest, Mrs Duncan."

"That's real kind of you," Aunt Isa said. "But if you'll just wait until Kathy's able to sit up."

There was a pause in the conversation, and Isa Duncan roused herself.

"You'll take a cup of tea, Miss Boswell and –"

"Thank you, but I'm afraid I can't wait. We're having guests and I must get the seven o'clock bus back. I promised Mother I'd give a hand with the sandwiches."

"Haven't you got your car?" Ewen asked.

Alice shook her head.

"It's laid up with back axle trouble."

"I'll run you home, then."

The colour in her cheeks grew deeper.

"But it's out of your way!"

Ewen grinned.

"What's a few miles in a car? Besides, I'm – I'm a free agent this evening."

Alice looked at him and then went on quickly.

"We're having a few friends in to play bridge. Would you like to join us since you're free? No, you wouldn't be intruding nor would you be odd man out. Mother only plays when we can't get anyone to take her place. She's never been a bridge fiend."

"That's very nice of you, Alice! I'd like that."

When they left, ten minutes later, Isa Duncan saw them to the door. In spite of the snell wind stirring the leaves on the path she waited until they drove away.

She watched as Alice laughed happily at some remark Ewen made. They made a handsome couple. But it would be a pity if Alice Boswell had any notion of Ewen Gilmour. There was only one girl in his life. That was Kathy. But Kathy had no thought or eyes for anyone but Craig Carmichael!

As she turned into the house and closed the door behind her Isa Duncan sighed heavily. Sometimes life could be an awful tangle – even to folk who least deserved it! She shivered and blamed the thought for feeling cold and disturbed.

Aunt Isa had just got Kathleen settled for the night when Craig Carmichael arrived. He apologised for the lateness of his visit.

"I've been busy at the office. I've got to go to Liverpool tomorrow, so I had to get things cleared up. I'll be away a week –"

"Have you had any tea?" Aunt Isa asked.

"I had a cup of tea and a biscuit at the office. No, please, don't bother. My housekeeper will have left sandwiches."

Aunt Isa voiced her opinion of sandwiches for a hungry man, and went to put on the frying-pan. Craig followed and stood leaning on the jamb of the kitchen door to hear all the news of Kathleen.

"Heard from Kenny?" he asked.

"He was in this afternoon. As bright as a bee he was!" She cracked an egg on the side of the pan.

She couldn't help wondering what Ewen Gilmour would think if he knew one of his eggs from Carnbo was going to feed his rival. The thought made her smile, and Craig mistook the reason.

"You're quite happy now about Kenny being at Finnard?"

"Well, not exactly happy, but I've got used to it. I didn't like it at first – and neither did you."

"I wouldn't say I didn't like it! In view of all that's happened it surprised me. But, of course, it was the only thing to do under the circumstances. And who knows, it may be all for the best.

"Nursing a grievance – and Kathleen had reason if any

269

woman had – never does any good. The Lauries are slowly beginning to realise that. But don't you worry about Kenny. He won't be a day longer at Finnard than I can help. As soon as Kathleen is better we'll get married and Kenny's home will be with us."

Aunt Isa opened the tea caddy and made no comment. Craig moved into the kitchen and placed something on the table.

"What's that you're doing?" Aunt Isa asked quickly.

"It's Kathleen's pay packet."

"You shouldn't have bothered about that!" She smiled. "Things are not as bad as that yet. I can aye pay the rent."

"I should hope so!" Craig grinned. "But that'll be the least of your worries. Laurie won't put you out."

The lid of the teapot dropped from Isa Duncan's fingers and fell with a clatter on the polished linoleum.

"Laurie! Put us out! What are you saying?"

Craig straightened himself and met her incredulous gaze.

"But, of course, you know –"

"Know what?" Her voice was harsh.

"That this is James's house – look out! The bacon's burning!"

Aunt Isa gave short shrift to the bacon. She shot it on to the plate which had been heating above the gas. Then she turned to face Craig. She tried to keep her voice down, but it was shrill.

"Are you telling me we've been living all this time in a house that belongs to James Laurie?"

"Didn't you know?"

"Know!" Aunt Isa echoed breathlessly. "D'you think I'd ever have set food in this house if I'd known? I only knew old Wylie was the factor. But are you sure?"

"Quite sure. I only heard about it a little while back, but I thought you and Kathleen knew all the time. It seemed a natural thing –"

"There's nothing natural about it!" Aunt Isa broke in fiercely. "Kathy's a Laurie in name only. She's never accepted any favours from that man – never known any kindness, either."

"Mind you, I don't think it was always Laurie's house –" Craig began.

"That's neither here nor there," Aunt Isa interrupted. "It's his now! I don't know what Kathy will think!"

"You won't tell her!" There was an emphatic ring in his voice. "She has got to be kept perfectly quiet and free from worry of any kind. You mustn't tell her!"

"Do you think I'm daft?" Aunt Isa said sharply, irritated by his aggressive manner. Then her voice grew softer. "Now go and sit in at the table. I'll bring your supper."

Sharing a cup of tea with Craig, Aunt Isa began to simmer down. She began to view the situation with interest instead of the shock which Craig's disclosure had first aroused in her.

"But what did he do it for?" she asked helplessly, sugaring his tea with a liberal hand.

Craig grinned.

"He wouldn't be James Laurie if he didn't have his reasons."

Aunt Isa snorted, then pursed her small mouth thoughtfully.

"But one thing's certain. He didn't do it for me. And he didn't do it for Kathy, either. She could have lived in the Vennel for the rest of her life and it would never have lost him a minute's sleep!" She raised her head and her eyes widened.

"He did it for Kenny!"

"I think you're right." Craig stirred his tea slowly.

"Blood's thicker than water – and Kenny's his grandson. It would never do for a Laurie to be brought up in the Vennel." The hardness had crept into her voice again.

"But you forget something," he argued calmly. "In making life easier for Kenny, Laurie was also making it easier for Kathleen – and for you.

"Don't you see? Kenny had been happy here – so has Kathleen. And haven't you? Just think of the pleasure your little garden has given you. A home anywhere is what you make it, but admit it, Mrs Duncan, you've enjoyed certain comforts here that you would never have enjoyed in the Vennel. Isn't that right?"

A ghost of a smile played round the old woman's lips.

"You've a rare gift o' the gab," she said, and it was as near to admitting he was right that she would go for the present!

By the time Craig left, Aunt Isa was still full of speculation, but she was no longer ruffled. No matter whose house it was, she was paying the rent. That was the main thing. It might be James Laurie's house, but it was her home!

At times it was a queer world. But this was the queerest thing that had ever happened to her. It made her smile, thinking how sure she'd been that Wylie had given her the chance of the house because she'd scrubbed out his office all these years.

But no matter why they'd got the house, they'd got it! She'd been lifted out of the Vennel when she was resigned to spending the rest of her life there.

She had good friends in the Vennel, but Craig Carmichael was right! This bungalow was a palace compared to the house there. Here she had no stairs to climb. A kitchen that would make her old neighbours green with envy. A garden that brought rest and peace to her heart.

And as long as she paid the rent who was to put them out? Not fifty James Lauries!

But what if Kathy married? The thought struck Isa Duncan with new force. She couldn't afford to stay here alone. She'd need to look for something else with a smaller rent. Oh, well, maybe houses would be easier got later on. She'd cross that bridge when she came to it. Meantime she'd be thankful for what she'd got. Even if she had got it by the grace of James Laurie!

She lifted the dish-towel from the hook, then paused. He couldn't be quite so black as she'd painted him. The man had a heart, after all – even though he didn't show it. He'd thought about the bairn and there couldn't be much wrong with any man who gives a bairn a home. Nor had Laurie ever cast up what he'd done. That was the most surprising thing of all!

As she dried the supper dishes Isa Duncan found herself humming one of her favourite hymns.

Stretch forth Thine hand to heal our sore;
And make us rise to fall no more;
Once more upon Thy people shine
And fill the world with love divine.

CHAPTER TWENTY-SEVEN

A WEEK slipped past, and then another. Kathleen was improving. She was still very weak and so listless that Aunt Isa worried about her. They had been busy weeks for her. But she'd found help and encouragement on every side, and strength when she least expected it.

Ray Balfour was a daily visitor, doing the shopping and making little dishes to tempt the invalid's appetite. Despite all protests, she went on doing all the household washing and ironing. Aunt Isa had become increasingly fond of the bright young woman, always so ready with a smile and an offer of help.

There were other visitors: Nan Webb, Aileen Gilmour, Alice Boswell and Miss Gemmell, who brought Kathleen's pay packet while Craig was away. She also brought a lovely basket of fruit from the office staff.

Aunt Isa liked Miss Gemmell at once. They discovered a mutual interest in crochet, and Miss Gemmell was invited back.

"Haste ye back!" Approval with Aunt Isa could reach no greater heights.

Then there was Mr Jardine, the minister, whose visits brought real comfort to her. He was a fine preacher and a man who could give a lovely prayer. He was sympathetic in trouble, yet no matter how depressed you felt he had the gift of leaving you with a feeling that the sun was shining.

"It's in time of trouble that you ken your friends," Isa Duncan told him, "and we've been truly blessed."

Flowers came from the church on that second Sunday. Shaggy-headed chrysanthemums they were, and very beautiful. Aunt Isa arranged them lovingly and stood them on a low table where Kathleen could see them.

The cloud had gone from her eyes and she was smiling from the propped pillows. Aunt Isa forgot her own weariness in a silent prayer of thankfulness. Kathy had got over the worst, thank God.

After his return from Liverpool Craig Carmichael was a frequent visitor. He was at the bungalow the day Kathleen was allowed into the living-room for the first time. She was pale and wan. But she was more like herself again, and Craig rejoiced to see the evidences of her recovery.

They talked about Kenny, whom Craig had not seen since the boy went to Finnard. He came every day on his way home from school. It was obvious he was quite happy with his grandparents.

"Peter Balfour's been up to play with him once or twice," Aunt Isa said.

"And they had Peter out in the car last Saturday," Kathleen put in. "They went to Saltcoats, and Kenny brought me back that egg-timer on the mantelpiece." She smiled. "He had to have an egg for his tea right away so that he could see it work!"

Craig smiled with her, delighting in her happiness.

"We'll soon have him home again," Kathleen went on.

Aunt Isa nodded. That Kathy was wearying for her boy was the best sign yet. It had worried her, seeing Kathy so weary that she didn't seem to care. If she had her own way Kenny would be home tomorrow.

But Dr Dallas had advised leaving him where he was for a while yet. There was no hurry, he said, and Aunt Isa didn't argue. She could see the boy was well looked after, and another week wasn't going to make any difference!

Besides, she herself was more tired than she cared to admit. Now the strain had lessened she knew reaction, and was doubly weary.

"It's good to see you up again, Kathleen." Craig was sitting in the chair beside her and he leaned forward to touch her hand.

She smiled gently. She was very thin and against the pallor of her face her hair flamed like fire.

"You need a holiday," he went on.

"I've been invited to Carnbo for as long as I care to stay. Aileen and Ewen were in yesterday. They wanted to know when I'll be ready. Wasn't that nice of them?"

His brows slanted.

"Yes – very nice of them, but that's not the kind of holiday you need! Carnbo's too close to Kilmarford. What you need is a complete change of atmosphere – where you'll get plenty of sunshine –"

He broke off because Kathleen's smile had widened.

"I'll soon be back to the office."

"You're not coming back there!" His voice became urgent. "Kathleen, let me take care of you – and Kenny. I've got such wonderful plans. All the time you've been ill –"

Isa Duncan rose quietly and went into the kitchen, closing the door after her. Craig was scarcely aware of her departure, but Kathleen was and she frowned.

"Please, Craig! I'm – never going to marry. My father –"

"Darling, we've gone over all that before. Your father doesn't matter."

She drew away from his touch.

"He does to me! I've got to make a home for him to come back to. That's my responsibility. And it's mine alone. I'm not going to involve you. I couldn't, Craig. It would ruin you –"

"Surely I'm the best judge of that!" He was white-lipped, hurt by her attitude. The thought of the invitation to Carnbo rankled, and Ewen Gilmour loomed large in his mind. It was an image not easily dislodged.

It was fully ten minutes before Isa Duncan returned to the room, but she knew by their faces that Craig had accomplished nothing. Kathleen's mouth was set, and there was no smile now in her expressive eyes.

Craig left soon afterwards. His face was thoughtful.

* * * *

It was a crisp Saturday afternoon when the car from Finnard drew up at the door of the bungalow. Kathleen and

Aunt Isa were waiting for it.

"Now are you sure you're warm enough, Kathy? That's a chilly wind."

"I'm fine, Auntie!" She smiled and spoke to the chauffeur, whom she knew quite well. He had often collected Kenny for his Sunday visits to his grandparents.

As they turned into the drive at Finnard, Kathleen found herself remembering her first visit there. She remembered the bitterness which had flamed in her then, how she had leaned against that very gatepost trying to steady herself.

It was over a year ago. Yet it seemed a whole lifetime. Here she was visiting Finnard again as an invited guest. Her son had spent weeks under the roof she had once sworn in her heart would never shelter him.

How had the change come about? It wasn't that anything had happened, or anyone had done anything. It was just time. There had been no sudden or sweeping changes in attitude or in views. Just a gentle softening, a mellowing perhaps that only time and experience can bring. An acceptance of life as it was.

Lying in bed she had thought a lot about things. She knew the changes were not all on the side of the Lauries. The year had brought a deepening of emotions to her own life.

Love had come to her unsought. The second summer, the incredible blooming of the flower for which she had never wished and could not take.

But it gave a deeper meaning to her life. A greater sorrow and a sweeter joy. She loved Craig with all her heart. She

279

thought, fleetingly, as she had thought often and long in these past weeks, that she could have married Craig even in these circumstances if she had loved him less.

But her love had deep roots. It was not only to give joy to her. It had to give every happiness to Craig and that she knew it could not give.

* * * *

Mildred Laurie received them gracefully as she did most things, and the presence of Kenny soothed away any momentary awkwardness there might have been. He was immensely proud to show his mummy and Aunt Isa into the lounge. His eyes sparkled under his bright hair which Kathleen noticed had been cut.

She mentioned it and he laughed.

"Grandpa took me to the barber's," he said proudly. "His barber's!"

"I'm sorry my husband isn't in at the moment, but he'll be back shortly," Mildred Laurie said, ringing for tea.

Isa Duncan took the chair her hostess indicated. She sat completely silent, leaving to Kathleen the entire responsibility of making conversation. Kenny returned to the model of a windmill on the floor by the window. Watching him, Aunt Isa reflected how much at home he was in this big room. A great deal more at home than herself.

Her lack of ease began to leave her as she sipped her tea from a wide, delicate cup and nibbled at a sandwich. Her mind was registering every detail of the beautifully furnished room.

"Kenny has been round the mills with his grandfather." Mildred Laurie was telling Kathleen, trying to hide the pride in her voice.

At that Kenny bounced up from the windmill. He went to Kathleen and began to fill in the details of a wonderful morning, which, being only a few hours away, was vivid in his mind.

"It was super, Mummy!" he exclaimed excitedly. "Grandpa says he will take me back again – and perhaps Peter can come, too!"

Kenny was still talking excitedly about his visit to the mill when James Laurie appeared in the doorway. Kathleen felt a catch at her heart when she saw how her son ran across the room to meet him.

The feeling changed to something approaching wonder when she realised that Laurie's manner to Kenny was something she herself had never seen. She was not to know that until now, only his wife had seen that gentleness. Nor was she to know that James Laurie had come to love his grandson with a more demonstrative affection than he had ever shown his sons. He had never been a man who wore his feelings on his sleeve.

But Kenny was rebirth. The continuance of the name of Laurie, the security of the future when there had seemed no future at all.

James Laurie ruffled the little red head as he produced

copies of "Beano" and "Dandy." He was still smiling when he greeted Kathleen.

"It's nice to see you out again, Kathleen."

She smiled faintly, slightly at a loss for words. It was the first time he had ever addressed her by her Christian name.

He nodded and smiled at Aunt Isa, took a cup of tea from his wife, and then gave his entire attention to Kathleen.

"You're looking very pale," he said sympathetically. "But that's not surprising. You've had a bad time and you'll need to be careful. What you need now is a holiday – something to build up your strength."

"I've been invited by Mr Gilmour and his sister to stay at Carnbo."

"I've heard Alice Boswell speak about it. She's been there once or twice," Mildred Laurie put in, passing the biscuits to Aunt Isa. "The Gilmours seem very nice people. Alice had them to supper last week. General and Mrs Boswell were most impressed with them."

James Laurie passed his cup for more tea, but his eyes never left Kathleen.

"That's very nice of them," he said. "But what you need is a complete change of air with plenty of sunshine."

Isa Duncan stirred her tea thoughtfully. She was puzzled. Then she reflected that the conversation was remarkably like one she had heard before, between Kathy and Craig.

James Laurie cleared his throat and went on carefully, after a slight pause.

"My wife and I have been talking about this. We've been

282

talking a lot about you and Kenny recently, and we – we'd like you to have a real holiday, a complete change – in Madeira –"

"Madeira!" Kathleen echoed in surprise. But despite the appeal in his eyes she shook her head. "But – but I couldn't!"

"We rather expected you to say that, Kathleen." He leaned forward and smiled. "That's why I've only made the reservations provisional – two single cabins –"

"Oh, James! How badly you explain things," Mildred Laurie interrupted, seeing the look of amazement on Kathleen's face. "We knew you wouldn't like to go alone. I would be going with you – if you want to come, of course. We do hope you will."

Isa Duncan clicked her cup on its saucer. She was beginning to doubt the evidence of her own ears. Was she dreaming? Where was all this leading? What was behind it? She looked at the out-thrusting jaw and the deep-set eyes of James Laurie.

He was talking so persuasively, so gently, she was almost believing his good intentions herself!

"You know we went on a cruise last winter. At the time of Roger's" – James Laurie glanced at his wife and faltered – "when – when Roger died," he finished simply.

"Yes," Kathleen said hastily. "Yes, I remember."

"It didn't do either of us much good. One just can't close a door and hope to forget. Nor can one run away from life." His voice was gentle.

"But things are different now. I'm sure Mildred would benefit from a real holiday. And young company like your own." He smiled.

"I thought of another cruise to Bermuda, but there are snags. It would mean being away about three months. I knew you wouldn't want to leave Kenny for so long –"

"I couldn't leave him at all!"

"Don't be too hasty, my dear."

Kenny, who had been deep in his comics, chose that moment to run outside to where the chauffeur-gardener had started up the motor mower. James Laurie spoke more freely.

"Things have been – unfortunate between us for long enough. I've been wrong in some things. I realise that now. Please let me – let us do this for you!"

"But I couldn't –" Kathleen protested again.

"Don't think of it as a one-sided arrangement," Mildred Laurie said gently. "I would be very glad to have your company."

Kathleen swallowed as her eyes met Isa Duncan's.

"There's Kenny –" she said helplessly.

"Kenny could stay here," James Laurie said. "He's been very happy –"

"And who'll look after him?" Isa Duncan spoke for the first time since he entered the room.

James Laurie swung round to her and his voice was oddly quiet.

"We've thought of that, too, Mrs Duncan. We know how

much the boy means to you and how much you mean to him. While Kathleen and Mrs Laurie are away you can come and stay here. You will have complete charge of him."

Aunt Isa drew a long breath and gripped the arm of her chair to steady herself. She felt giddy. She couldn't believe it. James Laurie, the man she had always despised, was inviting her to come and stay in his house! Words formed in her mind, but they never reached her lips.

He was speaking to Kathleen again.

"Please understand, Kathleen, we are not forcing you. We can't. The decision must be your own. But it would give us both great pleasure –"

Silently Isa Duncan watched the three of them. The Lauries hopefully expectant; Kathleen still hesitant but wavering. The Lauries were winning. Aunt Isa could see that. But she could stop it!

She knew she had only to say the word, say she would never stay at Finnard, and Kathy would refuse to go. The poor lassie was still weak physically; torn between conflicting loyalties. She needed someone to tip the scales one way or another. It would be so easy.

But Isa Duncan knew she had no right to say that word. It would deprive Kathy of a wonderful holiday she badly needed. At Carnbo she would be made welcome. Ewen and his sister would look after her with loving care and kindness.

But at this time of the year Carnbo would be like any other place in Ayrshire. And already winter was stretching out its long, cold fingers.

Madeira! It was only a foreign place on the map to Isa Duncan, but the Lauries made it sound wonderful. So inviting. Sunshine and warmth . . . blue skies and tropical flowers . . . What right had she to deprive Kathy of such a chance?

So Isa Duncan was silent. But the smile she gave Kathleen was more eloquent than words.

There was more talk and in the end Kathleen decided to go. The Lauries brushed aside her efforts at thanks during the discussion on dates. It seemed that there was little time left for all the preparations that would have to be made.

James Laurie didn't believe in letting the grass grow under his feet. Aunt Isa smiled to herself as she listened to his voice raised in excitement.

At his suggestion it was decided Kenny should return home with them that night so his mother could have him for ten days before she left.

CHAPTER TWENTY-EIGHT

AN hour later the Lauries stood on the steps of Finnard saying good-bye. The car had been brought round, and Kenny sat in the front beside the window, waving to his grandparents, as the car drove away.

James Laurie slipped his hand through his wife's arm as they went back into the house. No words were spoken. No words were needed at that moment.

They went back to the sitting-room and sat talking for a time. Then Mildred Laurie said she had things to do upstairs and left the room. James Laurie lit a cigar carefully and drew on it gently with satisfaction. Then his face suddenly darkened. "I must be getting into my dotage, forgetting such a thing."

He stepped over to the telephone and dialled a number. While he waited for an answer his fingers tapped on the side table impatiently.

"Oh, that's you, Carmichael. Well, I've arranged all that, just as you wanted. Kathleen is going to Madeira with my wife. See you Monday to fix things as we arranged. Yes, that will do."

He replaced the receiver and turned to leave the room, but stopped when he saw his wife in the doorway.

"James! What does that mean? What has Mr Carmichael to

do with my holiday with Kathleen? Oh, James, you're not spoiling things when everything is so happy?"

Mrs Laurie spread her thin fingers on the edge of the door. Her eyes, wide with amazement, never left her husband's face.

"What does it all mean, James?" she asked, surprised at the steadiness of her voice. "What have you and Craig Carmichael been up to?"

He slipped her hand through his arm and led her to a fireside chair.

"There is no mystery, my dear," he said gently. "And certainly nothing to cause you any concern. I was going to tell you all about it –"

"But Carmichael," she broke in impatiently. "What has he got to do with the cruise?"

Laurie settled himself in a chair opposite her, his eyes twinkling almost mischievously.

"Call it a little conspiracy if you like." He smiled. "But it's all for a good cause. Let me tell you how it all started. The other day I received a phone call from Carmichael. He seemed rather upset, so we arranged to have a coffee at Fenwick's . . ."

Carefully he recounted that meeting, describing Craig's concern about Kathleen and the need for her to have a complete change.

"It seems that Kathleen was invited to stay with the Gilmours at their farm," Laurie went on, "but Carmichael didn't think that was good enough. What she needed was a complete change of atmosphere, with plenty of warmth and sunshine. And I agreed with him. But Carmichael couldn't force her –"

"So he asked you to help him?" Mildred Laurie sat forward in her chair.

"That's right. He thought if the suggestion came from me it might carry more weight."

"And so you went right ahead and made the reservations. Weren't you taking a risk without first getting Kathleen's approval?"

"The cabins were only provisionally reserved," he reminded her. "And I've never been afraid of taking a risk, my dear. Sometimes it's the only way to get things done."

"Of course, Kathleen doesn't suspect that Carmichael has anything to do with –"

"No, and you must never tell her," Laurie broke in quickly. "That's our secret – ours and Carmichael's."

While he was speaking Mildred rose to her feet and moved silently over the thick fireside rug. She laid her hand on his shoulder.

"Oh, James," she said with a quiver in her voice. "I'm so glad things are turning out so well. Better, indeed, than I had ever any reason to hope."

He felt the gentle pressure of her fingers as she turned away and left the room.

She was relieved and happy to know that James and young Carmichael were on better terms now. It would all help towards the amalgamation that James had set his heart on.

And anything that pleased him pleased her.

Unconsciously Mildred Laurie's steps led her upstairs to the bedroom Kenny had used. It was really the dressing-room to their own room. It had a connecting door. She'd put him there in case he was nervous.

But he hadn't been nervous at all. He was a sturdy, self-reliant child – but so lovable.

Cleared of most of his belongings, the room looked bare – and cold. They'd left one or two things, though, because he'd be back. A pair of scuffed sandals lay under the window, toes together and heels apart. They looked forlorn, as if they missed the eager feet which were so often thrust into them. She picked them up and handled them almost tenderly. Many years ago the rooms and staircase of Finnard rang with the patter of such sandals. Kenneth's and Roger's . . .

Mildred Laurie looked out on the garden where dusk was already falling. After having him all these weeks she was going to miss Kenny, miss him almost unbearably. Of course, he would be back – but she wouldn't be here.

She saw a shadowy shape racing across the lawn as if in search of something. It was Roy, the spaniel that James had bought specially for their grandson. He, too, would be missing Kenny after those happy weeks together.

Finnard stood on a rising knoll, and she could see lights pricking out on the south side of the town. One of these might even be at Kathleen's bungalow. They should have reached home by now. She wondered what they were thinking, what they were discussing – especially that shrewd old woman, Mrs Duncan.

She had taken little or no part in the talk about the cruise. Yet it was her opposition to the trip, more than Kathleen's, that James had feared. She was a strong-willed woman, and Kathleen respected her view. Yet Mrs Laurie felt Mrs Duncan would never stand in the way of something which was so obviously to Kathleen's benefit. The bond of affection between these two was strong – and mutual. Anyone could see that.

Mildred Laurie laced her fingers together and smiled. She would like to have known what Mrs Duncan was really thinking . . .

* * * *

At that moment Isa Duncan was thinking a home without a bairn was like a clock without a tick. Now Kenny was back, his red head in its rightful place at the side of the table and his tongue wagging endlessly. The three of them seated round the table together! That was the way it should be.

No mention was made of the trip until after Kenny was in bed. Then Isa Duncan darned a pair of stockings, while Kathleen did a few half-hearted rows of the pale-yellow matinee jacket she was knitting for Nan Webb's expected baby. But her mind wasn't on it. Every now and again she would pause and gaze into the fire.

"I wish – I hadn't said I would go," Kathleen said, as if

speaking her thoughts aloud.

Isa Duncan looked up.

"Now, what's making you say a daft thing like that? Think what it means, lassie! A sail in a ship, seeing wonderful places, and lots of sunshine to put colour into your cheeks again. It's a chance of a lifetime!"

"Yes, I know all that – but if I could pay my own way –"

Aunt Isa snorted.

"Why bother your head about that? They asked you to go, didn't they? Besides, it's little enough the Lauries ever did for you, and you their son's widow. Don't forget that!"

Kathleen smiled wanly.

"I suppose you're right."

"Of course I'm right! Didn't Mrs Laurie say she'd be glad of your company? You go with her and enjoy yourself."

"But Kenny –"

"I'll look after Kenny as I've done before today."

"You mean you'll go to Finnard?" Kathleen asked.

"Yes, if it's going to make you easier in mind. And you know something, Kathy?" A smile, with more than a hint of mischief in it, spread over the round face. "Maybe it'll be a great experience for me, too!

"Aye –" The smile widened. "Like enough I'll have a grand time. Leading a lady's life – with nothing to do but get waited on! But I never thought I'd see the day when Isa Duncan would set foot inside Finnard – far less move in, bag and baggage!"

She was rewarded by an answering smile on Kathleen's

face and a lightening of the shadow in the grey eyes.

But later, when Isa Duncan was lying in bed with her toes on the piggy she'd brought from the Vennel, the memory of those brave words came back to mock her. At Finnard she would be like a fish out of water. She'd be as much at home as a daisy in a vase of begonias! But she'd go. She'd do anything – for Kathy!

Isa Duncan turned over on her back and looked up at the ceiling. There was a street lamp opposite the gate. A shaft of light pierced through a chink in the curtains and made a small pool on the ceiling.

She frowned. The curtain swayed and the little pool of light on the ceiling widened. She wished she could see what was behind James Laurie's sudden generosity. What was the real purpose of this trip abroad? Where was it all leading?

Why had Laurie completely changed his attitude to Kathy? Today he couldn't have been nicer.

Anyone present at Finnard this afternoon and listening to the concern and pleading in his voice would have been justified in thinking James Laurie was the kindest father-in-law in the world.

Yes until a few weeks ago he'd treated Kathy like an outsider. Refused to acknowledge her – or his grandson.

Aunt Isa put her hands behind her head, pushing a curler out of the way.

Maybe she was being too suspicious. But the more she thought about it the more she pictured James Laurie at Finnard as a spider sitting securely in the middle of his web.

And they were the innocent flies, being invited in – and going!

* * * *

The following day was Sunday, and in the afternoon Ray Balfour appeared and invited Kathleen and Kenny for tea. Aunt Isa was asked, too, but she declined. She was now on such good terms with young Mrs Balfour that she knew she could decline without giving offence.

She was going to put her feet up and read what "The Sunday Post" had to say about the General Election.

She had hardly settled when the door bell rang. With a few pithy whispered remarks about visitors she pushed her feet into her slippers and went lazily to the door.

It was Craig Carmichael. Her irritation vanished and she smiled broadly. They hadn't seen much of him for a week or two.

"Come in, Craig! Kathy's out. She's just round at the Balfours'. Maybe she'll see the car . . . ." Aunt Isa chatted on while he followed her into the room.

"I hear you've got Kenny back," he said, lifting the paper which had slipped on to the floor.

"Oh!" Aunt Isa looked surprised. "How did you know?"

She was even more surprised when he flushed.

"I – " He shrugged his broad shoulders and felt in his pocket for his cigarette case. "You know how news gets around."

"Aye, it's amazing, isn't it? He only got back home yesterday."

She settled herself in the chair opposite him and he switched the conversation to Kathleen. How was she?

Aunt Isa told him, then poured out the good story of the cruise to Madeira. It was good to be able to talk about it.

"What do you think?" she asked, leaning forward in her earnestness. "What do you really think?"

"I'm very glad Kathleen's going. It will do her a world of good."

"Then you think we did the right thing?"

"The right thing? I don't understand –"

Aunt Isa broke in impulsively.

"I can't help feeling there's something behind all this. It's not like James Laurie to give anybody something for nothing – especially Kathy!"

"But he's doing it!"

"That's what's bothering me! He's doing far too much. He's even getting me to come up and stay at Finnard with Kenny. Can you imagine it?"

Craig laughed.

"Why not? I'd say you'd be a match for James Laurie any day."

She laughed, too, infected by his twinkling eyes. She was beginning to feel much better.

"I hope you're right."

The twinkle in his eyes deepened, but he shook his head reprovingly.

"You're an awful woman for looking a gift horse in the mouth!"

She smiled at that, but her voice was serious.

"It's just that Kathy and the bairn mean that much to me –"

"I know that. They mean a lot to me, too. That's why I don't want you to worry about this – or let Kathleen worry about it. When we're married everything'll sort itself out."

"You're gey sure of yourself, lad." Aunt Isa's tone was a great deal gentler than her words.

"I've got to be, Aunt Isa." It was the first time he had called her that, but she scarcely noticed. It seemed natural, somehow. "If I lost confidence in myself I'd give up trying. And she's everything to me."

They heard the scamper of feet round the end of the house, and Kenny burst into the room.

"I saw the car, Uncle Craig! I told Mummy it was yours. She's coming!"

When Kathleen followed a few minutes later Craig suggested a short spin in the car, although the light was already going from the day.

"If you don't mind, Craig, I'm rather tired –"

"That's all right." He smiled. "Some other time!"

He went on to speak quite naturally about the trip to Madeira, but Kathleen had little to say on the subject.

When he left half an hour later Kathleen went with him to the front door.

"I'm glad you're going, Kathleen. You're certainly

needing a holiday."

"I've got rather mixed feelings about it," she admitted frankly. "My mind was more or less made up to go to Carnbo."

They lingered in the doorway because he would not let her come out to the car. The street light gleamed on the brightness of her hair.

"Forget everything and enjoy yourself – and get really well again!"

"This holiday means I won't be back at the office for a while."

"When you get back there'll be other things to think about – a different future altogether."

Once again his tone implied much that his words left unsaid. But he let it go at that, and for a moment she did not know whether she was relieved or not.

"Will you write to me while you're away, Kathleen?"

"But Craig –"

"You'll have plenty to write about. Think of all the wonderful experiences you'll be having. Don't keep them to yourself."

"But –" She hesitated again, conscious of his nearness, of how much – fight against it as she would – she loved him.

"Aren't we friends?" he asked gently.

Kathleen nodded. Craig put his hands on her shoulders and kissed her cheek. It was unexpected, and he was gone, clicking the garden gate after him, almost before she realised what he had done.

He started up the car and drove away, but she still stood in the doorway, her hand against her cheek.

She was still weak physically and far more easily moved than usual. Perhaps that was why the lamp at the gate melted into a golden gaze, and the fingers on her cheek became suddenly wet.

If Aunt Isa noticed her abstraction when she came in she gave no sign of it. Later in the evening she began a lively discussion about the clothes which Kathleen would be taking with her.

Soon Kathleen was as animated about it as the older woman herself, and it was into the midst of this discussion that Alice Boswell walked some time later.

"I've just come from Finnard," she told them, drawing off her gloves.

"Yes" – she answered Isa Duncan – "I got my car back on Wednesday. I've been lost without it. How are you, Kathleen? It's grand to see you up and out again?"

She was wearing a blue dress under her loosened coat, and it deepened the colour of her infectious enthusiasm soon affected the others. Talk turned again to the subject of clothes, and Alice – who had once accompanied her parents on a cruise to the Mediterranean – was soon giving her opinions and her advice.

When she left after supper the atmosphere in the bungalow was extremely cheerful, and both Kathleen and Aunt Isa went to bed to sleep dreamlessly.

Last night Kathleen had been full of doubts. Now, with

Alice's gay chatter still ringing in her ears, the idea of the trip became suddenly exciting. Alice assured her she would like Mrs Laurie, too, when she got to know her. Now the prospect of a few weeks in the company of her mother-in-law – a woman she hardly knew – no longer appeared such an ordeal.

CHAPTER TWENTY-NINE

ON a bleak afternoon in November Isa Duncan sat before a brisk fire in the lounge at Finnard with a writing pad on her knee. She was writing to Kathleen.

She was used to writing air-letters to Alec, but today she was having trouble with her pen. She had much to say and she bent her head over the pad again. Agnes would bring her in a cup of tea about three o'clock, and she was determined to have her letter finished before then.

It is Thursday and I'm going to the church guild meeting tonight. When I told Mr Laurie this morning he said he'd send the car for me afterwards.

I had to put my foot down on that! Imagine what folk would say if a braw car and a chauffeur rolled up at the hall door for Isa Duncan!

We've got settled down fine. I'm not saying I didn't feel like I had two left feet at first, and I was fair homesick for our own fireside. But I must say Mr Laurie has been very good – my, he fair dotes on Kenny. He gives him far too much, but there's no use me saying anything. I might as well talk to the wall!

I make my own bed and keep my room, but other than that I don't have to do a hand's turn. I was fair lost at first, but I've got used to it now. So I'm just sitting back and having a real rest myself.

There's plenty of help in the house, and I could see I wouldn't be welcome if I meddled.

I've been down to the Vennel once or twice. Old Mary Kerr isn't well. This damp weather doesn't do with her at all. I walked past the bungalow and picked the last of the chrysanthemums to take to her. They're gey wurly wee things, but she was fair charmed, poor old soul.

I looked in on Mrs Balfour when I was there. She was showing me the postcards you sent her and Peter. She made tea and I got a slice of vanilla sponge she'd been baking. She wrote down the recipe for me. We'll need to try it when you get home.

I was very glad to get your long letter, and that relieved to know you're feeling such a lot better. Imagine you sitting out in a summer dress and me here sitting almost on top of the fire, listening to the rain dripping down outside!

It was a nice day on Sunday, though. We all went to the church in the morning, and Kenny sat in the pew beside his grandfather. I made an excuse about the gallery stairs and slipped in at the back downstairs.

I just couldn't face sitting beside James Laurie for all the congregation to see! It weighs on my conscience, Kathy, but I just couldn't help it!

It was a fine day in the afternoon. Mr Laurie told the chauffeur to take us for a drive. We went to Largs and had a dander along the front. It was nice of Mr Laurie to do it.

I wish I could like him – like you tell me you're getting to like Mrs Laurie. Mind you, I don't dislike him – but I don't know what's going on in his mind, and I'm sure there's plenty. I keep these deep folk at arm's length. We're that polite to each other it makes me want to laugh sometimes. But I mustn't be ungrateful. I'm very comfortable here so don't worry about me.

Isa Duncan sat back in her chair and bit thoughtfully on the end of her pen. She was remembering her conversation with James Laurie the previous evening, on one of the few occasions she was alone with him.

"I believe," she said, meeting him on the landing as she came out of Kenny's room, "you're my landlord."

She saw his chin thrust out, his brows draw down. She knew she had caught him off guard.

"Who's told you that?" he asked.

"I've my own way o' finding out things," she replied, determined not to give Craig away.

His hand gripped the banister rail.

"Any complaints?" he asked gruffly.

She shook her head.

"None. It's a grand house," she said. "And it was kind of you to give it to us."

He shrugged and went on downstairs, but she had a feeling he was pleased. Halfway down he turned back.

"I forgot to tell you I've invited Mr Carmichael and Miss Boswell for dinner tomorrow. I'd like you to join us." Then he stumped on without waiting for an answer.

She always had high tea with Kenny and then spent the evening in her own room. After suggesting once or twice that she spend the evening in the lounge, James Laurie seemed very pleased to fall in with her wishes.

Although she had an electric fire in her bedroom, she found now that a coal fire was lit in the evenings, and a small portable wireless transferred from the lounge to her room.

James Laurie spent most of his evenings in his study or entertaining business friends in the lounge. This was an arrangement which suited everyone.

Now on this wet afternoon Isa Duncan suddenly realised time was flying and her letter was not finished. She must tell Kathleen about the dinner party tonight. But just as she poised the pen over the paper the door opened and Agnes brought in the tray.

Maybe she should keep the letter open and tell Kathy about the dinner party after it was over. That was an idea! She poured out her tea. That was one thing about Agnes. She could make a good pot of tea!

* * * *

It was midnight when the letter to Kathleen was finished. Aunt Isa sat up in bed, a pink bed-jacket Kathleen had knitted for her birthday round her shoulders.

This time she wrote in pencil in case she should get ink on the sheets.

. . . a very nice evening, Kathy. I'll say this for Miss Boswell, she's a grand one for keeping the talk going. And she's got a knack of easing Mr Laurie off business which he'd talk every minute of the day if he got the chance! From what I could gather, he and Craig seem to be making some big business deal. I just hope Craig knows what he's doing!

Miss Boswell was looking very pretty. She had on yon same blue dress and it fairly sets her. I heard her asking Craig if he'd had a postcard from you, like she had. He said he'd had a letter. He seemed very pleased.

Here Aunt Isa's eyes grew warm with a smile, and she carefully traced the last words over again, making them so black that they stood out from all the rest.

Presently the muted tick of the clock by her elbow drew her attention to the lateness of the hour. Hurriedly she began to finish off.

I'm enclosing this letter of Kenny's. He wrote it himself and I haven't done a thing to it. He's fine, and he's been very good. He often asks for his mummy, and remembers her every night in his prayers. Mr Laurie brought one of these globe things in one day – you know, a map of the world. Now Kenny shows everybody who comes in just where you are –

Soon the letter was finished. Isa Duncan tucked it into an envelope, addressed it, and switched off the light.

Another week slipped in, and on the Friday Kenny came home with the news that Peter Balfour had been absent from school. He'd gone round to Peter's on his way home, and Mrs Balfour hadn't let him in. That was a great grievance to him.

"I hope it's nothing catching," said Isa Duncan.

"You'd better phone Mrs Balfour and find out." James Laurie was home early from the mill.

Aunt Isa was not happy using a telephone, but she would never have admitted that to James Laurie. She went into the study, having to send Kenny running upstairs for her glasses because she couldn't read the print in the directory without them.

"I haven't had the doctor yet, Mrs Duncan, but I think it's chickenpox." Mrs Balfour's voice came clearly over the wire.

When she described the spots Aunt Isa was sure it was chickenpox. She went back to the lounge and told James Laurie.

"Is there anything we can do?" he asked anxiously.

His anxiety made her warm to him.

"Not a thing!" she answered cheerfully. "Peter and Kenny are never out of each other's pockets, so he'll likely take it. But you never can tell. I slept with my sister and she took scarlet fever and I didn't."

Kenny did develop chickenpox – a fairy mild attack. On the second night he was slightly feverish and James Laurie insisted on phoning for Dr Dallas at ten o'clock.

Aunt Isa went upstairs with the white-haired doctor.

"This is none of my doing," she told him in an undertone. "Mr Laurie will not take my word for it that the bairn's all right! I never saw a man make such a fuss!"

Dr Dallas smiled.

"Isn't that natural? By the way, how are you liking it here?"

"Oh, I'm fitting in not so badly."

"No recurrence of your old trouble?"

"I feel better than I've done for years!"

"Changes are lightsome," said the doctor, pushing open the bedroom door. "I only hope young Mrs Laurie's as much the better for her change as you are of yours."

When they came downstairs ten minutes later James Laurie was waiting anxiously in the hall.

"How is he, Doctor?"

"He'll be all right. No need to worry –"

"Should I get a nurse?"

The doctor felt Aunt Isa stiffen beside him and hid a smile.

"That's not necessary. Mrs Duncan is quite capable of seeing to everything. He'll be able to be up in a couple of days. Keep him in the house where it's warm."

"You'll be in tomorrow?"

"I will," Dr Dallas promised, opening the front door.

After Kenny was asleep, with a night-light beside him, Aunt Isa went downstairs to collect a magazine she had left on the sofa. James Laurie opened the study door.

"Is Kenny all right?" he asked.

"He's asleep. You should look in and see him. I've left a night-light."

He opened the door wider and she saw there was a glowing fire in the grate. The roll-top desk was strewn with papers.

"I'm just going to ring for coffee. Will you join me?"

She was too surprised at this unexpected invitation to tell him coffee at night would keep her from sleeping. Instead, she took the seat he indicated at the fireside. At first they talked about Kenny, but presently the conversation drifted to Kathleen and her mother-in-law.

"My wife seems to be enjoying her holiday." He put another spoonful of sugar into his coffee. "I had a very cheerful letter from her this morning."

"I had one from Kathy, too."

"They seem to be getting on well."

Aunt Isa stirred her own coffee and made no reply.

He cleared his throat and began to talk – choosing his words carefully. Aunt Isa listened with growing surprise. She had never associated tact with James Laurie, but what he was saying about Craig Carmichael and Kathy was so nicely put that no one could have taken exception to it.

But it all boiled down to the fact that he'd been given to understand there was some kind of attachment between the two young people and he'd like some confirmation of it – of Kathleen's attitude – from Mrs Duncan.

Aunt Isa took some time to reply, and when she did it was brief.

"All I can say is – she doesn't want to marry him."

She felt his surprise, which he tried to conceal. He looked at her as if weighing the possibilities of continuing the conversation, but there was something unyielding in the round face opposite which warned him further questions would elicit nothing.

Smoothly he turned the conversation to other things. The unyielding quality in her he recognised and admired. It was familiar, because it was part of his own nature . . .

* * * *

Kenny still had spots, but he was convalescent, when Mrs Duncan visited Mary Kerr in the Vennel one wet Tuesday at the beginning of December.

When she left the Vennel there were sharp needles of rain to prick her face, and the brief daylight of a winter afternoon was already waning. The shop windows were brightly lit and cheerful, though, and already there were signs of Christmas in the goods displayed.

She reflected that it was time she got Alec's Christmas card away. The parcel to the family had been sent off some time ago, but she liked to send the card separately – and she liked to get a really nice one.

Agnes was with Kenny and they were great pals, so there was no need to hurry back. She went into a stationer's in the high street and spent some minutes choosing a really nice card – one with a verse on it.

When she left the shop the bright windows of Fenwick's attracted her, and the thought of treating herself to a hot cup of tea and a cake attracted her even more. She was almost at the doorway when a familiar voice hailed her.

"Hello, Mrs Duncan. Gallivanting?"

She smiled at Ewen Gilmour, who had materialised from nowhere at her elbow. She greeted him with pleasure. It was some time since she had seen him.

"You'll have been at the market, Ewen?"

He nodded.

"I'm just going to pick up Aileen along at Forrester's. She's buying a new hat!"

The rain was becoming heavier and he drew her into the doorway where they were jostled by people entering and leaving the shop – but sheltered.

"How's Kathleen?" he asked.

"She's grand! I had a long letter yesterday. Have you heard yourself?"

He moved aside to let a stout woman pass.

"I had a postcard," he said with elaborate casualness.

"Oh," Mrs Duncan murmured, by no means deceived by his tone.

"I suppose you get lots of letters?" he asked.

"Yes –"

He looked down at her from his great height. He was hatless and the rain had made his hair curl. He looked boyish, and his expression – no longer casual – caught at Aunt Isa's heart.

She had always liked Ewen – more than liked him.

"Does she ever say anything about me?"

Isa Duncan felt herself droop. Why did she have to be the one to do this – because she knew this was no casual question?

They were separated momentarily by a young woman with a small girl, and then came together again. Aunt Isa lifted her head bravely in the brown felt hat and looked up at him. Her eyes said a great deal her voice could not say.

"No, Ewen, she doesn't. I'm sorry."

He looked away from her face to the steadily falling rain.

"I could – have got very fond of Kathleen," he said, "but I've had a feeling for a long time – " He broke off. "It is Craig Carmichael, isn't it?"

She put her hand on his arm against the rough tweed of his jacket.

"I'm sorry, Ewen," she repeated gently.

"I had to know," he said.

Her hand slipped down his arm and was enveloped in his.

"I'd better be getting along," he said.

With a tight feeling in her heart she watched him go, bending his fair head against the driving rain.

CHAPTER THIRTY

IN Fenwick's tearoom Isa Duncan settled herself at a table for two. It was beside a window which looked down on the high street. She looked down, wondering if she could see Ewen Gilmour's fair head among the passers-by.

But she failed. Ewen had gone, perhaps out of all their lives. The thought saddened her. What a pity things had to be that way. The rain now running down the window seemed in keeping with her own depression.

When a waitress came she ordered tea. But the savour was gone out of her little outing. What she had told Ewen Gilmour had done that.

She could still see his face, the disappointment in his eyes when he admitted that there was no hope for him with Kathy. She was very sorry for him. Sorry, too, that Kathy could never find happiness with him.

Ewen would gladly have spent the rest of his life making her happy. And that's the way she, Isa Duncan, had hoped it would be. Silly, wishful woman that she was!

She chose a cake from the stand and cut it thoughtfully, her brows forming themselves into deep furrows. It was all wrong that Kathy was going to be denied happiness, denied the reblossoming of love. It was her right, the birthright of every young woman.

It was not so much that Kathy was being denied it but that

she was denying it to herself! She was sacrificing herself and love.

Aunt Isa scooped up a fragment of icing from her plate. Yet who was to say Kathy was wrong? Loyalty was a strange thing, and no one could understand the claims it made until it touched one's own life.

She sighed heavily. Ewen hadn't a fair chance with Kathy. But he'd get over it. He was a fine and a good man with an assured future for himself, and for his wife, when he did marry, in his own world.

And what was left for Kathy? What was her future?

Widowed almost as soon as she wed, she'd been left with a bairn to raise and no home of her own. She'd been real brave about that. And she'd done well. But now, when life should have been brightening for her, it was all spoiled by that father of hers. Could anyone have any future when it was burdened like that?

Aunt Isa caught the waitress's eye and signalled for her bill. It was time she was getting back to Finnard and Kenny. All the thinking she could do wasn't going to straighten out this sorry tangle or make anything easier for Kathy.

It was still raining the following morning, the solid grey downpour the West Country can get at the back end of the year. When Isa Duncan took her place with Kenny at the breakfast table, James Laurie was reading a letter. A gaily coloured envelope lay on the tablecloth.

"'Morning, Mrs Duncan," he said shortly but politely. Then he laid aside the letter and began talking to Kenny about everything and anything that came to their minds.

Aunt Isa had a broad smile for Agnes, who brought in Kenny's porridge. Agnes Wilson was a rosy-cheeked girl whose home was in central Perthshire. Her friendly manner had made Aunt Isa's stay at Finnard more homely than it might have been. And Aunt Isa was deeply grateful for that.

This morning she had scarcely enough time to exchange smiles with Agnes before James Laurie began talking to her.

"I had a letter from my wife this morning." He pointed to the thin, grey sheet beside his plate. "Anything from Kathleen?"

"No – but I had a postcard from her yesterday."

He lifted the letter in his blunt fingers.

"They seem to be having a good time."

She expected him at the most to read just a few lines. But James Laurie pushed aside his plate, sat back in settled comfort, and began to read at length.

This will have to be a quick letter because Kathleen and I sat up late in the lounge tonight and I am rather tired. We met some people from South Africa. Their talk was so interesting that the time simply flew past. In fact, that's what it is doing all the time here. But isn't that always the way when one is happy?

I am feeling very well, my dear. Better than I have done for a long time. This holiday has been a wonderful tonic to me. And a more wonderful experience.

At first I did my best to look after Kathleen, but now I'm

afraid it's the other way round. She rested for the first few
days, now she says she cannot believe she was ever ill at all!
She's taken on a lovely tan. Kenny wouldn't know her.

Kathleen could have plenty of young company in the hotel,
but she spends most of her time with me. She is a very
charming girl, James, kind, thoughtful, and warm-hearted. I
realise now how much we have lost in not knowing her all
these years. We were the ones who really suffered – not
Kathleen. I am sorry for all these months since she came to
Kilmarford. We should have opened our door to her. I no
longer wonder why Kenneth married her. He chose
wisely –

James Laurie's measured voice went on. But Isa Duncan
never heard him. She could only stare and wonder.

James Laurie seemed quite unaware of anything unusual in
these references to Kathleen. Did they register at all? Did
they mean anything to him?

"A kind, warm-hearted girl. . . He chose wisely . . ."

Questions chased each other through her mind. Could
James Laurie be so blind to this change in his wife's attitude
to her daughter-in-law as he pretended to be? Could he have
some purpose in reading aloud this letter to her?

He was folding the letter up.

"I'm real glad to see that everything's going so well," he
commented.

"Yes," Aunt Isa answered him dazedly. She took a piece of
toast from the silver rack, then realised she already had a

slice on her plate.

"So they'll be home in time for Christmas! That will be splendid, won't it? Don't you think, Mrs Duncan, it would be a good idea to stay on here over Christmas? I mean, there's no special hurry to get back to the bungalow. We could have a real family reunion. What do you think?"

Aunt Isa gathered her scattered wits.

"I really think Kathy would like to go home, Mr Laurie. After that long sea voyage and train journey she'll be wearying for her own place."

"Maybe you're right." He did not press the point. He looked at the clock on the mantelpiece, then pushed his chair back.

"It's time I was getting to the mill. There's a lot to do – too much for a man of my age."

* * * *

The days slipped by quickly. The weather improved. Kenny lost the last of his spots and was happy to get back to school. The voyagers were on their way home, and Isa Duncan began trotting between Finnard and Dalreoch getting everything in order for Kathleen's return.

Craig Carmichael found her there on Saturday afternoon when the brief hours of daylight were almost gone. He gave the bell three sharp rings, his usual signal, and walked in.

"Thought I'd find you here. I noticed the door was open when I came along."

Aunt Isa greeted him with a smile.

"I was just making myself a cup of tea before I started to walk back to Finnard. Can you take tea without milk?"

He replied that he could.

"Have you heard from Kathleen today?"

Aunt Isa raked in the sideboard for a box of biscuits.

"I had a postcard this morning. The boat's due at Plymouth on Wednesday evening. Mr Laurie thinks they'll stay overnight in London and travel home the next day."

"Is Kathleen coming back here?"

"Yes. I'm coming down here on Monday, but Kenny will stay at Finnard till Thursday. This house hasn't much firing, and I don't want to risk burst pipes in the cold weather."

"Aunt Isa – I've a great idea! What about having a party here on Thursday night?" he said enthusiastically. "Just a few friends. I'll see –"

Aunt Isa bit into a soft ginger snap.

"On Thursday night!" She repeated the day in a tone which brought him up short. "Don't be daft! Kathy'll no' be thinking of a party that night! She'll be needing her bed!"

"Of course. How stupid of me!" He looked so crestfallen that she immediately softened.

"But it's a good idea. Now, if you're so keen on a party, why not make it Friday? But who will we ask?"

So over another cup of tea it was decided to ask the Balfours with Peter as company for Kenny; Ewen and Aileen Gilmour and Alice Boswell. The Gilmours were Aunt Isa's suggestion. Craig's blue eyes narrowed at their mention, but he made no comment.

"I'll see Mrs Balfour," said Aunt Isa.

"I'll phone Alice Boswell and ask her to get in touch with the Gilmours. I understand they are very friendly. In fact, I saw Alice and Aileen at a concert the other night."

So it was left, and presently Craig ran Isa Duncan back to Finnard through the frosty darkness.

"I'll see you again before Friday, Aunt Isa." He opened the car door for her. "I'm pretty good at arranging parties!"

"I'm wearying for the time to pass," she said, easing herself out of the seat.

"So am I – more than I can tell you." With a smile and a wave of his hand he was gone.

* * * *

The time passed in a flurry of growing excitement. Dalreoch shone like a new pin and a cheery fire burned brightly when Kathleen returned on a sparkling, frosty evening. The car had first taken her and Mrs Laurie to Finnard.

She brought Kenny with her. He was speechless with excitement, every red hair electric with life. But for once Aunt Isa had no eyes for him. Her gaze was for Kathy. A smiling Kathy with the flush of health on her cheeks and an overflowing vitality that reached out to enfold the older woman, even as Kathy's arms did.

"Aunt Isa!" The beautiful grey eyes shone with happy

317

tears. "Oh, how good it is to be home!"

The suitcases were carried into the small hall and the door closed. The little house smiled with warmth and love. Kathleen could feel it as her eyes went round familiar objects. The table was set for a meal, and there were flowers on the sideboard.

"How lovely everything looks – and smells! Roses, Aunt Isa? At this time of year!"

"They came from a florist this morning. There's a card, but I might as well tell you I looked! They're from Craig."

"They're beautiful!" Kathleen touched one of the pink blooms gently. But her expression did not change; at least, not so that Aunt Isa could notice.

There was so much to talk about that time ceased to matter. When nine o'clock struck they were still sitting at the table. Even Kenny protested when bed was suggested.

But he was finally persuaded after being told about the party for the third time.

"We'll have a job getting him up for school in the morning," said Aunt Isa, busy drying dishes when Kathleen came back from the bedroom. "But what does it matter? You don't come home from Madeira every day."

Kathleen smiled, putting away the cutlery.

"He won't be separated from that little carved wooden donkey I brought him. He's got it in bed! There were some lovely things, Aunt Isa. I wished I'd had more money –"

"I think you did gey well, considering all you've brought back. That beautiful cloth and napkins for me. We'll use them tomorrow night!"

"You'd have loved the shops." They went back to the living-room and Kathleen poked up the fire. "But what about your own news? I've been talking non-stop ever since I came home! How did you get on at Finnard?"

Aunt Isa plumped up a cushion and pushed it behind her back.

"A lot better than I expected, and that's the truth. Mind you, I wasn't keen to go, but as I said in my letters, James Laurie couldn't have been nicer. Treated me like a real lady, he did. But you wouldn't believe the way he carried on when Kenny had chickenpox! It took me all my time to keep my temper. When he dragged out the doctor at that time of night – and him not needed – I was fair affronted!"

Kathleen laughed.

"Any news from Chicago?"

"Yes. I was to tell you. At first Alec and his wife thought of coming at the turn of the year, but they're putting it off till the summer. They can bring the bairns with them and stay a longer while."

"That's good news."

Then for a while they were content to sit silently with their thoughts. Later Isa Duncan cocked her head and spoke of something which was on her mind.

"You haven't said much about Mrs Laurie."

Kathleen took her time about answering. She rose to her feet and looked into the glowing fire.

"I feel quite different about her now I've got to know her.

She's a good woman but a lonely woman." She paused. But Aunt Isa made no effort to break the silence. She just sat waiting, a thoughtful look on her round face.

"We talked about Kenneth and Roger. There was so much bottled up inside her it was a relief for her to talk. You know, Aunt Isa, she has suffered a lot. Losing both sons – losing practically everything she lived for –"

"She had her man," Aunt Isa broke in, a trifle stubbornly. "And she could have had you – and the bairn if she'd gone about it the right way."

"I think she realises that now."

"She and that man of hers treated you gey badly, Kathy." Kathleen rested her hand on the mantelpiece.

"Maybe – but does it matter so much – now? Why waste time in vain regrets? The past is over. If we can learn something from it we can avoid making the same mistakes in the future. That's what Mrs Laurie said, and I agree.

"And let us be fair, Aunt Isa. They have been very kind to me, to Kenny – and to you. Once they closed the door on us, but they are trying to open their hearts now."

Isa Duncan shifted her gaze from the sweet face beneath the gleaming auburn hair to the fire.

"The day's coming sooner or later when you and Kenny will be living at Finnard. That's what the Lauries want, of course. It's as plain as the nose on my face!" She cleared her throat.

"Hasn't she asked you yet?"

"As a matter of fact, she did. More than once. But I told

her it was quite impossible."

"Why?"

"Need you ask that, Aunt Isa? My future isn't at Finnard. Or here, either!"

"What are you talking about, lassie?" Isa Duncan was shaken. "This is your home – as much as mine. Where else would you bide?"

Kathleen shook her head. "You're forgetting my father will be out of prison soon. I've got to find a place for him and look after him. This is your house. And you'd never let him come here –"

"But I would, dearie! I would! For your sake!"

Kathleen leaned over and patted the plump hand.

"Bless you for saying that, Auntie. I believe you. But I would never ask you to do it. It would never work. My father's my responsibility. Not yours, nor – " She was about to say "Craig's," but checked herself.

"I'm not going to pretend life will be easy. But that's my problem. Besides, you'll have Alec and his family here. There'll be no room! I'll find a place –"

"If anyone goes out of this house to find another place it will have to be me!" Aunt Isa blew her nose but spoke firmly.

"While you were away I got to know something. It will surprise you. We're sitting in this house by the grace of James Laurie! Yes, it's his house. And he never gave it to us for the sake of Isa Duncan."

She recounted what she had been told. Kathy listened

silently, but her eyes strayed to the bedroom where her son was fast asleep.

James Laurie had done it for Kenny.

Gradually the talk drifted to other things and Jock Todd was not mentioned again. Kathleen went to make another cup of tea, and the two of them sat until the fire was almost out. It was after midnight when they went to bed.

"A fine thing this," Aunt Isa sighed. But whether she was referring to the lateness of the hour or what the future held Kathleen would never know.

CHAPTER THIRTY-ONE

IT was half-past six the following evening when Kathleen joined Aunt Isa in the kitchen. In her best brown moire silk dress and pendant crystal earrings the older woman poked anxiously at a raspberry jelly.

"You'd think with the weather as cold as it is the jelly would set like a block of ice," she complained. "It's as wobbly as –" She broke off and gave a gasp of delight. "My, Kathy, you're as bonnie as a picture!"

Kathleen blushed.

"I've always said green's your colour. I like the neck of that dress, too. It suits you, dearie."

"You look charming, too, Mrs Duncan!"

"Get away with you!" Aunt Isa shook her head reprovingly. "Where's Kenny?"

"He's at the front window looking out for the first of the visitors. At least it's keeping him out of mischief. Everything's looking very nice."

"I think so, m'dear. What a help Mrs Balfour's been making that trifle and all these little sausage rolls. I never thought we'd be ready on time, but we're early –"

Kathleen laughed.

"You sit down and I'll make a cup of coffee. You were too excited to take any tea."

"I wasn't going to! Not with all this grand food to eat later.

What do you think of Craig sending all that fruit and nuts and boxes of crackers? I'll have something to say to him!"

Ten minutes later they heard Kenny shout, "Here's Peter with his mummy and daddy!"

Kathleen went to greet Don and Ray Balfour.

"We're early," Ray Balfour apologised, "but we couldn't hold Peter back another minute!"

"How well you're looking, Mrs Laurie." Don Balfour smiled. "Obviously Madeira's the place for a holiday!"

"We'll go some day, darling!" laughed his wife.

"When our boat comes in!" He grinned.

Soon the door bell was ringing again and Kathleen ushered in Alice Boswell and Ewen Gilmour. She looked over his shoulder for Aileen.

"Ewen picked me up at the house," Alice broke in. "How lovely to see you again! You're looking wonderfully fit."

Kathleen felt her hand taken in Ewen's firm grasp.

"I'm sorry Aileen couldn't come. She's got a frightful cold. I think it's flu. So she thought she'd better keep her germs to herself and not bring them along to a party. It's nice to see you back again, Kathleen. Had a good time?"

"Wonderful," she said.

"Well, you didn't have that holiday at Carnbo. I doubt if it would have put such lovely colour in your cheeks anyway." He smiled at her.

Aunt Isa appeared and he turned to greet her. Kathleen took Alice into the bedroom so that she could leave her coat. Alice was looking charming in blue, her straight, fair hair drawn smoothly back from her broad brow and coiled in the nape of her neck.

Craig was the last to arrive. When the bell rang Kathleen was pulling a cracker with Peter. She hesitated and looked at Aunt Isa who was making for the kitchen.

"You'd better answer it, Kathy."

Craig held out both hands as he stepped inside the door.

"Hello, darling! Welcome back!"

"Hello, Craig." She spoke lightly, trying to still the hammering of her heart. The remembered face, the sudden flashing smile, the familiar tones of the beloved voice.

She would have evaded his grasp, but he was too quick. His hands were cold but his lips were warm. The kiss was brief, but it was enough to make Kathy's confidence crumble. She had been so sure she would be able to withstand him – and her own heart.

"You're looking lovely!" He released her and turned to hang his coat on the hallstand.

She managed a smile.

"I've never felt better. I'll be ready to start work on Monday. Will that be all right?"

Kenny and Peter scampered noisily across the narrow passage and vanished into another room. Craig hung his scarf on the peg and turned to her.

"You're not coming back to the office – not on Monday or any other day. You're going to marry me, my darling," he said.

"Craig" – she lowered her voice, almost whispering.

"Must I remind you again? My father. I must look after him."

He smiled at her.

"I haven't forgotten about your father. Let's look after him together. From now on I want all your problems to be my problems. Do you understand, Kathleen?"

Kathleen shook her head, and at that moment Aunt Isa called from the living-room.

"Is that Craig?"

They went into the room together, and soon the small house was ringing with laughter. Everyone voted it a wonderful party. Because of the children they played all kinds of childish games. Everyone entered into them with zest – including Aunt Isa. But for all that her bright eyes were busy.

It was obvious to anyone, she reflected, that Craig couldn't see past Kathy. He hardly took his eyes off her all night! And Kathy? Well, a woman was always better at hiding her feelings. But she'd never looked prettier. Her large grey eyes sparkled, and the waves of her auburn hair shone.

She had competition, too. There was Alice Boswell, looking so perfectly groomed, and Ray Balfour. She wasn't pretty, but she was so full of life and looked as warm and friendly as a candle flame.

At first Aunt Isa had been rather shy of Ewen, remembering their last meeting in Fenwick's doorway. But Ewen seemed quite at ease. If his eyes sometimes had a wistful look when they rested on Kathy, he was as often laughing with Alice, teasing her in that deep, friendly voice of his.

The door bell rang again just when they were finishing supper.

"I'll answer it," said Craig, already on his way to the hall for another packet of cigarettes from his coat pocket.

It was raining heavily and the policeman was wearing his cape. The light from the lamp-post at the gate shone on his peaked cap.

"Does Mrs Laurie – Mrs Kathleen Laurie – live here?" he asked.

Touched by a premonition, Craig pulled the glass door behind him and stood in the tiny vestibule.

"Yes, but I'm sorry – she's not available at the moment. Could I take the message?"

The policeman hesitated.

"Well, I don't know about that. You see, it's about her father."

"Her father!" Craig tried to keep his voice steady. "I know all about him. I'm a close friend of Mrs Laurie's."

"We've just had word from Manchester – from Strangeways Prison. John Todd died late this afternoon. The authorities want to know what's to be done. Will Mrs Laurie want him brought here –"

A burst of laughter came from the living-room right out to the vestibule. Craig thought quickly.

"Look here," he said. "Suppose I get in touch with you later tonight. I'll talk it over with Mrs Laurie and let you know what's going to happen."

Having watched the policeman mount his cycle and ride away, Craig re-entered the house.

"Who was it at the door?" Aunt Isa asked as he took his place again at the table.

The smiling faces looked at him expectantly.

"Someone looking for people called – Sinclair. I said I didn't know"

"Sinclair? There aren't any Sinclairs about here – at least, not that I know of."

So it was passed off. Soon the room was ringing with talk and laughter again.

The Balfours left first, with a yawning Peter who protested he "wasn't a bit sleepy." Ewen and Alice followed shortly afterwards. Ewen was to drive Alice home.

"I've had a lovely time, Kathleen!" Alice tied a scarf over her smooth hair.

"And me!" Ewen was smiling. "Now you'll all come out to Carnbo during the school holidays. I'll kill the fatted calf especially for you, Aunt Isa!"

"You'd better wait and see your sister's well enough before you start handing out invitations."

"Alice'll come and help, won't you, Alice?" They went out into the darkness, arm in arm, and Aunt Isa gave a contented smile.

Craig made no move to leave. He helped Aunt Isa clear away the dishes while Kathleen put Kenny to bed. Then he sat at the fire and seemed unaware that Aunt Isa was looking pointedly at the clock.

He waited till Kathleen came back into the room, then rose to his feet and stood beside her. She looked at him in surprise.

"I'm afraid I've got rather bad news for you, Kathleen," he said quietly.

"What is it, Craig?" Kathleen asked.

"You'd better sit down." He led her to a chair and stood facing her. "The caller at the door tonight was a policeman." His eyes never left her face as he broke the news.

"When you decide what's to be done I'll call at the police station on my way home," he finished.

Kathleen had gone pale, but her voice was steady.

"I'll go to Manchester first thing tomorrow."

Craig leaned over and took her hand.

"I'm going," he told her calmly. "You can follow later in the day. I'll make all the necessary arrangements if you tell me what you want done. The funeral can be there. No-one in Kilmarford need ever know. Is that what you want?"

"Yes – yes, I think that would be best," she said shakily. She wasn't thinking about Kilmarford or what people would say. She wasn't thinking about her friends or the Lauries – or even herself. She was thinking of Kenny. He must never know . . .

Kathleen went with him to the front door.

"Thank you, Craig, for keeping the news from the others – for not spoiling the party."

He looked at her. All the gaiety was gone from her face.

"That's all right, darling," he said. "We'll look after him together. Just as I said."

When he was gone Kathleen went quietly back into the living-room. Aunt Isa was still sitting by the dying fire. She looked up.

"I was just thinking we should have a cup of tea." It was her unfailing remedy in times of stress.

Kathleen put on the kettle and they had the tea, but they took it silently. After all the happiness of the last few hours it was as if a cold hand had been laid on the house. Neither of them felt like talking about Jock Todd, but each had her thoughts.

Finally Aunt Isa stirred.

"So he's away," she said with a heavy sigh. "God rest him."

Kathleen said nothing, but her sweet mouth gave a slight tremor.

When she went to bed Kathleen took a long time to fall asleep. She found herself remembering vividly that last time she saw her father. How glad she was now that she had gone to him then; and that she had promised to look after him. He had known, at least, that there was a home waiting for him.

In the other bed Kenny was breathing evenly in the darkness. The shadow had passed away from him. Her fears for him had been brushed aside. Now Kenny need never know his grandfather was different from other men.

CHAPTER THIRTY-TWO

JUST after nine next morning, as Kathleen slipped on her coat in the bedroom, the door bell rang.

"That'll be the taxi!" Isa Duncan called from the living-room. "He's early. I'll go, Kathy."

But it was not the taxi. On the doorstep stood Mr and Mrs James Laurie.

Aunt Isa's face betrayed her surprise, and Mrs Laurie hastened to apologise.

"We're very early to be calling, Mrs Duncan, but my husband's running me to Ayr to have a look at the shops. I wondered if Kathleen and Kenny would like to come, too."

"You'd better come in." Isa Duncan was conscious of the curlers still in her hair, of the old slippers on her feet.

But the living-room had been tidied and a bright fire burned in the hearth. In the middle of the floor in a travelling coat and with a small case at her feet stood Kathleen.

Mildred Laurie took in every detail.

"You – you're going away!"

"I'm going to Manchester," Kathleen replied quietly. "I'm leaving at once."

"Manchester!" James Laurie looked at his wife. "Surely a sudden decision –"

"My father has died." In a few words she told them everything.

"Oh – how sad." Mildred Laurie changed colour, glanced at her husband, and then recovered herself. "Can – can we be of assistance? You'll be going by train? We'll run you to the station."

"Thank you, but there's a taxi ordered. It should be here any minute."

Mildred Laurie gave a rather strained smile.

"I was just telling Mrs Duncan we hoped you would join us in a run to Ayr – with Kenny."

"Kenny's round at the Balfours. But I'm sure he'd – "

"No, my dear, we won't bother. Not under the circumstances. But we'll see you off at the station if we may."

"Of course." James Laurie was content to follow his wife's lead. "We'll follow your taxi."

"That's it now," said Isa Duncan. She kissed Kathleen and hugged her tightly. "I'll be waiting, dearie, when you come home," she whispered.

There was only time at the station to get her ticket before the train came in. James Laurie pushed a box of chocolates and a couple of magazines into Kathleen's hand.

"Let us know when you get back," he said.

Mildred Laurie kissed Kathleen's cold cheek and noted her shadowy grey eyes.

"Look after yourself, Kathleen," she said gently.

Kathleen stood by the window, waving when the train drew out. When it had disappeared James Laurie turned to his wife.

"Where now, Mildred? Do you still feel like going to Ayr?"

"No – let's just go home, James."

Back at Finnard they sat on either side of the newly lit fire.

"Would you like some coffee, Mrs Laurie?" Agnes asked, putting another log on the fire. "You look cold."

"That would be nice, Agnes."

The door closed after the girl. Mrs Laurie stretched her thin hands out to the blaze. But James Laurie sat back in the armchair, his shoulders hunched.

"So Jock Todd's dead," he muttered finally.

"Poor Kathleen," his wife sighed. "If we'd treated her as we should she wouldn't have been facing this alone. The more I know her the more I admire her."

James Laurie hunched his body deeper into the chair. He made no response except for a nod of his grey head.

It was at that moment Agnes brought him the telegram.

"What is it, James?" Mildred Laurie did not like telegrams.

"Just business, my dear. It's from young Carmichael, reminding me of some business we were to do on Monday. But he won't be back by then, he says."

"Is he out of town?"

"Yes. He phoned me late last night to say he'd been called south urgently and would drive down overnight."

"By the way, James, have you bought over Carmichael's?"

"No, Mildred. No-one could ever buy Carmichael's. We're amalgamating, and it's a good arrangement that suits me. I'll be able to shed some of the responsibility now. Carmichael and I don't see eye to eye on some things, but he's a go-getter. Knows what he wants and generally gets it – " He broke off abruptly, looking again at the telegram.

"Mildred, d'you see the postmark on this? It was handed in at Manchester!"

"Manchester?"

A gleam came into the eyes beneath James Laurie's shaggy brows.

"Don't you see? Craig Carmichael is there, waiting for Kathleen. He's not going to let any grass grow under his feet. There'll be a marriage between them before long, Mildred, or my name's not Laurie!"

His wife shook her head.

"I think you're wrong, James. I talked a lot with Kathleen during our trip. I don't know whether to be pleased about it or not; but Kathleen has no intention of ever marrying again."

James Laurie bent down and put his cup and saucer inside the hearth. Then he leaned back in his chair and stretched out his long legs.

"I wouldn't count on that, my dear. Perhaps it's what you would like – what we would both like, if it comes to that. But we mustn't close our eyes to the obvious. Kathleen's friendship with Craig Carmichael.

"I'm beginning to have a very healthy respect for that young man. Once his mind's made up about a thing he'll not give in without a struggle."

Mildred Laurie shrugged her shoulders and smiled.

"Neither will Kathleen. Don't we know that ourselves, James? I grant you Carmichael is showing plenty of interest in her –"

Her husband bounced his fist gently on the arm of the chair.

"Interest? Is that what you call it? He's in Manchester at the moment waiting for her. It's obvious he knows everything. He shares her confidence; he knows about her father. And remember how upset he was over her illness and the fact that she was going to spend a holiday on that farm with the Gilmours?

"Come to that, Mildred, who suggested the trip to Madeira? Wasn't it Carmichael's idea? Let's face facts, my dear. It might save you a lot of disappointment and hurt."

Mrs Laurie switched from the main point of their conversation.

"I wonder if they'll be bringing him back to Kilmarford."

"Jock Todd, you mean?" he asked bluntly. "Do you think it would be wise?"

She evaded the question, and didn't speak for a moment.

"It'll take a lot of courage for her to face up to what all this could mean, James."

He nodded, his head sinking on his chest, his eyes hooded beneath his drooping brows. Finally it was Mrs Laurie who broke the silence.

"I wonder what's happening in Manchester . . . I wonder if her father's death will make any difference to Kathleen's future plans? I would give much to know."

The grunt from her husband might have meant anything. Through half-closed eyes he studied her face. It was still a beautiful face despite the heavy lines of doubt and uncertainty. Dear Mildred! There was still loneliness in her heart, a loneliness which she hoped would be eased by the presence of Kathleen and Kenny at Finnard. But James Laurie, reared in a hard, practical school, knew it was a forlorn hope.

* * * *

If there was concern for Kathleen at Finnard, there was even greater concern at the small bungalow on the South Road. On Monday morning Isa Duncan was trying to work off some of her restlessness by attempting a most elaborate icing of her Christmas cake. She was dipping her knife in a jug of hot water when the front door bell rang.

"Drat!" she said, opening her mouth to call Kenny to answer it, and then remembering he had gone round to play with Peter Balfour.

"Maybe it's the postie with a letter from Manchester," she thought, hurrying to the door.

But it was not the post. James Laurie, a few bright spots of sleet on his overcoated shoulders, stood in the doorway.

Aunt Isa felt a momentary pang of fear, thinking this unexpected visit might mean a phone call from Kathleen in Manchester. It vanished at once, however, when she saw the small Christmas tree in one large hand and the box under the other arm.

"Is Kenny in?" he whispered, and peered mischievously over her shoulder. "I've brought a tree for him, and would like to surprise him. I noticed you didn't have one when I was here on Saturday."

"No, he's not in. He's playing with Peter Balfour." Aunt Isa's voice was rather stiff, but she opened the door and invited James Laurie to come in.

"You won't mind if I fix it before he comes back. I've brought a box of coloured lights, and I thought you might like the tree in the front window. When my boys were young they always had a Christmas tree – the biggest in the district."

"We don't have a plug near the window." Aunt Isa's voice was unhelpful, but James Laurie didn't seem to hear her.

"These lights work off a small battery." He was smiling like an excited schoolboy, and Aunt Isa felt her own lips parting most unwillingly into an answering smile.

"I haven't brought any presents for Kenny," he explained. "They're at Finnard. We hope to have you all up later in the week. Tell Kathleen to keep one night free."

Aunt Isa moved a blue bowl of hyacinths off the round table in the window and helped him steady the small tree. He admired her bulbs and Aunt Isa expanded a trifle more as she always did when people mentioned flowers to her.

"Any idea when Kathleen will be home?" he asked, his blunt fingers remarkably nimble as he began to fix the lights.

"I've had no word from her yet. But she'll no' stay away a

day longer than is necessary."

James Laurie poked at one of the green branches and kept his head down.

"Is she – bringing her father – home?"

"No. I can tell you that!" The words sprang from her lips, and the grey head was tilted defiantly. Her mouth thinned.

"But Kathy's not thinking of herself. She's faced idle talk and gossip afore the day. She knows what it is to have the sins of her father visited on her. She's had cause to, poor lassie!

"She's thinking of Kenny. She's trying to protect him – as she's always done!"

The accusation in her voice was unmistakable. But as soon as she saw the dark colour rising in James Laurie's cheeks she regretted her hastiness.

"Well, Mrs Duncan, I'll wish you a merry Christmas. We'll be looking for the three of you at Finnard – say Friday evening? Kathleen is sure to be home by then."

Aunt Isa put her small, work-roughened hand into his large one.

"Will you take a cup of tea before you go?" she asked. The words came out with difficulty. She felt he had cut the feet from her, and a faint, unwilling liking for this thrawn, proud man was stirring her heart.

"Thank you, Mrs Duncan, but there'll be coffee ready at the mill when I get there. I – I hope you'll find Kathleen all right."

Aunt Isa saw him off and watched the black car drive

away. Then she returned to the kitchen, where the icing had hardened in uneven, crumbling streaks on her cake. The water in the jug was cool, and she switched on the kettle.

"It's high time you learned to curb your tongue, Isa Duncan!" she reprimanded herself. "But that James Laurie is a bit too clever at asking questions to suit me! Aye, and if he doesn't know anything it's not for the want of speiring!"

At Finnard, over the lunch table, Mildred Laurie was to say much the same to her husband, but in gentler terms.

"Don't tell me you went to the bungalow specially to ask Mrs Duncan a lot of questions?"

James Laurie took a spoonful of custard before answering. It was unusual for Mildred to criticise him even in the mildest of terms.

"Of course not! I had the Christmas tree to deliver, and the rest just came out in the course of talk. Mrs Duncan is a shrewd old body, but when she's roused she can become very talkative."

Mildred Laurie smiled.

"Just when she wants to be."

"Well, doesn't that prove she'd never tell me anything she didn't want us to know!"

"I'm glad Kathleen's not bringing her father home. Poor girl! It will be difficult enough for her as it is –"

"I wish" – he gave his head an impatient jerk – "I knew how things stood between her and Craig Carmichael! What do you think about Ewen Gilmour, too?"

"I'll be very glad if it's right about Alice," she replied.

That momentarily diverted James Laurie. It was not until afterwards he realised he had never mentioned Alice Boswell at all during this conversation.

"I like Alice," he said now heavily. "She'd have made Roger a good wife."

They looked at each other wordlessly over the table. Then James Laurie cleared his throat.

"We're still not any wiser about Kathleen, though. But Mrs Duncan is right. Kathleen must find her own happiness. And this time we must not interfere."

Their eyes met, and there was a wealth of meaning – and understanding – in their depths.

CHAPTER THIRTY-THREE

ISA DUNCAN came out of Kenny's bedroom and pulled the door closed after her. At last he was asleep, his round face buried in the pillow, his red hair flaming against the freshly laundered white of the slip.

Over the end of the bed his stocking hung, limp and empty. She wouldn't risk doing anything about that for a while yet. He was so excited he might still wake again before he was really settled for the night.

She crossed the little hall and went into her own bedroom. She was tired. She was worried, too, about Kathy. She hadn't expected a letter, but all the same she'd scanned the many envelopes the postman had brought during the day. She had hoped one might be addressed in Kathy's familiar handwriting.

Surely there would be news tomorrow! It was a holiday, of course, but there would be one delivery of the post.

Isa Duncan's thoughts kept her busy as she put her sparse grey hair in curlers.

She decided she would leave Kenny's stocking till the very last minute. She stood up on a chair in her faded blue dressing-gown and lifted a few mysterious looking parcels from the top of her wardrobe.

What a lot Kathy was missing! These were the years you could never bring back; when your bairn was young enough to go to sleep dreaming about Santa Claus.

She put the snib on the front door and went to fill the kettle for her hot water bottle. The iced cake, brave with its pink and white decorations, was there for her to admire. She was touching the tiny fir tree she had stuck in the middle when the doorbell rang.

"Who on earth can that be, and me looking a sight. Maybe it's the carol singers again." She padded through the kitchen. "I'll just take a look out my bedroom window and see."

What she did see sent her flying back through the lobby. She fumbled with the catch of the door then threw it open. Words of welcome fell in a torrent from her lips.

"Kathy! Oh, lassie, it's good to see you! There was a prayer in my heart all day that you'd get home tonight. Is Craig coming in and me looking like this –"

Kathleen hugged her tightly, her face cold against the older woman's cheek.

"He's not coming in, Aunt Isa. He said he'd just wait till he saw you open the door. That's the car moving off now."

Arm in arm they went into the warm living-room. Aunt Isa poked up the fire and put on a log before she took a good look at Kathleen's face.

"You'll be needing a meal, lass?"

Kathy shook her head, taking off her coat and laying it on a chair.

"We stopped for supper at Crawford. But I could do with a cup of tea! Is Kenny asleep?"

"Just –" Aunt Isa smiled. "Away and have a look at him

and I'll make tea. I had the kettle on anyway, so it should be boiling."

A few minutes later they were sitting at the fire, with a tray on the stool between them.

"The first thing I saw was the tree," said Kathleen. "What a lovely sight – like someone holding out their arms in welcome. I could hardly believe it was our window! Where did it come from?"

Aunt Isa briefly explained briefly then changed the subject. She was more interested in what had happened in Manchester. Kathleen told her everything. Though she spoke calmly, Aunt Isa's observant eyes noted that the hand which held the cup trembled slightly.

"Thank God you had Craig to help you," she said.

"Yes – he was wonderful. It wasn't only what he did or said. It was just him – being there. To lean on, to stretch out his hand when – when –"

"Fine I ken." Aunt Isa swallowed a lump in her throat. Now that the first excitement of home-coming was over, she saw that Kathleen was pale. There were a few fine lines at the corners of her eyes.

"Has there been any talk here?" Kathleen asked.

"Not that I've heard. But I haven't been over the door since you left. But of course there'll be no talk, Kathy! That part of your life is over and done with for all time. Put it behind you and look to the future."

When Kathleen made no response, Aunt Isa looked at her anxiously, seeing the droop to the full generous mouth.

"No one in Kilmarford knows what's happened, Kathy –"
Kathleen stirred herself.

"But it's bound to come out. The Lauries know."

"They'll never talk! You can be sure of that!"

Kathleen smiled faintly.

"Probably you're right, Auntie. But others know. There's the police and I think my father kept up with a man in the Vennel. It's too much to hope that the news won't leak out. But not much of it, I hope and pray, for Kenny's sake."

"The worst's past, Kathy," Isa Duncan spoke with determined cheerfulness. "You've just got to look ahead and think of what's best for yourself and Kenny. Have you any plans?"

"You mean about work?"

"Aye, about that – and other things."

"I'm starting at the office the first Monday of the new year."

"Carmichael's office?"

"Yes."

"So he gave in? You know that lad's never given in half as much in his life before as he's done to you!"

* * * *

Kenny was on holiday and the days flew past. In no time at all it seemed to Aunt Isa she was laying out the black bun and shortbread and sitting up with Kathleen to welcome a New Year.

"I hope Craig's our first-foot," she said, polishing a glass with a clean cloth.

Kathy was threading ribbon through the little jacket she had knitted for Nan Webb's baby, due in a few weeks. It was on Aunt Isa's insistence she was finishing it at eleven o'clock on the last night of the year. The old woman was against leaving any job undone which could be done. It was a good thing, she said, to start a new year with your feet clear.

"Next year," Kathleen said, tying a bow neatly at the neck, "we'll let Kenny stay up."

"Next year," observed Aunt Isa, laying a lace-edged cloth on the table and frowning over a tiny frayed bit at the corner, "is a long way ahead."

Kathleen laughed.

"It's just yesterday I heard you saying the years were flying so fast now you hardly could keep up with them!"

Aunt Isa made no response. She lifted the cloth and relaid it so that the frayed bit was at the side next to the sideboard, where it wouldn't show.

Kathleen folded the little jacket neatly.

"It was nice of the Lauries to give you that bowl of tulips on Friday. I think everyone knows your weakness for flowers."

"I really shouldn't have them in here. The heat's not good for them. Aye, it was thoughtful of them to give me a minding as well as you and Kenny."

"We've had some lovely presents, haven't we? That turkey

345

from Carnbo –"

"The biggest one on the farm, I think! What a job we had getting it into the oven!" Aunt Isa looked up from the shortbread. "I see you're wearing Craig's brooch," she remarked with elaborate casualness.

Kathleen fingered the delicate gold filigree in which the fine amethysts gleamed.

"It was his mother's," she said.

Isa Duncan kept her thoughts to herself. They were puzzled thoughts. It was his mother's and it was also very valuable. Well, only time could tell.

Then, standing there with a paper doily in her fingers, Isa Duncan was struck by a thought which made her stiffen and draw in her breath sharply. For a moment she tried to check it, but in spite of herself it persisted.

Could it possibly be the reason why Kathy was not marrying Craig? Could she have been so blind and never realised it before? Her rounded cheeks lost some of their colour and she moved away from the table, forgetting all her preparations.

"Kathy! Tell me truthfully – is it me that's keeping you from getting married? Are you thinking you're needing to make a home for me?" She stretched out her fat little hands and the words tumbled out.

"Never give that a thought! I could manage fine. I'd find myself a place. Just last week when I saw Mary Kerr at the Vennel she said her back room was empty. I know she'd let me have it. You're not needing –"

346

"Auntie, Auntie –" Kathleen caught at the warm, work-roughened hands. "What are you talking about? You're never going to leave Dalreoch. This is your home. Your home for as long as you need a place of your own – whether I'm living in it or not!

"Sit down, Auntie. I was going to tell you as the first bit of good news for the new year, but I'll just have to show you now."

"Show me what?" Aunt Isa asked in a mystified voice as she sank into a chair. "What do you mean, dearie?"

"Sit still for a moment. I've got it in the bedroom. I'll bring it."

Two minutes later a manilla envelope was in Aunt Isa's lap.

"The title deeds to the house, Aunt Isa! It's mine. Mr Laurie gave me Dalreoch on Friday as a Christmas gift."

"Kathy –"

"I know! I could hardly believe it myself. But it's true, Auntie. The house is mine – yours! No matter what happens this will always be home for you."

Isa Duncan looked round the comfortable room with the red tulips opening their petals on the sideboard and Kenny's paper chains looped across the ceiling. She looked at the holly tucked behind the pictures and the new curtains drawn cosily across the window.

Her eyes filled with tears and spilled over, so that a drop fell on the envelope in her lap.

"Auntie, darling – I thought you'd be happy."

Aunt Isa gulped. "Happy? You don't think I am? Oh, Kathy" – the old voice trembled – "this is the happiest day of my life!"

CHAPTER THIRTY-FOUR

ON the day Kathleen returned to the office it was raining heavily, and Isa Duncan had a cheery fire on for her return. Sitting curled up in a chair, Kenny was engrossed in the pages of a boys' annual he received from Peter at Christmas. When he was interested in a story he was completely oblivious to everything else.

Isa Duncan reflected that she'd missed Kathleen very much all day. Having had her at home for so long made it much worse. The afternoon seemed to drag on, and she'd spent more time on the daily paper than she'd done for weeks.

There had been a long report about the places Princess Elizabeth and the Duke would visit South Africa. They were flying at the end of the month. Aunt Isa would have felt a lot happier if the young Royal couple had been going in a boat. She was not too happy about these flying machines.

She was real glad her Alec and his family were coming home by boat, on one of the Queens – the bigger the boat the better, thought Aunt Isa.

The front door clicked and Kathleen came in, her hair damp at the front where her hood had not covered it.

"How did you get on today?" Aunt Isa pricked the sausages with a fork and set them in the pan.

"Fine!" Kathleen lifted her apron from its hook at the back

of the kitchen door.

"Ten minutes after I was in the office I felt as if I'd never been away. Everyone was so glad to see me. Miss Gemmell and Jenny and all the others."

"Did you not find any changes?"

"A few. In fact, I'd have been a bit at sea, but Miss Gemmell soon brought me up to date. She's got her finger on everything. Craig's lucky to have such an efficient woman."

"She's a nice body," said Aunt Isa.

"There's a lot of work because of this amalgamation with Laurie's, but I don't think it'll mean too many changes when it comes to the bit. Carmichael's will still carry on pretty well as an independent firm within the company.

"Craig insisted on that, and I'm glad. Carmichael's is a real family concern. It's got a personality."

It was when they were still seated at the tea table and Kenny returned to his annual that Kathleen said suddenly: "I nearly forgot – I've got news for you. I met George Webb on the way home. He'd just come from the nursing home. Nan had a baby girl this morning."

Aunt Isa beamed.

"Isn't that fine! I knew she was away. Mrs Balfour said she'd seen the car. A wee girl! Now that'll just please her. I must look out that head-shawl I knitted."

"I'll go in and see her on Saturday," said Kathleen. "I asked George and he said they only allow fathers in the evening during the first week, so I can't go before my half-holiday. I'm so glad for Nan. She's had to wait a long time."

"It'll be all the greater happiness for her now. It's always the same with something that doesn't come too easily." Aunt Isa passed the jam to Kathleen and remarked with a strange note in her voice: "And how about Craig? Was he pleased to see you back?"

"I think he was," Kathleen answered lightly and switched the conversation.

* * * *

It was just after three o'clock when Kathleen turned out of the nursing home gates on Saturday. She had not stayed with Nan long because several other visitors had arrived. But it had been a pleasure to see Nan looking so well and so happy.

The baby was to be called Muriel Anne. It was a pretty name. She was a pretty baby, much smaller and more delicate-looking than the eight-pound, noisy young gentleman Kenny had been at that age, Kathleen remembered.

She was still thinking about Nan when the car drew up beside her.

"Hello, Kathleen!" said Alice Boswell. "I called round at the house, but Mrs Duncan told me you were up here. I was hoping I would catch you."

Kathleen returned her greeting, and, rather to her surprise,

Alice left the driving seat and came out on the pavement beside her. The nursing home was in a secluded part of the town, and the road was practically deserted.

"I've got something to tell you, Kathleen."

It was then that Kathleen became aware of the subdued excitement that was making Alice's clear blue eyes glow and giving a tremor to her usually serene voice.

"What news, Alice?"

"I wanted you to be the first to know." She put her hand on Kathleen's arm. "Ewen has asked me to marry him! See –"

Kathleen looked from the diamond and sapphire ring on Alice's finger to the flushed face and the glowing eyes.

"Alice –" Kathleen took the slim hand in both hers. "I'm so happy for you – for you both!"

"And I'm so happy I'm almost afraid! Can you understand?"

"Yes, I understand."

They looked at each other. Many things which could not be spoken in words passed between them in that revealing look, drawing them together so that their friendship deepened into an emotion stronger and more enduring than either of them realised at the time.

There are degrees of friendship. But only to the few are our hearts ever opened without a word being spoken.

Alice swung open the car door.

"Will you do me a great favour, Kathleen? Will you come with me – somewhere?"

"Where?" asked Kathleen in surprise.

"I want to tell Roger's parents. I'd like them to know at once." She sighed and some of the glow faded from her eyes. "I hope they'll take it all right – especially Mrs Laurie."

"Of course I'll come." Kathleen slipped into the seat beside Alice.

Alice pressed the self-starter.

"It's not," she said awkwardly, "that I've forgotten Roger –"

Kathleen halted her swiftly.

"You don't have to tell me that!"

"No." Alice let in the clutch. "No, Kathleen, I was sure you would understand. But Mrs Laurie –"

"She may surprise you," Kathleen replied.

She did. James Laurie was out and it was Mildred Laurie, smiling and almost bright-faced who greeted the girls and took them into the lounge. She stopped Alice's halting explanation almost before it had begun.

"My dear – I'm so happy for you!" she echoed the words Kathleen had used earlier. "I've met Ewen Gilmour and he's a fine young man. James will be delighted, too."

Alice expanded like a flower to the sun.

"I was afraid – Roger –" she stammered.

"Life must go on – for all of us, my dear. I would have loved to have you for a daughter-in-law and you know you will always be more than welcome in our home.

"But I would not have cut yourself off from happiness and normal living because of a – because of the past. That's something we can never bring back. I tried to live on memories. It was a mistake – in more ways than one. In your case, a young girl like you – it would have been a tragedy –"

Shortly afterwards Alice rose to go.

"I'm sorry to rush away like this, but I promised Mother I'd be back in an hour. We're expecting guests. Can I drive you home, Kathleen?"

Kathleen made a move to rise, but Mrs Laurie held out her hand.

"Now you're here – please wait and have tea, Kathleen. We haven't had a real talk since we came back from Madeira. Perhaps if Alice wouldn't mind stopping at Dalreoch and telling Mrs Duncan where you are –"

They both went to the front door to see Alice off, waving as the small car turned out of sight down the drive. There was a pale, wintry sun and the air was cold.

"She's a sweet girl," murmured Mrs Laurie, making no move to go in.

"Yes," Kathleen agreed. "It's wonderful to see her so happy."

* * * *

The same subject kept Aunt Isa's tongue wagging after Kathleen's return to Dalreoch.

"I could have almost wept for joy when Alice told me this afternoon," she went on excitedly. "She's a lucky lass. Ewen will make her a grand husband."

She followed Kathleen into the bathroom where she was hanging up the towels after Kenny's bath.

"I'm no' a good hand at writing letters, but there's one I'm writing this very night – a wee note of congratulations to Ewen." There was pride in the old woman's voice. "Will I tell him you were real pleased, too, Kathy?"

"Yes, of course," she replied.

There was little time for talk because Kathleen was going out with Craig. He was expected at half-past seven and he was never late. Aunt Isa stayed with Kathleen while she dressed, admiring the burnished hair which was being brushed so vigorously.

The old woman said little, but her eyes missed nothing. Kathy had always taken a pride in her appearance. But tonight she seemed even more particular.

"I've very glad for Alice," said Kathleen, pushing in the deep wave above her brow. "She deserves happiness after the way it was snatched away from her almost two years ago."

Aunt Isa nodded.

"And I'm real pleased for Ewen's sake," she said rather tersely. "We all have our share of disappointments and Ewen's had his – as if you didn't know!"

Kathleen slipped her arms into her clean blouse.

"All right, you old schemer. He's found real happiness now," she said gently. Then her voice changed.

"That's the bell. Will you go, Auntie? Tell Craig I won't be a minute."

Isa Duncan walked to the door then paused.

"Where are you going? Anywhere special tonight?"

"No. Just a short run and supper somewhere, I suppose."
Kathleen smiled and gently pushed the plump figure through
the doorway.

She lifted the jacket of her suit, tested the centre button
that Kenny had almost pulled off the day before. It would
hold. But it wasn't neat. She sewed it quickly, put the jacket
on and took another look in the mirror.

When she came into the living-room a few moments later,
Kathleen heard Aunt Isa telling Craig about the engagement.
They lingered only a short time chatting and then left, with
Kathleen saying she would be home no later than ten.

As she closed the front door behind them, Aunt Isa shook
her head in bewilderment. Young folk were queer "kittle
cattle" nowadays!

It was a beautiful night, clear and frosty, with moonlight
sparkling on the roadway. Craig laid the travelling rug over
Kathleen's knee and smiled at her as he switched on the
engine. The moonlight glistened on his even teeth, white
against his shadowed face.

"I must say I am relieved to hear about Ewen and Alice."
There was a teasing note in his voice.

"Relieved? Why?" Kathleen asked innocently.

"Because for a long time I regarded him as my rival,"
Craig replied frankly. "I'm sure he would have married you
if –"

"What nonsense!" Kathleen laughed. "You're almost as bad as –" She broke off quickly and bit her lip.

"Almost as bad as Aunt Isa," he finished for her. "It's all right, my dear. I'll never hold it against Ewen Gilmour for wanting to marry you. I've been trying to do the same thing for a long time. I know what you're going to say, but it seems long to me! Oh, by the way, Kathleen, I've got a surprise for you."

She pushed her hands deeper into the woolly gloves which were Aunt Isa's latest gift to her.

"What is it?"

He turned his head and laughed.

"Wait and see!"

For almost an hour they drove on through the countryside, flooded in magic moonlight. A silence fell between them, deep and companionable. Kathleen paid little attention to where they were going. So it was with surprise – and not a little astonishment – she recognised the familiar landmarks of Kilmarford drawing nearer in an irregular line of winking lights.

She sat up and stared through the windscreen.

"We're home again!" she exclaimed.

"Home," he replied, an undercurrent of deep seriousness in his voice, "is where we're going!"

Some instinct held her in its grip until he drew up outside a house which stood on a high banking. A flight of steps led up through a rockery garden.

"The only way I can get into the garage is through the lane

357

at the back," said Craig, switching off the engine. "I'll just leave the car here for the time being."

The moonlight sparkled on the frost on the roof and on the panes of the darkened windows. It was a house which had more length than height, but the high banking gave it a commanding, if somewhat dejected appearance.

"Know where you are, Kathleen?"

She nodded.

"It's time you saw the inside of my home, Kathleen. I had to arrange it this way to make sure of you coming. Forgive me?"

He saw her smile. Then she turned and looked at him.

"Would it matter?" she asked softly.

He opened the door and led her into the dimly-lit hall.

"Mrs Fisher is rather deaf. If you speak slowly she'll understand. She's very good at lip-reading."

Later Kathleen was to remember the heavy, old-fashioned furniture, the large mahogany sideboard with its towering overmantel, the thick fringed shades on the lights which left the ceilings in deep shadow.

That was her first impression of the interior of the house. It was rather depressing. It puzzled her for a while – then she understood.

It was not a home, but an old-fashioned, over-furnished house, lacking warmth and that friendly feeling of being "lived in." No carpet in that house had been worn by the tread of little, rushing feet.

It was a lonely house that seemed to cry out for company;

for the echo of happy voices from its walls, for the friendly intimacy of family life.

Mrs Fisher was a wisp of a woman with the soft, unaccented voice of the deaf. Her hair was quite white, her small, claw-like hands heavily veined. She wore unrelieved black with a small cameo brooch at the neck of her dress.

She was frail and slow-moving. Kathleen realised her reserved manner was partly shyness and partly brought about by her deafness. She could only smile warmly and be glad because an answering smile darted across the thin little face whose skin was like cream parchment.

After the meal Craig showed her over the house.

"I suppose you'll think I'm silly," he said boyishly. "I should have done this in daylight!"

Kathleen smiled and assured him she was interested. And she was. It was a roomy house, and there were many things which caught her fancy.

There was the deep, embrasured window on the stairs and the brass-faced grandfather clock which ticked majestically on the upper landing.

"I wondered" – Craig opened another door – "if Kenny might like this room. It used to be mine."

It had a dormer window and a corner fireplace. The roof was low, so that the wardrobe almost touched it. There was a marble-topped washstand and two rush-bottomed chairs.

"Is that your old tennis racket?" she asked quickly. "And your football boots?"

He nodded.

"I haven't really been in here for years. It was my room when I came to live with my uncle – after my parents died."

"Oh," Kathleen murmured gently.

"I was eleven when Mother died and Dad followed six months later." He took a small, oval frame from the mantelshelf. "That was my mother."

Kathleen held the old-fashioned frame under the light. The face that looked back at her was sweet and smiling. A gracious and young face.

"It must have been dreadful for you, Craig."

"It was – at first. My uncle was an old bachelor. He didn't understand children, especially a wild one like me. He was rather like James Laurie – he lived for his mill. I'm afraid I was always a disappointment because I didn't share his enthusiasm.

"It was almost a relief when the war came so that I could get away. I joined the R.A.F. I never expected to inherit the mill, and when I did, I certainly never expected to run it. My ambition was to settle in Australia."

"But you came back?"

"I came back and stayed – and how glad I am today. My uncle left Mrs Fisher well provided for, but I managed to persuade her to stay on and look after me. But this house is too much for her. She deserves a rest."

Craig returned the oval frame to its place on the end of the mantelshelf.

"I think I've shown you everything, Kathleen. I can't expect you to be impressed. But meantime I'm content to believe that it's a house with possibilities. A house that could easily become a home one day."

Kathleen put her hand on the door handle and gave him a half smile. She swallowed hard then gave a sigh of relief when he switched off the light.

CHAPTER THIRTY-FIVE

AUNT ISA intended to have a bath, so the living-room fire was well stoked up when they arrived back at Dalreoch. The room was warm and the tulips which had come from Finnard were opening their petals widely.

Kathleen smiled.

"You'll never guess where I've been! I've had dinner at Craig's home."

"Well, now." Aunt Isa spoke mildly, as she always did when she was surprised. She looked at Craig standing with his hands in his pockets.

"You know the house, Aunt Isa." Kathleen took off her coat and put it over her arm. "The one on the left at the top of the hill with the rockery in front of it. Balmullo, it's called."

"Fine I know it – and well I remember Andra Carmichael, your uncle, Craig. He was an old curmudgeon!" She laughed and Craig joined in.

After a time the talk reverted to Alice Boswell's engagement.

"I wonder if Aileen will stay on at Carnbo after the wedding?" Aunt Isa crossed her plump feet. She had been persuaded to sit down while Kathleen set the tray.

Kathleen halted with the sugar bowl in her hand.

"I remember Aileen saying that they have an uncle in

Canada she's always wanted to visit. He has a farm in Ontario."

"Then there's the housekeeper," Aunt Isa went on thoughtfully.

Kathleen took teaspoons from the drawer.

"I don't think she'll stay on. She's getting old. She has a younger sister in the village who would be glad to have her."

"Is she as old as Mrs Fisher?" Craig asked.

"No – I don't think so."

"Mine would have been retired years ago, but I couldn't get anyone suitable to take on the job. And Mrs Fisher has a soft spot for me. But I'll have to do something about it soon."

They heard Kenny whimpering and Kathleen hurried into the bedroom. They heard her quieten him and then heard her go to the kitchen.

"So you'll be looking for another housekeeper?" Aunt Isa asked Craig.

"Are you thinking of applying for the job?"

"A body might do worse," she answered primly.

"She might –" he agreed with a laugh. "But it's not a housekeeper I'm looking for, Aunt Isa. It's a wife. And I mean to have the one I want!"

Aunt Isa smiled.

"You know something, Craig. My man proposed to me in the kitchen – with the door shut!"

Craig rose to his feet and had disappeared through the doorway into the small kitchen almost before she had finished speaking.

Kathleen was making the tea when she heard the kitchen door close.

"What is –"

As she began to speak she turned round and saw Craig. Something she saw in his eyes stopped the words on her lips.

Craig said nothing, either. He stood looking at her, taking in every detail. Her hair burnished under the light, her pretty face, her neat figure, its curves more sharply defined because she held her body tense.

Then in one quick step he was beside her. His arms went round her, crushing her to him. At the same time he bent his head and his lips sought hers. At first tenderly seeking, then eagerly strong.

No two women ever accept love and all it means to them in the same way. But always when the citadel of their hearts are stormed there is a reluctance to surrender. All are slow to accept at once the joy love brings.

And it was so with Kathleen.

Taken by surprise she strained away from Craig's arms, her body tended and unyielding, her head moving from side to side to evade his hungry lips.

But it was only for a time. His lips were warm. Gradually her own responded. Joy flooded through her. She closed her eyes and suddenly happiness cascaded over her. Slowly her arms were raised to encircle Craig's neck and she returned his kisses. Love's second blossoming, in a beauty more mature and, she prayed, more enduring, was her own.

Feeling her yielding Craig tightened his arms around her.

"I'll never let you go now, darling – never!" he whispered.

Kathleen's lips moved but no words came. She looked up at him. His face was touched with tenderness, and when he kissed her again his lips were soft and caressing. This was the Craig she loved.

All the problems that had beset her were suddenly as nothing. In taking her for his own, Craig took them also. For the first time in many years she had found safety and security – in his arms. All the hurt, the bewilderment of the past was blotted out.

She pushed him away from her, then as soon as she was free she raised her lips to his. Her first real kiss, the seal of her surrender. Tears like tiny mother-of-pearl beads filled her eyes, trickled down her burning cheeks.

"Oh, Craig!" Her voice trembled. "And I thought I was always to be alone!"

"You've never been alone, not since I met you, Kathleen. You've always been in my heart and mind, dear. You've just been a long time in finding that out. Now you know, you'll never feel alone again."

He bent and kissed her softly, reverently.

"Now, we'll tell Aunt Isa," he said. "Although I think she'll know already!"

* * * *

Isa Duncan sat in the study of a manse in Balornock struggling to keep back the tears. Weddings always had the same effect on her, but this was no ordinary wedding. It was Kathy's.

There were three guests. Just herself and the Lauries. The thought made her smile inwardly. She, Isa Duncan from the Vennel, and James Laurie, Kilmarford's biggest millowner, together in a Glasgow manse to see Kathy become Craig Carmichael's wife.

The young minister, the son of an Ayrshire farmer, was a friend of Craig's. Aunt Isa liked him. He was solemn faced but he had a kind generous mouth, the sort of mouth that could make you laugh or comfort you in time of trouble. His wife was small and pretty, with red hair as bright as Kathy's. It wasn't often you saw two such red-heads in the one room, Aunt Isa decided, as she waited for the wedding service to begin.

But if it came to that, there was a red head missing! Kenny! He'd been left at Finnard with Agnes, Imp that he was, he could twist poor Agnes round his little finger! He'd be having a grand day to himself, or Aunt Isa was much mistaken.

The Rev. James Dundas began the simple ceremony, and Isa Duncan clutched at the silk handkerchief buried in the palm of her hand.

Kathleen looked very pretty in her blue dress. She had taken off her coat, and it lay over a chair. Her hat matched her coat and her lovely hair gleamed beneath the light. It was a dull day and although it was mid-afternoon the lights had already been switched on.

Mrs Laurie was wearing a rose spray in her coat. Standing beside her husband, she was pale but composed.

Aunt Isa looked at Kathleen's red head – at Craig's dark one. This was their great moment and she thanked God that in her own humble way she'd helped to bring it about.

"Do you, Kathleen, take Craig –"

Aunt Isa blinked hard and two tears ran down her cheeks and plopped on to her coat.

"Whom God has joined together, let no man put asunder."

Isa Duncan bowed her head and silently added her own simple benediction.

Afterwards there were smiles and congratulations – and many kisses. Fancy Craig kissing her and thanking her for looking after Kathleen and Kenny. In front of the Lauries, too! As if she deserved any thanks for looking after two who had come to mean as much to her as her own flesh and blood!

They all went to the Grosvenor for a meal, and Aunt Isa learned she had been right about the young minister. He was full of fun and sound commonsense.

In no time it seemed they were leaving and Kathleen, her eyes misty, was hugging Aunt Isa tightly.

"Bless you for everything Auntie. Now look after yourself while I'm away."

"Goodbye, Kathy. God bless you and make you happy – and you, too, Craig."

"Goodbye, Aunt Isa!" He stooped to kiss her wet cheek. "You'll remember to go up to Balmullo and hustle the painters. They said they'd be out by next week."

"I'll see to that!" she promised.

"Goodbye!"

They were gone, and the young minister and his wife had said goodbye, too.

"We'll take you home, Mrs Duncan," said James Laurie.

The car was warm and comfortable. Laurie sat in front with the chauffeur, his wife and Aunt Isa in the back.

The two women chatted about the wedding as they crossed Jamaica Bridge and drove south.

"Do you know where they're going for their honeymoon, Mrs Duncan?"

"A wee place in Somerset. Kathy left me the address. They meant to go to London, but they changed their plans because of the King's death. The news fair upset me. It was like a personal loss. I think we all felt like that. King George was a good man – an example to all of us."

"That's true. It was a sad homecoming for the young Queen," said Mrs Laurie.

"Ay, it was." Aunt Isa agreed softly. "She'll have to carry a heavy burden on her young shoulders. But she's got a fine man to lean on."

The miles rolled on beneath the wheels of the luxurious car.

"Are you sure you'll not change your mind and come back to us to Finnard? You've stayed there before and you should feel at home. And Kenny's there. Won't you be lonely all on your own?"

Aunt Isa clasped her gloved hands firmly on the travelling rug.

"Thank you, Mrs Laurie, but I'll be better in my own place. With all the excitement of Kathy's wedding I've been neglecting the house and garden. There is a lot to do, and the sooner I start the better."

"Just as you like. But you'll come on Saturday afternoon to have tea with us?"

"I'll be there! I'll not weary, Mrs Laurie. The house went like a bell all last week when we had Kathy's show of presents, and it's never been right tidied since."

"She had some lovely gifts."

"Yes, lovely," Aunt Isa replied proudly. "Did you see the crystal bowl she got from the Boswells and the lovely china tea set from Carnbo?"

"Yes. It was beautiful."

"The blankets were from my son and his wife in Chicago. They were bound with satin ribbon. The things they do in America –"

"You have a son in America?"

That subject kept them going until the car stopped at the small green gate of Dalreoch. Isa Duncan got out on to the pavement and stood until the black car turned out of sight round the bend.

For all her brave words, her spirits fell as she fitted the key in the lock and went into the tiny lobby. It was almost dark and the living-room fire was out. She went into the bedroom and took off her coat and hat, hanging the coat on the back of the door.

A sense of loneliness crept round Aunt Isa's heart. After the fuss and bustle of the last week or two, the solitude and quietness touched her like a cold hand.

She sank wearily into a chair and took off her new shoes. Then she put an apron over her dress and relit the fire. So long as she kept busy it would not be so bad. She must keep busy. She'd put on the kettle and get herself something to eat – although there wasn't the same pleasure in food when you had to take it alone.

But she'd have to get used to that. She'd been used to it before; she could get used to it again. But it wouldn't be easy. It would be two years come August since Kathy and Kenny came. That was a long time – and much had happened.

This would never be Kathy's home again. From now on her home would be the grand house up on the hill, where an army of painters had been busy for weeks. She smiled remembering the happy hours she'd spent with Kathy choosing new furniture, carpets and curtains.

Craig grudged her nothing. Balmullo was Kathy's to do with as she pleased – and she'd soon make it a lovely, comfortable home. Aunt Isa was sure of that.

Dalreoch was no longer Kathy's home – nor was it Kenny's. When Kathy came back from her honeymoon he would go from Finnard to begin a new life with a father as well as a mother.

Which was as it should be, but . . .

Aunt Isa set the table, but looked at it without appetite. All she had was a cup of tea and a digestive biscuit.

She was filling her hot-water bottle when the doorbell rang. Who could it be at this time of night? The only neighbour given to looking in at any hour was Mrs Balfour. But she and her husband had been called away because of the illness of an elderly relative.

Aunt Isa walked cheerfully to the door. No matter who it was, a visitor was welcome!

There was no one at the front door, but the church magazine lay on the mat. Aunt Isa bent to lift it, and beneath it found a thin blue letter. An air mail from Alec!

She pounced on it eagerly. It must have been there when she came in, but she hadn't seen it in the bad light. She carried it into the fire and sat down, her loneliness forgotten. The thin sheets were closely written, half by Alec and half by his wife, as usual.

Eagerly she devoured the pages, her eyes growing bright. They were coming home earlier than expected. Their passages were booked! They had decided a few weeks off school wouldn't harm the children, and they would be home the first week in June!

June! Aunt Isa's gaze flew to the calendar. It was soon, much sooner than she expected. She'd have to spring-clean the whole house to have it ready for her family.

Her own family – her own son, his wife and bairns.

He'd be home again and the house would be full of voices and laughter, and two grandchildren running about the place. She'd never have a minute to weary.

Isa Duncan got to her feet and tucked the precious letter into the pocket of her apron. All weariness, all loneliness had suddenly vanished. Staring into the fire she remembered a favourite quotation of her old mother's – "God moves in a mysterious way His wonders to perform."

Later that night, in the quietness of her own room, Isa Duncan knelt at the side of her bed. Her grey head was bent and her lips moved in a simple prayer of thankfulness.

CHAPTER THIRTY-SIX

THE day before the return of Kathleen and Craig, Aunt Isa hurried the last of the painters out of Balmullo.

Standing in the dining-room on a February afternoon, with the pale sunlight filtering through the branches of the tree outside the window, Aunt Isa knew Kathleen would find her new home a welcoming place.

Of course, there would be changes Kathy would want to make later, but wasn't that part of the happiness of building up a home? She'd have to be patient, and make the changes with time – although by the looks of things, Craig would give her the moon if she asked for it!

Kathy and Craig were coming to the bungalow for a meal before they went to Finnard to collect Kenny.

Aunt Isa left the house and closed the door behind her. She'd come back in the morning and light one or two fires. She rounded the corner into South Road, then drew up with a start. A car – a familiar car – stood at the gate.

She hurried along the pavement and through the garden gate.

"We're home!" Kathleen was running to meet her. "I still had my key so we were able to get in." Aunt Isa had never seen her face look so tranquil and radiant.

She kissed Kathy and turned her cheek to Craig.

The next hour passed on magic wings while they sat round

the fire and talked. Then at last they made a move to go.

"But you'll need to stay here. The paint is not dry yet!"

Craig put his arm around Kathleen's shoulder.

"We're going to have one night alone in our own house – wet paint or no wet paint! That's what we came home a day early for!"

"Well, you can't take Kenny!"

Kathleen laughed.

"We'll leave Kenny till tomorrow," she said. She and Craig went out together with such radiance on their face that Aunt Isa found her own eyes were wet . . .

The first few days passed, and life began to assume a more routine order for Kathleen. Her marriage had caused much talk in Kilmarford, but she knew she had the good wishes of most people. If news of her father's death had reached the town it had been kept very quiet.

Kathleen was busy in the house on the hill, but not too busy to find time often to run round to the bungalow where she and Kenny had known so much happiness. There she would sit and talk to the wonderful old woman whom she knew was missing them – although she would have denied it stoutly.

The first Sunday she and Craig attended church together was the day Nan Webb's baby was christened. It brought back the old days to Kathleen, the less happy days when Nan's friendship had been the one bright spot in her life.

She felt a new surge of warmth towards Nan as she saw her with the tiny white-clad bundle in her arms, and George standing rather self-consciously beside her.

Those days in the Vennel, with the perpetual shadow over her – they seemed very far away now. She was secure, secure in the love of a husband whose worth she realised more fully with every passing day.

Kathleen looked down. Kenny stood between them, his red head bare. She was blessed, many times blessed . . .

In the weeks that followed she and Craig did a lot of entertaining. Mrs Laurie and Ray Balfour were frequent visitors, as were Alice Boswell and Aileen Gilmour.

It was a soft day in late May, when the trees in the garden were budding and the rockery at the front was ablaze with aubretia, that Alice came climbing up the steps from the street. She was wearing a tartan skirt and blouse. She was hatless.

"Come in." Kathleen had seen her coming and opened the door before she rang the bell. "I'm just going to make coffee. I've been expecting Aunt Isa, but she must have been delayed. You didn't see her on the road?"

"She was just turning the corner as I came in the gate, but I saw her stop to speak to someone."

"Well, I might as well start to heat the milk. Will you come into the kitchen, or will you wait in the dining-room?"

"What do you think?" Alice laughed and followed her into the kitchen. "What a lovely place this is, Kathleen. Look at that sink and those built-in cupboards! It's enough to delight any housewife's heart."

"If you'd seen it at first . . ." Kathleen poured milk into the pan. "What's new with you, Alice? There is something, isn't there? I can see it in your eyes."

"Well – " Alice perched herself on the edge of the table and swung her long legs. "We've fixed our wedding date – late October – after the harvest."

"That's lovely!" Kathleen was smiling. "I'm so glad for you."

"Of course you and Craig will be there. You see – " She broke off and looked at Kathleen questioningly.

Kathleen smiled and shook her head.

"I'm afraid I won't be there, Alice – I'm sorry. I'm having a baby."

* * * *

A stillness lay over Kilmarford that Sunday morning, a stillness broken only by the pealing of church bells.

Standing at the sitting-room window of Dalreoch, Isa Duncan looked out at the wintry sunshine, flooding South Road in golden light.

As always the sound of the bells uplifted her heart. This day they seemed to ring out with a special message. There was a gladsome note about their peals. It was as though they were aware something wonderful was going to happen that morning.

And it was!

As she turned from the window Aunt Isa's eyes were tender. Softly she began to sing a verse from the baptismal hymn: –

Lo! Such a child whose early feet
The paths of peace had trod,
Whose secret heart with influence sweet
Is upward drawn to God.

As the last words trailed away in a throaty note she looked
at the clock – for the fourth time within the last twenty
minutes.

She couldn't settle. She was too excited. It showed in her
eyes, in the tinge of colour in her cheeks, in the way she kept
touching the feather in her hat.

It was the hat she wore at Kathy's wedding a year ago. It
was only worn on special occasions. And this was a very
special occasion.

She was dressed far too early, of course, but Isa Duncan
was determined not to be late. She was not going to keep
Kathy and the taxi waiting.

She was about to sit down by the fire, but she checked
herself in time. She mustn't crease her coat. Instead she
reached out her hand to an airmail letter resting against a
brass vase on the mantelpiece.

Dear Alec! His letters arrived regularly as clockwork. And
now that she was alone again, they were welcome more than
ever.

Every letter from Chicago made some lovely reference to
Alec's visit home with his wife and family. It seemed just

like yesterday that Dalreoch rang with the happy laughter of her grandchildren; with the attractive voice of her American daughter-in-law.

Four months they all stayed. And they were wonderful months.

The ringing of the front doorbell broke into Isa Duncan's thoughts. She gave a final touch to her hat, smoothed the front of her coat and hurried outside.

The driver was holding the door open. In the taxi was Kathleen, in her favourite green with a new and pretty velvet hat. The baby, wrapped in a beautiful shawl, was on her knees.

Isa Duncan sat beside Kathleen and looked at the pink little face.

"He's sleeping, the wee lamb."

"Yes, but wait until we get to church." Kathleen smiled.

Aunt Isa straightened the brown feather in her hat. She had brushed it against the door getting into the car.

"There were no tears in my cup this morning. I looked specially. He won't cry. Will I take him now?"

Kathleen smiled.

"He couldn't be in better hands."

"He's a darling." The older woman held the shawled bundle on her knee. "I – I'm real proud to be carrying him today. An auntie to Kenny; a granny to Alec's bairns – and now a godmother. Could any woman ask more from life?"

"Who else would I have had but you, Auntie?"

The older woman's small mouth quivered at Kathleen's

kind words. They were sweet to her ear. Because she was deeply touched by them and the occasion she hurriedly looked out of the car window. Her eyes caught the buildings that made up Laurie's Mill, spreading out like the fingers of a great hand.

"Never did I think," she said, "that I'd carry a bairn called Roger Laurie Carmichael to his christening!"

"Look, Auntie!"

Kathleen was sitting upright, staring out at Laurie's Mill. Across the skyline the name stood out boldly. Because it was newly painted it stood out even more boldly than it had that day when Kathleen returned to Kilmarford two and a half years ago.

That day it had sent a chill through her. It reminded her of all the hurt, the heartache and loneliness she had known since Kenneth died. She was a Laurie, but in name only. The proud Lauries of Finnard would not acknowledge her. They had closed their doors and hearts on herself and Kenny.

But that was a long time ago. Time's gentle fingers had worked a wondrous miracle, wiping out all bitterness and hurt. And if proof were needed, there it was, proudly displayed for all Kilmarford and the world beyond to see.

"Laurie and Son" now read "Laurie and Sons."

Fascinated, Kathleen continued to stare as the dark cloud, forming in the background to the huge sign, began to disperse.

Slowly she turned her head away and her misty eyes rested on the sleeping child. James Laurie had accepted him as his own, as Kenny's brother.

This precious little bundle was the symbol of the future.

The future of a family that had known sorrow and tasted grief; that had learned the folly of misunderstanding and foolish pride, and was now united by the unbreakable bonds of love.

Into Kathleen's mind returned the first prayer, Grace, her mother, had taught her. Her lips moved in silence as she said it.

"Thank you, God, for everything."